The Other Mother

The Other Mother

A Novel

Gwendolen Gross

SHAYE AREHEART BOOKS / NEW YORK

Copyright © 2007 by Gwendolen Gross

All rights reserved.
Published in the United States by Shaye Areheart Books, an imprint of the
Crown Publishing Group,
a division of Random House, Inc., New York.
www.crownpublishing.com

Shaye Areheart Books and colophon are trademarks of Random House, Inc.

Library of Congress Cataloging-in-Publication Data

Gross, Gwendolen,
The other mother: a novel / Gwendolen Gross. – 1st ed.
1. Neighbors–Fiction.   2. Women editors–Fiction.   3. Stay-at-home
mothers–Fiction. 4. Motherhood–Fiction.   5. Work and family–Fiction.
6. Psychological fiction. I. Title.
PS3557.R568O84 2007
813'.6–dc22   2006033211
ISBN 978-0-307-35292-7

Printed in the United States of America

Design by Chris Welch

10   9   8   7   6   5   4   3   2   1

First Edition

For Mom
and for Carina

The Other Mother

Thea

I t started with a mangled squirrel. I hadn't swept the front porch in weeks; the wind's offerings hid like shy children behind our antique milk jug. Twigs twined with dead moss, credit-card offers, and Sears Photo Studio fliers lifted from my neighbors' recycling bins and collected into nests, growing snowballs of lost words. Usually, I was diligent about the condition of the front porch—usually I was also diligent about swim-team carpool and a weekly menu and freezing two meals from each spinach lasagna so the freezer offered Friday-night answers other than plain ground beef stuck to itself in a wad. But that spring I was wanton with chores, wanton with the ordinary bricks of tasks that held up my family's house of days. There was an unseen listing in the foundation.

Perhaps the squirrel had crept unaided into the nest of refuse after a close encounter with a Volvo, a clip that didn't splatter but crippled. There was blood, but just a crust. The head was slightly flat but not flattened; it had a two-dimensional quality, as if it had been copied from a cartoon. It smelled but was not rancid, only vaguely green, with the hint of salt. I whisked my three-year-old, Iris, past it without comment and went inside to give her raisins and peanut butter on graham crackers, ants on a raft, we called it.

It should have been the end when I turned the blue *New York Times* bag inside out, picked up the squirrel, and carried the carrion to the edge of the woods and flung it in. But the squirrel was just the first. In two weeks we had a series: two squirrels, one with entrails exposed, one long since desiccated, clearly roadkill reassigned to our stoop. Then there was a house finch, the red cast of its breast dissectible, up close, into red-tipped feathers, as if just those plumes had been blessed by a certain heat. Then a mouse, which I almost missed. It was so small and so light that when I bagged it (this one I cast into the trash, impatient with the business of decay), I might have been casting a wrapped puffball into the garbage can. Iris missed them all, and Carra and Oliver, my other children, were always away in their respective worlds, and at first I didn't tell Caius, my husband, partly because he might have suspicions and partly because he might not.

I hoarded my own theories like Halloween candy still held in January closets. It could be a feline gift, or something about our porch that inspired animals to come there to die, or it could be a person, a sick practical joke. It could be *her.*

Once these offerings were presented to me, I felt I had to own them somehow, their finishedness, their objectness. I started a sketchbook of evidence and kept it in the bottom drawer of my rolltop desk; I didn't want anyone to think I was preoccupied. And I wasn't, at least at first.

Then there was the groundhog. It was huge, the size of a fat cat, too heavy to be the offering of any animal other than human. Too gruesome and pathetic and fresh, a pool of blood losing itself to the porous nature of the concrete porch floor, a last autonomic twitch of the feet, the belly ticking into stillness. And worst of all, Iris saw it, too. We'd just come back from her preschool open house. Iris had wanted to take Miss Leigh's piggy puppet with her and had cried in the car on the way home, unable to relinquish her disappointment until I pulled the parking brake. I let her pick a Johnny-jump-up in the backyard, and then we came around to the front to collect the mail. Iris liked reaching into the box for me. She liked dropping everything in the front hall, too, saying "Uh-oh" and then smiling as if it hadn't been on purpose. She helped me sort, she scribbled on the castoffs, and sometimes on important things, too, and I tried not to scold her too much, because I felt my voice making me older with unnecessary corrections. Iris ran for the mail, taking the steps too fast. She slipped and landed on the top step, skinning her knee and tearing her one new dress among the hand-me-downs from her sister. Iris started to wail as I caught up with her, then stopped abruptly when she saw the groundhog.

"Fog juice!" she said. "Mommy, what's that? Fog?"

"A groundhog," I said, confirming her identification. "Dirty, too—don't touch!" I said, inelegantly swooping up her and the mail and my keys, and unlocking the front door. I bumped her head and my shoulder against the latch, but then we were inside, safe from the onslaught of dead things without. Once Iris had seen the groundhog, I couldn't help but let suspicion leak from the container of my heart. I suspected malevolence. I suspected the spleen of another mother. I suspected Amanda.

September
2000

1

Thea

I had already lost Iris in the Rite Aid. She'd begged and begged to get school supplies, in her sweet-voiced, slightly lisping two-year-old language that unfailingly invites patience on my part just when I'm about to despair of ever managing a simple errand. I told her if she stayed close, she could pick out something, a notebook or a box of crayons, or markers if she promised not to suck the tips to blue her mouth, and we could have some school projects together. But as soon as we got to the store—my son, Oliver, was stepping from one foot to the other without traveling anywhere, and my oldest, Carra, was sorting through the stacks of three-ring-binders as if they'd each delivered a personal insult—Iris slipped into the aisles and was gone.

Rite Aid wasn't the best place to shop for school supplies, but I was too busy to manage a trip to the mall. Carra, who had recently turned twelve and was as serious about middle school as the rest of us had been about enrolling in college, showed her displeasure in every gesture on the way there. Not good enough, said the snap of her seatbelt, no special cartridge-filled fountain pens like her best friend Lizzie had. No rainbow-laser binders, only babyish unicorn decals, her sigh said, as we drove the mile into town. She let out a little grumble of disgust as I parallel parked, badly, leaving my wheels at least eight inches from the curb.

But for some reason I wasn't frustrated with Carra. She was simply navigating the new with her best coping mechanism, disapproval, for guidance. When Carra was first born, and I was deeply in love and in the thick thrall of milky exhaustion, almost like drowning, my friend Tia came to visit. She held Carra and looked into her wrinkled infant face and said, "She'll break your heart when she's a teen."

Oliver wouldn't get anything he needed and would require a separate trip the next day because he forgot "pencils, and oh, a big gummy eraser thing, and Mom, I think I need paper but I don't remember which kind." It wasn't that Oliver was oblivious to everything. At ten he had a very good memory for the books he loved, which characters were in which series, and which movie—his most serious passion besides his bicycle—was coming to the Sylvan Glen Theater. Oliver went to see whatever wasn't rated R, even if it was considered a girl movie or something that featured kissing. It was Oliver who noticed Iris wasn't with us.

"Ma," he said, more interested in the meager shelf of paperbacks and the greeting-card aisle than the things he'd need for fifth grade. "Ma, I think Iris went that way." He nodded his head.

I hated the feeling that I'd lost control. With the first two, there had been some chasing, some games of run-away-from-Mommy, but it was long enough ago I'd already forgotten. And Iris was different. She was as wild at one as my others had been at two, and now that she was two, she was uninterested in her mother's suggestions, pleas, and demands, and passionately interested in whatever I didn't want her to have because it might hurt her. She put everything into her mouth, still, long after Dr. Goodberg, in her calm and slightly condescending lecture voice, had told me she would grow out of it.

"I-ris," I called, trying not to let panic spread its wide wings in my chest.

"I-ris," called Oliver, right behind me. He still liked to help, and he still liked to please me. Though Iris's disappearances made him a little too happy in the look-at-me-I'm-being-good department. He'd adjusted well at seven, when he learned he'd have to share his mommy with a small, shrieking person who would probably never be old enough to play with him. Along with his beauty, Oliver was blessed on occasion with dazzlingly clear perceptions. "It's better that she's a girl," he'd said that first week, when I hardly had time to look into his face for Iris's needs. "That way I won't have to be as jealous."

A small cloud of red hair dashed around the corner of the aisle I was entering. I could hear her demonic little laugh. It was funny for a second, but then she wasn't in the next aisle.

"I-ris, I need you to come here *now*," I said. I could hear the automatic doors hissing open, closed, open, and the high-speed traffic out on Sylvan Avenue made me nervous. My other two had known, somehow, without more than half a dozen didactic lessons on my part, that streets were dangerous. Iris had already run out into our cul-de-sac dancing, and on a previous shopping trip she'd made it off the curb on Sylvan, though I'd grabbed her before she had a chance to take a second step. Iris would go right out those automatic doors, she'd run right out under the wheels of a giant SUV; she'd be a low and unavoidable target. I felt this possibility weighting me, fear unfurling, and started running toward the entrance, pulled by gravity and danger and responsibility.

"Mo-om," called Oliver. "I got her."

I rounded the aisle, but I didn't see them. I had to squeeze by a pair of teens necking in the candy aisle. I thought I recognized my neighbor's daughter, half-mashed, half-wrapped around a young man with straight hair that fell below his angular jaw, but I couldn't stop to really see. I passed the pair and ran toward the entrance, but my children weren't there.

"Mo-om!" Oliver yelled. I could hear Iris's cry. It wasn't an easy cry, it was a loud, angry, word-filled cry, as if she had things she couldn't say in such a state of agitation. Because of the cacophony surrounding her intent, we'd probably never know what she was saying. Often, I was too annoyed to *want* to know what she was saying. I was a bad mother, already thinking about preschool, wishing she'd been born two months earlier so she could enroll this year. An hour or two of freedom, freedom for both of us, I had told myself when I fingered the brochure from the new Montessori school. This was my last go at raising a toddler. I'd thought I had known what I was doing. Even when I'd told Caius I was pregnant, even when I'd believed I was surprised, part of me had expected this last round all along. But none of me had expected Iris to be the challenge that she was.

"Myma-ahhh!" cried Iris. They stood back near the binders. Iris was clutching two jumbo packs of Pez; maybe she'd have become Sylvan Glen's youngest shoplifter, the poster child for a stop negligent mothers campaign. Oliver triumphantly gripped her arm. Iris was flopping, flailing. His grip was a little harder than necessary, but Iris did try, strenuously, to escape.

And I adored her, my last little one, my jitterbug. Guilt and relief soaked into me. I took my baby in my arms, despite her resistance, despite the bruises her pink-sneakered feet would leave on my thighs where she kicked me. My knees made a sound like gum bubbles popping as I stood. I kissed the top of her head. She let the Pez fall to the floor. I hadn't lost her yet.

"Mine plies," she sobbed.

"I know, your supplies," I said.

"They don't have the right kind," said Carra, looking bereft by the big bin of loose-leaf paper. "We'll have to go to the mall."

Sometimes, when they were all in the car, if Iris was sleeping in her seat and Oliver and Carra were in their private looking-out-the-window worlds, dreaming of things I wasn't sure I wanted to know about, I forgot, for a guilty, delicious moment or two, that I was a mother of three, on errands, the person in charge. Sometimes I was my college self, home for the dregs of summer, relishing the last of languid August, full of the details of my summer jobs and summer crushes and the cicadas starting their song of sex and death in the late afternoons. I slowed down as I neared Tia's old house, remembering the time when she was home, still my best friend, and forecasting our future together: we'd work as raft guides on African rivers, trek in the Himalayas, join sky-top bird studies in the Amazon, meet our mates at bars in Amsterdam, and come home to Sylvan Glen, New Jersey, to raise our broods across the fence from each other, where they could make their own bug collections and later, fall in love.

But the house next door wasn't Tia's anymore; it wasn't even Tia's mother's house. I'd seen the For Sale signs a few months ago and had left three unreturned messages for Tia. Even after the Sale Pending notice went up over the original placard, I'd fantasized about buying it myself so it wouldn't be invaded by strangers. Not that we could afford a second house. I felt as if I'd lost Tia's mother, Phoebe Larkspur, though she'd only moved across the woods to the assisted-care facility. When the Bergen Sunset Home was built five years ago, I'd stood in the cul-de-sac with my neighbors listening to the grand-opening party. Even Jillian Martin emerged, with her suspiciously fraternal-looking husband, Jack, who rarely came out of his house except to push snow around in his drive with a leaf blower and to weed and deadhead his perennial garden with his chain saw. They stood there with their matching narrow foreheads and bitter sucked-lemon expressions. At nine o'clock on a summer weeknight, the polka was so loud it blasted across the maple-and-sassafras-filled woods like a storm. Then the announcer started yelling instructions through his bullhorn, "Walkers on the *left!* C'mon ladies. *Ladies,*" and Jillian Martin screwed up her sour face and laughed.

"Stupid," muttered Jack. "Stupid old people."

It wasn't as if Mrs. Larkspur had done cartwheels under the pink dogwood on her front lawn, but at least I'd seen her over the back fence sometimes, clasping grocery bags against her chest like little children.

I captained the van into the driveway, Iris asleep after the indignities in the Rite Aid. I gasped a little at the sight next door—almost like driving past a wreck. I hadn't expected new neighbors so soon, and I felt a vague crushing sensation in my chest, tempered by a little hope. They were here already. The moving vans were dribbling the new family's belongings out into the yard like a tree spilling leaves, the only order that of gravity and wind. A huge buffet sat squat under the dogwood, scuffing the soil with its feet. It looked too large and ominous for the open dining room I'd sprinted through a thousand times, playing sardines with Tia and my brother Oren. The lawn was littered with boxes and boxes and boxes marked BOOKS, with letters for alphabetizing added in a cramped scrawl.

I pressed the buttons on the van to release Oliver and Carra, who would get out, be on their own, who wouldn't need me now for a while.

"When can we go to the mall?" Carra asked, but she was already running away from the driveway and toward her friend Vivian Morocco's house.

Leaving Iris asleep in the car seat, I went inside. I opened the back door so I could hear her from the kitchen when she woke. I felt a compulsion when there were new neighbors. It was selfish, but I just wanted all new people to like me, and I harbored a fantasy each time that there would be a best friend for me.

Carra, at six, would recite when she'd met each neighborhood friend, "When I was two, I met Vivian, when I was three . . ." Iris was two, and we hadn't found anyone for her yet. Maybe her best friend would live in Tia's old house. Maybe they would be horrible nouveax riches and tear the whole thing down to make a McMansion stretching to the edges of the lawn. Maybe they would take down the slowly dying dogwood. Maybe if I brought them brownies, they would be more likely to keep things as they should be, as they were.

I unearthed chocolate, sugar, flour, nuts, eggs, relishing the shape of each object that would participate in the whole. With my first two children, I cooked and baked all the time while they played with muffin tins and dried pasta on the floor. Carra pointed out the shapes she recognized in her board books, and Oliver swung in a bouncy seat suspended from the doorway. Iris hardly ever let me bake, so when she woke a few minutes before I spread the brownies into the pan, I let her talk and fuss alone in the car; I even let her scream as I opened the oven and slid them in, telling her, "It's okay, lovey, just a second," though of course she couldn't hear me.

I never expected to live in the house I grew up in. I never expected to lose my mother before I became a mother myself. I never expected the losses and the gains, the shapes they took in the corners of days, of years, shifting in their chairs like visiting aunts.

When we all lived in the house, my mother, my father, my four brothers—three older, one younger—we filled the rooms with the scents of half-peeled oranges and new notebook paper and the blue chemical odor of dittoed homework sheets. My mother had had us each two years apart—"regular as eggs," she said. My father, a math-ematician at Columbia, was often at conferences or at his office over the garage, where piles of papers leaned against each other like tired soldiers. He had chosen my name after Theano, the wife of Pythagoras, a mathematician in her own right. Still, she was mostly known as someone's wife. My mother was mainly a mother, though even then I knew there were other things she loved: making small drawings she kept in a drawer and tending her roses and vegetable gardens.

She talked about her garden all winter, about places she'd been and planned to take us: the brilliant blooming grounds at Versailles when the jasmine spread scent all over the green trimmed lawns; snorkeling among a riot of tropical fish off the coast of Israel. She talked about places she hadn't been, sighing loudly, her chest and shoulders rising and dropping into brief defeat.

Then my brother Oren died a few months before his twentieth birthday. I knew in some ways my mother, the first Iris, felt a failure for losing her son. Now that I was a mother myself, I knew my mother probably dug deep into the history of her child rearing to determine how it was her fault, what she'd done wrong. And a little part of her was broken, like a dead limb on an otherwise healthy tree, after he was gone. The rest of us were grown, or mostly grown, and her work was over, despite the undug soil and untraveled terrain.

There was a lot of time before that, though, living in the house. I was a girl with four brothers, and my life was generally blithe. I was a little sister and big sister both, and I ran around with my brothers catching toads and holding them gently, feeling the pulse of strange cold life in my hands.

It wasn't until Tia moved in the summer before third grade that I realized I'd been missing something, a sister, girl company and competition. Her parents had just divorced, and her father had kept their apartment in the city. Tia pretended she'd been in the suburbs all along, as if she'd been living in her house before I lived in my own. When we played outside she invented histories—the secret spirits of the woods, the right way to catch a salamander, the house she knew had burned down with people trapped in the attic. And she knew that the junior high school principal was secretly gay, that our baby-sitter Leslie Chen's parents were getting a divorce.

We practiced kissing on each other; her tongue tasted like wood sorrel, a tangy green flavor. And of course Tia fell in love with my older brothers. First, she had a crush on Clark, who was six years older and looked like a man to us at sixteen, with his broad chest and long messy hair; then Lloyd, who was only four years older, but inaccessible as Dad, locked in the quiet of his own important thoughts, behind light blue eyes like Oliver's now; then Fred, who was the most fun because he actually played hide-and-seek with us instead of asking us to hide and never coming to look, like Clark and Lloyd.

By the time we went to college—Tia to Berkeley and I to Amherst—she had dated both Lloyd and Fred, and when Oren told me he had a crush on her, I told him to leave her alone and try for someone his own age. Tia gave him rides with us to high school; she burrowed her tricolored nails through his dark blond hair, and I pretended not to see the way he couldn't look into her face, the way he gazed at her ear or her neck as if avoiding the blinding light of the sun.

Iris stopped crying because I let her lick the batter from the beaters. She was so fleetingly beautiful, chocolate smudges on her nose, her forehead, her cheeks, her chin, that I looked around the kitchen, as if someone might be watching, and then cleaned her face the way she always wanted me to—not with an offending paper towel, but by licking her off.

"Joshua Giraffe," she said, referring to her favorite Raffi song. His mommy didn't lick him. Most mommies in their right minds wouldn't lick their children—what if she licked her friends on a play date to be like me? But she was my last, my most difficult; she was sweet and chocolatey and it kept her, for the moment, from protesting. We both changed clothes, putting on summer dresses so we would look like a welcoming committee, and I bribed her to be good by pilfering one brownie from the plate and putting it on the counter, "for when you come back after doing a very good job being a big girl."

"Mine," she said, pointing to the plate. She started to sob again and wiped her wet face on the front of my dress as I held her. I took her upstairs and put her on my bed, where she chortled and hid under the covers, and I changed again. Jeans and a T-shirt. It wasn't a dress, but nor was I naked or snot coated or chocolate stained for the moment. That would just have to do.

2

Amanda

All my moving-into-our-first-house fantasies were tempered by the vomiting. It was Saturday, September second, hot and drizzling, and Aaron directed the moving men like Moses parting the Red Sea. Arms overhead, his voice majestic and vibrant with authority, he ordered them through the silty spray. Aaron liked exerting authority. He sent the living room couches into the family room and the office bookshelf and night tables into the living room and the wardrobe containing his suits into the basement, and somehow there were eight boxes of books in the front hall bathroom. Which is where I spent the entire day, pressing my hands against the cream-colored tiles, trying to find a cool spot even though everything was hot and humid and nauseating. I knew this room best of all already, the single cracked tile by the southwest corner, the faint scent of sanded oak, the window's webby paint, the bubble in the wallpaper behind the tiny sink. The yellow-flowered wallpaper itself was cheerful enough on our first visit, months ago, when we decided to bid on the house. Years ago it seemed now, when I was still ordinary, before my hormones set about their work in my body, like a contractor ordering building and landscape work everywhere. I was sick all the time; my wretchedness became the unsolicited center of my universe.

Everyone lied to me about morning sickness. The TV and movies lied, showing a quick purge and then laughter; the books and doctors lied, saying it would be uncomfortable, yes, but it would surely pass by the end of the first trimester. The mild precautions were laughable, but I tried them: Get out of bed slowly, eat a cracker before you get up, avoid strong smells. Try sniffing a lemon, try sucking a lemon, try thinking about a lemon. Try seasickness pressure points, try staying in bed, get up, try exercise, take it easy. There was nothing easy about it. I was in my seventh month, and I still fumbled from bed to toilet as soon as I woke and sometimes twice in the middle of the night. I was sick everywhere, all day: On the train I'd given up trying to be discreet with my plastic bag and gravelly retching; in the office, I no longer fumbled to start the sink water running before slamming into the too-small stalls. I had a favorite stall almost everywhere, the one with the quickest lock or least disgusting floor.

I threw up at movie theaters and restaurants, when I was still trying to go to restaurants. I threw up in the employee bathroom at the gourmet foods store while clutching the smoked, braided mozzarella I'd needed, desperately, just moments before, until the salty smell reached my nose. I hated crackers—I hated people who mentioned crackers. I imagined a snow of crushed crackers falling on them, salting their heads as they spoke.

The receptionist at my dentist's office—where I had to leave my appointment because I couldn't keep from gagging with rubber-gloved hands in my mouth—told me when she was nauseated and sick three decades ago, her doctor told her it was her fault, that she was clearly feeling ambivalent about the pregnancy.

"It was planned," she said, holding her hands in the air. She was about my mother's age and still remembered her own sickness with a grimace.

"That doctor should have had court-enforced nausea," I said, appalled.

"He's dead." She offered a diminutive smile. "And things are better now."

Yes, I thought, *but I'm still sick.*

I wasn't even pregnant yet when we found the house, just trying. The widow who sold it to us, Mrs. Larkspur, had Alzheimer's disease and was moving into a retirement community across the woods. You could see the roof of the Bergen Sunset Home if you stood in our backyard by the slanted little shed with a rattly window. Her daughter, who lived in California, had hired the real estate agent and organized the sale. On our first visit, Mrs. Larkspur appeared perfectly ordinary, her freshly dyed brown hair curved into a short, sprayed bob. But the second time we visited, with our earnest money, she had lined up more than a dozen pairs of shoes on the front porch, and she was arranging stones in a spiral on the living room floor. We waited by the open front door for the agent, watching as she patted the stones—round granite, chunks of quartz—and mumbled happily to them.

From my crouch in the bathroom I could hear the moving truck starting up. The late afternoon had smeared into an ambiguous gray, but the rain had stopped. I got up, slowly. I heard shuffling, then Aaron's sigh.

"It's safe," he said. "If you can come out, Mango, come on out."

"Okay." I braved the doorway. Our doorway. Our house. No rent, no elevator, no neighbors sharing walls, no crazies shouting out the lost pieces of their minds on the street below our windows. I was exhausted, but Aaron, standing there looking strong and fine in his cutoff shorts and frayed green law school T-shirt soaked from shoulders to midchest, was wearing a spectacular grin.

"So, shall I carry you over the threshold?"

"Um, I'm kind of heavy. And I'm already inside." I wanted him to, part of me really did, but I was also afraid we'd sprain his back.

"I could," he said.

"How about we christen the bedroom, like good Jews." I felt suddenly romantic, having watched him at his finest, directing traffic in Our New House.

"Do you think the neighbors will hear?" Aaron was already halfway up the stairs. I was trying to convince my legs to take a single step while the baby twisted and pounded, doing laps and flip turns in the womb pool.

I looked at Aaron as he pulled me by my arms into the bedroom. My gigantic ship of a body followed. Nothing was imperative these days, no matter how much I wanted him, wanted to feel as urgent as we had before, wanted to look down at his face as he concentrated, waiting for me to give him permission. Here we were, in our box-furnished room, where one dresser lay on its side below the window and the mattress was crammed into a corner, half-obscured by disassembled head- and footboards, a left-behind industrial packing strap that smelled of motor oil, a wooden dowel which belonged to I did not know what piece of our furniture—or someone else's—and a little bamboo tea strainer resting on the single rescued pillow.

I began the elaborate crouching and bending required to get my body down to the mattress, and Aaron, his eyes incandescent green, took my arms and lowered me down like a crane laying a steel beam to rest. I tried not to notice the baby's sloshing, but it was everything, being at the center of my body.

"Our house," sang Aaron, "is a very very very fine house."

"No more super! No more laundromat! No more takeout from Mr. Garlic's Pizza," I finished, slightly sad.

"I'll garlic pizza you," said Aaron, starting to kiss me, tasting my cheeks and lips, letting his fingers measure my collarbone. I shivered despite my distraction. I started to cool and heat, a geothermal map of the possibilities of passion.

"Do, please," I said, reaching as far as the fabric allowed up his cut-offs. Sometimes I couldn't believe he still found me desirable in my gravid state, a vast vessel, redistributed material with the purpose of procreation. Aaron loved my breasts, loved to trace and squeeze, to taste and heft them. But in the last few months, they were unbearably tender and enormous due to their upcoming employment. I hated it; they were too sore for much handling, but he said in some ways, it made him more eager when I pushed his hands or mouth away.

"Can I?" Aaron tugged at my voluminous flag of maternity shirt. He pulled it up and pulled my skirt down over the dome of my belly.

"The baby's den." He patted me. I cooled a few degrees. I did feel like a building.

"May I," I said.

"What? Of course, whatever it is."

"No, I mean, you said 'Can I?', but you should have said, 'May—'"

"Shh," said Aaron. "Tell the editor to take a nap. And the baby, too. It's you I'm interested in." He slid down below my belly, so I couldn't see where he was kissing. But I felt it. It was as if he was trying to melt chocolate in his mouth, and I was trying to let myself be melted. It was hard to relax, hard to let him do everything. It was hard not to be able to see him while I felt him, his hands inside my thighs, the damp spot of the T-shirt he was still wearing. I tried to imagine us in our apartment, my own body as it used to be, and the way he used to lift my dress up and open the top buttons so I was still dressed and entirely exposed. The way he used watch me as I opened my lips around him, though since the morning sickness I couldn't take him in my mouth without gagging. I wanted this pleasure for me, but even more, for him. He could tell when I pretended, as I'd done the last few times, and though he didn't say anything, I knew he felt it was a small failure on his part.

I felt like solid wax. I breathed deeply and felt a jab at the bottom of my lungs. Aaron loved me, and some orderly part of him wanted everything to be *fair,* couldn't sleep as easily if he knew I hadn't been as satisfied as he had.

"What's that?" He stopped for a second.

I looked at the boxes and felt the baby shifting. I tried to ignore my stomach as something—an elbow or a foot—lumped along the surface.

"Don't stop," I said.

"Um, I think that's the doorbell. Do you think they want their strap back?"

"I don't give a shit about their strap," I said, sitting up with great effort and leaning on my elbows. I pulled my maternity shirt down over my chest, as if I could cover myself with anything short of a tall-ship's sail. Sex was not going to work. Especially if Aaron wasn't going to pay attention.

"I'll be right back," said Aaron, bouncing up, wiping his mouth. His percussive steps irritated me. Down the stairs to the door's demands. I resented him for wiping his mouth of me, for stopping, and most of all, for his ease.

I listened. Birds were congratulating themselves on the banquet of drowned worms left by the rain. Aaron's voice, words indistinguishable, lifted and dropped with his mesmerizing friendliness. When I heard him laugh, I knew I had to forgive him. It took three tries to heave my body up. I saw he'd forgotten the strap; if we weren't going to finish our business, at least someone should get what they needed. I lurched back into my clothes. As I started down the hall the other voice came clear, a bright, bell-like woman's voice—not the movers. I clutched the strap and waded my way down the stairs.

Aaron was leaning against the doorjamb, casual and sexy, his earlier intentions still visible in his posture, his thickened lips. He was talking to a beautiful woman, her hair sunlit, her body pale and small in a skinny black tank top and jeans. She was a little bony, and she had a lantern jaw, but these idiosyncrasies made her lovely. I envied her small chest, the quirky mole by the corner of her mouth, her ordinary state. A toddler with red Botticelli curls knitted herself in and out of the door, and in and out between her mother's long legs.

Perhaps she wasn't the mother; she could be a nanny. She offered Aaron a big glass plate covered with foil, and I hoped it was something delicious, though I didn't really want to think about food. And when she smiled, I couldn't help liking her.

"Brownies," she said, pushing the plate into Aaron's hands. He didn't see me, so I cleared my throat.

This was good, I thought, recovering from my snit. This neighborhood has stunning, friendly neighbors who bring chocolate. "We thought you were the moving men," I said, wading down the last of the stairs.

"Oh, wonderful!" She held her hand out toward my belly as if introducing herself to the baby, letting me be special. "I'm Thea— from over the fence," she said. "Iris is my third." She waved toward the little girl. No chance she was a nanny; probably a stay-at-home mom.

"My best friend used to live here," she said, glowing at me again, and even though I wasn't looking for a friend, I felt deeply comforted. Was she for real? Never mind sex, this was a welcoming committee. If I needed help when the baby was born, I might even call this perfect, calm mother next door.

"Brownies," said Aaron, holding onto the plate with an almost-religious reverence. Before we moved in, he'd constructed a lot of what-ifs for us. What if our neighbors brought us a pie? What if the people next door were expecting, too? What if our kids could all play together? What if we had barbecues in our backyard all summer? What if we lived next to born-again Christians who hated kids? I'd added, but I was laughing. Aaron held up the egg of suburban possibility with greater thrill than anyone I knew. He'd never really had it, a solid, predictable place to live, and even though he'd loved the adventures of his childhood, he imagined something calmer for his own children.

"Yes, I see," I said. "We're Amanda and Aaron, and thank you." I took the brownies from Aaron and set them on a box. The thick cocoa scent made me hungry, not nauseated, and I reached under the foil. "Want one?" I asked the toddler, who was singing about baby ducks going over the hill and far away as she bounced and wove. I started eating when she didn't answer, but then offered another when she came over with both hands up.

"Say thank you, Iris," said Thea.

"Thank you Iris," said the girl.

We three adults stood still while Iris ran and shed crumbs. Outside, the birds continued their proclamations, and inside, our quiet filled the room. I watched Aaron trying not to stare at Thea. Iris didn't stop moving. I appreciated the welcome, but now I wanted to lie down. With or without Aaron. Just eating the brownie had exhausted me.

I asked some chocolatey questions to break the silence. "Maybe you know which grocery store is best? Do you have a good pediatrician?" She just let me ramble on, looking clean and pretty. It was so sweet it almost seemed artificial. If I was going to live here, I was obviously going to have to employ a better-dressed, more-cheerful self. In Manhattan, the general approach to neighbors was courteous disregard. With the ones I liked, I exchanged greetings in the lobby; with those I didn't, I just avoided eye contact if I met them when they left for their morning commute. Here, clearly, the distance between houses didn't mean more anonymity but less.

"Oh, my," said Thea, smiling at Aaron, indulging my patter. "Just call me—I'll leave my number. I've lived here a long time, so I can tell you all about those things." I was intimidated by her ease. I guessed she'd gone to the same supermarket on the same day for the past ten years. Eaten the same brand of eggs. She and her husband had sex the same way every Saturday night. *Stop being mean*, I told myself. *Welcome to Jersey: check your sarcasm at the GW Bridge.*

"You're from the city, I assume?"

I nodded instead of saying something cynical. "I'm going to miss all the restaurants," I said. Aaron was eating a brownie; his chewing noise embarrassed me, the crumbs on his lips like a greedy six-year-old.

"Oh, we have plenty of those, not that you'll have any time for that." She nodded toward my belly. I smiled but hoped she was wrong. Maybe she'd want to baby-sit.

Aaron brought her a piece of paper—the invoice from the movers, I noticed—and a ballpoint pen with ink all over the barrel. She wrote her number and checked her fingers for smudges. The little girl was twirling through my rhododendrons, snapping off leaves. She picked the only zinnia, red, in the whole front garden, and tore the petals off, littering the lawn.

"Iris, stop that!" Thea said, without making a move to bring her command to fruition. I waved my hand to say *never mind.* I could forgive them a flower. I could do this good neighbor thing, too.

"Well," said Aaron. "Thank you so much for coming." He reached out to shake her hand, but Thea didn't understand. She leaned in as if to kiss his cheek, but her mouth didn't touch him. She walked out the door again. The air was thick with sidewalk steam, the rain trying its best to evaporate and rise before the sun set again.

"Let me know if you need anything," she said. "I'm right over the fence in the back." The picturesque Iris had chocolate on her cheeks and chocolate-covered baby teeth, and she started singing about the ducks again. Thea took Iris's hand, and even though her daughter resisted at first, she led her back down the walkway. The suburbs looked even better than I'd imagined—maybe Thea would have another baby and we could do strollercize together on the weekends. Maybe we'd have family picnics together and her older kids would take care of the younger ones and the grown-ups would go off to those myriad restaurants. It was such a generous gesture, so foreign to my experience; I told myself I'd make brownies if we ever got new neighbors. Of course, I'd be at work, but I could do it on weekends. Or holidays.

Aaron shut the door against the early-evening sun.

"Shall I make dinner?" he asked, pulling a whisk from a box by the steps. I sighed and reached for his waist. He rummaged in another box and pulled out a huge art history textbook. He held book and whisk triumphantly in the air.

"Mmm, whipped rococo," he said.

"I think we're going to like living here," I said. "Let's have brownies for dinner."

3

Amanda

After the move, I went in to the office two days a week. Perhaps I was still adapting to the commute, but the train ride felt interminable—I was sure I would vomit each time we passed through Hawthorne, Paterson, and Passaic. By Secaucus, though, I had usually settled in to thinking about something, dwelling even, the way I'd always focused too long on both things that mattered and those that didn't: The strange ticking in the wall when we ran the kitchen faucet, the art that was late for our new hardcover series on ducks in the ocean, the little bump inside my hand that my friend Rosanna in the art department had assured me was a ganglionic cyst, which I could have drained after I was done "cooking," as she put it. I was massaging the cyst on a too-hot September Monday, thinking it was maybe not a ganglionic cyst— maybe it was a tumor, maybe I needed to get it checked out *today* so I wouldn't die before I saw my baby born—when a string bean of a man, curved posture, barb tail of black hair, said, "Um, you're going to miss your transfer if you stay here."

The train had stopped, and I was just sitting. I'd seen string-bean man before—he boarded at my station. I thanked him and waddled over to transfer to my train, at first worrying that he was one of those weird men who became obsessed with pregnant women, and then realizing I was being absurd and that he was probably just a dad who lived in my town, who kissed his three kids and wife good-bye before he left. His wife was an optometrist, I decided as I huffed up the steps to my platform, looking out at the tangled root ball of train tracks leading into the station. They were probably as friendly as my new neighbor. This friendliness thing was going to take some effort to master. And I would have to switch it off once my train reached the city.

I was only a little late, and I was sure no one would notice. It had taken approximately a half hour to go six blocks from the PATH station to the office. Six sticky-skinned, achey-ankled blocks. The baby banged around inside me, her sharp ends asserting themselves against the spongy resistances of my liver, bladder, spine.

"You're late," said Neethi, walking past my office bearing a thick brown binder. I knew that binder. I remembered that binder from sometime last week. It had nothing to do with books, though—why couldn't I remember why that binder was important?

"We're due in the conference room to start this thing now."

"Of course," I said, ducking into my office. I had one of those binders, too, buried under the horrible pink stack of messages (They were supposed to forward calls home! How could I have so many messages? It had only been since Thursday!) and a loveseat-sized black portfolio that was hopefully the art for the ducks-in-the-ocean book. I grabbed my brown binder and took it to the conference room, hoping whatever thing this was wouldn't last more than an hour.

It did.

We had signed up for the Franklin Day Planner training day about seven months ago, when I'd imagined somehow I could reschedule, or that I might accidentally miss it; when I wasn't thinking about how devastating the loss of an entire day's work might be. That I might start crying if I didn't get to work today.

"Let's get started," said the oddly perfect-featured man in a dark blue suit who was animating the conference room with his picket-fence-white smile. His nose was narrow, not too long. His lips were embarrassingly bowed. His eyebrows were a few shades darker than his sleek russet hair.

"We're going to transform your lives today—together. We're going to improve how you work and how you play. This is a place of work," he continued. It almost sounded like *place of worship* to me. I looked around the conference room. Three editorial assistants. The director of production, two designers. Neethi, someone from accounting, someone from legal—our in-house council. I recognized her from the single legal issue I'd dealt with in eight years in publishing. Maybe her job was perfect—one lawyer among bookmakers. I should get a job as a publications director for a law firm. One bookmaker among lawyers. I think she mostly was left alone in her glassy corner office. I knew she had kids.

"So." I'd already missed a few Power Point presentation slides thinking about the in-house council. What was her name? Aliza?

"We're going to start with the personal before we move to the professional. I want you to write out a list of hopes and dreams. We're going to start here and work into concrete goals. But think big here, think personal."

"Um, Neethi?"

Neethi glared at me. She had a smudge of jelly on her collar and I thought, Doughnut.

"May I borrow a pen?"

I wrote out my dreams—wrote them down! Right in the room with Neethi and the director of production! I wrote: Healthy baby. Easy delivery. No more barfing. Good sex again. Keep my job. That was all I wanted, I thought. Then I added: Become editorial director. Have own imprint. Plumber finished by the time I get home.

"Now we're going to share them." Everyone groaned. I cupped my hand over my list. No way. "You have to open up and dig deep to change your life," said Mr. Perfect. He smiled, big teeth.

"I want to live on a boat," said our director of production, looking down at his paper, then out the window. "I always have."

Neethi gasped a little, then looked at me and smiled conspiratorially.

"I want a better job," said one of the editorial assistants, looking at the man as if he held the power to get this for her. "I want her job," she said, tilting her head toward me. The other assistants tittered, and the in-house council yawned.

When it was my turn, all I could say was, "I want to get back to work soon after the baby." It made my throat close up to say it. I wasn't a liar. "I mean, part-time at first—" Then I covered my mouth, not because I was afraid to say more, but because I had to run from the room to throw up. When I came back, it was coffee break time.

Three days a week I was supposed to work at home. So three days a week I hid upstairs or on the old beanbag chair in the half-finished basement, hoping not to encounter Mark the carpenter, who smelled of cigarettes and old cheese, or Ronnie the plumber, who was replacing lead pipes with some fancy new plastic ones, which would probably turn out, in fifteen years, to be more hazardous than lead. They weren't awful; I was simply intolerant of anyone in my space, and they always had questions. Ronnie had an assistant he called Wheeze, who actually was awful. He habitually requested root beer, as if I were the operator of a soda fountain. Wheeze left half-crushed soda cans behind the toilet and open potato chip bags on the mail table like a cat's carrion gifts. He never flushed.

On the Wednesday after the Franklin Day Planner Time Suck Day that made me think about what I really wanted, that made me break down my goals into small, attainable tasks—really nice stuff, except perhaps for the fact that breaking down labor into small, attainable moments of anticipated agony wasn't going to help much—I was trying to work in the bedroom. I lay on the bed letting the light from the windows cast beams on my legs. The walls, freshly painted, were pale green and soothing. I brought the cordless phone in with me, a svelte black dolphin with a hideous, sharp ringing sound. It rang all the time, sometimes waking me from a terrifically uncomfortable sleep during which I firmly believed I was editing the Rose manuscript, a young adult novel about a girl who becomes a world-class rock climber. Sometimes the phone was work. Assistants with questions, bosses with questions, marketing managers with questions. They were letting me be, they each said, they just had a quick issue. The quick issue often turned out to be checking to see whether I was really working and not wastefully lounging with the whole ocean inside me, gobbling Halloween candy a month in advance.

Even more often than work, the phone was my mother, my sister, my friend Rosanna, who was technically from work but only called to gossip, or Aaron. Aaron called six times a day, with not much to say, but always with a special ring of anticipation in his voice. I hated to disappoint him with the bland news of my discomforts. "Threw up again . . . yes, twice . . . I have an incredible charley horse. . . . Can you pick up more Tums on the way home?" When it was my sister, I felt as if I ought to woo her with interesting details. "Oooh, that was a kick," I'd say, sometimes even when I felt nothing.

When we were little girls, Jane was the one who played mommy all the time. She diapered her stuffed animals with paper towels and Scotch tape. She had triplet dolls she named Dolora, Adora, and Mora, whom she spoon-fed and offered milk, and whose naptime inspired fervent hushing sounds. I, on the other hand, was busy designing dioramas of Salem after our witch-hunt unit at school. My friend Diana came over and we held tiny trials with paper dolls. At her house we tapped at the hornets' nests under the giant rhododendrons in the backyard. We climbed the pine trees that secluded her family's deck and ate peanut butter sandwiches while talking about boys. I didn't spend a lot of time practicing for motherhood.

But despite marrying Cornelius years before I'd even met Aaron, Jane had put her child rearing on hold. At first we never talked about it, because it wasn't interesting to either of us. But once I knew I was pregnant, it was the magnetic core of my universe. All other topics swirled around with the dull import of cold stones. Pregnancy, babies, details, and due dates were hot and dazzling. So after I told Jane, I'd waited through weeks of conversations for her to say something about herself. And I'd waited more. And now I was in my third trimester, and the ridiculousness of being just a vessel made me brazen.

"So, Janey, when are you going to make a cousin for my baby?"

"Oh," she said, "so that's what you're after."

We'd just finished talking about her newest research paper, on symbolic metallurgy in *Dracula*. Jane would be up for tenure at Columbia, where she taught literature and feminist studies, in a year. While personally I felt that *Dracula* was a good story that had been absurdly overanalyzed, Jane was an academic, always looking for minutiae to reconstruct and reconstrue, to own and give to others as a gift, wrapped in polysyllabic discourse. Jane would probably get tenure. Her papers were published, her dissertation had been made into an academic tome, and her students adored her, leaving questions on the subtext of heroine worship in cramped blue pen on quartered sheets of notebook paper under her office door.

"No," I said. "I just thought we were done talking about *Dracula*. But I guess we'll never be done talking about *Dracula*."

"Or hemorrhoids," said Jane.

"Fair enough."

The phone buzzed with empty seconds between us.

"Okay," she said. "We are waiting until after tenure review. You can't tell Mom. And even then, I'm not sure; I might want another few years to try for full professor. I want to able to be home with a baby, if I have a baby. Sabbatical or something."

"Oh, Jane!" I took this as a big yes, soon.

"Subject closed." she said. "Deal?"

"Deal."

The phone clicked in a second of truceful silence.

"So," I said. "I have this great new neighbor." I'd been wondering when I'd see Thea again. We'd finished the brownies, and I knew I should return the plate. "She brought welcome food."

"Wow," said Jane. "Stepford wife?"

"Don't be mean," I said.

"Does she work?"

"I would guess not." I said. "Three young kids." I was proud of myself for not following that up with anything sarcastic. My graciousness campaign continued.

After we hung up, I fell asleep again and drooled on a particularly exhilarating rappelling scene in the Rose manuscript. I dreamed my father came to see my house. Dad had remarried six years ago and lived in a London suburb with his wealthy widowed wife and her two children, the boggy Diana, who was too sad for even my sister to ridicule, and hyperactive Henry, to whom Jane referred as Henry the Eighth with a surprising snideness. Mom and Dad divorced amicably, a sort of truce that frightened both Jane and me, because despite their very different ways, we'd never imagined they'd been anything but happy in their separate worlds of the marriage.

Now retired from teaching, Dad volunteered as a tutor at Henry the Eighth's prep school. I missed him and his quiet presence. I called him when I learned the news about the baby, and he had sent a giant teddy bear with HARROD'S printed on its chest. I hadn't been able to find it since the move—yet another unimportant detail that plagued me.

The phone woke me again. I gagged but recovered, picking it up.

"Darling," my mother said. "I'm on the cell. I've got half an hour until I have to be in the city."

"You're in New York?"

"Of course not, I'm home."

"You said the city."

My mother sighed. "Boston is a city, too," she said. "Darling, do you have stretch marks yet?"

Once upon a time, I'd been a Boston snob, too. I thought New Jersey, even the name, was a joke, unless you were talking about milk or tomatoes. I grew up in the suburbs, and my first real city experience was in Providence, Rhode Island, where I rented an apartment off campus and felt cosmopolitan. After Brown I thought about graduate school, but instead I moved to New York City with two other English majors, and we all got jobs in publishing and argued over whose turn it was to buy toilet paper.

I started in magazines and found the frenetic pace and emphasis on personal attire exhausting. One of my roommates worked in children's books, so I made the switch. For the first few years, I imagined this was a temporary job, that I'd get a degree in something else, but after a while I got promoted. The corner offices and the senior editors' correspondence files stuffed with author endearments and discussions of tense, or the symbolism of red hats, or reading level, looked fascinating. The Frankfurt Book Fair and Bologna beckoned. When my boss, Neethi, returned, aglow with the marvelous projects she'd acquired, the party gossip and agent lunches and author parties scheduled like bright lights through the gray tunnel of winter, I knew I wanted to keep doing this until I became her.

It wasn't only the glamour that drew me, it was the books. I fell in love with them, especially picture books, the marriage of a slim little bride of a tale or a flamboyant bride with unusual adjectives and leaping syntax, and a groom, artwork, plain and clean or dazzling with color, shape, excitement. Silver dragons, zinnias with silky purple petals and secret faces.

Some projects didn't actually seem to be for children; they were really for parents who had to read aloud every night, stories built with morality and double entendre and, often, a wildness bordering on sacrilege. Children, though, were part of the vision for me; the words were meant to be read aloud, the details of the art highlighted by a questioning toddler finger. But the wholeness of the project—buying a manuscript, simply words printed out on a sheet of paper, and pairing it with someone's fanciful, purposeful style of painting or drawing, someone's interpretation—was a thrill. It was as mysterious and chemical as baking: ingredients and temperature were just the details, the outcome as miraculous (and potentially disastrous) a convergence as chocolate-orange soufflé.

Because she was still talking about stretch marks, I interrupted my mother.

"Did you save anything from when we were babies, Mom? Do you have any blankets or anything?"

She was not distractible.

"My dermatologist recommends the most delicious-smelling cream. Of course there's the real stuff, Retin-A, but you can't use that until after you've popped."

"Ugh. You make it sound so gruesome."

"It is gruesome, hon. But at least you'll get your epidural as soon as you arrive. I only wish they had them for me."

"So, did you keep anything?"

"I'll look. Anyway, you can get the stretch-mark cream at this place in the city—I mean *your* city this time—"

"I'm kind of not making a lot of special trips, Mom."

"And what about that nausea? Still chucking? I didn't, you know. Not a single day, though I had horrible water retention. My feet swelled terribly, and they've never been the same."

"You did tell me, Mom."

"The stretch marks are pretty bad, but C-section scars are worse."

"I'm not planning to wear bikinis soon, Mom. You know, I'm trying to get my layette in order. I was wondering about nightgowns."

"Don't put yourself down, darling, you have a perfectly lovely body."

My mother could say this because she was thin. And at the moment, thin was not only something I was generally not, it was something I was specifically miles away from.

"Especially those little feet. I always loved your feet. Are they swollen?" She sighed.

I looked down in the direction of my feet. They itched, but I wasn't sure how I could get them somewhere I could reach to scratch, or even close enough to see whether they were swollen. All I wore these days were clogs. A knee or an elbow surfaced and ran along my belly like a shark's fin cutting through surf.

"She's kicking, Mom. I can see. It's incredible."

"My signal's fading, sweetie," said my mother.

I wished my mother would send something, a nightgown, a onesie, a blanket. I wished most for something from my own infancy, which seemed as incomprehensible to me as a Mars landing. But three days later when I tore open the firmly wrapped, priority-mail package that arrived with my mother's handwriting on the address label, I discovered she'd sent the special stretch-mark cream with no note. It smelled like coconut and made me hungry. I wanted to appreciate it, but like most other things in the last weeks of pregnancy, this not-quite-right gesture made me retreat to the beanbag in the basement where I could weep in my hormonal, self-sorry state without interruption from the carpenter.

October

4

Thea

Someone had been stealing pumpkins from the walkways and porches in the neighborhood, and it wasn't the ordinary teen demolition, where the evidence would be smashed on the sidewalk, sad smeared orange skin and flesh, seeds spread like obscenities. Instead, the pumpkins were vanishing. It didn't happen overnight, or in the evening, when I was out in the garden, mournful of the clamping hand of cold and the early dew and the last of the roses, their heads bowed with defeat. Someone had found some sliver of daytime when no one was around, and had taken the Turners' giant pumpkin and the Martins' stingy miniature gourd and the tall lean one they'd set at the base of a porch pillar.

The second Wednesday in October, I carved our pumpkins at night, after cleaning up, and Caius watched from a collapsed posture in a chair and made suggestions while I tried not to resent the intrusion. When we were first married, we'd collaborated on a jack-o'-lantern for our apartment, each cutting an eye, an ear. Caius made the mouth and the nose was mine. It was ghoulish. Caius's eye was an uneven slit; mine was enormous and round. The nose and mouth were inverted, a fermata. We'd smeared each other with the goop; we'd eaten burned roasted pumpkin seeds and made love still salty and squash scented, tasting each other's autumn mouths in the deep inside of the city. The nest within a nest of our apartment. No kids had come for our candy, so we ate coconut chocolate and miniature bars of Special Dark and went to bed without brushing our teeth.

On Thursday, our jack-o'-lanterns vanished. Sometime between picking up Oliver and bringing Carra to swim practice, while Iris chewed a crayon in the backseat, purpling her teeth, they went missing. I tried not to take it personally, noticing that my scarecrow, though slightly soggy from a storm, was still intact, corncob pipe and all.

The new neighbors' porch was empty, and I wondered whether their pumpkin had been stolen or whether, pregnant as she was, she had overlooked this detail. Perhaps they were the kind of people who got their pumpkin on October thirtieth. I didn't really know what kind of people they were and kept wondering whether I was supposed to visit or keep my distance. She'd asked so many questions—did she expect me to stop by with the plumber's number? I saw her bundling off to the train many mornings, but this afternoon the car was parked in the drive.

When I'd stopped by with the brownies, I'd been struck by her particular kind of attractiveness—not at all typical, she was zaftig in the best sense. Her short, dark hair was rich; her smile was opulent and ironic. Of course, she was pregnant, but there was something about her body's roundness that made me see why men might like to watch her. As someone who had often been called pretty—a plain word, actually, almost a minor put-down—I felt as though I recognized a different kind of beauty in her, or maybe it wasn't beauty, maybe she was just plain sexy. Or maybe I was jealous of her pregnancy, though I ought not to be. Perhaps when she wasn't holding someone else inside her skin she was ordinary.

I watched Iris dig at the edge of the fence—close to their property—while bread baked in our kitchen. Maybe Amanda would come out to the fence. Maybe I was being overeager. I had friends, after all, and she probably did, too. But she was new here, and having her next door seemed so auspicious.

"Don't dig there, Jitterbug!" I called out to Iris. "Want to come inside?"

The sky was bright and suddenly it was cold enough for a sweater. I wondered what had changed—the wind, the intensity of the sun? It was a matter of a few degrees, like everything else, like the zone of fertility, like the waking of yeast, short sleeves to sweater.

"No, Mama," said Iris. She looked me in the eye and started to eat the dirt.

"Iris, love, that's yucky," I said, sweeping her up. She wailed but wasn't fully committed to a tantrum, at least not yet.

Caius hadn't really wanted three. We had our heirs, he joked, the boy, the girl. I had, though; I had needed to refill my arms as soon as Oliver left them. Now, I surely didn't want four, but sometimes I wondered if we ought to have one more, partly to clear our mouths, like sorbet, after the heavy meal of Iris's infancy. Ridiculous—who was to say another baby wouldn't be as difficult as Iris, or even *more* difficult? I was staring down thirty-seven. It was getting late; my body was getting tired of the great feat of growing babies. We didn't have room, we didn't have *that* much money for college, and I surely didn't have the energy. But I thought it anyway. If I got pregnant now, we'd have our own new one next summer, right before Iris headed off for preschool. She or he could play with the older baby next door. I wiped my hands on my jeans, ridding myself of the ridiculous idea.

"Fog!" yelled Iris. I'd just rested her on the back steps to open the door, but she darted down again and scrambled across the lawn, chasing something, a bunny perhaps.

"Not dog. Bunny?" I asked.

"Fog," said Iris again as she ran to the fence, then recommenced digging in the cold dirt like a puppy.

"Don't dig," I said.

"Fog," she said. I scooped her up to bring her inside. My knees cracked and ached. Transitions were never easy. It was hard for Iris to give up on what she was doing for what I decided she would be doing next. For several months I tried giving her warnings, since that had worked with the other two, but Iris invariably tried to escape as soon as I told her my plans. Change was hard for all toddlers, but especially Iris, who started screaming and kicking. Her sneakers thumped my thighs as I held her tight. My hip ached. I didn't like transitions myself. It was the least I could do to make her feel strongly held, even if she had no choice about when she had to come inside.

From the back step I could see the "fog" of her exclamations. A pudgy groundhog shuffled and sniffed the air in Amanda's yard. I wondered how Iris had named it—I didn't remember ever seeing one with her, except from the car, since they loved to graze alongside the Garden State Parkway. It had squashed itself under the fence from our yard to Amanda's, where probably the grass was sweeter with possibility.

"Hi lady!" Iris yelled across the lawn, forgetting her dramatic sorrow. "Hi!"

Our new neighbor looked up and waved lightly, a noncommittal sort of wave. I felt the rush of change. Suddenly I wasn't alone with Iris, I had an audience, I had company. Adult company, maybe a little understanding. Little girls are so temperamental, I said silently, raising my eyebrows.

"I like what you've done," I called to her, walking over to the fence, relinquishing a squirmy Iris. Amanda stood with her back to me, running her fingertip over the pickets of the fence they'd had put in on the other side, between their lot and the Martins'. The wood looked raw, ready to suck in rain or paint.

"Well," said Amanda, turning to face me as if we always talked across the lawns, "I didn't want to say anything, but . . . well . . . are they"—she jutted her elbow in the direction of the Martins' house—"are they always, um, territorial?"

I laughed. I'd wondered what it would be like, moving in beside the Martins, your first house. When Tia had lived there, we could hear the Martins arguing from her bedroom, through layers of glass and wood and the spindly fir trees. They'd yelled often, at each other, at their children; they'd yelled when alone on the telephone. Usually I couldn't make out the words, but Tia said they fought about "how stupid they are—she tells him he's an idiot and he calls her the *B* word." Still, they sometimes held hands when they were walking the rat terrier they had for two years before Jack Martin crushed it backing out of the driveway in one of his trucks.

"You know," I said, leaning as far as I could over the fence. "He has a plate in his head," I whispered. I felt childish saying it this way, but it was true. Perhaps it would help to know. "He was hurt in a machinery accident at work—"

Amanda waded closer to the fence; she was wearing a nightgown under her coat.

"Oh, are you on bed rest?"

She looked at me sharply. Maybe I shouldn't have asked. *Well, you really shouldn't be up if you are*, I thought, worrying for her.

"I just got up for a minute. To see the fence. We wanted to get it painted before it gets cold." She looked at the red-slashed maples.

"Oh, I know. I hated bed rest. So anyway, the Martins aren't that bad—but they aren't that good. What happened with the fence?"

Amanda leaned on the post. She smiled a little. "We went over to tell them, because we had the survey done when we were inspected? Anyway, we wanted to tell them we were putting in a little strip here, and that we'd match their fence if they wanted. They have a piece in the back—"

I knew this. I knew the inside of her backyard from a dozen years ago. More.

"—though theirs is facing the wrong direction so we thought it might be ours. You're supposed to face the smooth side out. And when we did the survey their fence was on our property. Three feet in, actually. Aaron wanted to have it moved, but I thought that might be too much." She ran her fingers through her hair, a five-pronged comb. Her hair was thick and brown, with gold and red glints in the sunlight.

"Anyway, we said we'd match their fence and he said, 'You'd better not be getting a dog. I don't like dogs—' and he did this thing with his hand, like a gun! Can you believe that? Like he'd shoot a dog if we had a dog? God, I had no idea people would be so hostile. We were just trying to be polite. Then when my fencing contractor was here, he came out and argued with him about the posts. We did it inside the survey line but he accused my contractor of lying—I couldn't believe it! I stayed inside and steamed, but I really wanted to come out and tell him off. I wouldn't. I just wanted to. I'm *supposed* to be on bed rest." She patted her stomach, as if I didn't already know.

"They're not the easiest neighbors," I said, laughing lightly. "But they'll leave you alone."

"As long as they don't shoot my dog," said Amanda.

"You have a dog?"

"No," she smiled. I knew that smile, the secret smile of feeling wretched and also able to fight dragons. Of having to pee every six seconds. It was a brief communication, her smile. We both knew what it was like.

"Are you going back to work after the baby?" I asked. Something flashed across her face, too quickly for me to tell what emotional lightning it was. I was only asking; everyone asked this question, didn't they?

"After leave," she said.

I nodded, hating the awkward pause.

"Well, welcome to the neighborhood," I said. I couldn't decide whether she made me nervous or comfortable—there was some-thing about her, something almost aggressive. Maybe it was just her city skin. Or maybe I was being defensive; after all, I had had the same neighbor almost all my life.

"Ha! Thank you. Glad *you're* the one on the other side."

Me, too, I thought. I was going to enjoy having a baby next door.

"Don't worry about the Martins. Once you're established, I don't think they'll bother you much. They're too confined by the storms of their own small systems of strife."

"Yikes, how poetic." Was she serious or sarcastic?

"That's the suburbs for you," I tried.

Amanda rubbed her belly and didn't meet my eye. My phone rang; I said good-bye, scooped up Iris, and went inside feeling slightly puzzled but flushed nonetheless with the briefest moment of neighborly bonding.

5

Amanda

Less than a week before Halloween, there were pumpkins out on everyone's porches except for ours. I couldn't bear a trip in the car, not to mention heaving a giant gourd into the trunk, and I hoped Aaron would volunteer to go. But when he finally got home from work, after a long stretch of my pretending to myself I wasn't waiting for his company, he had things other than Halloween decor that required his attention. Like unpacking the groceries I'd had to leave in the car, and making dinner, and finding his dress shirts among the remaining boxes. And sleep. His slouch and the down-turned corners of his eyes made him appear even more tired than I felt, so I didn't bring up the issue of porch decorations. I wondered who we were becoming; I was beached on the couch and he was a work zombie. When I'd met him, Aaron was already working for the firm, but he'd still been different—still been a man who didn't quite belong where he was, who held foreignness in his smile, an attractive otherness.

Aaron and I met at an author's vacation house in Vermont one winter weekend; I drove up in a rented car in time to watch him grappling with too many logs from the well-stocked woodpile, spilling most of his load onto the path and wiggling his slipper-shod feet like a cat to shake off the snow. The author was having a weekend-long book party, and she hadn't told me she'd invited Aaron, her husband's lawyer. I saw him and laughed as I sunk the car's wheels too deep in a crusty snowbank. I thought, nice Jewish New York boy, probably born and raised on the Upper West Side.

My instinct was wrong: Aaron wasn't from New York, though he looked as prissy about the splinters and woodpile cobwebs as the best city boy. He was a year younger than I was, and he had been born and had spent his first decade in Kenya, where his father was working for a hospital and his mother was learning not to feel too guilty about dirt cheap domestic help. Then they moved many times: Hawaii, D.C., Brazil, the French Congo, and ultimately, as I'd guessed from my faulty first impression, New York. NYU undergrad, NYU law school. Aaron tried to make up for his childhood peregrinations by staying put in his adult life. He still spoke a few words of Swahili and wore a braided metal bracelet on the weekends, and the cultures of his childhood wove through his perspective like a gold thread in an ordinary gray suit.

"You should do a book on spiders," Aaron said to the author, sitting on her couch and looking at me, enough, not too much.

"I was bitten by a brown recluse once," I said.

"Can't blame him," said Aaron, his forehead revealingly flushed.

"My, my," said the author, smiling at me. She had long gray hair and attractive big teeth. "You've got an admirer," she said.

"Oh, I'm afraid I killed her," I said. "It was a girl—she had eggs."

"As long as you're not so rough with all your aficionados," said Aaron. He got up to clear our plates of lemon cake, comfortable in the task. I admit, I watched him walk away and knew he knew I was watching.

I found myself thinking about him all the time when I got back to the city.

Aaron called me cute things, things I wouldn't have let other boyfriends call me: Manda, Panda, Mango. He sang "Brown-Eyed Girl," a little bit out of tune; it was gorgeous. When we were first living together, he brought me small gifts from his day—a cookie from his client lunch, wrapped in a cloth napkin stolen from some posh restaurant and taped with masking tape from his desk; Post-its with my name doodled during a meeting; tiny origami birds he made with exquisite expensive papers from Dokument, a gorgeous, expensive little stationery shop near Sutton Place. He brought me the last bite of his cake, he brought me matchbooks and, instead of hotel soaps and shampoos, the sewing kit from every place he'd had to go on business without me. Which was very often. I kept the little threads wound and intact, the tiny scissors folded. A catalogue of sewing kits rested neatly beneath the knee-highs in my drawer.

Now that I was home, full-time, I was supposed to lie on the couch and let the gravity of pregnancy overtake me. My blood pressure was up a bit, and my doctor suggested that I quit the commute entirely and only come in for appointments and soon, very soon, the delivery. Soon couldn't possibly be soon enough, because I was a vast balloon with legs, enormous and weary and ready to have her out, to hold my baby, my real pumpkin, instead of carrying her inside, with her portable swimming pool beneath my freshly stretch-marked skin.

Maybe it was my mother's fault for mentioning it so often. For the first seven and a half months, I made it without a single red complaint on my belly, but the lines began to appear, bright as magic marker, right after I'd convinced myself I'd escape unscathed. It wasn't that I was obsessed with my body. I was never thin, but I had spent lunch breaks and nights at the gym, keeping my body in check. The red cracks looked hideous, and there was nothing I could do about them; they itched and I despised them.

She was worth it, of course, my still-indoors baby girl. Most of the time I believed myself when I said that, "Worth it, all of it," about the vomiting and the stabbing pains in my lower back and the heartburn and, now, the lines. So I could only joke about how much I really detested pregnancy.

"At least you get a big present at the end," I said to the cashier at Rite Aid, who was kind enough not to comment on my prune juice, panty liner, and candy bar purchase.

"Yeah, but you won't sleep for *years*," she said, and she looked like she hadn't.

Aaron and I had picked out the baby's name, Malena Greenberg-Katz, as soon as we knew the gender from the amnio. We'd narrowed down our list from ten names we each liked—there was no intersection—and then I found Malena on the M page and remembered it was mentioned in a Hans Christian Andersen tale. We both liked it, at last, bleary headed from scanning the name books. It wasn't after anyone, and we chose no middle name since the hyphenated last was so long. Because we didn't want too many opinions, we told only one person each and made them promise not to leak. I told my sister, Jane, and Aaron told his best friend at work. I kept thinking of my mother's reaction to New Jersey, and I was afraid she'd say something subtly damning, like, "Are you *sure*?" or "Well, that's an interesting possibility."

Years before, when I first started my job—waking to the shrill complaint of the alarm, taking time for a shower and layers of makeup and hair stuff and a bagel with cream cheese from the shop one door down from my apartment and one block from the subway—I fantasized about a week to myself, all free, when I would sleep late, wake to eat, sleep some more, read books, and sleep.

But now that I was plunked like a gigantic water balloon in the suburbs, with nothing to do but lounge, I thought about everything I couldn't do, and when I tried to nap, I worried instead. From the living room couch, I could see out onto the front walks of half a dozen neighbors, and I knew that I was falling behind at this house-ownership game. There were tall bound sheaves of autumn wheat, festive skeleton and witch flags, pumpkins round with jack-o'-lantern potential, even a few scarecrows stuffed with the dried remains of summer grasses and dressed in red-checked shirts that once graced the broad suburban shoulders of men who climbed ladders to clean out the gutters with leather-gloved hands.

I missed seeing Rosanna at work, getting lunch at the falafel cart and sitting on a bench gossiping, napkins covering our clothes so we wouldn't come back covered with tahini sauce. Rosanna and her ridiculous office, a fire hazard, piles and piles of artwork, illustrations for books, manuscripts marked up for design. We never discussed it, but the only reason she hadn't been fired for her extraordinary mess was because she was an utterly brilliant designer, sometimes too avant-garde but always original. She had tantrums when the art director asked her to "tone down" a book jacket where the title was illegible but the overall design was mesmerizing. She lost important projects in her piles daily, but she won awards. She also knew all the gossip. Since I'd been pregnant, though, we had less to gossip about. Rosanna was single and an exercise addict—she went to the gym before and after work every day, ran marathons, met men at Hudson River swims, and had never learned to drive. She said she'd come out to see me at the house, but I knew that might only happen once, when I had a baby to show for all the complaining I'd done. I tried to ration my calls to Rosanna, because I needed to have something new to say. I was sure our growing home-improvement list would be less than riveting.

I wanted to fix the shed with the rattly glass window—actually, I thought we should tear the whole thing down, but Aaron loved the idea of a shed. "For our skis and your garden stuff and the kids' Rollerblades and all the bikes that won't fit in the garage!" he'd kvelled, even when I pointed out that we had a perfectly good garage. "Since when do I garden?" I'd asked, but he'd only kissed my intentionally sour face.

I needed to find a lawn service, because our grass was an embarrassing forest where the bunnies hid. In the back, some animal had dug a hole under the fence. Aaron saw it on the third morning I was staying home, and he came upstairs to tell me about it at six-thirty, when the light on the window shades was still thin with ambition. He didn't know what it was.

"It's huge and furry and kind of looks like a hedgehog or maybe not, because it isn't spiky. Are there some kind of very small bears here? Or giant wild guinea pigs?" He smelled of aftershave, musky.

"I don't know, honey. I think we'll have to get a field guide to suburban wildlife."

Aaron laughed. "Then we'd be able to identify all these massive cars, and we could tell roofers from landscapers from plumbers."

"I can tell. Just read their trucks."

"That's cheating. Do you see it? Get up for a second, Mango, look out the window—it's amazing and gigantic and furry."

"And you're late," I said.

"Oh, man," said Aaron. He looked at the clock and ran down the stairs. I heard the car start—the small car, a sporty Honda with low tires and ordinary seats, into which I could no longer easily fit—and I envied his quick escape. I envied his full, important day, so unlike mine, which was long and hollow and ornamented with physical discomforts.

Still, I was curious, so I waddled down the stairs. By the time I made it down, I had to sprint to the kitchen sink to throw up. I rinsed my mouth and looked out the window, but didn't see any small hairy bearlike beast. But finally, after Aaron called me from work, three times, to ask me how I was and had I seen it, I looked out the back window and saw the groundhog. I automatically knew what it was, but I looked it up online anyway, enjoying the photos of fat furries, the nickname (whistlepig), the details (groundhog gestation is only thirty days). Lucky fur balls. I hoped they didn't wreck the yard with their tunneling.

"Your bear, your invader, your wild thing," I said to Aaron on our fourth call, "is a whistlepig."

"A whistlepig! What is that? Is it poisonous?"

"I'm not planning to eat it, are you? A groundhog."

"Oh, just a groundhog," he said. He was disappointed that it wasn't something more exotic, he who had grown up with monkeys who stole dried-fruit provisions and hyenas laughing up the night. But he said he'd love going around his office telling people he'd seen a groundhog in his own backyard. Now that his intrigue had waned, mine grew. Was it burrowing under the house? Would it have babies of its own in the spring? Would it poop all over the lawn? Would it bite my baby, or could we make a pet of it?

Instead of tackling my list of home improvements, I lay on the couch and thought about whistlepigs and tried to nap and finally called work, checking my voice mail and feeling weepy when I listened to a message one of my authors left about something I couldn't do anything about from home. I tried to respond to anything I could—I called back, checked in with the design director and production, agonized over a project whose pub date had been bumped an entire list because the galleys were a wreck with the author's alterations. I knew I ought to let it go. In a week or so I wouldn't be able to do anything, at least for a few more weeks. My mother called and suggested I get a manicure.

"It'll be months before you can get out again," she said.

"I don't like manicures," I said. "Remember?"

"And eat out," she said. "And get yourself a haircut."

"What's wrong with my hair?" I touched the even ends of my bob. Since pregnancy, my hair had gotten thick and heavy, and at night I sweated until my head was soaked.

"Pumpkins," I thought she said.

"Excuse me?" I plugged my other ear so I could hear her more clearly over the chorus of leaf blowers outside.

"My silly cell phone—I said, perfect, your hair is perfect. But you won't have time to have it done, later. No time whatsoever."

It had sounded like *pumpkins* to me. I went out to the front porch to sit in the late-afternoon light, the soft orange cool. For a minute, all was peaceful. I was going to have a baby, miracle of miracles. Leaves rose in drifts on our unmowed lawn. Down the street, I saw a lone figure negotiate a walkway, then another. The person appeared to be inspecting the porch pumpkins, and I wondered whether this was some strange suburban ritual I hadn't learned growing up in Massachusetts. Down the block, three teenagers laughed and walked along—hunched, furtive, nervous, but mostly just adolescent. They stepped up to a neighbor's scarecrow and one guy chucked it on the head, but even the hat stayed in place. Then they jogged off down the cul-de-sac toward the woods.

I worried about the woods. Who knew what was going on down there, what rituals and leaf fires and what dangerous play in the creek? There was a rope swing over the water—I'd seen it dangling, nooselike, when we took a reconnaissance trip down the path before we put our bid in on the house. Then it had seemed like a quaint place, like a respite from the evenness of lawns. But now I felt menaced by all those trees, all that cover for lurkers or mean-derers, so close to home. Aaron said I was being silly and it was probably just pregnancy hormones at work again.

The pumpkin inspector crossed the street and started down the cul-de-sac after the teens. I couldn't tell, for the big sail of a hat, whether it was a man or a woman who shuttled, quick but awk-ward, toward the woods.

The orange light collapsed into a chilly evening. It was sudden that way here, and I felt mournful for long summer evenings, though I'd grown weary of the heat, the slovenly spray of the sum-mer rain. What was left of the light showed a spot of dark gray advancing from the east above the roofs. In the city, you never saw a storm coming this way—either there was bad weather, or there wasn't; the buildings seemed to hold systems between them. And sometimes I was inside so much that I didn't have time to notice it was raining until it was finished, and I went out into slicked streets and lamps haloed by the steam of heated water rising from the concrete.

I shivered and went inside, relinquishing the magic of the outside world. Even though it was too late, I had to do something; I got out the yellow pages and left messages for a landscaper, for

Bobby the painter, and for the Chipper Cleaning Service! Bonded! Licensed! First Visit Free!

I called Aaron, got voice mail. "Come home soon," I said. "Stop spreading groundhog rumors. It's too quiet here."

I noticed the baby had stopped moving as much. I'd grown used to her kick turns at the end of the womb pool, to internal battering or quick flicks of limbs. Sometimes her butt pressed up against my ribs and the pain was sharp, like heartburn, which I also had, constantly. Aaron called and said he wouldn't be home for dinner. I looked in the fridge and took two bites from a block of cheese. Then I leafed through the half-eaten bags of pretzels in the cabinet and decided I really needed to eat the canned baby corn. The tiny kernels felt good against my teeth, but after three miniears, I felt very green and didn't want them anymore.

As night settled in, the storm crept closer, the thunder like a band playing in the next town. I waited for the sound on the roof, and I waited for the baby to move. I gave up on TV and tried to read the manuscripts I'd brought home from the slush pile, something I usually left to my assistant, but something I could do, with no time limit, at home. The first was a young-adult novel set in New Orleans about a child who witnessed a murder, and I sighed. I didn't even want to assess the writing. The world was far too full of dangers to invent more peril in the world of fiction. I turned on the CD player and turned *The Marriage of Figaro* up loud, giving the baby a dose of classical music, giving myself a manageable drama other than my own.

The storm finally reached the house, and the air split with the cracking sound of thunder. I liked it and how it made my blood race into my fingers, pulsing in my throat. The baby still didn't shift, and I put my hands on my belly, willing her to let me know everything was okay. I thought about calling my doctor, after-hours, on his special number for labor or important questions, but I wasn't that kind of patient. All along I had planned to be brave and to be no trouble, to tough out labor or have an epidural if my body told me to, and if

Dr. Papageno thought it was prudent; to nurse immediately, as La Leche League and all my books recommended; to show Malena the view from the hospital window and tell her that this was New York City, where she had been conceived. Forever she would write NEW YORK, NEW YORK, on forms that requested place of birth.

Another splitting sound, a tear in the wet fabric of the air, and the lamps all went out at once. I sat in the dark for a second, thrilling. But after three more seconds, with Malena quiet inside me, I got nervous. What if Aaron's train couldn't make it home? What if everything in the fridge spoiled? What if marauding bandits took advantage of the storm and came barging right through the front door to steal our cash and Aaron's undiscovered boxes of dress shirts? I was absurdly nervous, both sweating and cold. Then Malena shifted slightly. Relief—at least she was okay in there.

The dark grew increasingly malevolent. I groped in the kitchen until I found something I thought was a flashlight, but it was the turkey baster. Finally I found a match, and then, in my purse, the penlight I always kept for emergencies. Was this an emergency? The phone was dead, so I couldn't call Aaron's cell phone to see if he was on his way. I'd left my own cell at the office by mistake.

Then, as I stood in the kitchen shining that feeble light onto the items in the cabinet, I was ravenous for almonds. Rummaging through the olives and the rice and ancient jarred macadamias we'd brought from our minuscule kitchen in the city, I found a pristine can of cocktail nuts. I opened it and sifted through it for the almonds, which were the most delicious thing I'd ever tasted. And for the first time since my first few weeks of pregnancy, I felt good.

The storm had stopped crackling and thunking, and now only a thin drumming of rain punctuated the night. A bird sang inexplicably, joyous and doodly, as I finished the almonds and started in on hazelnuts, which were not as good but certainly better than Brazils or piddly peanuts.

Someone thumped on the door.

A burglar. Someone who wanted to steal the silver. Or worse.

Thump-thump.

Burglars didn't knock.

I went to the door armed with the nut-jar lid and my penlight and steeled myself to open it. There was the sunny face of Thea the neighbor. She was holding something orange, about the size of a soup pot, and in front of it she gripped an old-fashioned hurricane lantern, the light so bright I couldn't look directly into her face.

"Hello," she said, as my eyes adjusted. "I've meant to bring you this for days now. It's been so busy."

It was surprisingly warm outside, with cold close on the storm's steamy heels. The air smelled of torn green and soil and worms.

Thea's hair had escaped her raincoat hood and lay in slick blond strings around her face. I'd forgiven her for asking about work with that *look* on her face. Maybe I'd imagined the look. Everyone asked. Besides, if I could be as content and fulfilled a stay-at-home mom as she appeared to be, I'd probably do that, too. But that wasn't me— it wouldn't ever be me.

Thea held out a pumpkin. I almost loved her.

"Oh," she said. She put it down on the porch instead of into my open hands. "I didn't mean to make you lift. I came over because of the storm. I mean, is everything okay? Do you need anything?"

"To get this baby out of me," I said out loud, before I had a chance to think. My mouth felt crusty with salt and nuts.

"Um? I'll just put this here." She pointed at the pumpkin.

"Thank you so much. I wanted to get a pumpkin—I kept meaning to—it seems like pumpkins are essential here." I gripped the doorframe. "But I couldn't go out to get one."

"Bed rest." She smiled knowingly. "It'll be done soon. I know, I always hated the last few weeks." She stood for a second, looking picturesque: Her casually soaked hair, the pumpkin she'd placed on the stoop like a sentry. Probably I should invite her inside, I thought, without moving. This was a neighbor, a real neighbor. And unlike anyone I'd ever only just met, I trusted her.

"Were your labors tough?" I knew I shouldn't ask, for my sake more than hers.

She smiled, but the joy was reserved. "It seems huge, but it's over very quickly in the scheme of things," she said. "Are you scared?"

No one had ever asked that outright. And I was, I was so scared I didn't want to admit it.

"Yes?" I said. "But Aaron will be there. . . ."

"He's charming, your husband." I looked at her luminous face—I almost asked her to come with me when I delivered. I realized I'd had her standing on my porch in the dark this whole time.

"Oh, do you want to come in?" She was dripping on the porch, a small rain beneath the roof.

"No, thanks. I've got to get back to the kids—unless—are you okay? These blackouts can be a little spooky. You could come over."

I pictured a warm, yellow kitchen. Fresh-baked bread—probably pumpkin—milk in jelly-jar glasses. I needed to stay home, though. Besides, it was hard to tell when people were offering because they felt they ought to and when it was courtesy, even with Thea, who was so even and warm it felt authentic.

"Thank you, but I need to unpack some boxes."

She raised an eyebrow. "Nesting," she said. "That usually means you're in the homestretch. If you need anything—" She pointed toward her house, her arm a single soldier in a yellow raincoat, lit by the lantern. This way to safety. I leaned over the threshold and kissed her cheek, more grateful for a gourd than my ordinary self would allow.

I was calmer after Thea's visit, but I couldn't stop digging for sudden necessary treasures. For three hours I sorted the contents of the remaining boxes in the basement by the waning penlight, until I found Aaron's shirts packed in with his record collection. We no longer had a turntable, and the shirts were wrinkled.

When Aaron came home I didn't even hear him at the door. But as he started down the steps, calling for me, all the lights came back on, and the clock radios blinked and the CD player started playing

Cecelia Bartoli singing "Porgi Amor" at top volume. I looked up at my husband and felt the strangest urge to get to the bathroom.

"Honey," he said, "what are you doing? Was the power off long? Are you okay? I tried to call. The train was stopped and they put us on buses. There's a tree down at the end of the block, so I had to climb through someone's lilacs to get home."

"My water just broke," I said as the gush wet my pants, every inch of them, and filled my shoes with warm amniotic fluid, which smelled ever so slightly of almonds.

November

6

Thea

I shouldn't have expected a call, but I somehow wished I could've been involved, could have helped. Amanda had seemed both tough and vulnerable—like most first-time moms—when I came with the pumpkin, and that ended up being her big night. She had driven to the city despite the storm's mess to have her baby. I tried to imagine feeling so devoted to the place, to the tiny hospital rooms, to the gritty streets. I remembered how the subways smelled like rotted cabbage, even in the winter. Of course, her doctor was there, and that made sense. I'd moved from Manhattan and had all my babies at the hospital in Ridgewood, six miles from Sylvan Glen, where the doctors were perfectly good and where they'd delivered a dozen sets of triplets, hundreds of preemies, and one set of quints without incident. We'd gone there as kids for broken bones or swallowed objects; we'd each been born there ourselves. But when Oren was dying, we'd trooped into the city to the special hospitals where they were expert at prolonging his death, though that wasn't what they called it. They called it experimental treatment.

Jillian Martin was the first to tell me the Birth Story. She was watering her hanging pots, the impatiens mostly dead, the mums brown from overwatering. I could tell she couldn't wait to share the news, starting in as I walked down the drive from the backyard.

"It was a very, very long labor," she called to me with vibrating authority, as if she'd been there. I wondered whether Amanda could hear her over at her house.

"Oh, I didn't know." I was out for a quick breather, collecting fallen branches and twigs from the most recent downpour. I brought them to the curb. The sky was the bleached blue that comes after a squall and the air felt clean.

"In the morning, two weeks ago, after that big storm," she said. "Her water broke first. Her husband took her into the *city*." She yelled this word like an expletive, and I put down the last of the debris and walked around to her porch.

Two days after I brought Amanda a pumpkin, I'd seen the pink balloons tied out on their tree and supposed that was announcement enough. They were allowed to be private. And overwhelmed. Then everyone at my house got sick, so I hadn't brought anything over. "A covered dish," my mother used to say, "maintains a civil society." I hadn't really been out of my own house recently, except to go get soup ingredients and Children's Tylenol and rental movies.

"And she went for eight hours with no progress, so they started the Pitocin, you know, that drug that stimulates labor? But that didn't help, so it was another eight hours, and then it was a C-section."

"Oh, that's too bad. Boy or girl?" I knew from the balloons, but I asked reflexively.

"No shame in a C-section. My aunt had a C-section. They thought my cousin had spinal problems because of it but that wasn't the reason."

"No, it probably wouldn't be—"

"Wasn't your father a doctor?"

"Mathematician," I said.

"I saw her yesterday—bringing the baby outside *already?* We waited a month at least. And anyway they already knew it was a girl."

"I have to go," I said, wishing I were inventing the excuse. "Everyone's home sick today."

It wasn't even two weeks into November, and everyone—except me—had been coughing on each other, snuffling and moaning about for days. Caius had gone to work, but as I walked toward the backdoor I saw him lumping up the steps ahead of me like an injured giant.

"Oh," he said, smiling weakly. "I'm glad you're here. I came home because I think I have a fever." He pulled my hand to his forehead, as if that confirmed it.

"Poor sweetheart," I said, but my heart wasn't in it. I was nurtured out. Caius was supposed to be the one person who didn't need a lot from me.

"Can you take my temperature?" he asked, as we walked into the house. He lay down on the couch and pulled the blankets all around himself.

"Let's just give you Advil," I said. He was flushed, his eyes terribly blue.

"But I want to know how bad it is," he said, his face under the fleece.

"It's bad," I said, sighing. "Would you like soup?"

"Angie in reception said I looked awful." He was relishing this. Caius was rarely sick, but when he was, he usually took to his bed. I thought of the last time I was allowed to convalesce: In the hospital, after Iris was born. It had felt like a vacation, not having to cook for two whole days, not having to help anyone else in the bathroom.

I sat in the kitchen with my own headache while Iris pulled all the plastic containers from the drawer, sticking germs to them with eager little fingers. Caius started moaning something about wanting a cool cloth and a ginger ale. I pretended I couldn't hear him. Sweet potatoes and the last of the corn and a smooth-hipped butternut squash sat in the basket on the counter. I had meant to start a new soup but I felt too exhausted, so instead I sat on the kitchen floor with Iris, pressing my thumbs into my temples, hoping to grind the headache away.

"Dada," said Iris. "Dada's sick."

"I know, love," I said. "But at least *you're* feeling better." Iris was fascinated that he was here; she wanted to go visit, she wanted to be the one to bring the ginger ale, the newspaper. And I didn't.

"Why don't you bring this to Dada?" I creaked myself off the floor to give her a can of ginger ale for one hand, a straw for the other. The can was cold and Iris winced—she hated cold against her skin—but she didn't drop it. She liked her mission.

"Take it to the living room for Dada," I said, feeling a little sly and temporarily relieved. Soon enough, I would have to make this soup for everyone, soup they might or might not eat, and toast, and a salad, and probably someone would require a hamburger, someone who looked terribly hungry and made me feel like a wretched mother for suggesting vegetables and bread might be enough. Probably Oliver, but maybe Iris, who was learning how to play the mealtime game. I didn't want to have a game. I wanted to take a nap.

"Are you okay, Mom?" I felt Oliver touching the ends of my hair as if they needed surreptitious tenderness.

"Why?" I asked, sitting up. I had fallen asleep on the linoleum, and I could feel a hot line where my cheek had been pressed against a seam. Dreams slid off me and my body felt heavy, but my head felt light. Asleep on the kitchen floor. I sighed, and Oliver stepped back and inspected me, as if he might be able to see where the pod person had faulted in replicating his mother. Then he grabbed an apple from the basket on the counter and bounced out the door.

"Are you better?" I called after him.

"Going for a bike ride," was his answer.

"Iris threw up," yelled Caius, who'd gone upstairs to rest.

Carra was next to appear. "Do you have my sick note?" she asked, standing with her hip pressed against the doorframe as if holding up the whole house. "I'm going back tomorrow."

I could hear Iris crying upstairs.

"I'm okay now. And it's Vivian's birthday." Carra looked pale.

"*No one is to be sick anymore,*" I declared, still sitting on the kitchen floor. "*I hereby declare it—the sickness allowance is now bankrupted.*"

"Iris threw up again," said Carra. "And I don't think you can bankrupt an allowance." She sneezed twice and started up the stairs. Iris cried a long stream of indecipherable grievance. I felt a curse inside my throat—a good, satisfying *goddamn,* the kind of word that would have sent my mother into a tizzy. Now that *I* was the mother, I didn't say those words, either. But sometimes they sat in my throat like half-swallowed bread.

"I'm coming," I said. I got up and followed Carra to take care of Iris. Mop, bathe, soothe, feed, read, cuddle, read, get drink of milk, get drink of water, read again.

That night after the soup, and grilled cheese for Carra and Caius, and peanut butter and jelly for Iris, I went out to the garden in the dark. I was beginning to have a fever myself and could feel the scratchy throat that meant I would lose my voice in a day or two. I'd have to croak to my children and would not have the luxury of an afternoon in bed, the way Caius did. I went outside anyway. I surveyed my garden, where I hadn't readied anything for winter, where the mums I'd ordered from the girls' field hockey fund-raiser and the cabbage plants from Carra's swim team plant sale sat in their plastic containers, despairing of water and new homes for their pot-bound roots.

It all made me sad: November, the early dark, Iris's surrender to sleep, Caius holding his feverish head and taking over with Oliver and his catch-up homework; the good continuance made me almost as sad as the gray-nipped ends of things. I loved to watch things growing dormant, though, the trees settling in for sleep between leaves, their sap slowing. The plants that quit aboveground and crept silently through the winter, growth as unostentatious as the body's aging. I wanted everyone to be well. I wanted to take Iris to town to pick out a beautiful outfit for our neighbors' infant, to bring it over with homemade food, to hold the baby and smell that inexplicable glorious perfume of the newly born. These pleasures would come soon, I consoled myself.

Iris would go to preschool next fall. She'd start to choose her own friends, bringing home stories about the toughest boys or the shy ones, exerting her self in her choices. She'd be three and independent; she'd learn things I hadn't taught her, my Jitterbug. It was a relief and a despair. That was when I started thinking of more, inevitably, of more children to dilute the pain of loving them each too much even as I had to let go. I secretly loathed the parent-teacher conferences, resented hearing who my children were without me, even as I was proud of them. Or I was resentful of the teachers for not noticing the same talents I saw. It was like long division, and I was the number being divided as they grew in steps, as I broke myself apart to let them loose. But having another wasn't the answer anymore; I wasn't sure it had ever been. Each letting go was equally intense.

I'd never discovered what happened to the pumpkins. Halloween had come and gone, Spirit Night first, when the kids played hide-and-seek in the woods and shaving creamed the stop signs and toilet papered trees. Amanda never carved hers, but she had had a baby, so I probably shouldn't have noticed. It was just that I felt a mild proprietary interest in the gourd I'd given her. Down the street, Mike Reading instructed his thirteen-year-old son, Joey, to shaving cream only his own house, to use as many eggs as he'd like, keeping in mind that he'd have to clean up the next day. Oliver was invited, though he was three years younger, and he went as cheerfully to the cleanup as he had to the mess making. He came home with a store-bought orange-and-black-frosted cupcake from Mrs. Reading, shaving cream crusted on his jeans, and a great grin.

"I used a squeegee," he said. "You should have seen how clean I got the windows."

"You can wash Daddy's car anytime," I said. "Or mine."

"No way." Oliver said, running upstairs.

Now that it was November, the pumpkins were gone or eaten into rinds by the relentless squirrels. I'd made pumpkin pie and pumpkin soup and pumpkin bread, and Caius and Oliver had pitched the spent and nibbled jack-o'-lanterns into the compost heap with grand flourish. The shops had started in on Thanksgiving displays, and the outlet on Route 17 was already selling Christmas lights and wreaths and candy canes. We'd have Thanksgiving ourselves again; all my brothers had other plans. Maybe a stray single or couple from Caius's office would come, but no family. I was a little disappointed and a little relieved. The few times my brothers had come, they'd appeared uncomfortable in the house, as if my family were somehow usurping their memories of the place. My mother had always managed to make everyone's favorite dishes, to serve everything warm, to orchestrate the kind of strifeless joyful family gatherings that usually only occurred in nineteenth-century novels. There was singing, and my father's face was rosy with uncomplicated pleasure and turkey and wine. My holidays could never compete, even with the same kitchen, the same dining room at my disposal.

Tonight I noticed that Mrs. Martin had put out her snowflake flag, which was flapping in the November night. Iris would love the flag; one of her rare easy enthusiasms was for holiday decorations. I started to dig in the cold earth with a spade, hoping I wouldn't disturb a tulip for a measly purple cabbage plant. I thought about Iris's new two-year-old tricks and my battles with her. Iris's will was different from the others'—it demanded that I pay attention, full attention. She wouldn't tolerate my weeding or cooking or even dressing while we talked. She hung on me or grabbed the spade or spatula or hairbrush. And part of me resisted this need and part of me knew it was just for now, that she'd grow up soon enough and I'd have mornings to myself, and then afternoons, and in November the garden hardly needs a full day. But somehow I couldn't bring myself to belong entirely to her the way I could with the others. I had less, but I needed a bit more time, for my weeding and mulching, for the seedpods snapped off the irises, for pruning the forsythias, wintering over the strawberry beds.

7

Amanda

Four weeks after Malena was born, my body was completely unprepared for sex of any kind, but I kept thinking about it, longing for it, the old languorous days, partly craving the accoutrements—unbuttoning, socks kicked off under the sheets, the salt of Aaron's skin right above the hair on his chest, his taste on my tongue, the tender green smell of him, the thick sleep afterward—the way one longs for a bath when it's really the smell of almond soap and not the hot soaking itself that sings a siren song. My senses were sleeping, lost in weary, milky baby mode, and when I watched my husband knotting his tie, adjusting the ends, and tucking in his shirt, I envied the shirt. I wanted sex because I wanted normal, self-indulgent life in my body again. But I couldn't imagine I'd ever have that back, exactly, and I couldn't imagine we'd have sex for a long time either. Even though it appeared when was mostly up to me—even if the traditional version would have to wait for more healing. How of any variety seemed too unbearable in my bruised and sutured state. So I longed and said nothing and went about the excruciating, delicious stream of hours caring for Malena.

I had actually been ambivalent about children in our early days; it was Aaron who knew he wanted kids, always knew he wanted them, and more than one. That was our first argument; he'd asked me, over chocolate cake with gold leaf and a single, surgically sliced raspberry at Le Cirque—our one-month anniversary dinner—how many I wanted.

"Oh," I said, surprised because the look in his face had been so intense, almost like the look he got when he climaxed. I'd felt a shock of embarrassment that he'd get that look in public, but then, no one else at the restaurant knew what it meant.

"I mean, I always wanted half a dozen," he said. "Before I learned how much private colleges cost."

"Oh," I said again, trying to excise the gold leaf with my fork. I couldn't bear that face again.

"I guess—" I started, but then he put his hand over mine.

"It doesn't have to be that many," he whispered, his tone suddenly subdued.

"No, I mean, I was never completely sure I want any at all," I said. But then the thought of seeing the grief I knew was there if I looked up made me add, "Until I met you, of course."

I had lied. He knew and I knew, and the sex was dulled and I sniped at him for little things like leaving his underwear in my bed. And he started to work more and kiss less, and I was afraid we were lost. The anticipatory grief gripped me, twisted me—I couldn't lose him. So it didn't take any thought to tell him that I would never rule it out, that I was on the fence, but that he could ask me again in a year if we were still dating. The grief vanished. In a year, we were engaged. Two years later we were both fully committed to having a little one and even to living in the suburbs. We had sex at least once a day, and even though my friends told me getting-pregnant sex could be a chore, it wasn't. We took the project seriously, and we were both people who liked to succeed. It was a marathon, and our earnestness reminded me of our earliest days. It worked within a month. Because of Aaron, I'd lost my ambivalence—what we had together was too good not to expand.

After the parade of visitors, it was only our little family. My mother hired a visiting nurse—what I wanted from her was something less expensive and more personal, but Mary did help. The visitors had been exhausting and a somewhat pleasant distraction. I'd fallen asleep against my great-aunt's arm; I'd breast-fed in front of Aaron's nervous group of coworkers, all prebaby husbands themselves. It made me feel daring and old, though generally I was too dazed to pay attention to anything.

My mother, though: I'd paid attention to my mother. She visited when Malena was two weeks old, having canceled three times in the first week, leaving me nervous with the anticipation of who she would be when she finally came, now that I'd made her a grandmother. When we were little, her own parents came to visit only once or twice a year, filling the house with cigar smoke and the scent of gardenia hand cream. When she finally did visit on her way home from a conference in Philadelphia, my sister had to come out from the city, too, though she'd already met Malena in the hospital and had driven out twice to cook us dinner. On the first two visits, I was thrilled to have her chopping onions in my kitchen, thrilled even to have her onion-scented hands holding her niece. But coming for my mother's visit was an obvious assertion of territory, clear-cut competition.

Ultimately, it didn't matter. My mom looked at Malena, her face stretched into an approximation of approval. She pressed on the baby's chin to look inside her mouth, like someone inspecting a horse for sale. She kissed my cheek and her mouth felt cold.

"I'd like some tea, please," she instructed the nurse, who looked put out but went to the kitchen. Malena fell asleep on Aaron's chest and my mother fell asleep on the couch and Jane and I nervously pretended to look through magazines—when I should have been sleeping myself. An hour later, my mother woke up, cleared her throat, and asked Aaron to take her to the train so she wouldn't miss her connection back to Boston—in three hours at Penn Station.

I didn't protest; I was weary from waiting for the visit, weary from waiting for my mother to wake up, and most of all, worn-out from having grown and delivered a small human who woke every few hours demanding my milk. Aaron took my mother and Jane to the station and I tried not to feel too wistful for nonspecific grandmotherly attention for my daughter.

"She's not psychologically prepared to be a grandmother," said Aaron, when he got home. "She'll come around."

"I wish my father lived in the States," I said.

"He said he'd come in the spring, right?"

"Malena will be driving by then." I sighed. "She bought Malena a *sled*," I said. "I don't think our daughter will need a Flexible Flyer for about six years."

Four weeks had felt like a year. A good year. A torturous year. Aaron was back at work; it was our last day with the nurse service. I couldn't wait to be alone in the house—not just alone, *responsible*— but it also terrified me. I was up every three hours at night, and then Aaron took one shift, bottle-feeding Malena before he left in the morning, and then the day was a blur of nursing, crying, napping, diapers. I could fall asleep nursing her in a hard-backed chair, and I did, only the nurse woke me, tapping my shoulder as if it were a recalcitrant IV bag.

"You could drop her," she said, taking Malena from me. "You go to sleep now and I'll hold."

But by then, of course, I was nervously awake, my absurd fantasies of Mary the nurse dropping the baby herself, of sudden choking, of SIDS jittering my mind while my body ached for sleep.

Mostly, the interruptions were horrible. I knew babies cried at night. I knew mothers nursed them back to sleep. I never looked at that equation, at the logical reality that mothers, or fathers, would be waking up to do that nursing or bottle-feeding, that they'd have to get up and manage in the middle of the night, that they'd have to interrupt dreams they had barely started. I felt as if my dreams were a story waiting to happen, the book I'd started six times and loved but left languishing on the nightstand because I couldn't get back to it.

I was tired of feeling inadequate as Mary changed or swaddled Malena. I was embarrassed that she'd helped me with my "lactation issues"—she'd squeezed my nipple to show me how to express milk as unceremoniously as she might wash and dry dishes. And I was nervous to let her go, because it was an enormous relief that she was there to let me nap and to do a bottle-feeding when I was asleep. Four hours slipped past as fast as ten minutes. And she did wash and dry dishes. She concerned herself with food, too, when I was ravenous and I didn't have a clue how to scramble an egg. Nothing had ever been this difficult. I thought I was awake, sitting on the couch, but I wasn't, and I woke up feeling as if a gray fuzz coated my eyes. I put on my glasses to see where Malena was—with Mary—and the world was far too bright.

But Malena. It hurt to love like that; it reminded me of how it felt when Aaron was first in my life, when I wanted to think about him, when thinking about him filled me enough that I had no time to think about anything else. But that sort of love had made me sharper, and barely one month into motherhood, I was blissful, exhausted, and afraid I was irrevocably dulled to the rest of the world.

Mary recommended not going outside with her until four months, and then, since Malena was a fall baby, she didn't recommend going outside until spring.

Packing up to leave, she said, "Hon, you have a nice place here. Set up your fort. Keep her warm. Not like that—" She adjusted my hold on Malena, though the nursing felt fine to me. "She's hardly getting anything."

Apparently Mary had a direct line to Malena's stomach. She could see things no one else could. But she also made me pancakes. And that very afternoon, after Malena fell asleep in my arms and Mary relieved me of my perfect burden and rested her in the mostly unused bassinet, Mary had brushed my hair.

"You could use it, hon," she'd said. And I didn't mind that she meant I looked awful, because I did. And because it felt delicious, the brush tugging through my hair, short strokes, gentle and sure. Then at last, she was gone.

The first thing I did when Mary left for good was to go outside with Malena. It was the second week of November, and our back-yard was mowed and leafless and trimmed now, though I'd never connected the hideous drone of mowers and blowers to the people I'd hired right before my water broke. That had been then, when I'd had a whole lapful of time to complain about my physical state, to obsess about stretch marks and heartburn; and this was now, when my body no longer belonged to me. Instead, I had temporary own-ership of a new and fascinating body, one that hadn't been budded with sexuality yet, one that was only doing the work of waking to the world.

No more Mary, at last. Outside, five o'clock was vaguely lit by a fading sun. The trees tilted against the sky and the landscape looked like a movie screen's grainy vista, a pan of New England with the house lights still on. But it wasn't New England. We had two patchy-skinned sycamores in the backyard, and the air smelled of mostly finished roses. Still, the cold backing the last of the light was unmistakable. No more autumn. Winter twining its fingers in the night's hair.

Grainy clouds marred the final smudge of afternoon blue. Over the fence I heard children yelling. Somehow, they seemed unrelated to my Malena, a different species, so rough and big. Malena's mouth opened in her sleep—she was rooting for a nipple. I touched the tiny bow of lips with my pinkie. If Mary were here, she'd be watching; she'd remind me to wash my hands before touching her.

The yard looked so bare; our groundhog was gone, and I worried for it. Was it just hibernating or had something eaten it? What ate groundhogs? I made myself feel almost sick, imagining a hawk swooping up baby groundhogs in my own safe backyard. I was so lost in my baby that everything was about babies now.

Something tapped my head, and though I couldn't reach up to test, it felt like a raindrop. I looked at the sky, where a bank of dark gray had blocked out the thin new moon. Rain. I held Malena close and scuttled back inside.

The phone was ringing as I settled in on the couch to nurse. In my last life, I might have answered it, but now that I was a mother, now that I belonged to someone else's needs, I let the machine answer. The whole house buzzed, and the lights went off, on, and off again. The storm was a few miles away; I counted between thunder and lightning, one mile per "one Mississippi." Malena started to cry. The last storm had been her birthday. To what backwater had we moved? Why did we have so many power outages in New Jersey? I settled Malena to my breast as I sat in the grainy evening light. The maroon upholstery smelled of milk.

I wondered whether I could ever bear to have another child— whether it was possible to sustain this intensity of having and giving up. Whether another child would be Malena's friend and frustration and greatest competition, the way Jane and I had been. I thought about Aaron standing by the hospital bed, telling me to breathe and concentrate on my focus object, his braided metal bracelet. Of course, in the end focusing hadn't been enough, and I'd had the C-section—the hard light, the quick sensation of being unzipped, and it was done. I hadn't seen him wearing the bracelet since, and I felt a completely unnecessary pang of nostalgia. If his bracelet had gone missing in the hospital, was he still the same man who wanted roots after childhood peregrination? Would he tell Malena his monkey tales and all about the Hawaiian rainforest? Did he still have any explorer left in him? Did I?

I woke up because the lights were on and the doorbell was chiming. Upstairs, our stereo was making unnecessary music; I didn't remember leaving it on. Though I'd learned about leaving the phone unanswered, I still couldn't bring myself to ignore the door. What if someone spied me through the window? I tried to get up without separating Malena's sleeping mouth from my breast, but of course she woke and cried as I carried her to the door with my robe clamped closed with one elbow.

"How hard it is, being born," said Thea when I opened the door. She was wearing lipstick. I would never have time for lipstick again.

There were two children with her, a boy and the little girl, and she held out a foil-covered casserole. The rain had stopped. Her daughter clung to a gift wrapped in paper with pink clouds.

"Vegetable lasagna?" she offered.

In the city, no one would stop by with vegetable lasagna. My boss, Neethi, might have sent some bagels, but she wouldn't have come to the apartment. In fact, she'd messengered a scratchy, frilly pink dress Malena couldn't wear for two years at least to New Jersey on the company dime.

"And this is for the baby—" Thea wrestled with her daughter for a minute, trying to gain possession of the gift. The silver bow tore off in the girl's hands.

"I would have come sooner," she started, before commanding, "Enough, Iris," as she put her hands firmly around the gift.

"Mom-eeeeeeeeeeeeee," said Iris. But she let go of the package and ran down the walkway in the dusk, gripping the bow in her teeth.

"Oliver, can you please . . .?" Thea had such a yielding voice, a mother voice, even when she was scolding. She smiled at me. "Is everything okay? I mean, did your power cut out, too?"

"Yes," I said. The boy caught the little girl's hand and held tight while the girl sunk down to the sidewalk and whined.

"She's gorgeous," said Thea. I looked down at Malena, who had stopped fussing and was looking out at the world with that enormous expression of hers, a wide-eyed recognition, a sort of wise gaze. I also noticed that my breast was half out of my robe like an offering from my open-flapped nursing bra.

"You're nursing?" said Thea.

"Yes," I said, covering myself. "Though we supplement." I didn't know why I was volunteering this information. Iris stopped struggling and got up to see what all the fuss was about. She ran over to me, to Malena, and pointed one fat finger at Malena's face.

"Sorry," Thea said. She reached down herself then and stole a short stroke of Malena's cheek. I kept hearing Mary's voice, "Visitors must wash hands," as she had instructed Cornelius and Jane; my friend Rosanna, who brought the baby her very own Janson's art history tome and brought me a silk shirt that wouldn't fit me for months, if ever; my aunt Ronnie; even my doctor mother, guiding them to the powder room and the antibacterial pump soap. But Thea knew what she was doing; surely Thea meant no harm. She probably washed her hands at home. I hoped.

"Shall I put this—" Thea gestured toward our dining room table with her gift and food. I didn't want to let her in to see the mess, but I didn't have a free hand for the loot. And I did appreciate it. I was suddenly famished. I could smell good cheese from under the foil, aged Cheddar or Gouda or something. I nodded. Iris ran a circle around her mom, and I couldn't help noticing her nose was crusty with a cold.

"Does supplementing mean formula?" Thea was standing in my dining room, and Iris was picking things up: unopened gifts, the mail, the breast pump briefcase Mary had packed up for Aaron to return to the rental place at the drug store in town. Her pink slicker dripped with leftover tears from the trees and shrubs.

"I gave up on the pump. It was awful," I said, tilting my head to ease a neck cramp. I wondered what planet she was from— everyone knew what *supplementing* meant, and some people, the breast police, Aaron called them, seemed to think it was a crime. Tough luck for them. I sincerely hoped Thea wasn't one of the breast police.

"Iris, will you help me?" I wanted to be generous. I pointed to the gift, and Iris smiled and helped tear open the package, revealing a heaven-soft yellow blanket with Malena's name and birthdate—all correct—and a matching cap and booties. Iris tried to wear the hat. It was so wonderful I almost wept, but stopped myself by offering everyone shortbread cookies from a tin I'd received.

Under her unzipped raincoat, Thea wore a tank top and her husband's old button-down tucked into her jeans. She looked like something out of a catalogue, casually elegant. And part of me wanted to hand her Malena, to run upstairs and take a shower and get right into bed. If anyone knew how to care for a baby, this woman did.

"Would you like some tea?" I asked, because I was going to be nice to this lovely woman if it killed me.

"Absolutely not," said Thea, closing the cookie tin, to Iris's disappointment. "We've exhausted you enough."

She knew when to come, and when to leave.

After they departed, the two children still chewing cookies, I washed my hands and ran a washcloth along Malena's cheek. She squirmed, then fell asleep, and for once, she didn't wake up when I transferred her to the bassinet. I would survive without Mary after all. I stood at the dining room table with a fork and the lasagna, thinking I should have been more gracious, more thankful. It was overwhelming when she came with her kids—and that was just two of the three. Would I ever be that calm again? Had I ever been that calm to begin with?

The food was delicious. I was ravenous, and I was an enormous, lumpy, milk-engorged, stitched and sleepless blob. Thea and her husband were probably having fabulous sex. Their children slept in their own beds, I was sure, slept as peacefully as babies in television commercials. She probably tiptoed in with her husband and looked down on their angelic faces before their own blissful bedtime. They never were tainted with formula; she probably breast-fed them all until age four and grew her own organic vegetables to make her own organic baby food. I could never compete. But then, I didn't really want to be her, I just wanted her to mother me.

As usual, right around the time Aaron came home, Malena entered a sort of witching hour of inconsolability. If we were lucky, she'd nurse for an hour or so and I'd be sore, but we'd have some peace while she sucked. But more often, she settled and unsettled in her bassinet, then whimpered until we picked her up, rocked, walked around the room. And for almost an hour, she'd yell, or whine, or hoot her baby noises no matter what we did. But if we put her down again, she'd scream, a pure, angry, open-mouthed new-born rage.

When she cried, Aaron got very calm. When she cried, I felt helpless unless it was nursing she wanted.

I ate two thirds of the giant pan of casserole before Aaron came home. He was whistling, his eyes dark with exhaustion, and the minute he put his keys on the table, Malena woke up.

"That looks good," he said, despite the crying. "Did you make it?"

Do I look like I have time to cook? I thought, but checked myself. "The neighbor, Thea," I said.

"She's really nice."

Of course she was. She was nice and perfect and gorgeous, and I remembered how he'd looked at her, a happy, tiny assessment, when she'd first come to our door. I envied him for getting to be the father; I envied him for being allowed to think lustful thoughts about the neighbor.

"But she's kind of skinny," he said, clearly thinking I was brewing the bitter potion of jealousy. The baby's fuss turned to a thin wail.

"Not really," I said, feeling full enough to remain serene.

"I'll get her," he said, picking up a fork and Malena at the same time. I watched him eat the rest of the cold vegetable lasagna, a speck of oily spinach stuck to his chin. Malena spat a little yellow blob on the shoulder of his white dress shirt.

December

· 8 ·

Thea

Even though everyone was recovered, back at work and at school, I still felt claustrophobic in the evenings. Though it was too late in the year, I was out in the garden again, trying to set everything to rest for the winter. Before bed, Iris had told me she wanted to sleep with Mommy, and I'd said, "No, you're too big," more harshly than I'd meant to. She hadn't cried, but the quick cross of grief on her face stayed in my chest. Guilty again.

I told myself I'd been short tempered because of the electricity of the impending storm. As I returned to the cold-nipped mums with an armload of hay, I could feel the air growing heavier with rain, the pressure like a need in my own body. The soil was damp and cold, still unfrozen, and I tucked a mum in, singing to it a little, the way I'd tucked Carra in until last year, when she decided she didn't need me or the "dream abouts" she'd asked for since she was four, something to think of to help her fall asleep. Sometimes I used them myself: "a thin river with birds telling secrets" or "a long green field" or "eating apples," though this last made me hungry, hungry for the crisp sour of a first Paula apple of the fall.

The rain watered my mum, fat drops, and then the thunder started. I felt a thrill, a slight scare from the sound. The mums were getting soaked, the dirt becoming rivulets of mud as the rain intensified. Lightning split the sky, cutting across the tops of the oaks in the woods—a quick strap of light.

I walked toward the house to get my raincoat. Through the window upstairs, I could see Caius putting Iris to bed for the third time, the form of man holding child lit like a shadow puppet.

I fished my gloves from the half-filled wheelbarrow and searched for my clippers on the sponge of grass. It was dark outside, and all the houses were lit. I could see the TV's glow in Amanda's window, in the windows of the Martins' house and Mrs. Chen's, that oddly soothing flicker. Rooted like a peony in the mud, I saw my own family room dazzled by the light of Carra and Oliver's last show before bed. I saw Caius back in the kitchen, dumping soup bowls in the dishwasher without rinsing, so I would have to run the machine twice. I wouldn't say anything, it wasn't worth it. I loved him for certain ineptitudes, and though I didn't like to think it, I liked being needed, even for small domestic things like rewashing soup-crusted bowls.

Storms also reminded me of my father, how he'd go out despite the rain, walking to the bus station for work with his mouse-gray trench coat and hat, carrying his newspaper outside his briefcase as if he'd forgotten rain would ruin the stories. In the summer, sometimes, he'd take a break from his equations and take us out in the backyard in the rain. Oren and I would each hold one of his hands and he'd dance us in a circle. My father was not a smooth dancer. He jerked his knees up in an odd march; he'd wave his arms at funny elbow angles like a marionette. We'd tip our mouths open while we danced, catching what raindrops we could and gargling.

My mother would stand at the backdoor, watching us with proprietary pleasure. She didn't tell us to put on raincoats; instead, she put towels in the dryer so she could swaddle us with them, warm and ready, when we came back inside.

None of my children had met their grandfather or gone out dancing in the rain without their shoes. They hadn't met their grandmother, either. They hadn't met their uncle Oren, and the other uncles could not compensate for the loss. I carried my brother's death with me, a gap, a hole in my fabric where I held the ends together and tried not to look at what was exposed beneath.

The storm started to settle into a slow slog of rain, a low roll of thunder, as the time between flashes and growls spread, the electric air traveling past Sylvan Glen and on to Ridgewood, Fair Lawn, Paterson. I was past needing a raincoat; my jeans were soaked, and my sweater sagged with water. And then, as I flipped the wheelbarrow, not wanting to let it fill, the wind wrapped around the houses and knocked against me, almost like a punch, as the storm picked up again. I stumbled against the wheelbarrow, scraping my arm against the metal stays. There was a thud, and then it was dark. I looked up at the house and the lights were gone.

Inside when the power went out, I always felt prepared. But outside it was almost as if my own house had disappeared into the storm. The rain wasn't quaint and cozy, and I could hardly see as I sloshed toward the house. My heart worked too hard—I wanted to be inside with them, I wanted to give them safety. It was unnecessary, the weight of worry I always carried right behind my breastbone. Worry for my children, that they wouldn't be safe without me, as if somehow my presence could keep the light on when the power was gone.

After an hour, and after peeling off my wet clothes for sweatpants and Caius's hooded sweatshirt from college, softly shrunken and mostly mine, I was sitting on my bed with Oliver and Iris and Caius. I knew Carra wanted to be on the bed with us, but she sat in the rocking chair by the bay windows, her voice tilting back and forth as she rocked.

We were telling a story, taking turns. Carra was pretending she wasn't scared and Oliver was pretending he was. I could tell from the steady sound of his voice that he loved this adventure, this excuse to be all together under one blanket.

"She didn't know where her house was," said Caius on his turn, talking about the bear in our story.

"Because of the rain," said Oliver.

"It was my turn," Carra mumbled.

"But you didn't want to go," said Oliver.

"So she dug in the earth looking for her house, and instead of her house she found birds," said Carra.

"What kind of birds?" Caius asked. I was leaning against him, so his voice vibrated in my chest as he spoke.

"Flamingos," I said. Caius slipped his hand inside the sweatshirt. I wasn't wearing anything beneath it and my nipples responded to his touch. I felt warm and soothed, though this attention made a small electric current travel from my breasts to my thighs.

The sirens had been a background to our story all along, but now they grew louder. Thunder and rain rattled the windows, pounded the roof.

"And they sounded like sirens," said Oliver.

"And ravens," said Carra. "Did you know ravens are really smart? They can hide stuff and find it later."

"Dat," said Iris, pretending she'd forgotten how to say "that"; it was a regular nighttime regression. She started burrowing under the covers, nuzzling my belly and interrupting Caius's casual sexy touching.

A police car parked on our street, lights illuminating the houses and the trees, oak leaves everywhere in the spots of red and blue light.

"Dat," said Iris again. She was enormously sleepy now, and everything was funny or made her cry.

"You can say *th*-at," said Caius.

Another emergency vehicle made a *blat* of passing sound, and Iris commenced crying. The wind had calmed and the rain had tapered to a faint drizzle. I pushed Caius's hands from my body and stood to look out the window. The great corpse of an oak tree lay across the power lines, pinning them down, pressing a snapped utility pole into Tia's mother's lawn. The tree itself had fallen right on the house. Into the house.

Iris grabbed my leg and I eased her up onto my hip. There were wires everywhere, and a man was barking something through a bullhorn, something about the house, the word *okay* and the word *unsafe*. Tia's mother's house had been cracked, smashed, punched in by the tree and the pole. In the light, I could see glass on the lawn.

"Live wires," whispered Caius, who was standing behind Carra now, his hand on her head.

"That looks so cool," said Oliver. "Can we go see?"

"No," said Caius.

"I'm going," I said. I handed Iris to Caius, put on slippers, and ran down to get my raincoat, stumbling in the dark.

Tia's mother's house was wrecked. Only it wasn't Tia's mother's house anymore, it was Amanda's, and Amanda had a baby, and as far as I knew, the baby had been inside the house.

9

Amanda

That soft slumping sound, then the music of glass breaking, and at first I'd thought I was still in the apartment. I reached for where my lamp used to be and found a night table instead, but the light wouldn't switch on, and I felt guilty that I'd forgotten, for just a second, about the baby. Then I was terrified that somehow Malena was being taken from me. I rushed into her room and found the crib was empty, and there was a limb of an oak penetrating one crushed wall, obscene as an old man exposing himself. But the windows were intact, though exposed bones of lathe jutted naked in the night air and there was crumbled plaster on the rug, like sand and stone. I ran frantically around the house and found Aaron downstairs, calling to me as if I were half-asleep, a lullaby of calling, and he held the baby in his casual, assured way, looking at what used to be the living room. I'd stepped on a sliver of glass and my foot throbbed, but it didn't matter because Malena was okay.

As I took her from him, he held us both for a minute—comforting, but a little too aggressive in his squeeze. Malena whimpered.

Outside had come in. The television was wedged between branches, and the bark looked heavy, menacing, and beautiful. It was confusing, everything was confusing and dark, and then the sirens. I stepped out the side door onto the lawn and looked out at the front of the house, where in the gray night light I saw wires threading out of the hole in my walls. It was drizzling; power lines were spread across the lawn, debris and flashing lights everywhere. A wreck.

They called out to us with bullhorns. There was a panic to extract us, a loud, steady call until we came, but once we emerged, we huddled under an umbrella by the police car and nothing happened.

"No one's hurt," Aaron told the policeman.

I said it aloud, twice, "No one's hurt," but I still shook, not sure this was true. Does "No one's hurt" mean "Everyone's okay"? It seemed like a math problem and I worried it, because that seemed like the right thing to do.

The policeman was young, with a birthmark on his cheek that captivated me. It was all I wanted to look at, the size of a dime, with little lumps on the top like mouse ears and a tiny tail at the bottom. He was clean shaven in the middle of the night, he smelled like lime cologne, and all I wanted to do was look at his birthmark. I remembered the glass and my foot—which was still bare—and went to the ambulance to have the sliver tweezed out. I returned Malena to Aaron; he wrapped both arms around her. I was afraid I'd forgotten how to hold her until she started crying for food and I asked to sit in the squad car to nurse her. Someone gave me a pair of men's slippers, and with the bandage over it, I could barely feel the tiny angry mouth of cut on my foot.

Our neighbors emerged from their own houses in pairs, alone, and with children clinging to their legs. I sat nursing Malena, letting the nursing hormones take over—this time the surge in my body was peace, though sometimes it was sadness, sometimes pure sleep. I closed my eyes and imagined I was in the rocking chair in her room, only I still smelled the officer's lime cologne, intensified by exposure in the car's upholstery.

Then someone tapped on the window. It was Thea and her husband, whom I'd only seen across the lawns. He looked at me and looked at Malena and smiled. Even inside a squad car on the night my house had been squashed by a tree, I noticed he was handsome, a man in striped pajamas and a trench coat, his jaw square, eyes blue even in the vague glow of the emergency lights, his smile as light as if we were meeting at a garden party.

"You must be Amanda," he mouthed.

I knocked on the window and fumbled for a knob or button, but there was none; I couldn't roll it down. The officer in the front seat pressed something and the window slid down to reveal their whole voices and the humid air.

"Is everything okay?" said Thea. "I mean," she turned to the house, "is everyone okay? I mean, obviously, everything isn't okay. Are you okay?"

I wondered where their kids were. I wondered if they married because their jaws matched. Thea's hair was wet—she looked fresh from a shower. I caught her husband's glance. He was looking at my breast, not leering but fascinated, the way many men seemed to be about nursing babies, interested and usually embarrassed, though his gaze was firm.

"Well, the house is wrecked. We're not allowed back in. And the tree seems to have cut off all our power. Do you have power?" I asked, feeling confused.

I could hear the low melody of Aaron's voice as he talked with the officer. He was joking. It made sense, though at first I was bothered by the sacrilege, but what else was there to do? We could cry, but our house was still a half-smashed hazard of broken gas and electrical connections. Our safe place was dangerous. Our nest was ruined. I shivered. It was incongruous, almost comical, how much damage a storm could do, the vast damage caused by a single fallen tree.

"Can we help with anything?" Thea was looking at the house with an explicit sorrow.

"Oh, shit," I said. "You don't know a hotel we could go to, do you?" I winced as Malena started sucking again, hard. The sharp pain of it, the pleasure of the milk coming back in, coming out of the little knots inside my breast and into her. We had to find somewhere to sleep, as if sleep would ever come easy again.

"No," said the husband. "There's no question. You'll stay with us."

"Yes," said Thea. "Oh, of course." Those comforting eyes. She should work in an emergency room, I thought, or a nursery school.

"Oh," I said. "We couldn't." *Take me home with you,* I thought.

"You could," said the husband, glancing down again, approving of Malena's work, or mine, I wasn't sure. "And by the way, my name is Caius."

"Like Caesar," said Aaron, referring to Thea's husband when we were settled in their basement with Malena on the mattress between us. Malena didn't seem to notice anything, that the whole world, her whole tiny encapsulated world of sunlight through the windows, of her crib and mobile and monitor with its red eye aglow, had changed.

"He's very nice," I said.

"I thought he was kind of stiff," said Aaron, reaching around the baby to touch my shoulder. I was exhausted. I didn't want to move. I leaned into the gentle cheek of sleep, trying to let go. Malena shrilled and fussed. I tried to let her nurse again, but she wouldn't settle.

"No," I said. "He's nice." But Aaron was already sleeping.

The next day we weren't allowed back in, even to get baby things or clothes. It was like seeing myself in a movie—couple with baby moves into new neighbor's house. A newsreel, a clip about hurricanes. Only this was a localized crisis, a little flood, a few trees down. The traumas were purely personal. I felt lost in the action; a pin dot stabbed into a map of motion. All I knew was how to nurse, how to watch my child's mouth, how to concentrate on looking down for fear of what I would see if I looked up instead.

Early that morning, the police tape was up but no one was watching. Aaron sneaked into the wreck and found two outfits for Malena, a can of formula powder, some diapers, and two of his clean work suits. Caius stood outside and high-fived him when he came out; they were like boys on the street, proud and reckless. Not stiff, I thought, but said nothing, brewing other discontents.

I was glad of the diapers since the market was out of the small size—there'd been a run on everything, including formula. But I was furious about the suits. He didn't get the photo album or any clothes for me, no underwear or nursing pads, no baby wipes, no nasal bulb, no perfect yellow baby nightgowns, but he got suits. It ate at me through the morning, and while we were putting Malena down for a noontime nap, we quibbled in our neighbors' basement room.

"Why are you so snippy?" asked Aaron, after enduring my first three attempts at argument.

"I'm not snippy," I said. "Our house fell down and you risked your life to get suits."

"It didn't fall down, and I thought I'd spend my time off trying to get food and stuff we need for Malena instead of going out to buy new suits," he said. "I have to get back to work soon."

I didn't answer, because I couldn't imagine what he might say if I told him he would do no such thing.

That afternoon I left her house to go see mine, like lifting the bandage soon after the wound. I had to see it. The power was still out, but even in the daylight I could see it had come back on just one block down, porch lights and some windows aglow, like a demonstration of before and after Edison. The streets were sprinkled with spectators and utility trucks. One neighbor, a man with a face wrinkled as a walnut, tall and skinny in a flapping yellow coat, biked around the neighborhood relaying gossip. Wherever there was someone working, or not working—the phone company, gas and electric, postal carriers, cable TV—the town crier man was there, slowing progress through chatter.

The rain had stopped partway through the night, leaving muddy evidence. School was canceled due to flooding, so kids rode scooters and skateboards as close as they could to the POLICE LINE—DO NOT CROSS tape around our tree, our house, our modern ruin. Oliver, Thea's son, pedaled his bike past me three times, aglow with boy energy.

Walking along the street, I bounced and sang to Malena's disgruntled animal squeaks. Nothing felt ordinary. The light was dazzling and the storm's cool and humid bank had broken into beams of warm, clear light. The temperature belonged to early fall, wrong again. The houses in the powerless sector were disarmed without television or radios or telephones or even the casual beeping of answering machines, but still the leaf blowers made their last rounds, chewing the quiet.

I wanted to see it from a distance, our wreck. I wanted it to feel real, what I'd lost, what I hadn't, as I held Malena and looked at my ruined home. Trash trucks passed, overflowing with water and garbage. I watched a bag splat and split on the pavement, leaking evidence of ordinary life: banana peels, junk mail that should have been recycled, plastic packing peanuts, coffee grounds, the guts of a pumpkin. It made me sad, a quick surge, quick as a breath. The street stank of sour milk so I walked on, limping a little because of the cut on my sole. I listened to the gossip of the spectators as I neared our house.

"No power in the police station," called the walnut-faced man from his bike.

"Cool," said a boy on a skateboard to another on a low-slung, neon green bike, who was riding too close to his friend. "The whole football field is underwater."

"Did you see that tree across Sycamore?" said the bike boy as they started to leave.

"My dad had to drive over three lawns to get home last night," I heard as they rode away.

I watched Aaron call work repeatedly—until at last his cell phone ran out of juice. He slid around the side of their house as if meeting a lover up against the shaded clapboards. He phoned in the bathroom while I stood outside, bladder burning. I'd knock and he'd emerge with one hand up, a policeman—halt, silence, back off— the phone clamped to his ear, too precious.

I detested that phone. And his work. He called again from the bed, rousing a sleeping Malena. I wouldn't speak to him; despite his dullard drive to make those idiotic phone calls, he should be smart enough to glean my displeasure through silence. But he didn't. I sulked for several hours and he just went about his business, hanging his suit carefully to release the wrinkles, rubbing at a spot on the collar of his shirt with cold water, taking out the plastic stays and smoothing them flat like a boy readying a grass blade to whistle.

"Why do you have to keep doing that?" I snapped. I was lying on the bed, nursing.

"What?" Aaron looked at my breasts first.

"*Calling the goddamn office,*" I hollered. Malena coughed and spat up a wad of half-digested milk onto the sheet. I tucked her into the crib that they had brought down from the attic, settling her safely away from my wrath.

"I was just checking in," he said. "I really have to go back. This is killing my billables. And there are cases that really need me, I can't ask Leslie to do it."

I had never heard of Leslie. Who was Leslie?

"No one else is out," he grunted. What right did he have to be irritable? "One vacation day is all I can manage right now, Mango."

"*This* was vacation?"

"Mango," he said. He smiled that impossible smile. His teeth were even in the gray basement light. He still had a slight accent, from his long-ago years in Africa where he learned to speak. He sounded different and captivating and infuriatingly ordinary beneath it all. "I can't take infinite time off."

"Time off? It isn't time off, it isn't vacation. It's a fucking *disaster.*"

"Honey," said Aaron. He made a mock-shocked face over my expletive in front of the baby. Then he held out his arms.

"Okay, I know. But I can't stand it." I started to cry. This wasn't me. I didn't sob like a scared little girl over accidents that hadn't happened.

"I could have lost you when the tree fell. I can't lose you. I need you. I need our house, too. I have never been so squeezed in all my life, and I feel as if I should never go to sleep again in order to keep her safe, to keep you safe." I looked up at his face, steady as always, almost happy with my need. "Never mind," I snuffled, calming down. I looked at his clothes. "Maybe you could've borrowed a suit from Caius."

Aaron kissed my ear as I agreed to slip into his arms. Caius was tall and broad and Aaron wasn't. It would be like the house jacket at a restaurant, the 48 extra long that dwarfed your average patron.

Malena complained from the crib, but as soon as I picked her up she fell asleep again, her face squashed against my shoulder, her breath warm.

"I know you're still recovering," he said later, as he traced the line of my jaw. I shivered. Despite everything I wanted sex, but I wasn't sure my body was ready. Still, being in their basement—arguing, making up, the danger elapsed—made it feel urgent and possible. We were naughty guests. I wondered how much they could hear upstairs, what they were doing upstairs. Caius's office was closed, so he'd been home, too, all of us crammed in their house. The basement was our only privacy, although the kids ran down often to get some forgotten toy or implement of destruction, or simply to stake their claim on the space. They acted both more excited and more put out by the arrangement than their parents. The older girl,

Carra, was on the cusp of teenhood—she looked so sulky and gangly and big, not to mention about to be sexual, maybe already sexual, that it made me nervous to see her long limbs, her big feet, and sensuous mouth. Malena would never be that big.

I didn't know what Thea felt about our presence. At first, I was sure she wanted us there. She was a consummate hostess, making tea on a camp stove and bringing us extra towels. But I wasn't sure what she felt; it wasn't obvious from the motions of what she did.

Aaron reached inside my shirt, but I didn't like his hands on my breasts. They hurt, and they belonged to Malena, and though I wanted to please him and wanted to enjoy his touch the way I always had, I stopped him.

"Too much? They're really marvelous," he said.

"And really sore." I sighed.

"Can I touch you here instead?" I slid my hand inside his waistband. I wanted desire to overtake my body, the way it always had. But nothing was as it always had been. I kissed him hard, tasting his mouth, unfortunately aware of going through the motions.

"I'm not ready for, you know—," I said. It wasn't true, I was ready, it was the shell I lived in that wasn't cooperating. I was still wearing the same sweatpants and T-shirt with one of Caius's sweaters on top. I felt the opposite of leggy, the opposite of lithe. Not entirely unsexy, though, as I tongued the trail from Aaron's belly button downward. It made him feel better, and it made me want more, and I wished I could borrow someone else's skin for a while, not to mention someone else's unbattered insides. Still, I was proud of us, lying on the borrowed couch afterward, and I wondered again if they'd heard anything upstairs. I started to giggle.

"What?" Aaron sighed from his sleepy state and smiled.

"Just remembering what it was like at my mother's house," I said. I knew I would come close to sleep now, so close, but that the fear would eventually wake me.

"This," said Aaron, in a voice I didn't entirely believe, "was even better."

○

That night, Thea and Caius staged what they called an "eat it before it rots" party in their backyard. Neighbors I hadn't yet met came over with the contents of their freezers and refrigerators: turkey cutlets, ostrich burgers, steaks, and the ordinary burgers and chicken breasts. Caius presided over their giant chrome grill, wielding tongs and spreading marinades that sizzled, the oilier ones goading flames to fly up from the burners below.

"You need this," said Aaron, handing me a paper cup and taking the sleeping Malena into his arms. She was wrapped in one of Thea's beautiful crocheted blankets, quiet amid the din of neighbors chatting and laughing and eating in the dark. Lanterns dotted the yard, and I worried about the open flames but let it go. I needed to let more go.

I breathed in the wine and drank, though of course I was trying to stay away from alcohol because of the nursing. I felt like a clown in the mismatched clothes I'd borrowed, but still I managed to feel festive. Children wove in and out of the shrubbery, shrieking and eating grilled pineapple and cup after cup of too-soft ice cream.

"You really know how to have a party," I said to Thea, who was feeding Iris corn from her plate.

Thea laughed, a stage laugh, head back, eyes lit. "We haven't had a party in ages," she said. "We used to do it all the time. Are you cold?" She put down the plate and rubbed her hands against my shoulders, as if I were one of her children.

"Mom!" Iris yelled, pointing to her brother, who was spooning chocolate soup, his mouth mustached with whipped cream. "Bazerrt!"

"Might as well," Thea said to her youngest. She took her hands from my shoulders as if she'd just realized she was touching me, an almost stranger. Maybe it was a little weird, but it had felt good, after all that had happened. She had warmed me.

"Might as well," I said. "I want some, too." I started off toward the ice cream.

"I'll get it," said Thea.

"No," I said. "Let me get it for you—my hands are free."

"Oh, no," she said. "I can do it." It was awkward, one counter too many. We both started toward the table where Mrs. Chen was manning the myriad containers of storm-stranded frozen treats. We bumped arms on the narrow walkway, miscalculating the distance in the dark, and both lost our balance. Teetering, we started to laugh.

"You've had enough, then, Mango?" Aaron might have been joking, but I couldn't see his face.

"Not really," I said, but I was speaking to Thea. "I'm just starting." Thea laughed harder, but I straightened up and let Aaron hand me the baby, who was making hungry noises. "Time to get you home," I said to Malena, without thinking. "I mean, not home . . ."

"Now I can get ice cream for you," said Thea, starting off again.

"It's going to take a lot of ice cream to get over my house," I said, deflated. For just a minute, in the jovial dark of the party, I'd forgotten I didn't have a home to go to.

On the second day, Aaron went back to work. Though the electricity still wasn't on consistently, there were sporadic minutes of power, waking the electronic objects in the house and eliciting cheers from the children, but they never lasted more than an hour at a time.

Two hours after Aaron left, I was sitting with Malena on my lap on the living room couch, where I'd been when he left and where I imagined I might stay until he came home. Whatever room I was in, I felt unsettled. I didn't want to be settled; I didn't belong here.

"Muffin?" asked Thea, handing me a plate with a corn muffin and a little white ramekin with butter and strawberry jam. I didn't ask how she managed to have butter, or why she was giving me a real plate instead of paper. I was ravenous, and I ate the muffin spilling crumbs on Malena's toes and all over the couch. I waved my hand at them, as if that might help, then I tried to get up, because the crumbs looked like they were oiling up the pretty upholstery.

"Oh, just stay there, don't worry," said Thea. Didn't she ever get tired of being so helpful? Of caring for everyone? Malena opened her eyes as I lifted her onto my shoulder like a baby doll: baby up, eyes open.

"Really," said Thea, but now I was wandering around her kitchen hoping for a paper towel. She beat me to it, snapping a Dustbuster from under the sink.

"It still has power?" I stood back while she cleaned.

"Oh, I have hardly had to use it," she said. I couldn't let her do *everything*. For the first time, I noticed how adamantly she opposed help of any kind. Maybe she liked things a certain way—maybe it was her way of maintaining control—but it was almost hostile.

"Okay, okay," I said, putting my hands up in surrender. I tried to smile. It was her house, after all.

"By the way," I said, sitting again. "I've made a reservation at the Marriott. They don't have anything until Friday night, but they said they'd call if someone cancels—"

"Friday," said Thea, shutting off the Dustbuster and neatly tipping the crumb-filled container into the trash. "Two days from now? Oh, really, I really don't want you to go. I can't let you. Caius would think we'd turned you out—it's against his religion, you know."

"Really?" Malena felt heavy against my shoulder, then she emitted the telltale squirt sounds of an impending stinky diaper. *I'm out of wipes*, I thought. *And almost out of the entire four pack of double-roll toilet paper you gave us.* I didn't enjoy feeling beholden; I'd wait before I asked for more. Or maybe I could make it to the store with Malena by myself somehow.

"No, not really," said Thea. "Not really his religion, just his innermost Episcopalian psyche. He feels righting the injustices of the world are too much for one man, but helping your neighbors daily will help make up for your spiritual inadequacies."

"Really?" was all I could say again. *What do I know, I'm a Jew.* Malena's diaper was already starting to reek, and I felt a dangerous wet spot under my hand where I held her back.

"Want me to change the baby?" Thea asked.

"Oh, no, thank you!" I said too quickly, and much, much too loud. What did she think of me, that I was an incompetent new mother? No, I told myself, it was just her way of trying to help.

After I changed Malena, I came back up from the basement, hungry again and hoping for something to eat but too nervous about disrupting the kitchen's extreme order to help myself. Malena was hungry, too, so I sat back down on the site of my crumb crime, settling in to nurse again, again, again.

The back door slammed, and the boy, Oliver, came flying into the room like an untethered kite. He smiled, then bounced beside me on the sofa and stared.

"Does she eat anything else?" he asked. Then he flew into the kitchen and came back eating an apple. It looked good. I almost asked whether he could get me one.

"What does that feel like?" he continued, without waiting for an answer to his first question.

Malena fussed and wouldn't latch on and I felt like I was waving my nipple at this prepubescent child. He had an unnervingly beautiful face, open, innocent. Something about his eyes, that blue, and his lashes was arresting; you couldn't help looking. Which I did, for a second, while the baby cried.

"She just eats this, for now," I said. "But I'm sure she'll be up for a Big Mac shortly."

Oliver laughed and a tiny bit of apple flew out of his mouth and onto Malena's leg. By the time I brushed it off, he'd vanished.

I took an apple, feeling a little like a thief, and moved downstairs for a while to rest my eyes while Malena napped. Two days felt like forever. In the unfinished basement bathroom, the door didn't lock, so it was hard to relax enough even to pee when footsteps thumped on the steps. I missed my own shower and my bed. I should just be grateful, I thought, and fell asleep.

I woke up because someone was touching my foot. Someone small, with cold fingers. It was late afternoon, and the toddler, Iris, was gripping my instep.

"Hello?" I whispered, but Malena woke up anyway, her cries like a bark.

Iris wandered around the room while I bounced Malena to calm her.

"Whazzat?" she asked, fingering the few remaining diapers.

"Diapers!" I said, reaching over to save them from falling on the floor. Just that morning I'd ripped two from the dwindling pile, their little Velcro tabs tearing off in my hands. Defective! Too expensive! So annoying!

Now Iris was opening and touching the diapers, tasting the pacifier, squeezing the rattle, grabbing Malena's little onesies to test against her face. Innocent though she looked, I wanted to shoo her, to tell her to keep her germs away. Her curiosity was exhausting, invasive, and blameless.

Instead I herded Iris upstairs, and Thea brought me a cranberry-grape juice box she had chilled in a giant cooler with the butter and eggs. I sucked down the juice, desperate for sugar and liquid, feeling terribly selfish. Iris took my open juice when I wasn't looking and pulled the straw out of the hole, spilling bright purple onto the couch. She took sneaky touches of Malena's fuzzy head.

"Iris!" Thea called from the kitchen, where she was making something inventive for us to eat using only the camp stove. It smelled good. I had to pee. I couldn't possibly go back downstairs, too much effort.

"Go get your pretend baby from your room. The real baby's sleepy. As is her mommy. Leave them alone."

"I wanna juice!"

"You had two, love, let's wait for dinner."

"Milk! Milk! Milk!"

"Sorry, love, we don't have any." She peeked out at me. "If we don't get our power soon, I might have to send the kids out to the woods to hunt for berries and nuts."

"Berry! Mama, can I watch TV?"

"Sorry Iris," she said.

"Juice?"

"She's going to be a politician," she said, handing Iris a juice box after all.

"She has spunk," I said, trying not to say something wrong, wishing I didn't have to say anything.

It *was* Aaron's first day back at work, and he had said he might come home late, but it was even later than I'd expected, after ten, by the old silver watch Caius had given us to tell time downstairs.

I hadn't seen Thea for hours. I was in the basement, trying not to use up all the batteries in her emergency lantern but unable to turn it off entirely and leave Malena in the pure, soil-scented dark. So I had it on low while Malena was sleeping. I knew I wouldn't sleep and no one had made any noise in ages—the peace I'd coveted earlier made me nervous. I went upstairs.

The kitchen was hushed and dark. I carried a penlight as I wandered around. It felt like a haunted house—I didn't know when something would appear in my grainy spot of light. I looked at the photos on the fridge: smiling child after smiling child, maybe relatives, certainly friends. I looked at the calendar, reading out doctor's appointments, soccer games, dinner parties, symbols and notes I didn't understand, envying them their solid lives, their stable state. All three children born and already speaking, doing, almost all of them even dressing themselves. Aaron and I had talked about wanting two after I'd convinced him to whittle down his original plan of a dozen or so, but at the moment the idea of ever going through pregnancy again, let alone the incredible trauma of birth, was too awful to imagine.

I opened the cabinets, not knowing exactly what I was looking for, some secret stash of diet shakes, tattletale prescription drugs, something unseemly for their perfect bodies, their perfect routines. I wanted to find something to help me understand what kept this house standing. I straightened a tipped-over, open box of crackers. But nothing was unusual in my circle of investigatory light. The juice boxes Aaron had bought for me were stocked, almost lovingly, in rows beside the hot chocolate mix and cans of crushed tomatoes.

I was an awful snoop. Every time I heard the hum of tire noise on the road outside, I thought of what I should say when Aaron came inside. Not "Wow you're late," not "I was waiting." Perhaps "Hi, honey, you're home." I licked my lips, my mouth hungry for kisses. I wanted his attention, his unmixed understanding of my exhaustion.

I went to the drawers, which held the ordinary: rubber bands, coupon organizers, tape. I found a little notebook, and I knew I shouldn't look in it. It had a green cover, and three photographs spilled out as I held it. The first one showed Thea, very young, with a woman who had to be her mother. They were standing at the front of this house, and they were smiling matching smiles. The mother was shorter, darker, and surprisingly round. The second photo showed Thea, very young again, in a way that made me realize, even in the vague glow of my flashlight, that she'd been through many things since that moment. She was sitting in a chair, holding her arm up to a young man beside her, someone handsome in a fragile way, his eyes looked almost made up, their lashes impossibly long. He was about her age, or a little older, and Thea looked happy. Her arm's light gesture, fingers touching his sleeve, body full of light, eyes lit—she looked like someone in love.

I was focusing my circle of light on the last photo: a young girl, probably Thea again, by the back fence of this house. This house, I thought, recognizing the garage, the corner of my own house, soffits, a window—had she lived in this house as a girl?—when I heard the shuffling on the stairs. I turned, suddenly panicked, because I didn't know this kitchen, I didn't live here, and because I'd left my infant downstairs unattended. In the low light of a lantern, something that could catch fire, what was I doing, snooping around? I yelped, lightly, all feeling in my throat. Then I breathed. Even in the dark I recognized Caius's form. I slid across the kitchen and toward the basement steps, unsure whether I should say anything. He made his way toward the liquor cabinet.

" 'Night, Amanda," I thought I heard him say, but I wasn't sure, because of the loud hammering of my own heart.

" 'Night," I whispered, because it was.

10

Thea

"They get along so well," said Amanda, as Oliver and Iris sat together working on a puzzle.

I was sorting the recycling, newsprint smudging my hand like pollen on a nectar-drunk bee.

"When I was a kid," she continued, "my sister and I played these practical jokes . . . don't get me wrong, I love her, but we short sheeted each other's beds and dared each other to catch wasps with our hands and—oh, once I put Tabasco on her toothbrush." She grinned and I cringed. Really? I thought that seemed a little cruel.

"You have sisters?" she asked me, as Oliver grabbed the rest of the pieces and finished the puzzle.

"I win!" Oliver yelled, and Iris began to howl her protest. So much for sibling harmony, I thought, washing my hands and trying to verbally stanch the flood of my younger daughter's fury.

○

I will admit that it was thrilling at first to have an infant so close, the sweet smell, the incredible smallness of her, all her unknowns. She was a calm baby, and Amanda was unknowingly lucky to be up only once or twice a night already, at six weeks. The evening witching hour was brief and Malena barely cried—she made do with a little fuss between dinner and bedtime. She went down to bed in our old crib, and Amanda and her husband slumped around, bleary and yawning. They had no idea how bad it could be with a newborn, how some babies cried every hour to be fed, how even feeding didn't soothe some of them.

But I hadn't expected to have it all up close for so long. Two days, and two more until they went to the hotel. I thought of that saying about fish and houseguests. To be honest, I liked the idea of being a gracious hostess more than I actually liked keeping up that good front. My mother, who uncomplainingly catered to my father's col-leagues for month-long, math-madness visits where they stayed up late and talked too loud and left pale rings with their cups on her good wood and ate and drank all night, would've been disappointed in me.

Whenever the phone rang, I secretly hoped it would be a cancel-lation, a room opening up earlier for them. Though I didn't mind Amanda's company, I'd seen too much with her crammed into the microcosm of my family, spreading her belongings everywhere—a dirty washcloth-turned-burp-pad on the couch, her half-eaten banana abandoned on the coffee table, her shoes, Carra's old shoes, that is, beneath the kitchen table, a pair of my socks stuffed under the tongues.

At the very beginning, it had felt a little like an adventure. I cooked on my old Firefly single-burner camping stove; as I unpacked it, the pine and mildew odor of the trail had spilled into the unlit kitchen. A mom was always in charge. I'd learned about this work, I'd trained on the job from the minute I first went into labor, reorganizing all my impulses so others' necessities, comforts, and emotions went before my own. It was a relief in a way. It made my own needs dull.

Once, when Carra was one and a half or so and teething terribly—crying, drooling, stumbling around the house with her unstable walk, reaching for me all the time and then crying to be put back down—I had hired a baby-sitter, a grandmother from the retirement center around the block who'd advertised in the paper. She wanted to care for babies, and I had a headache, a backache, my old sore hip spot hurt, and I needed to go to the dentist to have a tooth refilled. Carra cried when I left. I could hear her howl of indignation as I walked from door to car.

And when the baby-sitter phoned the dentist, where I sat back in the powder blue chair with my mouth numb but not yet drilled, because Carra had thrown up with despair and could I please come home, she didn't know what to do in such an extreme case, it felt logical, almost expected. I smiled a crooked, Novocain smile as I grabbed my purse and left the office. It took a month before I left her with Caius on a weeknight, when the dentist's office was open late.

Since then things had gotten easier. Harder again, then easier.

In the few days the Katzes had been with us, Iris wasn't as clingy. Sometimes I thought I'd made her that way, I'd made her need me even more than the others, because she wasn't planned and I felt guilty, or because she was my last chance to be entirely essential.

"Do you think I can convince them not to bother with a hotel?" Caius asked on Wednesday night as he was brushing his teeth. "It's so expensive."

"Insurance," I said.

"I suppose they'd like their privacy at this point."

"Hm," I said, thinking me, too. Was I uncharitable, or was I just ready for things to get back to normal?

"She's a good one, isn't she," he said, teeth clean, climbing into bed. He snuggled against me and his feet were cold.

"Sweet," I said, not positive he meant Malena and not her mother.

"I think we should go to the shore next summer. Or up to the cape to see my mother."

For a moment I imagined both families camped out on the beach. I'd chase Iris and hold Malena. Aaron and Amanda would walk along the sand, holding hands. I'd watch Oliver jumping too deep out into the waves. I'd watch Carra tugging on an embarrassing bikini. Embarrassing to me, because I was used to her naked and tiny, not blooming. Everyone would need sandwiches.

". . . don't you think?" Caius asked. Now he had his arms behind his head, in the beach of the bed.

"Sure," I said, wondering how much of his summer musing I'd missed for my own.

The next day, the power burred and buzzed and came back on for good. The kids flocked to the TV like birds to bread loaves. Oliver proudly reset all the clocks. I brought out an old baby monitor for Amanda to use with Malena in the basement. With everything on, I noticed how much our house hummed.

"Do you mind if I make a phone call up here while Malena's sleeping?" asked Amanda. She looked exhausted: Her eyes looked bruised, her cheeks dry in tiny red patches.

"So sorry about this," she said, pointing to the infantile offenses—stains all over the sweatshirt she wore, which belonged to my husband.

"Oh, no," I said, "we should wash it. He has plenty of sweatshirts. And right now, you don't." I wasn't trying to remind her, but her lips grew tense with grief. I was afraid she'd cry. She hadn't yet, in her whole stay. I would've cried, at least privately.

"And of course, help yourself to the phone. I have to clean out the fridge, but I won't listen." As I said it I realized how silly that sounded. I might not listen, but of course I'd hear.

She sat down on the couch with a day planner and a pen and dialed.

"Work." She smiled, looking up at me. Her pen fell between the cushions, and when she picked it up, I saw the quick scratch of ballpoint ink on my fabric. *Argh. That stuff never comes out.*

I made myself busy, starting with the top shelf. A bottle of pineapple juice from before the industrial revolution, some cheese Oliver had to have but didn't like, Gruyère, now exquisitely molded. I unloaded the cooler. We had enough milk for another day or two, though I wasn't sure how much they were drinking. Aaron had it in his coffee, but that was just a little. Two dollops, a wrist twist each time. How strange to learn the intimate habits of strangers. Neighbors, not strangers. I took out the butter dish, scraped crumbs off the stick and pried it from the dish. Then I washed the dish itself, and replaced the butter.

"Hey, yeah, me too. I don't think I can, though . . . For Ethel? . . . I know, I should. It's just the house . . . no, I can leave the baby, it's not that. . . . You know I want to see CBF. God, the books alone! And I know Ethel loves having company. . . . No, she probably wouldn't like it as much with Jessica, you're right. And I love being there for the dinners. Someone always says something—what? Okay, I'll hold."

She leafed through her planner with a crooked tiny smile, one corner of her mouth up, the other flat. Disappointment. She looked up at me and I brandished the orange juice out of panic.

"Um, want some?"

"No thanks," she said.

"Yes," she said, back on the line. "Guess what—I think I can come. Just one day, and I don't think I can make the dinner. . . . Saturday, yeah. Tell Ethel I'll meet her at the signing booths in the morning. . . . I know. . . . Yeah. It's not much longer, I'll be back soon. So tell me about Herr Director. . . . What's going on with Harper? . . . No? Oh, well I . . . oh, okay, if you have to go—I'll see you Saturday the tenth. . . . Yes."

She put the phone down on the couch and picked up her planner again. Then she called her husband. I wasn't really listening, but I got the general idea that he'd take over with Malena, that she was going somewhere for work, that she was nervous about it. I couldn't imagine leaving one of my babies for a whole day, and so soon.

"You know," she said, softly enough so I wasn't sure she was speaking to me. I stuffed the browned bitty trees I'd cut from the broccoli down the garbage disposal and put the good remainder in the crisper drawer.

"I might like that juice if you're still offering."

"I am!" I said, a little too brightly. Malena's stirring sounds came over the monitor.

Amanda got up, shuffled downstairs toward her baby. I wasn't sure whether that meant she still wanted juice. I poured a glass and left it on the counter, and when she came back up again she took it along with Malena back to the couch.

"Thanks," she said, settling her girl in to nurse. She spilled a little juice on her chest, trying to drink and hold at the same time. I remembered that problem; it made me slightly wistful to recall.

"You know," said Amanda, though I was wiping down the bottom shelf now and couldn't hear her clearly.

"I really love my job. It's—"

"Sorry," I said, coming out and wiping off my hands. "I couldn't hear you."

"You know how you love certain things about your job, just certain ones? I mean, I could do without all the politicking—and I do it, too, so I'm guilty. But now that seems so petty. Still, all the brightness of the finished product, all that work gone into it. I really should go, it's like the big group book bat mitzvah or something."

"Where are you going?"

"Oh, CBF—Children's Book Fair—it's this new huge event. There are going to be talks and signings and dinners and authors and booths with a thousand free copies of books. It's been in the works forever. And one of my authors is this amazing old lady—she loves going to the fairs, and I love going with her because people want her to sign their books. Last year at the book expo she wore pink high-top sneakers with her dress; she's kind of a kook, but it isn't contrived, not like some kids' book authors who pretend to love kids and pretend to be spiritual and light. God, there are some huge egos. You should see the correspondence files. . . . Sorry, I'm just rambling."

Malena had dozed off at her breast. Amanda held the empty glass. I took it, then came back to the couch and sat down, two cushions between us.

"I just miss it all, I guess. Don't get me wrong; it's wonderful to be with my sweet pea." She gazed at Malena, dopey; I knew that look, the biggest love. "But it's kind of lonely, too. And I don't want to miss CBF—we've been talking about it forever. There's the political currency of going—I know I said I hate that, but it's just true—and there's also the fact that it's fun to see what everyone's doing. Maybe learn something. I got this book last year that had unbelievable pop-up cutouts, an astonishing feat of children's book engineering. I should show you. It ripped really easily, of course, but it was gorgeous the first time around. Like an ice sculpture or a paper snowflake or something." She yawned, a huge gasp for oxygen.

"But what about you? Was there something you loved about your job? Is there something you miss? I forget where you worked?"

How presumptuous of her to assume I worked. But I had. I thought immediately of being a naturalist at the Lakes of the Clouds. Then of being a school-group guide at the Museum of Natural History, which I'd done for quite a while but which never took much of my time. Then I thought of the bank. I laughed.

"I miss nothing about my job job. It was awful. A bank. But I also worked as a school guide at the Museum of Natural History—"

"Really?" Amanda interrupted. "Wow! I'd never have guessed. What was that like? That place is fabulous. It has that weird smell though, you know—in the hallways? Is that formaldehyde? What did you show the kids? Have you seen that new space wing? Aaron and I went when I was pregnant—" She yawned again. "I'm so sorry. I guess I have a lot of chatter stored up." She patted her lips like a child, zip your lips.

"It was fun, actually. But my favorite job was being a naturalist. At this hut in the White Mountains. Have you heard of them?"

"No way, really? Sure, isn't there one of those on the top of Mount Washington? Cloudy Hut or something?"

"Lakes of the Clouds. That was mine. Have you been there?" *No way*, she'd said, as if she didn't really believe me.

"Just to the top of Mount Washington. In a car. I'd love to take that train that goes up. It seems like a great thing to do with kids someday." Again, she yawned.

I'd always meant to bring my own kids, when they were older. Of course, they were older now, two of them, anyway. I wondered why I never took them, why we never went.

"That job I miss. It's how I met Caius," I said. I told her the story, as briefly as I could: He'd come on a whim to the hut with a client; he'd come back for me, playing hooky from his job. And ultimately, I'd left the mountain for him. I felt flushed and embarrassed toward the end, as if I'd just opened a journal and read her a week of entries.

"Amazing!" said Amanda. "You are more complicated than you seem. But you gave up your own life for this." She gestured around the living room, then clapped her hand over her mouth again. "I didn't mean it that way, I'm sorry. Sleep deprivation."

"I never imagined working while they were young," I said, sounding very brittle. I couldn't help it. I had given it all up for *this*, but it wasn't as if I'd walked down off the mountain and become a domesticated little Heidi. She didn't mean it. She'd said so. But she'd also said it. Who was she to tell me I'd given up my life?

"I never imagined *not* working," she said. "Until now . . . sometimes now I can imagine it. I just need to get a nanny, someone I can really trust, so I don't feel so terrified of leaving her."

"Oh, my mother always said, 'Why bother having children if you don't want to raise them?' " Had I really just said that?

For a minute, Amanda picked at a crusty spot on my couch. Then she barked at me, "Was she happy?" She glared. I couldn't bear her eyes, so I looked at Malena.

"My mother, you mean?"

"Yes, was she happy?"

The phone rang under her leg, and she jumped, and Malena started to cry. Amanda got up and stalked down to the basement, leaving me to pick up the phone, still warm from her body.

One of my high school friends, Belinda Crew, decided five months into motherhood that she wanted to be a screen actress. Since her husband was an investment banker and never home, it must have been sharply lonely in their big stone house in the Glens, the fanciest section of town, where all the lots were at least an acre. It had been part old-money estates, part farmland when I was growing up, but now it was all posh. In the Glens, neighbors cared what kind of car you drove. The residents frequented the outrageously overpriced supermarket right in town instead of going out half a mile to the shopping center and the giant A&P with double coupons on Fridays. The expensive supermarket was where you went if you didn't mind paying another three dollars for your loaf of bread because it would be a brioche loaf with blackened mustard seeds and because you'd have a chance to show off your right kind of car in the parking lot.

Belinda hired a nanny from Senegal and used her time to work out at the gym with a private trainer, to get an agent and a just-so haircut, to go in for photo shoots, and eventually, to get bit parts and advertisements—she was the dog walker in a New York sitcom one week; she posed boxes of tampons to show the flowery labels indicative of freshness the next. Meanwhile her little boy, Mitchell, never Mitch, learned to sit, stand, walk, and speak French and a few words in Wolof, and he went to his first day of kindergarten with his nanny. I was being terribly judgmental. But, tampons! I tried not to condescend. Belinda had been one of the Seven in school, the seven most-popular girls who had their own group number, who flocked through the hall all silver winged and desirable. Everyone wanted the Seven, girls and boys alike, for their good clothes, for their certain shades of lipstick—Pouty Pink and Smack Me Scarlet—for the power of being in that cream, the top. In high school I was popular enough, did well in my classes, had friends and a decent locker, and was caught up, but not too caught up, in the social swirl. I played the viola in the orchestra for the high school musicals and some of my drawings were chosen for the art and literary magazine. I still saw high school friends and nemeses all over town; I knew I'd left, but sometimes it felt as though I never had.

Caius told me he wasn't very popular in his high school; I thought probably he was beyond needing to be popular because he was smart and sufficiently entertained in the world of his own activities. He was captain of the debate team; he played rugby for two years and football for one, but he didn't date cheerleaders. In college he took advanced business courses, as well as philosophy and history and political science. He told me he was mainly interested in entrepreneurialism back then; he drove students to the airport from the isolated midwestern town where the college sat squat on a flat square of cornfield. He called his venture Red Ride, because the old Volkswagen he had inherited from his mother was a deep maroon. It paid for his books and room and board. And he implied that there were always interested women—a fact I had no trouble believing, partly because of his height and manner, partly because he had a deep vein of shyness, which was social gold with smart girls who thought they might bring him out, discover what deep riches lay below the surface.

I was right from the start, right to fall in love with him. He knew how to pay attention, he wanted to know people. He wanted to know me, even if usually the conversations we had now were about braces for Carra and something new and cute Iris said, about Oliver's dietary habits instead of about our deepest desires and needs. Theirs were our most immediate needs now.

That third afternoon, Aaron took a half day so they could visit day cares, and I relished the time to myself in my house. *You are more complicated than you seem,* I thought, remembering her audacity, still brewing a rich resentment. At a distance, her working-mom plan had seemed okay for her, but up close, couldn't she see what I saw? She hated the idea of leaving her child, despaired of being torn apart too soon. She needed to give up her vanity, change her plan—she had an actual baby now, not just the idea of a baby but someone who couldn't hold her own head up, someone who needed her mother.

I had so much cleaning to do. I ran the dishwasher with white vinegar to get rid of the smell and mineral deposits; I packed up the camp stove and cleaned the toilets and changed the vacuum bag. I peered into the basement but decided against cleaning down there. It was enough to remove evidence of our guests from the upstairs: her juice stains, her long hairs all over the couch cushions, her maxipads stuffed in my wastebaskets without being wrapped in toilet paper, so they curled open like wounded animals as I dumped the whole receptacle into a big black trash bag. Iris trolled behind me, trying to help or get my attention. It was tedious. When Carra was born, we'd hired a woman to clean every other week, but she never did things quite right. I'd had to leave the house so I wouldn't follow her around, noticing how she used Brillo on the chrome around the stove. But between Oliver and Iris, I'd taken over again. And most of the time, I didn't mind. I detested the cleaning itself, but I liked being in charge, being the one who said where the orange juice went in the fridge. It was an odd sort of power, I thought. Household power. Power over the ordinary.

I took Iris out for ice cream, bathed her, put her to bed. When Caius came home, I went out for an early evening walk, surveying the lawns. Sometimes I thought I should have a dog for the monotonous company, for the inspiration to leave my own house. It was as if the house had become an extension of my body, as though I needed the skin of walls and windows to keep the world at a distance. Amanda and Aaron's car was in our drive when I got back home. From outside, I could see Amanda's form as she lay on the couch with her baby. It looked as if they were sleeping, so I walked down the pebbly path into the woods. I hadn't been in months, and the carpet of leaves was over a foot deep. The trees had mostly

given up; the last few rainy nights had torn down even the recalcitrant unturned ash leaves. The sky was a clean gray, an early winter
sky, crisscrossed by the naked branches. The stream sang with
recent rain. I followed the main path, looking up and down, at puff-
balls and a crested nuthatch climbing backward down the thick-
barked trunk of a sassafras.

I wondered what I had done with all my quiet time before, and
what I'd do when they left and when Iris grew out of needing me.
Chipmunks flurried the leaves, and I saw a flash of orange between
tree trunks. Following a furrow in the blanket, I came upon a sort of
clearing and suddenly found myself facing over a hundred pumpkins half-covered with leaves. Their stems were still thick with
moisture, and most of their bellies still round. A few looked rot-soft
and slumped in the corners. Squirrels had chewed a select few to
bowls filled with black and orange crumbs. They were like a crowd,
all huddled together. I shivered and looked for any other evidence.
One pumpkin had mittens in front of it, crossed as if they contained a child's restrained hands. Another wore a wool cap. I wondered whether this was the work of teenagers, which teenagers,
and why; until now, I'd forgotten about Halloween's mysterious
vanishings. But some of the pumpkins were enormous, at least fifty
pounds, and it was hard to imagine the sleepy town teenagers slog-
ging though the woods with cumbersome orange burdens. I
laughed aloud. The pumpkins looked cozy beneath their blanket of
fallen oak leaves, sassafras, maple, beech, and sycamore.

11

Amanda

It was our third day as homeless people. Aaron, driving and whistling, acted as if this were a normal family outing. Malena fussed in the backseat—an uneasy sound, slightly hungry—but she didn't break into a wail, so I stayed in front, my stomach a wad of sick anxiety.

"Mozart, isn't that?" I asked, mainly to force his lips out of their energetic tune. Perfectly tuned. Aaron had unused musical talents. His mother had trained as an opera singer before she met his father, and she always encouraged Aaron with piano lessons and jazz saxophone, even in Kenya. He never practiced; he just kept his perfect pitch like a small stone in his pocket, something to take out and rub from time to time for its soothing surface.

"No." He stopped, but only for a note or two. "Sibelius." He resented another day away from work, but I couldn't do this alone. Later in the evening he'd shut himself in the bathroom to go over some briefs by phone.

"I hope it's not awful. It might be awful. Maybe I can get another month of leave. Maybe this is the wrong thing to do." My eyes felt dry and itchy from lack of sleep; my head a sandbag. Everything hurt, and I was tender and vulnerable when I was supposed to be in charge. A parent. Someone who is supposed to know all the answers, even when she forgets to brush her teeth for two days and neglects to tie her own shoes.

"We won't know if we don't go," said Aaron. He stopped whistling altogether, but instead of feeling relieved, I wanted the sound back for distraction. Malena, oblivious to the angst of every-thing, slept in the backseat in her own private nighttime.

Tot Time was in a new brick-and-clapboard building inside a fenced-in compound, with a parking lot so fresh it stank of tar and felt spongy as moss. We had to be buzzed in at the lot, and again at the gate. Before the tree wrecked our home, before I'd lost my sense of safety, I might've been able to see the order, the cleanliness, to see the place for all its good features. If I could sleep for more than thirty minutes at a time; if I didn't wake clammy and sweating. But in my current state, I reviled the cheerful woman at the desk who handed us brochures and made us sign in and showed us the moni-tors that displayed what was happening in every room at every moment. Malena started howling, so I sat down on a kiddie chair in the hall to nurse her.

"The tour," said a perky young teacher with a blond, starched face, wearing a Tot Time polo shirt and a big badge that said LIBBY—ONES. She stretched out her hand for us to follow, as if I didn't have an infant attached to my breast.

I stuck my pinkie finger between Malena's mouth and my nipple, bore her sweet, quick cry, then held her close and stood up.

"Shirt," Aaron whispered, pointing. My breast was still exposed in the orange fluorescent light of Tot Time.

"You go, I'll catch up." I said.

"Oh, no," Libby said. She tossed her hair, only it was sprayed into place so it didn't budge. "We have security measures."

She said "may-shures," like a midwesterner, which made me grin a little.

So I made them wait, and then Libby—Ones led us around Tot Time. The actual tots appeared happy enough, in the yard on the little slides and in the bright rooms, finger painting on an enormous sheet of newsprint. But in the infant room, the faces hurt me—tiny infants looking up from their swings, seats, and cribs with such anticipation, such open hunting, that I knew I couldn't do it. One woman, older and billowed with fat, rocked a child so tiny she looked too small to have been born. That child was cooing, look-ing deep into her caretaker's face, and I thought that this, though better for the baby, was even worse for me to see. Replaced. Malena's eyes searching someone else's in the waning months of our deepest attention to each other. It was impossible, and I started crying.

"My wife . . . ," said Aaron. "It's hard."

"We understand, here at Tot Time," said Libby, but her face said, Get me away from this ridiculous hormone-crazed mom and back to the ones, who appreciate their juice.

"Okay," said Aaron. We were sitting on Thea's couch after our afternoon of tours. Oliver was yelling to a friend in the dusk out-side. In the driveway a basketball thumped.

The couch was thick and cozy. Even though I sensed Thea's con-descension and resentment now, I had started to feel a little like it was my couch when Thea wasn't there because it smelled slightly of milk, because I'd fallen asleep there, and because despite the fact that she might actually loathe me for my choice to work "outside the home," her house was welcoming, comfortable, a grand lap. All the rooms on the first floor—I still hadn't been up to the second, though I was curious what her bedroom was like, especially whether it had flowery window treatments and a matching Laura Ashley duvet and pillowcases—smelled faintly of lavender and faintly of chocolate chip cookies. Comfort and more comfort. Girl and mom all at once. But was it all artificial? Did she really disrespect my choice to work? Did she respect *me* at all? One more day and it wouldn't matter what she thought.

Aaron continued. "So, we don't like Tot Time or Pear Tree or Becky's Day Care or the Early Childhood Center. We don't like any of them." He finished running his fingers down the list, which he'd typed on his computer at work. There were addresses, phone numbers, references, and I wanted to wrench it from his hands and fling it away from us.

"*You* don't like any of them," he continued. "I think Early Childhood's pretty nice."

"They didn't have room anyway."

"They have a waiting list."

"Shh," I said. "You'll wake her." The whole conversation revolted me. Aaron's breath was bitter.

"Mango, why don't you ask for another month off; you're clearly not ready."

"Why don't *you* take a month off? Why is this a *woman's* job? Why is it *me* who has to choose?"

"You don't have to choose." He took my left foot in his hands and started massaging the arch. It felt delicious, and it tickled. I wanted him to keep doing it, but I didn't want him to know that. "But I've got nothing on your lactation skills." He leered. Or maybe he just smiled. It was all so complicated. Had I said that to Thea— had I really said she was more *complicated* than I thought? I hadn't meant it in a bad way. I'd meant everything looked too easy. That I was jealous.

"Yes I do. If I take another month off they'll think I'm not really meant to ever be an editor in chief. They'll give my best books to Jessica Gravitas, who is only twenty-six and whose main talent is having a famous poet grandfather and who will never get married because she's so *mean*."

"People don't have to be married to have children."

"Fuck you," I said. "Fuck you for not having to choose." Even as I said it I felt as though I were reading a script from a daytime soap. This was not my house. This was not my life.

Aaron was still holding my foot, but he looked up. Thea was in the kitchen; I could hear the low hum of her voice. I wondered how long she'd been there, how much she'd heard. It was exquisitely clear she didn't approve of the day-care idea any more than a nanny. Part of me felt like mentioning it in front of her all the time, as if I could prove, somehow, that it wasn't bad and wrong by talking about it, by bringing the words into her house. Part of me thought it *was* bad and wrong. Especially now that I'd seen what day care looked like. It looked awful, it looked damaging. Even if it was clean and safe, it looked very selfish.

"Smells great," said Aaron, calling into the kitchen a little too loudly.

"Hmm? Oh, thanks," said Thea. Clearly, she'd heard everything.

That night after dinner, I called a nanny agency and arranged a day of interviews. I couldn't wait another day until we'd be in the hotel—by then it would be Friday evening, and a whole wasted weekend would be unbearable. Thea said she'd be out all morning anyway, and Aaron promised to come home early for the last few. So many people were ready to work it made me suspicious; if they were so capable and experienced, why were they unemployed?

Aaron took Malena downstairs after I'd nursed her to sleep. I could hear her little animal noises of protest, but I let him try to settle her, though my instinct was to bring instant contentment down after her. I had to practice letting go—just a little—giving her to Aaron. I'd never meant to be the only, the primary parent; I'd meant to be one of two, equal in our worship and responsibility.

Instead of going where my body leaned, I helped Thea with the dishes. She protested, as usual, but I hoped to move past our little spat, if I could. End our third—and almost last—day with Thea on a peaceful note. The younger kids had gone to watch TV, Carra had clomped off to her room to do whatever she did there, and Caius had gone upstairs to finish up some work in his office. Having not been upstairs, I hadn't seen his attic office, either; I imagined big leather furniture and a ridiculously manly pipe odor. So I was left with Thea, and she was left with a mess. I was determined to do something right, to show her I wasn't all lounging and profanity. My mostly healed stitches weren't so itchy, and though I was exhausted, dishes suddenly seemed like a novelty.

"You don't have to; I know you're tired," she said for the third time.

"We're going to the hotel tomorrow night," I said, though she already knew. "Just the interviews, then we'll be out of your hair."

"How will you manage in a hotel?" She tugged a strand of hair from her mouth and left a thin swipe of dish soap bubbles across her cheek. She looked tired, too. I took the dishes she prerinsed and fit them into the dishwasher.

"It'll be fine," I said, feeling like she'd lost the right to discuss this with me.

"No." I wasn't sure whether she meant the hotel or my dish loading. Thea took the dishes out after I put them in, rearranging. My placement looked perfectly fine to me, but I moved away anyway. I started on the drying rack, toweling off serving dishes, pots, the wine glasses with their pregnant glass bellies.

"What are you going to do, leave the nanny in the hotel?" She didn't look up.

One more day. We could check in tomorrow night. After our *discussion* about child care, I'd tried unsuccessfully to find somewhere for Aaron, Malena, and me to go right away, but everything within a thirty-mile radius was full. I'd tried to find something in Westchester, even in the city, but everything was booked. Aaron told me to suck it up. I told him he had no idea what it was like to suck it up, he was off having a fabulous time in his comfy office where the only obnoxious person was the scary secretary who wore gold appliqués on her talons. He told me I'd forgotten about the senior partners and the lobby attendant who pretended he didn't know you and wouldn't let you in if you forgot your ID badge. It didn't cheer me up, but it made me laugh a little.

As I tried to find homes for the serving dishes, Iris sprinted in from the TV room and started crawling on the floor, pretending to be a dog. Thea didn't protest, though I knew it was well past her bedtime. Mine, too.

"Ma," said Oliver, lighting the room as always with the sharp contrasts of his face, the brilliant blue eyes, the dark lashes. I started stacking placemats the way she always did.

"I need cookies for tomorrow. I forgot. I signed up."

"What?" said Thea. "What kind of cookies? Maybe we should buy Oreos." I was surprised to see she was grinning. "Maybe we'll get the lard-o-rama special at the bakery, the kind with that weird frosting in the shape of Mickey Mouse."

"It isn't lard, Mom," said Oliver, but he sensed her fun.

"I could make them," I said, feeling cavalier.

"I make!" said Iris. She climbed a stool by the counter, tugging on the flour bin at the back. Napkins rained on the floor as she reached.

"Love, wait," said Thea. "Chocolate chip? Banana nut? Oatmeal raisin? Spider fly?"

She had had one glass of wine with dinner; I'd had none, but I started to feel drunk with her silliness.

"I make!" Iris tipped the container, loosing the lid, and flour clouded the kitchen.

"I make!" yelled Oliver, waving his hands like a conductor through the airborne powder.

"I make!" yelled Thea, not yet bothering to rescue the flour from her daughter. Iris clapped hands full of flour into the room, a concert of mess.

"I make!" I yelled, too, waving a dish towel through the air.

"I make!" howled Oliver, lost in the invented absurdity.

"Lard special!" cried Thea.

"Ants and beans cookies!" I said.

"Ha! Ants and beans! Ants and larvae! Stumps and grubs!" Thea was laughing so hard her eyes produced a tear or two, or perhaps it was the flying flour.

It took at least five minutes to settle down from laughing. Thea sent Oliver upstairs with his dusted sister, who couldn't let go of her desire to bake and whimpered all the way to the bath.

"I think I'll take you up on that," said Thea, surprising me.

"On cleaning up?" I asked, mopping a gummy mixture of water and flour from the counter.

"On baking cookies," she said. Maybe it was a dare. "Here." She placed an index card on the counter, tugged the Mixmaster forth, brought eggs and butter and sugar and chocolate chips to me as I wiped.

"I'll just sit here and you can tell me how you met Aaron. Or you can tell me all about your first date. Or I can just close my floury eyes while you bake. Do you mind? All that laughing tired me out."

"No," I said. "I don't mind at all."

But she didn't just sit back, she cracked eggs with me, she scooped with a second tablespoon. She counted out chips as she ate them, licked batter from the bowl saying, "Who cares about salmonella?" It reminded me of an afternoon with Jane when we were kids, almost any afternoon we chose each other for company, a choice not entirely of accommodation and lack of options, but partly because we found ourselves fond of each other, if only for a short stretch of hours.

On the morning of our last day bunking with the Caldwells, after the men and half the children had left, Thea went over colors with Iris at the table, brandishing crayons and naming them before her daughter fisted them to mark a coloring book. I sat with Malena on my lap, opening the post-office-must-scented boxes of gifts Aaron had picked up from their holding bin in town. The gifts had started just before Malena was born and they continued, a tiny nightgown in yellow eyelet after fleece pajamas and impractical white tulle dresses, cot shoes that fell off before they were ever fully put on, toys Malena wouldn't play with for at least a year. I loved them all, loved the attention they represented, loved that other people were considering our girl from afar. And I was sorry to have to open them on someone else's couch, but I was too greedy to wait.

"I love the girl clothes," said Thea from the table. "The boy stuff is perfectly nice, overalls and blue boats, but the girl stuff is irresistible."

"You know," I said, wondering whether we could just agree to disagree about child care and move on. We didn't have to be friends, but we ought to be able to manage civility. "I never thought I'd be excited by girly things, but the socks just kill me. Pink ones. Flowers. It's absurd. I wasn't a huge clothes hound myself as a kid or anything." I thought of my mother's dresses, the way her closet smelled of Chanel, the way Jane had accidentally lost a lollipop to the lining of a blue crepe suit jacket.

"I wasn't either," said Thea.

"Actually, maybe I was," I said. "I loved my mother's things."

"My mother's things were pretty plain," said Thea. "*Green*," she said to Iris. "No, it's *green*." Somehow, it sounded like a judgment. I could just hear her thinking that I was going to hire someone else to teach my daughter her colors. No matter what, I would forgive Malena her lollipops on my hems. I wanted to tell Thea to just let her daughter draw, but each time Iris reached for a crayon, she held it back, naming it didactically.

"Hm, pretty plain," I said. Not voicing, Big surprise.

"Would you like me to stay upstairs while you finish up your interviews?" asked Thea. I could hardly ask her to hide in her own house, and Aaron wasn't there yet. I actually sort of wanted her company, or at least the safety of her presence.

"Oh, no, you can stay," I said. It seemed like she wasn't really asking, she was pointing out that I was making her a fugitive in her own house. Ah well, it was almost over. And I was too nervous to cope, anyway.

"Why are husbands always late at the exact wrong times?" I asked.

"Yes," said Thea. "And they're never late *leaving* on the day the car won't start and you're driving carpool and the gas guy comes to read the meter and someone suddenly develops a stomach virus and throws up scrambled eggs."

There she was again, the friendly Thea. I did appreciate her clearing out in the morning for my interviews. Why was Aaron so late? He'd said he was on the train in time to be home fifteen minutes before the interviewee arrived, and now there were only six minutes left.

I'd interviewed four women all on my own that morning, one so old and frail I couldn't imagine she could hold Malena without dropping her, one so sharp I thought she might smack me for impertinence, one sweet faced but so late and flustered I didn't trust her, and one who smelled, frankly, of garlic and farts, which she'd tried to mask with a brutally floral perfume. My first afternoon interview had canceled, and now I was waiting for the last hope of the day.

"And they're never late when you are busy conducting an affair in the bathroom with the boyfriend you had in high school who you met at the Stop & Shop by the frozen burritos and couldn't do without. Oh, or the UPS guy. I hate to say it, but he really is pretty wonderful looking."

"What?" I asked Thea. "*What* did you say?"

"Just kidding," she said. "Caius is home." She had a dog's hearing when it came to tires in the driveway. Thea shepherded a whiney Iris upstairs with the promise of a bubble bath "with bath paints, yes, yes, yes, with paints."

Before Malena was born, I had planned to go back to work the minute my leave was up; I couldn't let someone else take over the big angels book and the board-book series with the frisky ducklings and the cranky illustrator. Now part of me was impatient for selfish reasons. When I went back, during the day, I'd only have a boss, colleagues, deadlines, and work—all suddenly insignificant demands, all suddenly absurdly manageable. It would be easier. My life would be easier than it was right now, and I'd love every minute with my daughter and feel less like sobbing in the middle of the night, because being needed entirely for part of the time would be so much easier than being needed entirely all the time.

If I hired a nanny today, I could sleep on the train. I could go to the gym, every day, and though it wouldn't be normal again—it would never be normal again—I would have some sliver of self back. Not to mention my work. They needed me, my books, my authors. Without me there were quiet corruptions, diversions of the smooth stream of creation I'd built, stone by stone and drop by drop. Or worse, they might be getting along without me. I'd *tried* to make a greased machine, something that could flow on while I was gone but only barely manage until I came back in the glory of having completed my reproductive task.

But as much as I'd planned my quick getaway before the baby, it was different now. To be honest, I hardly thought about the books the way I had when I was forced to wait at home at the end. Then my nighttime worries had been about Marvin Mouse and the art for the story about stones. Now the questioning was not just because my house had been crushed by a tree, not just because I was woozy with sleep deprivation, not just because of Malena's exquisite, staring eyes, but also because of Thea. Because of what she had, that peace and evenness, that mother love like a dazzling light on her skin.

The last chance was here to interview. Her name was Prissy, a name subject to unavoidable judgment, and she arrived twenty minutes early and stood in front of the door with her hand poised over the bell, not ringing. I saw her from the living room window; I was trying to get Malena to nurse on the left side, because she'd been favoring the right, and I felt lopsided. There were hard, hot lumps in my right breast, and I didn't feel like doing anything about them, a hot weak-streamed basement shower or massage or self-expression.

"Self-expression!" Aaron had laughed the first time I'd had to follow the breast-feeding hotline's advice about engorgement. The lactation consultant had asked, "Do you have large bosoms?" To which I almost laughed, which was rare, because since when do lactation consultants have a hard time saying "breast"?

"I like your self-expression," said Aaron. "Can I watch?" I'd allowed his entertainment that time without complaint, because he held Malena while I showered, letting the water stain my skin with heat, letting the warmth mask the awful hurt of the milk lumps.

I watched Prissy from the couch. I was leaving this house tonight. Reservations aside, I needed a nanny now, because otherwise I'd have to ask for extended leave, and with extended leave, only *a* position was guaranteed when I returned, not *my* position.

She was the only white nanny I'd interviewed so far—not that I was any more likely to hire her because of her skin color. I kept wondering what kind of person could possibly want this kind of work. Sure, it was nicer to be with a baby all day than cleaning houses. But it was also bone-wearying work, and constant; you couldn't even be sure how long a nap would last. And not belonging to the baby, how could you suffer being needed so? Not to mention being told how to parent by a parent who wouldn't be there. Maybe you chose it because you had no choice. Maybe you were a pedophile. I wrung my hands, feeling old. I had to stop thinking that way. I reminded myself that I wanted to go back to work; I needed my work.

It was not abandonment.

Malena twisted her head and fussed, and Caius and Oliver fumbled around in the kitchen, having offered to clean up for Thea so she could have a break. Her break consisted of reading Iris another story, giving Iris a bath, getting Iris a glass of milk. Well, it was her fault I was so nervous, her fault her children relied on her too much.

Malena wasn't going to cooperate. I put her over my shoulder and patted and swayed. Out the window, Prissy was wearing a velvet hat. She had an ample wool poncho and I couldn't see her face, but her body looked nervous, lost, and tentative. I wasn't going to hire her.

When the doorbell finally rang, Caius answered it and let Prissy in with a courteous sweep of his hand. Malena was asleep on my arm, which was tingling, and Iris came running down the stairs yelling, *"No bedtime! No bedtime!"*

"I'll take her," said Oliver, proudly grasping Iris's wrist. She howled, and they started up the stairs.

"Am I in the right place?" said Prissy. "There's just one charge?" She had an accent, or possibly a lisp, and I sat still on the couch with my sleeping baby and a head full of unfair judgments.

"Yes," said Caius. He held his hand open toward me. I wanted Aaron to be there. I wanted Aaron to be courteous and calm like this, to have a small puff of dishwashing soap bubbles on his exposed elbow, his sleeve pushed up and his arms gold despite the short span of early winter's sunlight.

I started the interview in a whisper, asking simple questions about experience and abilities. Why she liked children, how long she'd lived in New Jersey. Prissy looked about twenty-five, though gray hair wound through her brown ponytail. Beneath the poncho she wore a red velour dress with small stains near the neck. They were pasty smears that could have been baby oatmeal or could have been some caustic substance from a drug habit or bleach spillage.

"Why are you looking for this sort of work?"

"Oh, loans. A little debt. It wasn't actually my fault—oh, and I *love* kids." Prissy answered in a loud, wavery voice. When she spoke Malena shifted, but never enough to relieve my arm's squashed state.

"Okay, uh, what do you do when the baby's crying?"

"Hm. Feed him, I think? Check the diaper?"

Her, I thought, *her.* More likely she'd turn her upside down and shake her for change.

Prissy and I looked at the coffee table. Cork coasters sat in a neat pile on one end. We were done, I thought.

I was thirsty and the room smelled delicious, buttery, like short-bread. Living at Thea's was making me fat, or at least keeping me in my maternity clothes, the one set I had with me. I had also borrowed three of Caius's shirts and had a pair of sweatpants Aaron bought for me on one of his lunch breaks.

Where was he?

"Would you like a cookie?" Thea appeared with a tray. She had tea, too, though she kept it on the far side of the coffee table, so it wouldn't be sipped or poured close to Malena's fragile skin.

"Aren't you a blessing." Prissy sighed. She took a cookie and leaned back on the couch.

"I've had nothing for hours. Actually, I've had nothing since breakfast. I'm kind of short on funds," she said. "Would I get paid at the *beginning* of the week?"

I didn't answer, and she didn't ask again. I thought of Aaron trying to quell my fears about the nanny interviews, explaining, "You only need one good one." So where was she, my one good one? And why had he said *I* needed one good one, instead of *we?*

I took a cookie, too, and leaned back against the couch. Malena stirred, and my arm went from numb to pins and needles. Butter in my mouth, I could think of nothing else to ask the nanny, whom I was certainly not going to hire. My baby woke up, and Prissy put out her hands. "I can try to calm her," she said.

"That's okay," I said.

"You could have tea," said Thea. She poured me a cup, on a tray, like an ordinary hostess.

"Oh," I said.

Thea nodded her head toward Prissy. *Let her hold the baby.* Of course Thea knew what to do. Though I wasn't sure. She nodded again and held out the teacup.

I stood and laid Malena in Prissy's arms, feeling the wrongness of it in my chest, not at all interested in seeing her succeed.

Malena's fuss escalated, but it probably would have even if I'd passed her to Aaron. I thought of how my mother had held Malena during her visit, like a fragile object, lacking the necessary firmness. I knew she'd been able to hold me properly, but somehow, she was pretending she'd forgotten how.

"Oh," said Prissy, "she smells nice." She snuffled her nose into Malena's hair tuft.

"Good, fine," said Thea. I sat down and took my tea in my hands, but I didn't commit to drinking, and I didn't stop watching.

"May I?" said Thea. She reached for Malena. A dozen times since we'd stayed with her, she'd offered to hold Malena. Once or twice I'd let her, but only for a second. I'd taken her back before her weight was entirely in Thea's arms, and I'd seen that flash of loss in Thea's expression, the quick eyes at half-mast, her mouth opened slightly.

"Oh," I said, starting to stand. It was one thing to see my baby held by a potential nanny, it was another for Thea to take over. She smiled, so pretty, even with that quirky mole by her mouth. I knew I'd have to let Malena go sometime, that the whole point of hiring a nanny was to lighten my arms so I could take them off to the city, take them to work.

Still holding Malena, Thea led Prissy to the door. Prissy gripped a cookie in her hand like a three-year-old with a party favor as she redonned the poncho and left.

"She wasn't right," said Thea. She supported Malena with expertise, with both strength and yield in her arms. It was all right, and I was empty and exhausted.

"I agree," I said, sighing.

"I never expected to move into my mother's house," said Thea, a non sequitur. I was fingering the molding by the window where I sat. "Never expected to come back to where I started."

Was she trying to excuse something? I smiled to show my interest, or maybe because she had my baby in her arms.

"After we married, Caius and I lived in Manhattan for a year— that's when I worked at the Museum—and I also took art classes. We used to think we'd move to Riverdale or Park Slope or something."

"But you didn't," I said, thinking of my own ideas of what it meant to settle down. That I wouldn't have guessed I'd end up in New Jersey. That it wasn't as unglamorous as I'd thought. That it wasn't about glamour anymore.

"My mother died of cancer, my father moved to California, and Clark—one of my brothers—suggested Caius and I buy all the brothers out. I was pregnant. I was scared, actually, of coming back here—it was so clean here, so orderly . . ."

I wasn't sure this was entirely addressed to me. Was I supposed to agree or dissent?

"Remember how the subway always smelled in the summer? Cabbage and sour milk?"

I laughed. "Yes. And I'll be back on it soon enough. Too soon. Sorry about your mother."

"Thank you."

"You're welcome."

"So, I could do it," said Thea.

"You could do . . . what?" I wondered whether she meant the hiring, or that Malena needed a diaper change. I felt the pull of my child in someone else's arms but resisted taking her back just yet. I sipped tea, which didn't calm me but tasted good. There was honey stirred in.

"I can be her sitter for a while."

I shivered, part fear and part relief. This was perfect, this was what I wanted, this was terrifying. Did she mean it? Maybe I could breathe easier with her caring for Malena. But wasn't she against the whole business of my going back to work?

"We'd have to pay you," I said. I'd meant to ask if she really wanted to, if she wasn't just being necessarily *kind* again, but I was afraid she'd change her mind.

"Okay," said Thea, archangel Thea.

"Honey," said Caius, thumping down the stairs with his son. "Oliver has a secret to tell you." Had she suggested the idea to Caius? Would she offer without even consulting him?

Oliver wrapped his arms around his mother's hip and whispered to her. She managed to bend and stay firm, holding my infant girl. Her hand cradled Malena's head. Malena wasn't crying. I tried not to watch too carefully.

Oliver glowed, his beauty disarming beneath the sugar and dirt smudges on his face. Thea smiled, and she had it, too, though her features were adult, imperfect compared to Oliver's uncanny balance. Caius had some of it, too. It was taken from each of them equally, like a pre-Mendel theory of heredity, and the whole was even greater than the sum of its parts.

"My secret," said Oliver, "is that there are enough cookies left for everyone to have two more."

At two thirty-three in the morning, I was nursing Malena on the couch because I didn't want to wake Aaron. We had to wait for Saturday morning to check into the hotel—Caius's idea again, but Aaron left us little choice. He was exhausted when he finally came home after midnight and apologized for missing everything— he had a new case, domestic abuse, which was horrible and consuming.

He told me about it, a little bit. I let him talk but I didn't want to hear any details. I nodded and pretended to listen for a while, but I fell asleep before he did, and when I woke to Malena's complaint, I almost said, "I'm listening, really."

Their house looked different at night, smaller, more held in by its own arms. The hums and clucks of heat and refrigerator and clocks were more pronounced in the dark. It even smelled different, as if the lavender and cookies of the day were sleeping beneath a gentle reign of dust and night-blooming jasmine.

I could do it, she'd said.

I hadn't told Aaron yet. I hadn't technically said yes, but already I couldn't imagine any other arrangement. Guilt edged my calm like frost on unfinished fall leaves. First we had moved in, eating her food and warming her couch with our expansive bodies, filling her kitchen with our noises, lying underneath her, a whole layer of her house made up with us, and now we were going to hire her away from her own children. She had Iris. Iris needed her and distracted her, and though I didn't doubt she could manage, I wondered why she'd ever want to. *If* she wanted to, or if she had been temporarily intoxicated by the sweet scent of Malena in her arms, the impossibly small weight, the enormous, exquisite need. I had wanted to write her off after our discussion about how we lived our lives, but I couldn't do it now, not if I was going to continue to need her. Pay or no pay, she was going to be part of our lives for a little longer at least.

The stairs complained; the person walking down them was the biggest one in the house.

"Hello," said Caius.

Malena was still nursing, and I didn't move to cover my breast. It would be wrong to say it felt entirely unsexual, nursing. But it wasn't about sex, it was simply of the same root, the way love and lovely were related.

"Sorry," I said. "I don't want to wake Aaron."

"Don't be sorry. It's good of you to let him sleep. Thea used to stay in their rooms sometimes. And you don't have rooms. It must feel pretty horrible to have no house. Bereft."

He was wearing flannel pajamas, the same ones he'd worn the night they'd rescued us in the storm. I was bereft, and all along I'd felt that it was mostly because I was recovering from having a baby, from being in this milk-filled bubble of her need, every few hours, of waking and waking. It felt like I never slept. But in fact I'd lost something, I'd lost a sense of safety. Maybe that was why I had such a hard time letting myself imagine Malena safe with anyone other than me. Or else that was natural. Sometimes the natural was counterproductive.

"You're right," I said, hearing my own voice crack.

"You probably would like something to drink," he said. "We'll miss you, you know—it's been nice to have a new one around."

I looked up from Malena; Caius was stealing a glance at my breast. It was almost chaste and almost covetous. I wondered whether he was like Aaron, entranced by the body when it was least accessible.

Caius brought me a tall glass of orange juice, watered down the way I liked it. He watched me drink, and we were tranquil together. I didn't ask why he was up, what he worried about. There was something solid and safe about not knowing, about assuming that Caius was simply the dad, the man who went to work and drove his son to the movies Oliver told me he loved. If Caius was blushing, I couldn't tell in the grainy light. It felt good, the quiet attention.

I remembered the men who flirted with me when I was first married, at work or at parties, how I knew they knew, how there was something especially exciting about knowing you'd never act, knowing the flirting was only flirting.

And now I felt like a big bag of milk, a great sea of mother, enormous, grown impossibly, grown uncomfortably. Aaron's clothes didn't even fit me, and sometimes, pathetically, though I'd never thought he was anything less than delicious and perfectly sized, I wished I had a big husband, so I could feel small beside him now.

"It's different for men and women, this whole thing." He nodded at Malena, then took a sip from a brandy glass. The scent was sharp and warm. "I think men are kind of surprised, the first time around. And even the second. But women, well, you seem to know exactly what to do."

"Thea does," I said. "But I'm still mostly at sea."

"Thea,"—Caius sighed—"is very good at this. But it's good to work, too, to have something for yourself."

Sometimes, when Aaron said it, it didn't feel important enough. When I said it, I felt as if I were trying to convince myself. But Caius wasn't allowed. Not with his perfect wife who stayed at home to care for his beautiful children, who volunteered to hold the Principal's Coffee in her yellow kitchen, all the milling mommies and daddies basking in the house's cookie smell. Hah, did she know of his treachery? Sweet schadenfreude. He secretly wished she worked.

Yet I wanted a Thea, someone to take over half the role, half the mommy job. And she'd volunteered. So why was I so uneasy? Why did I almost long for Thea to walk down the steps and interrupt our conversation, our mild form of subterfuge? I wondered what it meant to trust her, when the separation between us was dramatic as the wall that kept the night cold out and the grainy light and heat inside.

· 12 ·

Thea

I'd hatched the ludicrous idea on the spot, and who knew she'd agree, fingering a lock of her shiny brown hair and smiling so seriously? We said we'd try it for a few weeks, which grew after a week to a few months, which was how long they guessed it would take for their house to be habitable. It was an easy span to imagine— brief as a trimester. If I could stand Amanda that long, she'd become a bit of a tyrant when it came to Malena. How much did she eat? she asked, twice a day. What color was her poop? How long did you take her outside? Was she warm enough? How had I managed to let her become my boss? And whom was I rescuing—Malena or Amanda? When she was leaving my house, I thought I could go back to good-neighbor-at-a-distance status, maybe even a sociable acquaintance, but now we were too closely tied over a charming baby girl.

I tried not to be overcritical about the fact that Amanda's stains still graced my couch and every now and then I found a foreign brown sock that looked like a dead animal rotting in the corner of the basement bathroom. A wad of hair in the drain. A dirty diaper in the trash beneath the linen. Evidence of her occupation.

They had moved to a hotel on Route 80, so Amanda brought the baby to me before work—a bustle, a nervous separation. But then Malena stayed with me all day, three or four days a week. She didn't mind the bottle, and she didn't seem to be searching for her mother until evening. Amanda was habitually late picking her up, but at least I knew to expect it.

Malena was like an advertisement for a baby. She shifted— warm, exquisite, an object of need and fulfillment—against my chest in the Snugli. Her cry was rare and not at all grating; her requirements were easily met. She only fussed gently when her diaper was wet and she slept in her crib or in the car seat with equal ease. Because she didn't cry for constant holding, I wanted to hold her all the time—around the house, wearing her in the Snugli, or holding her against me in the porch swing, both of us bundled in my old sleeping bag while Iris did the Dance of the Dead Oak Leaves. It was already December, and only the dull red fists of the Japanese maple's finished leaves were left on the lawns.

I will admit that at first I loved it, that it felt almost as sweet as the new love of my own babies, only better for Malena's exoticness. Sometimes I dreamed Malena was mine. I woke content with having nursed her, with having sat on the porch swing in the summer while she slept, a baking loaf of bread on my shoulder, and it felt as real as our house, our floors, until Caius rolled over in his sleep and scratched my skin with a too sharp toenail. "Stop," he'd mumble in his sleep, and I would look at him in the grainy light of six A.M. with a little too much contempt. It wasn't his fault. It was my own for letting her settle into my heart, another valve.

I was never going to be a new mother again. Even if I dreamed it, it wasn't what I wanted. Perhaps, I thought indulgently, once everyone is older, if I'm not fully settled into some work of my own, I can adopt another child. I certainly wouldn't want to be pregnant again because, as my friend Vicky from the parents association said, "Pregnancy lasts but nine months, but hemorrhoids are forever."

Malena was the kind of baby who invited watching: when she was awake and taking in light, a plant turning her own hands slowly as if she could see her own growth; and when she was asleep, flying over the landscape of her own unconsciousness. I felt whole, I'm embarrassed to say. I felt necessary and satisfied, and I didn't have to wake at night but I did anyway, as if she were calling to me across the miles. I loved it, the sleepiness like a pleasant painkiller, the days lit with necessity.

But I didn't want to forget the ones who really belonged to me.

Iris was sometimes so affectionate with Malena I thought she'd have loved a little sister; sometimes, however, I caught her giving the car seat where Malena was sleeping a little shove, muttering, "*I'm* the baby," or scowling when Malena cried. I was trying to have projects with Iris the way I had with Oliver and Carra: we'd ironed leaves in waxed paper, drawn a map of the neighborhood in red and purple crayon on a giant sheet of newsprint, planted tiny peat pots with lima beans and peas and set them under lamps to keep something green growing even in winter. But Iris wasn't interested in looking at the different leaves; she only wanted to crumble them into dusty rain she could cast over the hibernating lawn.

Carra had thought the projects were fun until she was five. Then she'd been busy with her own work. But Oliver still wanted to be part of what I was doing; he wanted to follow my hands as I tied a bowline to hang a hammock, copying, learning by imitation. Even at ten, he liked to crack one of the eggs in the bowl for baking and help me close the garbage bags and lug the recycling out to the curb, his short intent form carrying one bin handle while I stooped with the other. Oliver always watched things. He was mesmerized by the visual world, staring at trees, even as an infant, my angel. His changing table view looked up at the crown of a maple, and he'd been dazzled by the green light in summer, lifted his fingers as if to stroke the twigs in winter. His first word, besides the requisite *da-da* and *ma-ma*, was *tree*, and he made me feel blessed, even now, when he came home with a pussy willow branch snapped off, so I could touch the velvety feet. "I didn't hurt the plant, did I, Mom? I mean, I only wanted a *sample*."

○

The May after Oren died, I was twenty-three. I read in the Appalachian Mountain Club newsletter about the visiting natural-ists at the AMC huts. I didn't imagine I was qualified, with only my undergraduate biology degree and my almost-finished Appalachian Trail excursion with Tia after we graduated from college. But I remembered how festive life at the huts had been when Tia and I had stayed there—skits for the campers and vast vats of oatmeal, happy gossip sounds in the lofts at night—and I wanted that, to be part of something instead of marooned and old, working at a bank and dating men who wanted to sleep with me or marry me, back in my childhood room with no fondness for its space and none of my brothers across the hall. So I sent out my letter and my résumé, composed at my dry metal desk at the bank, and less than a month later I was cramming my pack with rain gear and my mother's wild-flower guide and writing a postcard to Tia, who had long since left New Jersey, telling her I was going to the Lakes of the Clouds.

I loved the air there. I filled myself with the pure moistness of it when I was out with a group, pointing out the dwarf cinquefoil, the plants that grew to the size of a dime in a hundred years, touring the roped-off regions at the top of the world. My evening tours took us up to the rock with the best view of the stars scrolling over the sunset. Everything was extreme, the cold nights, the big winds that could pluck a hiker off a ridge like a great hand flicking a fly. The sky wrapped around the hut, and on nights when we had no visitors at all, weeknights in September, we sat out on a picnic table perched on a rock, higher than anything, with French toast for dinner, warming our hands in our sleeves and one another's. On days off, I hiked out to Lion's Head and the Alpine Garden, looking down at the world, refreshing my perspective from a height so great all plant life was shorter, smaller, took longer to grow against the great demands of their proximity to the sky. I made friends, but the crew shifted at the end of the summer, and no one was permanent.

I wrote letters to Tia. It felt like a conversation, like we hadn't lost anything between us by moving apart. In letters I said everything I wanted to say, and as a reader, I assumed, she listened. Tia sent me her letters from Colorado, where she was skiing and falling in love with Bozkurt, who was from Turkey and wanted her to be more traditional. Traditional or not, she wrote, the sex was fantastic. I still hadn't had sex. It wasn't that I didn't want to, I just hadn't found anyone I wanted to do it with. The men at the hut were too casual about everything. It wasn't that I planned to marry the first man I slept with, but I didn't want to watch him sleep with someone else the next night, a counselor whose campers were giggling in the bunkroom while I was banished, temporarily, from the loft.

We had too many visitors one weekend night, a big group from Outward Bound and a couple on a honeymoon and two men who had neglected to make reservations—a management consultant from New York who wanted a break and was out with an adventurous client leaf peeping and hiking. In the chaos of the hut after a meal, the consultant, Caius Caldwell, introduced himself, holding out his hand with a sunny smile. He was handsome, with a square jaw and big teeth. His eyes were pale blue and his brows looked as though they could use a tiny comb to put them back in order. When he smiled, one cheek dimpled. There was a scar running along his chin, and I noticed an awful lot more as he kept talking. I walked outside, stunned by all that attention, and he followed. His voice burbled—I wasn't sure whether he was responding to the mountain air or my fabulous talk about raptors during dinner. He went on about New York, how he'd grown up in Boston, which was much smaller, more provincial but comforting somehow, about the shades of the leaves, about the difference between working out in a gym and really being outside. The chatter surprised me and made me realize how lonely I'd been. We strode out into the great cold of just-past-dark together, and he asked me how I'd decided to be a hut naturalist, how I imagined my future.

"I do like learning and talking about the plants and the ecosystem, but I'm not sure I could live up here forever," I said, realizing

I meant it, realizing I'd never expected to stay even this long. "I'm too attached to comfort."

"Comfort's a good thing," said Caius. "Most people don't appreciate it." His back was broad and he stepped surely into the dark.

"I do, now. Maybe I should go back to school, study ecology. I don't mind the practical, either. Don't tell anyone here, but I was always interested in architecture. I'm definitely not cut out to be a biologist. Or an academic." I shuddered. I told him about my father's proofs, his webs of symbols and numbers, his way of learning by dissecting. It was his way, and it drove him. It didn't work for me. I needed to put things together instead of taking them apart.

"So much analysis—it's a good way of seeing, I suppose. But I like the idea of building, too. Maybe I just want to be God." I'd never said that. I sounded so casual and sure, I didn't recognize myself. Brave words in the cold air.

Caius laughed. "You could be a mom," he said.

I hadn't meant that. Or maybe I had. I was too young to think about children. Of course I'd have them, but not for a while. I blushed in the dark. "What about you?"

"It isn't anything so profound, but in my job, they have me do both: take the whole place apart—theoretically, of course—and imagine how the pieces could better fit together. Businesses are not the world, though. They matter, but they aren't everything. Anyone who prefers work to the world is running away—" His gloved fingers brushed mine; I felt the sweet shock through Gore-Tex and insulation.

"Keep looking, Miss Thea," he said. He had a slight Boston accent. "You'll find where to use all that talent."

"Thank you, Professor," I said, but I didn't mean it so cynically. I meant, Thank you. Thank you for asking, and thank you for listening.

We walked back into the hut, and my body buzzed beneath my coat. I wanted to sleep with this man. I wanted to undress him and taste him; I wanted to and I didn't care if he was leaving in the morning. His body sang out to me, its mysterious shapes beneath all those layers of clothing. His words were good; his listening had changed everything. I wanted us to be the ones in the loft.

At first we just kissed and held each other's forearms, stroking gently, as if there was a whole language to discover in the texture of the skin there. He put his hands inside my shirt, and I pressed mine inside his, my mouth tasting his skin, breathing the sharp, exquisite scent of exertion and arousal. But Caius didn't want to have sex. He stopped my hands, gently.

"I'm going," he said. "I have to go tomorrow. I couldn't stand to be with you and then just go." He whispered this, suddenly quiet.

"I couldn't either," I said, pretending.

We feigned sleep, entwined. Caius slept a little, but I was awake the whole night, wanting.

The next day, he and his client went on; Caius left me his card, and though I knew I'd never call, I put it in my journal and ran my fingers over the raised letters of his name. I wrote a letter to Tia, making it all sound casual, feeling tragedy blooming like a bruise under my breastbone.

I was still mooning the following day, while I led the Outward Bound group on a hike. The soldier lichens were redder than I'd ever seen them; the reindeer lichen silver in the late-afternoon light.

"This tiny thing, *Salix planifolia,* is a willow." I pointed. "*Rhododendron lapponicum,* Lapland rosebay."

"Is that a *tree?*" A young woman with a pointed face and cropped black hair asked, pointing at something smaller than the smallest bonsai.

"Gray birch," I said. "Dwarfed." I felt dwarfed, my voice snatched by the wind and sudden bursts of rain as I spoke. I wanted to be down the mountain; I wanted to be with the man I'd just met. I felt tragic and marooned. My cells were growing too fast for this severe environment, spreading spots of all-new skin where we'd touched.

I was leaning over a web-shaped patch of lichen, explaining, "the first thing to grow in a stony landscape, the first life," when I saw the shadow of a new form joining the group. Raincoats shushed as arms shifted to let him move to the front.

Caius joined us, grinning at me madly.

"Hey," he said, "want to teach an old man some new tricks?"

"A symbiotic relationship of fungus and algae," I continued, unable to say anything else.

"Sorry"—Caius nodded to the group, earnest teens with worry in their bodies—"but I have to borrow the teacher."

After that afternoon, I was the one having sex in the loft. Caius had let his client leave without him, though he was sure the firm would mind. Despite living in a city, I discovered, the backs of his knees smelled mossy, and his long legs were strong. I loved how they felt around mine—oaks among birches.

He stayed for three days of unclaimed vacation. He told me he was dating a woman in the city, nothing serious, he said, but he wanted me to know, and he would break up with her as soon as he got back. I didn't mind that I hadn't known before. We had just started, and I vowed not to care about history, even though I already felt a vague sense of ownership, of belonging. We kissed outside against the complaints of the wind. We fed each other oatmeal as if it were ambrosia. He told me he would wait until I was ready to come home, meaning ready to come to him.

We had a few months of passionate letters, letters with sex in the tiniest details, the meals he'd eaten without me, the scent of his pillowcase, the city's sounds. Then we had a winter visit to a resort hotel in Crawford Notch where I wanted to spend most of the afternoon in the shower, rinsing off the dirt of hut living. Caius scrubbed me until the hotel cloth was gray and called me his dirty girl. He fed me overpriced crab legs, expertly cracking the exoskeleton and prying the meat from the shell. Even the sweetest bit in the small of the claw came out intact, and he pushed it onto my tongue.

○

Sometimes I missed the Lakes of the Clouds, the living half-outside, the sense that I was more *of* the natural world than other people. Now I depended on it all, electric lights and heat, the cooked chicken from the market. Sometimes I missed the clouds in my hair, clouds around my head, like a cartoon. One morning Malena and Iris both napped—Iris falling asleep on Oliver's closet floor, gripping her rubber frog. I sat down at the computer and typed in Outward Bound. Need to Get Out? the website asked me. I did, I needed to get out. I scrolled down the list of trips. Two weeks in Costa Rica. Ten days in Alaska. It was hard to imagine what it would feel like to heave on my pack. I felt brittle, snapping my joints just to turn in the chair and check on Malena in her Pack 'n Play. Then there were one-week trips for women. Women over thirty. When had I become a category? Without thinking too hard, I filled in the online form, requested a brochure. I knew I'd never do it, but maybe I'd like looking at it, thinking about it. Maybe I'd enjoy my walks in the neighborhood more, remembering what it felt like at the top of the world. Maybe I had to get to Iris, who was wailing upstairs, causing Malena to stir as well, two bodies desperate for attention. I would need to make snacks quickly, to coax and carry them from their half-sleeping states back to reasonability.

By one o'clock Iris had recovered from sleeping, and Malena was ready to sleep again.

"My baby," Iris said, holding her hand up toward the Snugli on my chest. We were walking down Edgewood, and Iris pushed her baby doll's stroller in front of her, proud of her work. She stayed on the sidewalk. She didn't cry to be carried herself; she didn't flail and sit on the ground after three sidewalk squares. I felt an even happiness, things were going so well, minute to minute, the way they had not been for a while. The way they often did when the children were new.

"Oh," said Mrs. Chen, stepping out of her car in a woolly red coat. "I didn't know, how could I not know?"

"My baby," said Iris.

"It's Malena," I said. "I'm taking care of her for Amanda." I nodded toward her house, where several massive trucks and soda cans blotching the lawn indicated the slow work toward repair.

"She's already back at work?" Mrs. Chen looked surprised. "I don't understand why women do that if they don't have to."

"I don't either," I said.

"It's such a shame. I would've been there for all of high school if it weren't for the divorce. They need you. Even when they pretend they don't."

I nodded.

"You're not like that," she continued. "You're a good mother."

On cue, Malena's voice rose, a small star of sound.

"Feed me," said Iris, pointing to Malena with a long-dead, rust-colored mum she'd plucked from Mrs. Chen's walkway.

All the way home, offering my pinkie finger for Malena to suck, I tried to decide what reason Amanda really had for going back so soon. She loved her job? But not more than her child. They needed the money? Not sure about that. I didn't know all that much about Amanda's finances, but I did know everything was a choice—a smaller house, sharing a car. She didn't want to do the hardest work in the world? Still, who was I to judge? I had made my own choices, or at least, they'd been made.

By late afternoon, the weather of my occupation had changed. I had to strap Iris, whining, into her car seat, and clip Malena, who fussed as if to prove a point, into her car seat, and I forgot the bottle of formula to feed her while we waited in the parking lot of some school in Passaic County where Carra had a swim meet.

"Blankie!" Iris yelled in the backseat.

I kept the engine running. It was too warm in the car, but Carra would be wet from practice.

"Cookie!" yelled Iris.

Malena fussed. I reached back and stroked her cheek. She turned toward my fingers, but I had no food.

"No do that!" Iris grabbed at my fingers.

"Stop," I said, over the noise of the two of them. "It's 'Don't do that.' Carra's coming."

Finally, after a dozen other girls, Carra ran out to the chaos of the car, her hair still slick and the chlorine scent rising off her cold-coated-but-hot-from-exertion body like a chemical perfume.

"Mom," she said, ignoring me as I leaned toward her for a kiss. "Why don't you come to my meets? All the other moms were there." She pulled a box of chocolate-covered graham crackers from her backpack and started eating.

"No do!" Iris kicked mud onto the back of the front seat, regressed, wailing for cookies or for blankie or for God knows what, just wailing, and Malena was ready to be held, her fusses escalating into a serious complaint.

By the time we arrived home, Carra had grudgingly relinquished two from the box of cookies she'd stolen from the top shelf, Iris was chocolate coated and cranky, still, and Amanda was hovering inside the door, eager to nurse and go back to her hotel, annoyed with me for making her wait.

I knew it made sense for her to have our key, but sometimes, even though she entrusted me with her daughter, I didn't fully trust her with the key to my house. I was embarrassed to admit it, even to myself. I suppose it was our fundamental difference in belief— that hole in her heart by which she let herself leave her daughter— that made me unable to relinquish my suspiciousness. Sometimes I came home and she was there; I noticed the mail had moved on the table, the cupboards were open. I wanted to be generous, to share without reservation, but I couldn't shake the feeling of invasion.

Whenever the phone rang, it was for Carra, or it was Amanda, which meant it wasn't for me but for Malena through me.

"Hello?" I said one Wednesday afternoon, balancing Malena on my bent knee. She was propped in a sitting position, chewing on her sleeve with a profound look on her face, which meant she was probably about to poop. Amanda was an hour late on her half day.

"So, I can visit next week?" said a slightly husky, familiar voice. I tried to place it but then wondered whether this might be a wrong number. "There's a conference. It isn't mine—it's my, well, significant other's—but I can get a free plane ticket. I'd have to crash with you—"

"Tia?"

"Who do you think this is, Princess Diana?"

"Tia," I said. "Next week? Wow. That would be great. We're kind of busy, though, with swim meets, and I'm taking care of this baby—"

"Uh-oh," said Tia. "You're not thinking of having another, are you? Isn't it getting kind of late in the game? And seriously, I mean, three is a crowd already."

I bristled. Malena felt me stiffen and fussed quietly. Who did Tia think she was, calling me out of the blue and commenting on my fertility? *Was* I thinking about having another? I was getting too attached to Malena.

As if prompted, Amanda turned the key in the lock.

"You are *so* welcome to come, Tia. We're busy, but that doesn't mean we can't squeeze you in. I'd love to see you. It's been—well, almost three years, right?"

"More than three years, babe. Squeeze away. It may be next week—or the week after—not sure of my dates yet. Aren't you going to ask me about my significant other?"

Amanda bent to pick up her baby, looking at me sternly. I knew she disapproved of my being on the phone. My phone. Malena curled into her arms like an infant monkey. It was so beautiful it hurt a little to watch.

"How'd she sleep?" Amanda asked, sotto voce. She smelled the baby's behind. "I hope she doesn't have that hideous diaper rash again." She winced, holding the stained bottom up in the air.

"Can I call you back, Tia?"

"Sure. You'll need the number—I'm at a hotel—" She wanted me to ask why, ask more, she wanted to pick up the unplugged cord of our conversations and get instant electricity. But Amanda was standing there. And besides, I wasn't ready for Tia, wasn't ready for her brusque, honest questions. It felt like an assault after all this time.

"Hi," I said to Amanda after I hung up. She sat on the couch as if she still lived there.

Amanda was kissing her daughter's neck, unwrapping the poopy diaper on the couch without a cloth underneath.

The phone rang again. I knew before I picked it up that it would be Tia, impatient as always, and that I'd take it upstairs for privacy. That by the time I'd insisted yes, visit, and fended off the questions I didn't want to answer, hoping we could have a real conversation in person instead, I'd come back downstairs and mother and daughter would both be gone.

January

13

Amanda

At the beginning of January, we drove to my mother's apartment in Cambridge for a late Chanukah dinner. Since she'd moved from the big house in Auburndale, I'd always felt uncomfortable in her space, and the feeling intensified when I was there with Malena. Out the huge cold windows, I could see the Charles River lined with naked trees. Traffic on Storrow Drive hummed by, and the sky and river were the same gray. The kitchen was marble; the toilets were faux marble, and the bathroom fixtures real brass: furnishings my father would've felt uncomfortable around, until he remarried into money. The floors were clean wide oak, the tables sharp-cornered glass; there was nowhere to safely rest the baby. My mother's couch sported thin cream-colored wool on a dark mahogany frame. It bruised me as I sat, and I couldn't look up for the intense halogen track lights that broke the room into universes with tiny unbearable suns.

My mother, who had let my father do most of the cooking when they were still married, made beets and brisket. She bought the rest of the Chanukah items from a fabulous gourmet shop in Porter Square, except the because-you-missed-Thanksgiving, out-of-season strawberry-rhubarb pie, which my sister Jane and Cornelius made together, an event I could hardly imagine. Once Aaron and I had cooked together, but now the idea was laughable. Who'd hold Malena? Who'd be able to stay standing long enough to roll a crust? The edges were meticulously crimped and Jane's hair smelled of coconut shampoo and sleep when I hugged her.

This is my family, I thought, sitting at the table with an unfamiliar ornate crystal goblet in my hand. The wine tasted rich and good—just a few sips, I promised myself (and Aaron, who had developed an annoying habit of mentioning how much I liked to "get the baby sauced" whenever there was alcohol in our midst) as we toasted another year.

"To possibilities," my mother said. I looked at my husband and daughter and felt right and proud.

"Can you take her now?" Aaron asked. He started leaning Malena on my shoulder before I could answer. She coughed a little white blotch onto my black sweater.

I watched Aaron spooning kugel into his mouth and envied his taste buds the little burned bits.

"So, darling, you know I'd have you here for a while, what with your disaster and all," said my mother. She paused for a big mouthful of latke. Sour cream. Applesauce. I wanted to eat, but all I'd had time for in my baby-free shift was that single sip of wine and one forkful of beets. I tried to hold Malena and reach the brisket at the same time. Impossible. I managed a big wad of bread but swallowed too fast and felt the lump, an antelope in an anaconda's belly. I was a slob for having hunger.

"Oh, or we could have you." Jane's face was rosy. She held Cornelius's hand under the table; I could tell from the way her body overlapped his.

"You're pretty cramped in your apartment, Janey," I said. Malena's breathing deepened. "But thanks."

Malena sighed, a satisfied, gorgeous little sound, and grew heavy with sleep. As Aaron passed the plate I attempted to grab a slice of meat without waking her. Maybe I could come stay with my mother and she'd take over a night shift and she'd be so gentle with Malena I'd feel that surge of love for my own mother I'd had, deep and true, a few minutes after my daughter was born. But she'd done nothing to cultivate it; she'd done nothing, really, except make the brisket. Which I couldn't quite reach with my fork.

"I know," said Jane, as if she'd never offered anything.

"But I'm just *so* busy, and you'd never see your hubby," my mother finished.

I wasn't sure why they imagined I could just up and leave work.

"She is busy," said Jane, looking conspiratorial.

"Can you take her?" I asked Aaron. He turned to me with his mouth full and made a plaintive expression.

I knew it had only been about ten minutes, and he needed to eat, too.

"Fine," I grumbled, despite my reasonable thoughts. "I'm going to sit on the couch."

"Don't be ridiculous," said my mother. "I'll take her." She didn't get up. She had sharp objects at her plate, a carving knife, and breakable glass.

"You don't have to," I said. But I walked over to her just the same and tried resting Malena in her lap.

"Will your nanny want to celebrate *Christmas* with Malena?" My mother touched the baby's soft spot.

"I hardly think it matters," said Aaron, his mouth full.

"Oh, it matters," said my mother.

"An announcement," Jane interrupted, and I tried to thank her with my eyes.

I continued standing beside my mother, though Aaron gestured with a fork that I should eat while I had a chance. Suddenly, I wasn't hungry.

"I'm up for early tenure." Jane had a dot of sour cream on the corner of her mouth. Cornelius leaned in and kissed her.

"So maybe I can make a cousin for Malena sooner than I thought," said Jane.

"We," said Cornelius.

"No need to rush, darling," said my mother. She patted Malena's back in a short, brittle motion, and my daughter startled and began her hungry cry. I wished I was disappointed when I took her back, but really I was relieved. I didn't even mind that the brisket was cold by the time we finished nursing on the stiff couch and I made it back to the table. I thought of my own house the whole time we were there. Scaffolding, the cold coming in, the knitting of bones before we'd have it whole again.

I had been working in publishing for almost nine years; I'd been to ALA and BEA and had sat at awards dinners and author roundtables and a science-fiction conference. I'd been on panels where, all too often, the questions' underlying message was: Please publish my book. I'm an author. Okay, I want to be an author. I haven't quite finished my book yet, but I know it will be amazing, and also, I don't want to give an agent a cut of my advance. It will be a big advance. I am tired of my read-and-critique group, which thinks juvenile fiction is, well, juvenile. I know I'm going to hit it big. And all too often I answered their actual question, "Do you read unsolicited manuscripts?" or "How often do you buy new manuscripts? Do you have time after the panel to look at something, because I have something with me . . . ?" with a firm no, followed by a little talk on craft, or the way we try to work illustrations together with words in a picture book, or the changing shape of the young-adult audience.

The podiums all smelled of lemon furniture wax. My eyes stung by the end of the night from straining to watch the speakers in the lights. I had been part of a team that won awards—I'd sat holding an author's hand as she waited to give her speech, and then I applauded and even whistled, low, when she didn't get the medal but at least got an award. But I'd never been this directly involved before. My best-selling author, Ethel Vera—whose first book I'd acquired against the recommendation of four out of seven editorial committee members—was up for the Caldecott Medal for *Wild Aunt Safari*, her book about a girl who goes on a nature walk in the Bronx. Ethel's great depth of silly humor spilled out of her quick bright manuscripts with no space wasted—her acrostics had been popular, her silly snow day book had been big, and her getting-dressed story, *Bess Dressed Heifer*, had surprised everyone when it was both a Boston Globe–Horn Book Award winner and got a Golden Kite. *Wild Aunt Safari* was somewhat autobiographical, and it had been very rough. We'd revised and tinkered for five years before we finally found the right balance of humor and clarity and action. Most surprisingly, she had dedicated the book to me.

"To Amanda, who sees the life in small things," read the inscription. Seventy-two-year-old Ethel, with her almost lavender hair and surprising collection of scarves from street fairs—black women dancing on white silk, tiny red knitted squares with a purple background, cardinals made of sequins on a filmy flutter of polyester—couldn't be at the awards ceremony because her husband had fallen on a hike in the Adirondacks (Ethel had stayed at the campsite catching fish and working on a new manuscript) and was in the hospital for hip surgery. She wanted me there in her place, and it felt more important than any hand-holding. I was as nervous as I might have been if I'd written the book. My palms were sticky, my feet sweat in their hose and adhered to the new black pumps I'd bought for more than I wanted to spend at Nine West on the corner by my office, because the black pumps I kept in my drawer for events didn't fit me anymore.

Big feet, big boobs—I sat at the table and worried I'd leak through my breast pads. I swirled the tepid orange two-squash soup around in its bowl. My breasts hurt with milk, and I willed myself not to think about Malena while the author-and-illustrator husband-and-wife team for *Baby, Baby, Mama's Home*, a book about a stay-at-home daddy and a working mom and a big-eyed baby with a bottle—the book jacket was being shown up on the screen—delivered a talk about the marriage of art and words. The book was great, but I looked around the room at the authors in their tastefully original, deep blue, peacock-sequined blouses with slim black skirts, and the editors with tastefully decorous suits and silver scarves (the editorial director of Penguin was leaning a little too close to her soup, and an assistant tapped her sleeve to alert the executive to this potential disaster) and thought none of it had anything to do with children. If Malena were here, I thought, I would have spit-up on my shoulder. I wished I could drink the wine the server had poured, though I had held my hand over the glass to tell him no. If the editorial director had had a baby with a leaky diaper in her lap, I imagined, she'd leap up and hand the offending little one to the assistant.

I made it to dessert, poured cream in my coffee, and told myself, *Don't think about milk, don't think about milk.* I could smell it a little, almost a baby smell. I went to the rest room, though Ethel's book was up in a few minutes, and squeezed a tiny bit of milk out of each nipple in a panic, to release the pressure. I changed my bra pads. I sat on the toilet and noticed a rusty smell, then saw there was a little blood on the pad I wore in my nylons. If I sneezed, and peed a little, I prayed it wouldn't leak down my legs. "What a wreck," I mumbled to myself, realizing I was getting my period for the first time since Malena was born. My body was getting prepared for another siege. "Right," I said, also aloud, though I didn't realize it until someone said, "You okay in there?" and I knew from the voice it was Jessica Gravitas.

"Fine!" I chirped. "Just nerves!"

"You haven't won the Caldecott by now?" asked Jessica.

It was the convention to say we had won the medal if an author's book won. In my first year at the company, I said, "I didn't know you were also an author!" to Karen Woller, a kind woman with long white hair, when a book of hers was named. "Ha!" She laughed. "No, my author won it. We say we won it, though." I was glad it was her and not someone who would've deposited the coin of my naiveté in her piggy bank for future expenditure.

"Oh," I said, "my authors have won some honors, but never the medal."

"Oh," Jessica said. I could see slices of her through the space between the stall wall and door. "I think Dr. Stevens has a thing for you." She mentioned the art director from Harper, who was barely thirty and had a Ph.D. in art history, so everyone called him doctor. Wunderkind. Unmarried, with a reputation for frequent on-the-job dating.

I smiled to myself and mumbled, "Pull yourself together," as I adjusted pads and seams and zippers and tried not to gasp as I squeezed back into all my clothes. If Dr. Stevens had a thing for me, I could get out of the bathroom and on with this award ceremony. I had no interest in Dr. Stevens, though he had dazzling sapphire eyes and one very compelling crooked tooth. But having Jessica think I might be the object of Dr. Stevens's desire was enough to remind me of the big game I was playing here. And that I was just about to buy two hotels on Boardwalk if Ethel's book won the award. My book.

"I don't think so," I said to Jessica in the mirror. She looked earnest and beautiful and young, and smelled of a perfume that reminded me of sweet peas, though I could see where her roots were vague brown before the gold-blond began. I wondered why I'd ever felt threatened by Jessica. Sweet peas. She was someone's baby.

After I gave the speech I'd prepared with Ethel over the phone, and we had all clapped and raised our glasses (mine was water, at the podium) to the cover of *Wild Aunt Safari,* and the rest of the awards were over, Dr. Stevens came up to me in the lobby, where I was collecting good wishes for Ethel, feeling flush with our accomplishment, feeling as though I owned this award, too.

"Some of us are going to Downtown for a drink," he said. "Will you be one of some of us? Oh, and congratulations." He winked. A grown man winked at me. He was very good-looking, even if he wasn't my type. He was over six feet tall and I could tell he was looking down in the general direction of my cleavage. Which *was* rather impressive, though mostly I thought it was only supposed to be impressive to a two-month-old with an enormous appetite.

"Yes, I believe I will be some of us," I said. Not one ounce of me would ever be unfaithful to my family—and now it felt like my *family*, not just Aaron but the unit of home, even if we were sleeping in a hotel—but nonetheless, it was delicious to be the object of vaguely lustful attention.

Perhaps, I thought as I stood at the bar at Downtown and shouted a bit about my career to Dr. Stevens, and made a phone call to Ethel, whose husband was going to be fine and who congratulated me as if, once again, *I'd* won, perhaps no one even knows I'm lactating. Perhaps it's time to wean.

On the late train home, I called Aaron, though I'd told him to turn off the ringer if he was tired after he picked up Malena from Thea's. I squeezed my knees together, cramping slightly, letting mommyhood flow back into my shut-off brain. I'd had two glasses of wine after all, and one sip of Dr. Stevens's—"Mike, please," he'd told me, "the Dr. Stevens thing is getting old"—chocolate martini, which tasted medicinal but delightfully clandestine, as if I were underage again, and I was a bit foggy and high. The train was nearly empty and it was arid inside. My hands and lips both felt chapped; I was thirsty. At the front of the car a man in a dove gray suit snored so loudly I heard him over the rattle of the tracks.

"Hi," I was prepared to say into Aaron's cell phone voice mail. "I know it's really late." I looked at my watch as I thought it. One thirty-three A.M. I hadn't been out this late in a hundred years. I was suddenly sad Aaron wasn't with me.

There was a click, then a fumbling noise, as Aaron picked up on one of the last rings.

"Hi," he said, voice crackly with sleep. "Went late, eh? You win?"

"We won!" I said, a little louder than I'd intended. The snoring man shifted in his seat. "It was great! Some of us went to a bar afterward. Not that I'm really drinking—"

"Great, Panda, great," he said. He sounded distracted, breathing like a sleeping man, and then I heard a strange cough in the background. It was too loud and deep to be my baby.

"Is that a dog?" I asked. "Or did you bring a tubercular lover to the hotel?"

"Oh, it's Malena, Panda," said Aaron. He didn't even have a quick comeback for my joke. "She's okay, though. Thea took her to her pediatrician—Dr. Goodberg. Just croup. They all get it."

"They all get it? Croup?" My stomach was so tight, I thought I might throw up. I reached in my pocket out of habit, looking for a plastic bag. "She took her to the doctor? Why not Bergen Pediatric? How come she didn't call me? Will insurance even cover some other doctor? Are you sure she's okay? Who the hell gave her *croup?*"

"Honey, don't worry. We have a nebulizer—"

"A nebulizer? Does she need to go to the hospital? Jesus, one night, I go out one night—" I started to cry, my mouth and nose welling with phlegmy regret and fear.

"She's really okay, Panda, just—I have to go now, you'll be back soon." There was more barking, and he hung up.

A part of me knew croup was nothing to be worried about, that croup was common, that a nebulizer was not an iron lung, but a part of me felt punished for my sins—wanting the award, basking in my silly speech, and most of all, celebrating at a bar, flirting for even ten minutes with a man other than my daughter's father. It was too self-indulgent to cry. I stared at my hands, the hands of a mother who held her own daughter far too little, who'd assigned Thea the task of guarding Malena's health solely by not being there. Every time I picked her up after work, I felt so guilty and awkward that I asked a thousand questions. I knew that some sounded like blame. It wasn't blame, just guilt.

I took over for Aaron as soon as I got back to the hotel. I held and nursed my poor baby seal in the hotel bathroom with the shower on for steam without a break to change my clothes until Saturday at ten A.M., when Aaron finally woke up and I gave her to him so I could finally peel off my horrible panty hose.

February

14

Thea

On the eighth Friday of my tenure as nanny, Amanda was late, as usual. She was working full-time now, and their house was supposed to be habitable in a few days—but those few days kept racing ahead of the current days like a road-runner. It was early February, and the kids had started to bring home Valentine's Day projects, or in Carra's case, Valentine's Day angst.

I wanted things to be simple, the way they once were: I'd make heart-shaped cookies and doily valentines for each child, and they'd smile with the plain innocence of the loved. I was weary of the naked twigs of oaks poking the sky. I was tired of dry heat and dry skin and Malena's cradle cap, which I wanted to wash out gently, with olive oil and a comb, but Amanda didn't want me to bathe her. The one time I'd tried without a bath, Amanda had looked shocked by the slightly flattened hairdo and had asked me, please, not to "mess with her hair." I messed with her needs, with her food, with her poop, with her hard-felt work on her first tooth, so why not the condition of her scalp? But surely I'd be protective if I were the one leaving my child—not that I ever would, even if I was jealous, sometimes, of her suits and departures. Amanda relinquished all the responsibility and rode with empty arms on the train.

I had cleaned out the basement, changed the sheets for Tia, and then she'd postponed her visit until spring. *Hurry up and wait,* I thought, as I told her, "That's fine, no problem," on the phone. I had baked and frozen spanikopita, two pies, supplies for our nights of staying up late, talking. I served them to my family with a silent grudge. I was tired of waiting.

Fridays were especially intense mommy-chauffeur days. Today I had to pick up Oliver from a friend's house, shuttle Carra from a swim meet to a sleepover, and then go back to Oliver's friend's house because he forgot his backpack. Usually, I would have noticed whether or not he had his backpack. Usually, I paid more attention. But Malena was fussing in the car seat, and I had started a bottle at the high school when I picked up Carra. Oliver held the bottle for her to finish, but she began crying as soon as she was done, and I knew she probably needed burping, but it had to wait until we got home.

Home was chaos, because Iris had fallen asleep in the car and was furious when she woke up. This was left over from infancy, a resistance to sleep that was half excitement, half pure will. When she woke, she was angry that her body, or her mother, had tricked her into leaving her real world for the imaginary continuation in dreams. She hating waking almost as much as going to sleep, and she'd rail against the change in state for an hour or more. But she hadn't been this furious about it since she turned two. She woke as we pulled into the driveway. Oliver was trying to hold Malena's tiny hand, and Iris started to howl.

I picked up Iris first, feeling guilty for letting Malena cry, and patted her twice. Her face was pressed with sleep lines, red and woeful; her eyes were still seeing the stuff of her dreams, and her voice rose in a wail, a crescendo, a fury.

"Shush, Jitterbug," I said, as if she could hear me inside her pure bad mood.

"She's burpy," said Oliver, as Malena's hands waved and she joined in Iris's lament.

"I'm burpy," I said. Oliver laughed, a buoyant, happy sound over the wailing.

Sometimes I thought I was biased, that I loved Oliver more for his happiness, for his beauty, for his ease. They each had infant names I kept for them, saved like first hair cuttings from when they were small, pure weights I could hold across my chest. Oliver was my angel, always my angel, while Carra was my little bear, and Iris was my jitterbug. Why weren't they all angels? Carra was a bear because of her infant growling sounds; Iris was a jitterbug because even as an infant, she seemed to have that jerky, rhythmic dance in her body. Angel was no more endearment or less.

Of course I didn't love them unequally; each required a different way of expending attention. My mother would have had things to say about the three of them—things I wanted to hear about how I would appreciate them differently at different times. I didn't even know whether I was a difficult baby or as easy as Malena, as golden as Oliver.

I put Iris down on the lawn. She sat on the dead grass and wept and pounded the cold ground with her palms while I unstrapped Malena and burped her. Iris started to roll, her hair and coat decorated with wet patches and clumps of just-unfrozen leaves.

Malena obligingly burped and stopped crying. I looked at the chilly burned blue sky, at the fading light, and tried to remind myself of the good parts of winter. I always looked forward to the lit fireplace, chilly nights under the down comforter, to wearing sweaters and to the clean start afforded by a few inches of snow. But fall was over in a few minutes, and winter shut the days before I ever felt fully awake; there were snowsuits and wet socks and the musty smell that grew in the house with the windows shut. And we hadn't had a fire in the fireplace since I was pregnant with Iris, wading through the ease of days. The only good part of winter I could currently consider was its end.

I trundled Malena inside and put her down in her bassinet. I sent Oliver out to get his backpack from the car, then to get the bottle I'd forgotten in the backseat. Finally I went out after Iris. She was still rolling, but her crying had changed to a little song to herself. I sat down beside her and felt the cold damp soak from the earth through my jeans.

"Jitterbug," I said, "I hope you don't mind that I'm taking care of Malena. It's just for a while."

"Love my baby," said Iris, sitting up. Her face was bright and lucid.

"You're my baby, love," I said.

"Okay," said Iris. She patted my leg as if it were a small and unsettled child, folding her fingers under as she stroked. Such sweetness—it temporarily erased all the frustration. The sky stripped from blanched blue to gray, and it was already night.

Caius came home early and boiled water for spaghetti while we all took baths, including Malena. I wouldn't tell. I wouldn't mess with the scalp, but I wanted to warm and calm her. She'd be dry by the time Amanda came, and if she wasn't, well, Amanda wasn't following our agreement to the letter, either. She was later than late. I filled the infant tub and let the warm water thaw any winter from Malena's tender flesh. Amanda didn't call. Aaron didn't call.

"You'd think she might call. You'd think she might care to tell us when she's coming back for her baby," I said, sort of to Caius, sort of to myself.

"It isn't that bad," said Caius. "You seem happier when she works late, anyway, Thee."

"I'm not," I said, helping Caius set out the plates, but he was right. If she was late, pickups were abbreviated. We didn't have to talk so much.

"I read that suffragettes were sometimes called frigid," said Oliver, who I'd thought wasn't listening, from his homework site on the floor under the dining room table.

"Even though they were working for their country. We're pretty hippocratical about things like that."

"Hypocritical," said Caius.

"Hippo-critical," said Oliver.

We ate spaghetti, and Caius held Malena while he dropped salad into his lap. I held her during dessert, a sticky-frostinged poppy seed cake he'd bought on his way home. Without Carra, and with Oliver playing a video game in the family room and Iris, for the first time in her life, I thought, calmly working on a big-piece puzzle on the rug, the house was peaceful; it felt ordinary. In balance. I almost didn't want Amanda to come, but I was starting to worry. They ebbed and grew, my worries, and they were inexplicit. Something had happened: They'd simply run away, or they'd forgotten, even though I could never imagine being able to leave my child like this, all day and into the night, toward the witching hour, without nursing.

I dialed her office, but hung up on the voice mail. I tried her cell phone, but again, no answer.

I left the dishes; it was late. I took Iris up to bed, and during her story she didn't jump off my lap and run for the door in protest of impending sleep. She was subdued, and I'd started to imagine we'd made that change, we'd shifted from the clinging stage. Perhaps having a baby around was a good influence. Maybe it had made her aware of what she really wanted.

Then again, I was well beyond toddlerhood, and I still didn't know what I really wanted.

Perhaps I should tell Amanda about the bath, I thought. It was ridiculous, grown women keeping these secrets that held no harm, only a small power struggle.

I had to give Amanda notice, I decided, quit in this moment of peace, before it was urgent. I'd do it tonight. I'd explain that I wasn't able to keep up with my own parenting this way, that we'd never intended to keep our arrangement for more than a month or so. I'd give her three weeks' notice. Three weeks, and then I'd be back to wondering what was next. But at least I wouldn't be collecting money in an envelope for mothering, which felt wrong. And I wouldn't be almost hoping she wouldn't come back to get her daughter.

○

"No calls," said Caius when I came downstairs. He was standing over Malena stroking the fuzz on her head as she slept, swaddled and surrounded by cushion walls, on the chair. None of my children, even Oliver at his easiest, had slept through the witching hour at this age. The witching hour was the time between dinner and bedtime, the long evening when parents were weariest and needs escalated before the first collapse into sleep.

"She's great. I really like having her here," he said.

"It's okay," I said, and I kissed him. "I mean, she's sweet, but I'm thinking they should hire another mommy—I mean, *nanny*, geez, that was weird—soon."

"Really?" Caius was still gazing at the baby. He looked very appealing all of a sudden. For once, I thought about sex. For once, Caius settled down on the couch and sighed.

"Exhausted," he said, as if anticipating my overture. So I wouldn't do anything. I wouldn't caress his neck. I wouldn't want to be kissed. Besides, Malena might wake, or Amanda would come back. She had to, soon. Or Aaron might come instead. I started to worry a bit more earnestly. What if something had happened to one of them? To both of them? It was eight-thirty. Or—a little paranoia on my part—maybe they were having dinner together; maybe they'd conspired to defraud us of our own evening. I alternated, worried, then irritable.

We sat on the couch, and Caius read the paper until his head tilted back in a nap, his print-stained fingers hooked behind his head. I'd often find Oliver in the same position.

I tried her number at work, and her cell phone: voice mail, once again. What could I say, "Where the heck are you?" I tried Aaron instead, composing a message as the phone rang, trying for something calm; I didn't want to break the peace of the evening with panic. But he answered, instead of his *uber*-professional voice mail.

"Hey," he said, recognizing my voice, "is everything okay?"

"Amanda's not home yet," I said, listening to the word *home* in my own voice. Home. "And I was wondering if you knew anything, a meeting or something?"

"God, no," said Aaron. "I'd have thought she'd be there. I can come get the baby. There's a train in twenty minutes." I could hear paper shifting. His voice shifting, too.

"Everything's okay here," I said. "Just kind of worried about Amanda." At the same time, I was guilty of enjoying her absence. "I'm sure she's fine, just running late," I added.

"I'm coming," said Aaron. "I'm sure it's nothing. Do you need anything? Groceries or anything? I can stop on the way back from the train." As always he was shifting his attention to here, to now. I'd seen it those few days he was living here—when he came in from work, he'd unfetter himself of coat and briefcase and touch objects, the brass cat on the mail table, rooting himself in this world. And I often wondered how it felt to have lost his home, to have lost his apparent balance and calm, which he'd reclaimed as soon as he could, going right back to work, to daily life, to groceries and the law. Actually, I never minded having green-eyed Aaron around.

Nine o'clock, still no Amanda, and Malena began to fuss in earnest. She wasn't going to be put off by the bottle anymore; she wanted her mother's milk. I put a little honey in her bottle to make it sweeter, but she only took a sip. Caius went upstairs to take a shower. He'd had enough of our baby-memory moment, and I felt a familiar distancing on his part when Malena grew tired of the pacifier, my just-washed pinkie, the special bouncing-swaying on the shoulder movement he'd perfected for his take-over moments when Iris was colicky. *Colic*, I thought then and now, was a term invented to make desperate parents feel better. But Malena wasn't colicky, she wasn't ridiculously particular, she was only making reasonable demands.

I sighed and sang to her and turned off the TV, which Caius had left tuned to a show with inane laughter. It made me nervous. Iris called out and I hoped Caius would take care of her. It was a familiar place, alone and with a baby, downstairs while the others slept or got ready for sleep. But I was worried, and I had no one else to call.

I thought of rummaging through their few leftover things in the basement, looking for her mother's number. I could have dug up the phone bill for that, for all the unfamiliar calls from those few days— her sister, her parents, her friends, her assistant's home number. Or the police. I should call the police. Malena rooted and the house ticked as the hot water cycled through the radiator pipes.

Finally there was a scrabbling sound at the door. I got up, then sat back down on the couch. Malena had fussed herself back to a temporary sliver of sleep.

Amanda flurried into the kitchen. She sighed even as she opened the door. She dumped a briefcase and a coat on the kitchen floor. Her face was etched with worry, and with something else.

"I can't do this, I can't leave her," she said. Just as I was thinking, *I can't do this, I can't keep taking her.* But didn't say it. Amanda was crying. I'd never seen her cry, even on the night her house was crushed, even the first morning away from her baby, even with relief on the nights she came late to pick her up. But she'd never been this late.

"Why are you so late?" I asked, more snappish than I'd intended.

"God, Thea," she said. She sat beside me and reached for Malena, unbuttoning her blouse. "There was a train accident. I tried to call but there was no reception and then my battery died. It was stupid, and I didn't know what to do. Someone was hit by the train. Someone was so sad he jumped in front of the train. And the brake screamed and there was this *thunk,* even way back in my car. We killed him. I don't really want to think about it, but I still looked, really quickly, when they finally let us onto the platform to walk to the shuttles. I won't tell you what it looked like." She gasped, sobbed a little more.

"We had to wait for *hours,* and I was late to start with and then the bus got caught in traffic in Lyndhurst. It was so awful, his arm—I can't talk about this."

Malena had latched on, and Amanda's face softened with the relief and pleasure of nursing. In her cream-colored suit with her blouse unbuttoned, she leaned to the side while she nursed, slumping toward me, then resting against me. It didn't feel wrong. I wasn't angry with her anymore. I was trying to be nicer, to like her more. That had been my first instinct, to like Amanda. She was certainly heavier than a child, but as temporarily wretched as a two-year-old who's fallen off the bigger kids' slide at the playground. I let her lean. I could smell her milk, sweet and grassy.

"I can't leave her. It isn't worth it," she said again, turning her face to me. There was a ghost of plum-colored lipstick on her lips. I'd never noticed how soft her mouth looked, how the top lip peaked in a perfect bow.

"It's okay, sweetheart," I said, forgetting for a second that she wasn't one of mine.

And I don't know who leaned in first, but I do know the kiss felt logical, felt reassuring and calm and not unsexual. We opened our mouths a little, and her short hair fell against my cheek. I do know she tasted a little bit like chocolate, and I felt a warm flesh moon against my arm, her breast, and Malena's tender familiar form half in my lap, half in hers.

I heard the door open.

"Is she here yet? Good news—the contractor told me today we can move home this weekend. Only one bathroom and one bedroom, but we're finally getting out of the Marriott. I brought you a cantaloupe," said Aaron, as he deposited an I LOVE NY bag on the counter.

15

Thea

Never mind that I'd kissed a woman, that it had felt good. Never mind that that woman was Amanda. It was just a momentary thing—I'd been so relieved to see her. I was exhausted and angry and so blurry with family I'd called her "sweetheart," of all things. It certainly wasn't going to happen again. The world kept its pace around the sun, even if I felt tilted slightly out of orbit.

Over the weekend, Iris decided she *always* needed two sippy cups, one for juice and one for milk, and Oliver had a report due on the life cycle of a pond. We looked up *eutrophication* online. I found a half-frozen dead bird on the front porch and wondered what demented cats were hunting in winter, when they should be inside shedding and warming couch cushions.

On Sunday night I went to a fund-raiser dessert party, which Belinda Crew had organized as part of her work for the Junior Women's Club to benefit the Autism Society of America. My friend

Vicky from the parents association would be there, wearing a jet-beaded dress she'd picked out after our last lunch together.

Originally, Caius was coming to the benefit, and I'd hired the baby-sitter who lived down the block, a high school senior named Jasmine who had taken care of Iris once when Caius had a Christmas party at work and the other kids had sleepovers. That night I'd worn heels and the necklace he gave me for our tenth anniversary, jade with tiny gold beads, but he'd been as gossipy as a hen and had only noticed what *other* people wore. Or maybe he mentioned my dress, but it hadn't been enough for me. I didn't really enjoy his office Christmas party, all inside jokes and warm wine and catered chicken that tasted like the little propane burners they used to rewarm it. I remembered enjoying the first few because I'd been so proud of my important, clever husband. He was still important, I was still proud; it just didn't seem like the venue called attention to those facts anymore.

Sunday afternoon Jasmine called and explained that she hadn't finished her paper on organ donation for AP biology so she couldn't come. Carra said she could do it, Oliver winced; Iris threw up her lunch, but that may've been because she'd found some of Oliver's hoarded Halloween candy and had eaten three stale marshmallow pumpkins after her fish sticks.

"I guess I'm staying home!" said Caius, a little too happily.

The benefit was held at The Manor in West Orange, and despite the circumstances of my solo trek, I felt glamorous as I parked the van in the lot and clacked up the stone walkway to the grand house. The air smelled clean, the lights beckoned. So I wasn't with my husband; I was wearing eye shadow, wasn't I? And mascara with primer I'd gotten in the give-away gift they just happened to be offering when I went to Lord & Taylor to replace my nubby lipstick. My friends were inside—women whose babies had gone to kindergarten with Carra and Oliver, women who had gone back to work or stayed at home, had weathered the third-grade recorder recitals and summer camp waiting lists in concert with me.

"Oh, it's *Thea!*" gushed Belinda as I opened the thousand-pound front door. Chandeliers, candles, a string quartet playing Mozart, a long table laden with pear tarts and chocolate-macadamia indecencies. I was suddenly very hungry.

"How is your *job?*" asked the woman beside Belinda. I knew her, but I couldn't remember her name. She wore a parrot-feather hat. Her lips were enormous. I was looking at a woman's lips. I blushed.

"Thea is a child-care worker now!" said Belinda to Roberta Cross, who was the head of the Junior League. Roberta blinked at me.

"Oh, no," I said. "I'm just helping out a friend."

"You're working at a day care?" asked Roberta. Belinda had already spiraled out of our orbit, off into the glittering crowd. The ladies looked elegant, a hundred little black dresses and requisite diamonds and pearls, and a vast and shimmery violet silk muumuu on Francine LaBlanc, who was a cheerleader in high school and who lived not two blocks from me in her mother's house. I never saw her in town. Her wineglass was lipsticked and she was laughing with a gaggle of people I didn't recognize.

"No," I started, but Roberta was already gone, dragged inexorably into Belinda's wake.

I couldn't find Vicky. Roberta had said, "Oh, she's coming, I'm sure she'll be here," but an hour into the event, still no jet-beaded dress. I ate a slice of cappuccino cake, though I'd regret the caffeine later. I circled the tables and pretended I cared about the women I air kissed. It was a worthy cause. And the desserts were wonderful. When I finally sat down at my assigned table with two plates— because I had nothing else to do but try everything—half the chairs had been removed, crowded around other tables, and the only people sitting with me were the two husbands in attendance. They hovered over a tiny portable TV watching basketball.

"Where's Caius?" asked Belinda's husband, Jim, without looking up.

"Baby-sitting," I said, tucking into a coconut-lemon square.

I ate a rum-glazed chocolate tart, a raspberry–white chocolate layer cake, tiny handmade chocolates with real candied violets in their crowns. I thought about crowding around another table like the rest of the women, but I felt as though everyone was working so hard to belong, I just didn't have the will. I drank coffee, supposedly decaf but it made me jittery, so I tried talking with the men.

"How's the game?" I asked Jim.

"What?" Jim looked over his shoulder.

"Want some?" I held out a plate I'd filled with chocolate-covered strawberries. I felt a little sick but was unable to stop eating.

"Yeah," said Jim. "Thanks."

"You're still with Mattel?" I asked. He made no eye contact, though he'd plucked two berries by the stem.

"Oh, no, left three years ago," he said, eyes bonded to the tiny screen. "Toys R Us."

"Fun?" I asked.

"Pays the bills," he said.

There was a speaker, a college junior who'd been diagnosed with autism as a child and who was managing well enough to go to Princeton. A handsome young man, fidgeting with the button on his jacket while he read from a printed speech. I knew how lucky I was: three children, no disabilities, no illnesses. At least none yet. Just thinking myself lucky could be the punishable sin, I thought. I didn't stay for Belinda's bit; my stomach hurt. Maybe it was all the dessert, all the abandon of eating, all the abandon of feeling like an outsider. Maybe Iris had the stomach flu and I'd gotten it, too.

I'd wrapped a cheesecake brownie in a napkin for Caius, but I devoured it on the way home, despite my stomach. I carried my heels inside, tearing my stocking on the frozen ground, and Caius didn't get up from his lounging spot in front of the TV as I unlocked the door.

"How was your little escape?" Caius called from the couch. I could hear him picking his teeth with a card from a magazine— something I wasn't even sure he knew he did. I knew. Sometimes I knew too much.

"It was a benefit," I said. "Not an escape."

○

On Monday I trekked over to Amanda and Aaron's half-habitable house to pick up the baby at seven, because Amanda didn't have time to deliver Malena to me if she was going to make her train. I crossed the months-old POLICE LINE—DO NOT CROSS tape, which hung from the yews like leftover party streamers. I rang the bell, nervous that we'd kissed, wondering whether she'd hug me when she answered, wondering whether it would be strange. Or arousing. Or annoying.

Once, when Tia had visited her mother with a boyfriend from Colorado, Dav—"no *e*," he said, "not David"—a man whose dark brown hair looked expensively shellacked to his head and who stayed at the same level of unshavenness day after day, I'd leaned over to give him a perfunctory kiss good-bye on the cheek, the way one might kiss a brother. But Dav turned to face me and got my lips, full on. He blushed, I blushed, but I wasn't sure he hadn't done it intentionally. He'd held up the newspaper he gripped in his hands as if in explanation. Waved it a little, like a laconic fly swatter. I'd had to force myself to wait to wipe my mouth until I made it out the door. It wasn't that Dav was entirely repulsive, he wasn't. There was a certain charm in his flat vowels and goggle-eyed adoration of Tia. It was that I was not supposed to kiss him. It had been an accident.

Iris ran loops around the dogwood on their front lawn, tripping over a loose brick, saving her howl until I turned with the baby and sixteen items of urgent necessity in my arms.

"Careful!" said Amanda, sharply. She didn't look me in the eye. She wore a trim black suit and pulled on her overcoat and leather dress gloves as she told me she was about to miss the train. "Thanks," she said, without meaning it. Or maybe she meant it, but I'd expected something else, some warmth to explain what happened, to soften it. Something to bridge us as I carried her daughter back to my home.

"Mama!" yelled Iris. She flopped dramatically on the ground and rested her chin on the brick.

"Jitterbug, let's go," I said.

"I should be back by seven," yelled Amanda.

I dropped two bottles on my way home, and a packet of formula, and a long list of instructions, which Iris chased until it blew into the street and I told her to stop. After all, I had all the instructions I needed.

That afternoon I was sorting mail—cooking magazines I'd stopped reading, a gardening catalogue I wanted to moon over—when I spotted something from Outward Bound. I hadn't forgotten; I still needed to get out, but the thought was overwhelming and I tossed the brochure into the recycling. Malena napped in her basket by the couch; Iris unraveled an ancient knitting project I'd abandoned almost a decade ago. She brushed the yarn, a bright blue cotton-silk mix I'd intended to make into a light summer sweater, with her baby doll's brush. She said to it, "Your hair is messy!" Then, "Mama, I want more."

"More what, baby?"

"I'm not a baby!" She walked over to Malena with an extended finger, pointing. Her pointing became poking too quickly for me to stop her. Malena startled, getting ready to protest, though Iris didn't poke hard enough to leave a mark on her forehead.

"You don't do that, Iris," I said, trying to be firm while I lifted Malena from her basket and sighed.

"Mine," said Iris transparently, gripping my leg like a little tick.

We drove to the grocery store, only I couldn't find a parking space, and I didn't really need much. I had mainly wanted a drive to have the girls contained, to take a break. We looped back out the exit. On the drive home I hit a squirrel, something I'd only done once before and which had made me sob. This time I cursed the squirrel, then shushed myself for uttering the expletive. Iris was singing, and Malena had fallen back to sleep. The squirrel had been very fat and I could see it smeared and twitching on the slush-stained street in my rearview mirror, repulsive and pitiful. It was my fault, but it was a stupid squirrel. As soon as I parked the car Iris started whining. As I lifted Malena's seat from the back, Iris rubbed her hands along the filthy bumper.

"No, baby," I said, though I couldn't bring myself to be too urgent about it.

"Yes," said Iris, and she reached her finger toward the tailpipe.

"No," I said, gripping her arm. "That's dangerous!"

"No yelling! I'm not a baby!" yelled Iris. She cried, Malena cried. I herded them in, an inept shepherd. I scrubbed Iris's hands with antibacterial soap and kissed her arm where she said it hurt because I pulled her. I had, I had pulled her, and I felt pathetic for ruining so many things: an afternoon, a trip in the car, a squirrel, her unblemished arm, her sleeve, which was soaked now with soapy water.

"Now I get a present," said Iris. I looked at her sweet and self-important face, and thought probably I should say something, explain about good listening, explain about consequences, but Malena started to cry.

I handed Iris a wad of stickers from the kitchen drawer, and a small plastic dollhouse Carra had been given as a first birthday gift and which had housed a thousand dramas and domestic scenes in miniature.

"You can put stickers on that," I said, and she looked at me with delight and vague confusion. Usually I insisted that stickers were only for paper, but usually I didn't feel like I had to have more than a minute's peace or my head would explode. No, I did feel that way sometimes, I just bucked myself up and endured.

"Present," she whispered to herself with glee.

I put Malena back in her basket with a bottle, which was bad nanny form, as lying down to drink could be bad for the ears. So guilt perched on my shoulder like a monkey as I sat down at the laptop at my little desk. I could hear them both, though my back was to them. Malena made sucking noises. Iris sang to herself.

"I'm not afraid of storms, for I am learning to sail my ship" was the quote on the Outward Bound Web page. Louisa May Alcott.

I am not afraid of storms, I thought. But I was. This was exactly what was wrong with me, I was afraid of any storm outside the tiny snow globe of my domestic life. I opened a new Word document and typed: I am afraid I'm going to have to give notice at this point. Malena is darling, but I am unable to provide the level of service you need and . . . And what? And maintain my sanity? And not want your daughter to become mine? No, not really. I turned. Both girls were happy: Malena batting at a toy bee, Iris crumpling and uncrumpling a shiny Mickey Mouse sticker.

I would have to do it in person. I would have to tell her I was quitting. It was time to stop feeling lonely inside my own family— time to prune these extra limbs of work that sapped my strength, time to grow green again. Three weeks, she could have that long to find someone new. Someone who would work at her house and wash the bottles to her satisfaction and who wouldn't prop the baby in a basket with a bottle.

I closed my document without saving it and opened the Web page again. Maybe recycling the Outward Bound application had been hasty.

Twenty-one-day excursions. Or two weeks. Too long. I could never get away for that long. Who was I kidding? I couldn't get away for a weekend. I could tell Caius he should take vacation time. I could tell Caius I needed to go away or else I might quit. I laughed out loud. Quit my nanny job and my mommy job all at once. I could run away to California. The part of me that actually wanted to do that was small but painful, like a bee sting. Like a burn. Like a tumor. Southwest canyoneering. Dog sledding in the north woods of Minnesota. It looked hard, it looked exhilarating. There were trips for young women, for mothers and daughters, and for a minute I thought about taking Carra. Next time. This fantasy was for me. I typed in dates and looked at all the possibilities in winter. No, summer. Caius's office would be quieter then, and with effort, I could convince him. Or fall, better yet, when the kids were in school. When I wouldn't be leaving Iris *all* day. And best of all, I could hoard the plan to go for all these months. I could get back into shape, jogging with the all-terrain stroller; I'd take a class at the Y. I thought of the women I saw jogging every day as I drove the kids to their thousand engagements, how their faces looked lean and hard. But I didn't want to be hardened, I wanted to be opened.

My mother would not have approved. My mother never would have gone away for something so selfish—she never went away alone, never went away at all until she got sick. My devoted, adoring, lap-of-home mother had left me, though, had left us all, after Oren died. It was as if, since she couldn't have us all safe, she had covered herself in a cloak of failure. Not mourning, no. She'd pared herself from us neatly as she pared peel from a pear. The spring that came almost a year after Oren's funeral, soon before I went to the White Mountains, I'd found her in the kitchen, making lasagna with homemade tomato sauce, only she'd bought tomatoes instead of growing them. It was Oren's favorite.

"Can you put some meat in?" I asked, as I often had in childhood, loving her bolognese enough to eat it from the CorningWear in the fridge with a spoon.

"No," she said. "Because Oren likes it better without," she might as well have added. I was the only one there for dinner—Mom and me. Dad was at a conference and it was May and the evening light was already lingering too long.

"He's dead, Mom," I said, then touched my own mouth, surprised it had emitted those words.

My mother, my neat mother, always calm and organized and always kind ("If you can't say something nice," she'd singsong, and we knew to finish, "don't say anything at all" without her completion), lifted the big boiling sauce pot and turned it upside down on the stove, bloodying the gas burners with food-milled tomato, sautéed onions, garlic, perfect rounds of carrot, flecks of rosemary. The gas flame stung the sauce, then expired. And even though I wanted to go after her into the too-light evening garden, I'd stayed inside. I waited for her to come back to me and cleaned up the sauce, digging in the cracks around the igniter, sopping towels and sponges, trying to forgive myself for being among the living.

I downloaded and printed out the application for a trip the second week of September, western Maine backpacking, women only. I would resurrect my gear from the basement. I would tell Caius. No, I would ask Caius. No, I would *tell* Caius. He could shuttle the kids back and forth, he could manage dinners and diapers—or the potty—and bedtimes and waking. By then, Iris would go to preschool, and by then, he would understand why I needed this gift.

The girls were quiet. I started to fill out the paper longhand, though there was hardly anything to fill out, just the dates, my information. My credit card number. I could pay for it with the money I'd made as a nanny. Not that our money wasn't mutual, but somehow, if I needed this so selfishly, I felt I ought to be the one paying. I signed it and put it in an envelope, and Malena started coughing.

I didn't panic, exactly, but it was like being woken from a sleep you shouldn't have taken. Like discovering you were stealing some-thing, though you hadn't meant to, you'd just crammed it in your pocket because you needed both hands for your baby and then you forgot to fish it out at the register and the shoplifting alarm went off—this hadn't ever happened to me, I'd just imagined it, often. Nor had this: Malena coughed and I picked her up, afraid she might be choking. She coughed three times, hard, and dislodged a tiny clot of unmelted formula powder. Not enough to choke. Possi-bly enough to choke. But she was breathing, she was okay. I wouldn't have to tell Amanda. I was honest; I'd tell her. She might fire me. Then Malena started to cry, and I looked up for Iris, and Iris was not there.

o

First, I called around the house, trying not to sound afraid, for myself, for anyone who might hear. Why should she be in trouble? Just because she was no longer adhering foil hearts to the miniature kitchen didn't mean something terrible had happened. But my lapse, my moments of not looking—how long had it been? Ten minutes? Fifteen? It had felt like five, or less, but the sticker sheets were empty, her shoes were by the door. My lapse felt wrong, punishable. I had been dreaming of leaving them. Malena snuffled against my shoulder, looking for milk, or comfort, still helpless. I tried my best to support her head, though she hardly still needed that much support, as I rushed up the stairs calling, "Iris. Iris, honey. Iris, where are you? Iris, it isn't funny!"

She wasn't in the bathroom, she wasn't in her room. I knelt to check under my own bed, thinking perhaps she was playing a game. Not in the closets. I almost tripped on the stairs down to the basement, but caught myself, my big, irresponsible baby-holding self, by grabbing the wobbly rail.

Iris wasn't in the house.

Now I felt panic inching its way up my shoulders, around my throat, the windpipe clench of it, the clutch of fear, a squeeze, a giant muscle, an ache. It was like feeling pain and looking for the wound. I looked upstairs again, then laid the baby in the portacrib close to the door and ran outside.

It was warm for February, the gloaming was early, and the heat from the weak sun dissipated quickly. Both my older children would be home from their after-school business soon, and they would help me forget if I found her; they would help me search if I didn't. I didn't want to leave Malena, but I could run faster without her. I called out to the empty yard, to the few dead stalks of iris plants, to the yew bushes with their fat poisonous red berries.

"Iris," I called across the yard. "Iris!" I was almost screaming but not quite.

I ran now into the woods, because the back of our yard spilled me into them, because I could only think of the water and the stones of the river, of my daughter slipping down the banks with her careless enthusiasm for something, a stone, a stick letting go of its ice.

"Iris!" I called along the riverbank.

Now came the darkness, nagging at the last vestiges of day like a neighborhood crank, filling up the woods with its powdery damp.

I circled to the end of the right-of-way, ran up through the field where the high school band practiced in the fall, thumping the oaks and houses with sound, brass like birdcalls.

There were no birdcalls, just my voice too loud in the empty street as I walked across my neighbors' yards with the abandon of my emergency.

"Iris!"

I was back at my own house, with nothing to show but a stick I'd snapped off an elm in frustration and my voice growing raw.

"Iris!"

"Thea?" asked someone behind a hedge. "Is everything okay?"

"I can't find Iris!" It was Amanda—what the hell was she doing at home? Why hadn't she picked up Malena? It was *her* fault, I thought, feeling irrational—I didn't care that she knew, didn't care that I'd lost my own daughter in front of her.

"Just a minute," she said, her voice even. "I think I heard her in my backyard. Something about the groundhogs. Don't they hibernate?"

I pushed my way through the bushes, though I could've walked around in just a minute. There was no propriety in losing a child. A branch snapped back and scratched my cheek, but then I was in her yard. Amanda was walking across, a shadowy form in a long dark coat. She knelt down to the small person digging a hole in her cold-burned grass with a spade.

"Hi, Iris," I heard her say. "Are you digging for buried treasure?"

My daughter was fine, but adrenaline still gripped my limbs, making me one great muscle of anxious prey.

"Hi, Mama," said Iris, and the power of fear fell from me like a cloth, swept away into the sudden chill of the evening. I sat down on the grass and she ambled over to me. A foil heart dangled from her sweater's sleeve. She had no coat against the cold. I shivered.

"Saw a fog," she said. "Over there." She pointed to her dent in the earth. I kissed her soiled fingers.

"Thank you," I said to Amanda. She lifted a briefcase from her car.

"How was Malena today?" she asked without looking at me, without accusing me of anything.

I thought of her daughter, whom I'd abandoned in a portacrib by the door, and felt pathetic. By now, Oliver and Carra would both be home; perhaps one of them had taken her out to hold, to look out the window for the missing persons of the house. Perhaps they'd simply walked past the cot on their way to their own pursuits. She wasn't their job. She was mine.

"Don't do that, lovey," Amanda said, as Iris pulled away from me and started smearing soil on the white picket of her fence. It gave me an odd satisfaction, Iris's innocent defacement.

"She was fine," I said. "A little fussy, probably teething." I kissed the top of Iris's head. "Don't reprimand my daughter. And I quit," I said. I stood up and took my daughter's hand. Something bothered me about Amanda's endearment. Iris wasn't *her* lovey. "You can come pick Malena up. And her things. I quit." I said it again to convince myself.

Perhaps she had something to say, but I didn't want to hear it. I didn't feel respectful, or mournful, or wronged, only wrong myself, out of balance. I picked up Iris as if *she* were a baby, breathing in her safety, and walked her back home before anything could change my mind.

When I got back to my house, Malena was in Carra's arms, looking around with her perfect extrospection. My arms shook slightly with the departure of adrenaline. I told Carra to wait for Amanda, kissed baby Malena's cheeks good-bye, and took Iris upstairs. My chest hurt, and my heart; my heart hurt for my own mistakes—for God not cashing in on them. For luck and fear, for saying good-bye to my temporary baby. I did love her. I was a terrible coward, but mostly it was the baby I couldn't face when Amanda came; I started the bathwater running so I wouldn't hear her come and go.

16

Amanda

Whenever I thought of kissing her, I remembered how I'd been frantic—I wasn't myself. I'd seen a dead man on the train track, and I had been so desperate to get home to my baby. It didn't mean anything, that kiss. Then the Monday after it happened, she'd been in such a rush when she picked up Malena; she'd run off down the walkway before I could even explain about the new vitamin drops or ask about her weekend. I'd worried then that we'd crossed a line, that we couldn't make it work anymore. It was always such a delicate balance, making things work with a caregiver, especially one who was a neighbor and sort of a friend. Half of me had wondered, that day, whether I should just pitch it all in and stay home. Forever. But I hadn't.

I wondered whether she quit because we kissed. Whether the enormity of our momentary attraction was enough to send her fleeing. It had actually been nice, after all. She was afraid she was a lesbian, maybe; she was afraid of lesbians. Not that I was judging her—or maybe I was, because I felt as if she'd judged me all along, except in that one moment of confidence in her kitchen. It wasn't that I made a habit of kissing women—or anyone other than Aaron for that matter—but other people did, and I didn't think there was anything wrong with it. I had been exhausted, I had wanted comfort, and Aaron wasn't there. I hadn't thought it through or planned it. An accident of proximity.

Then the following Monday everything had happened at once: I had come home early because there was a leak in the plumbing and some problem with a fused circuit and the gas was off and Jeb the contractor, a smarmy guy hired by the insurance company and the last person I wanted to come home early for, told me we had no power, no heat, and no water. In February. But it was all under control.

"Under control" were his words, said with a sort of a hiss through his cracked front tooth. I abhorred that tooth, the way the hairline crack wasn't enough to split the enamel, to break the rock of his horrible cell matter into two pieces, to tear out his ability to bite into the ubiquitous meatball subs—with extra onions, extra peppers, and extra cheese—he left half-consumed and wrapped in greasy paper in my living room, in my one operational bathroom, on the windowsill.

We needed a plumber, and my contractor sat on the edge of my dining room table staining my telephone with sauce from his late-afternoon sub, nodding, yep, nope. "He's out," he said above the mouthpiece.

Then I walked outside and saw Iris, and Thea quit.

Actually, I'd been planning to talk about a transition in a few weeks, after things settled down with the house, to say perhaps it was time to change our arrangement. Perhaps it was time for me to try a day care after all, or to call the service again, didn't she need more time with her family? Only I'd felt squeamish and reliant. It wasn't ever going to be *firing* her, exactly, more like relinquishing her. Perhaps it was just because Malena was my child, my first child, that I couldn't *completely* trust her, but I couldn't imagine trusting anyone more. I was guilty of taking up her time, her mothering energy, taking advantage of her cookies and her home, and I felt beholden and embarrassed. *Don't reprimand my daughter,* she'd snapped at me, as if I was an ogre. As if I didn't entrust her with the most important person I'd ever met, my own, my Malena. Standing outside watching her tote her daughter back inside, I noticed how she moved like a spider, her legs and arms too long.

I suppose I had still thought Thea was my friend, in a marginal capacity, anyway. She had agreed to this job in my time of need. She loved Malena, though Malena was easy to love, but she also fed her honey, honey of all things, which could contain harmful bacteria—if you read anything in any pediatrician's waiting room you'd know that. And she was often late picking up in the morning so sometimes I missed my train. But she picked up. She did that for me. She'd washed my clothes and brought me juice boxes, and she'd given me so many things when I needed them that even though I knew things weren't working out—she didn't want to tell me what had really happened in my daughter's day, she was preoccupied, she'd let Malena go too long without changing so her bottom was pink and prickly with diaper rash—I felt obligated to keep her. Maybe I was an overprotective, guilty, first-time mom; I surely wasn't the first one. Underneath my criticism, I knew I'd been lucky, and I was afraid I'd never find someone else half as good for my daughter.

The next morning, it felt great to wear sweats. It felt great not to hand over my baby. Not to race for the train. For a few minutes, anyway. While I nursed Malena in the freezing bedroom with the door closed and a chair blocking any "accidental" entry on Jeb's part (I heard him guffawing downstairs, though there was no one with him), I called my boss, Neethi. She hadn't called me back after I left a message telling her I needed a few days of emergency leave. I left a message for our assistant, asking her to FedEx the dinosaur galleys and the middle-grade novel manuscript on my desk, just revised by the author. Honestly, I didn't care if neither arrived, but I needed to make a show of dedication.

"You know, Amanda," Neethi started, with an enormous sigh. "We have a lot of deadlines. I have to know you're committed. I don't want to lose you, but I've given Jessica the Smithe book. Walter says we can't miss deadline again."

"It was just galleys," I said, feeling my defenses rise. My checks heated, fight or flight. Malena, who'd been completely asleep in our bed, started to fuss.

"I know you have commitments," said Neethi. "And I'll keep your office open as long as I can—What? Oh, I'm sorry, production meeting's starting."

"Neethi? It's just a few days. I'm interviewing nannies, after all."

Neethi had children, too, but they were all driving. Two were voting. She couldn't possibly understand. She'd had a live-in nanny, she'd told me, it was the best. She still had a live-in nanny, though mostly Katia just helped with housekeeping and dinner prep. Dinner prep. For me that meant reviewing delivery menus.

"Neethi takes two-hour lunches," said Rosanna when I called her next. "She's either having an affair or getting deeply involved in off-track betting."

I laughed. Rosanna could always make me laugh.

"And you are the best editor they have, so I wouldn't worry."

"I'm worried."

"Did I tell you John-John in marketing made a pass at me? He must be all of twenty-two."

I hadn't even met the man, a new assistant. I let her tell me, hummed my feigned interest, but I was turning pages of the fax from the nanny agency all the while.

Part of me was afraid of losing my job. Part of me would be relieved. Those two parts inhabited the same sleep-deprived, itchy-skinned, still-baby-baggy body. I was hiding in my bedroom like an upper-middle-class refugee.

○

"They won't fire you," said Aaron that night. I had bought out Home Depot, and we now had three space heaters on high, since the electricity was the only thing working again. We drank bottled water, and I was planning to use baby wipes in lieu of a shower. Of course Aaron could shower at work. And it was warm there, too. He wore his winter coat inside the house, along with pink fluffy earmuffs my sister had given me as a joke and a black cashmere scarf. He was rubbing his hands over the Heat Master 2000 like a man at a campfire.

"No promises," I said. "Any chance you could take a few days?" Even as I asked him I knew the answer. There were new downtown clients who took him to important dinners twice a week and whose billable hours were more in a week than a whole client list would bill in some firms.

Aaron sighed. "I know it's not fair, Panda. I'll see what I can do." Which meant no. I felt like a petulant child. Diminished by his lack of flexibility, diminished by my own. Trapped and deeply in love with Malena at the same time.

I interviewed two women who came early and interrupted nursing and a nap, respectively. I sat by the heater in the living room trying to talk to twentysomething Terefa, who had brittle blond hair and frosty pink lipstick and answered her cell phone twice while we spoke. "All my friends are making twenty an hour," she said. "I'd have to know there'd be a raise in a few weeks."

"I lost my last job because my boss was a snob," said Xandra, who smelled unmistakably of pot. "She wanted me to wear shoes in the house. She didn't like my friends coming over. I can give you references, but don't call them, okay? They were snobs. Could I start in two weeks?"

Barbara had excellent references ("She's wonderful! I was so sorry we couldn't keep her, but Rebecca is twelve and I lost my job!") and she dressed neatly and had a green card and two grown sons. She came promptly and shook my hand—her own hand was soft and mildly fragrant. Jasmine. She spoke clearly and was respectful and I was awed. But nervous. Aaron and I went over my notes from the interview and agonized, and I worried the paper until it tore in my hands. I imagined it all night, Barbara at our frozen house in two days with Malena, this woman I'd only met one time. The smell of jasmine on my daughter's skin. Then I thought about the work I could get back to, I thought about walking into the office and telling Neethi I had a new nanny. I thought of spring with Barbara walking in our neighborhood, taking Malena out of our newly repaired house in her stroller to see the daffodils and watch our resident groundhog grazing like a cow on the lawn. I called her at the decent hour of nine-thirty and she respectfully told me she'd taken another position, with triplets, in a town much closer to her own. I was tempted to beg, but instead I hung up and tried to relinquish the images I'd invented as I dialed the agency again.

Next I interviewed Star, who'd gone to Yale and dropped out because of depression. Her hair was almost white, naturally, and I could see the pink of her scalp, which made her look vulnerable. She wore a dozen silver bangles and a thick silver nose ring, which fascinated Malena. I was considering her; she was soft-spoken, she was clearly intelligent, she wore neat clothes, and she had worked in three day cares that gave her reasonable references. I thought I ought to call her sooner rather than later. But when I went to tip the delivery guy from the Greek restaurant who knew our front door too well, I realized Star had taken all the cash from my wallet. I was not being paranoid. The wallet had been on the desk; I'd gone into the bathroom to throw away Malena's diaper, and now the three twenties and six ones I'd had right before the interview were gone. I looked around the room as if I might find the missing money, but I knew I wasn't at the end of my search. My black beaded sweater was also missing from the back of the couch, though I wasn't sure how she could've pocketed that as well. Star was not the one.

The fabulous Red Ruth came with weird recommendations, half enamored, half afraid, but I decided to interview her anyway. She had a grand sense of herself and her skills, and when I spoke to her on the phone, I was somehow lulled by her gravelly voice and her passionate claims about her deep and spiritual connection with children. She smoked. I could tell from her smell and the horrible rattly breaths between her words, but when I asked point-blank, "Do you smoke?" she said, "Not anymore." I felt like I shouldn't discriminate. Not anymore since the drive over? Ah, but I felt desperate.

I knew better than to call my mother after interviewing an entirely unacceptable nanny, but I needed to talk to someone, and I realized I couldn't talk to anyone from work, because that was dangerous. I couldn't tell my sister, because she wouldn't understand, and I couldn't call Thea . . . because. Remembering how I'd held that first round of interviews in her living room gave me a twinge not unlike an upset stomach.

"Hi, Mom," I said. The phone pipped a few times and my mother rustled around, clearly driving with her cell phone again.

"Is this okay?" she asked, the phone on speaker mode. "I have a headset, too."

"Headset, please," I said.

"Oh, it's you! I didn't look at the caller ID. I'm on the Mass Pike. There's this alumni dinner—oh, I won't bore you with it, but since it's you, I won't put on the headset. It's horrible against the earrings. They're crystal. Can you hear me okay?"

I could, but it was annoying and grainy.

"Sort of," I said. "I wanted to tell you about this awful interview."

"Oh, darling, are you on the market again? They're giving me an award or something, you know, that's why I don't want to take out my earrings. I'll forget them. I didn't realize you were getting out there again. Still publishing, or are you spreading your wings?"

"Mom,"—I winced, picking at an uneven edge of my fingernail—"I'm *in* the market, not *on* the market. I need a new nanny. Thea quit."

"She quit? Oh, darling. She was very good. But that's probably why. She probably got something better. You really were quite lucky you know. Damn! I should've taken Storrow Drive."

"No, she didn't get something else, she wasn't a professional nanny. She was mad at me—I don't really understand why. She was really good, but there were a few things . . ." I knew I was trying to console myself. "I mean, the day she quit, her daughter ran away and she left the baby with her little kids—well, her teenager, but still—and she gave her honey—"

"Oh, *honey*, that's not good, botulism, you know. Doesn't affect adults, but it can be serious—"

"I know, Mom. I know. I was just trying to tell you about this nanny I interviewed. She was scary, she had this dark, rattly voice, and she stank of cigarettes. And you won't believe this: She put on a clown mask, which of course made Malena cry. It almost made *me* cry. And she made this big deal about how great she was with kids, but I couldn't imagine her alone with a baby! She had a huge sharp chrome necklace like a barbed-wire fence and Day-Glo pink lips and a wig! A red wig! She told me the feng shui of our living room was horrible, and she scraped at a smudge on my sweater and pulled the thread and her nails were a thousand miles long—" The phone clicked. "Mom? Mom?" Two more clicks, and I got the "If you want to make a call . . ." recording.

"Argh," I said, when my mom picked up again.

"Oh, sorry, darling. I heard you say something about Thea and honey—honey just isn't safe for babies, you know—and then I had to go through a tunnel. The Big Dig is such a disaster!"

"Never mind."

"Never mind? Offer her more money. You should get her back. Wasn't she the one who thought women shouldn't work outside the home? Oh, I love that phrase, it's so old-fashioned. No gardening for you, missy!"

My mother sounded so perky, I knew she must be a little nervous about the dinner. But I'd wanted to confide, to tell her all about what had gone wrong with my day and that I was worried about my job, and here she'd gone and made me worry about her. Again.

"Yeah. That was her. She just quit point-blank, and she was mad at me."

"Well, my dear, all's fair."

I waited for the rest. "All's fair?"

"You know." The phone was clicking again.

"So do you mean it's love, or war?" I touched my mouth.

"I'm losing you," she said. "I'll call you later!"

And then all it took was one person and two days: we hired Carole. She had folded her hands in her lap on our couch, answering my questions, not worrying her wrists or fingers, just calm. She was a mom, she'd worked as a nanny, she was very neat, she didn't mind the workmen, and she adored being with babies. She knew not to give them honey. She'd start in two days. Just a weekend stood between me and a new beginning.

On Sunday morning, Aaron had to stop by Thea's house. He'd left his brown belt there all this time and didn't think my idea, *just get another fucking belt*, was practical. But when he came home, he acted as if he'd had to go behind enemy lines.

"*He* was there," he said. "Can you believe it—he said something about how we'd damaged the paint in the basement. That was two months ago. Such a *lawyer*."

"You're the lawyer," I said. "He's a management consultant."

Aaron scoffed.

"Was *she* there?" I asked.

"No," he said. "He was drinking. At noon on a *Sunday*."

Caius had never been bothersome. Caius had been gracious; he'd welcomed us and helped us put our things in the car when we left: a box of breast pads, Caius's own old French blue buttondown, which had become mine when I'd stained it past ordinary usefulness, little packets of formula, what seemed to be an endless supply of Aaron's work socks. Intimate things. Caius hadn't *quit* on me.

"He was kind to us," I said. "It was just her." I wasn't angry, exactly; I was embarrassed thinking about her, almost as if *I'd* done something wrong. Had I kissed her, really?

"They were kind to us," he said, "but they were never really our friends." Then, because it was what confused me most, I almost told him that Thea and I had kissed. I almost told him that she *was* my friend, just very different from me, but he was angry in a calm, organized way, as if he'd spent months collecting evidence against them.

"She was kind—" I started.

"Really?" he said, having none of it. "No matter how tired she was, we paid her, and she was working for us. She could've given appropriate notice. She should have. It was wrong of her. That's the only wrong here. There's nothing else. They helped us, we thanked them; she worked for us, she did something inappropriate. And very inconvenient." He sighed and put his arm around my waist. I didn't like my waist lately, but I pretended to. "That's all. Game over. New game."

Suddenly the shower upstairs and the kitchen faucet started simultaneously, hissing and banging like dying submarines.

"I guess we have water," said Aaron. "I'll call Jeb."

Malena, who had startled at the sound, started to babble, telling me very important syllables about nothing.

March

17

Thea

I'd been sketching lately, now that I had slivers of time formerly taken up by a baby. I drew the dead songbird—a thrush—I'd found on my porch the day after Amanda's late night, only I drew it alive, in a dozen poses, willing spring into my charcoal. Iris liked my drawings and I let her make her own on the good sketch pad, flush with patience. She smudged charcoal on her mouth and hands and smeared my sketches with her animated fingers, but it was easy to forgive her.

"That bird's lonely!" she told me. "She needs babies!"

I didn't tell her my inspiration had been cat kill; I just let the story become our shared entertainment.

Of course I thought about Malena. And Amanda. But I felt a thousand times more peaceful knowing I didn't have drop-offs and pickups, disruptions every day. I didn't have to love a baby I couldn't keep.

"I guess I'd be angry if I were her," I told Caius one evening after everyone was sleeping. I believed it, I worried it, I carried it in my pocket like a small stone. I'd be angry—not just angry, irate, confused, maybe bitter. I'd quit so abruptly, and I'd avoided really telling her why, the way friends might tell each other, even the way an employee might respectfully depart. But there hadn't been any choice. Quitting was choosing not to make any more mistakes.

"Did you know he came by to get his belt?"

"Aaron?" I was trying to get comfortable in the bed, but the sheets felt sandy.

"I told him about that scratched paint in the basement. Figured he ought to know we noticed."

"You told them? I just mentioned it to you; I wasn't trying to pick a fight with them or anything." Sand between my toes. Sand under my legs. Where had all this sand come from?

"Maybe that's the problem," said Caius. He leaned in to kiss me, but I gave him my cheek, feeling patronized.

"Maybe you were a little too nice to them," he finished.

I couldn't help it; I thought about kissing her. Had that been nice? Had that been the single time we agreed on something?

"I quit, Caius. That wasn't nice."

"I know you quit. What did you expect, that you'd stay with Malena until college?" he asked. He was picking at a toenail. It was yellowish and cracked and made me sad because it looked like an old person's toenail. I wasn't ready for any part of us to be old. I thought again about the Outward Bound trip. I hadn't told him yet—hadn't told anyone yet—though I had suggested Caius might take his vacation time then. I wrote the dates on the back of a receipt from the A&P and asked him to put them in his work calendar. He didn't ask about the plans, which was a little disappointing. I'd imagined myself answering both ways, truthfully and then with evasion, and got a chance to test neither.

"I expected that it wouldn't be for so long, I guess. I expected that she'd hire someone else." I leafed through the pages of a novel I'd had on my bedside table for months. My sketchbook with its pages of thrush mommy and thrush babies I'd made for Iris. Maybe I could sketch mountains and wildflowers on this theoretical trip.

"Or that she'd quit *her* job? Because I have this sneaking suspicion you expected her to join the other side."

"The other side?" I knew what he meant, but I was surprised. I'd make him articulate it.

"You know. That she'd stay at home like you do."

"No I didn't."

"It's not bad, Thee." He stopped picking and put his arm around me. I tried not to think about the toenail-y finger when he started playing with my hair. It wasn't as if my own hands were pristine. I'd helped Iris wipe her nose just before bed and the tissue wasn't quite in the right place. Had I washed my hands? I couldn't remember.

"Do you think you wanted her to be around, to be your friend? You were sort of friends, anyway."

"Sort of," I said. "But not everyone has to be a stay-at-home mom."

"Which 'leads to an overwhelming question . . .'"

"Ha. Since when do you quote T. S. Eliot in bed?" Maybe he didn't mean to patronize.

"'Oh, do not ask, "What is it?" Let us go and make our visit,'" he continued. "No, really. I was thinking you might be thinking about doing some of the other things that used to interest you now. I mean, won't Iris be in day care, too, in the fall?"

"Our kids go to *preschool*, not day care."

"Whatever. I was just thinking you might want to take a class or something. Don't get mad at me. I'm just thinking of you."

Me, too, I thought. *That's why I want to go away, without you, without any of you. Only you don't know yet, and I'm not sure I'm really going to do it.*

"That's very kind. I'll think about it." This should have been wonderful. This should have been my chance to make my trip his idea after all, even if that wasn't exactly what he meant. And even if we didn't operate that way—secrets and surprises. Not this kind, anyway. But I couldn't tell him yet. It was still only mine, a long way off, the way the children moving in my belly at night, before they were born, belonged to me. Except he knew about every one of them. It wasn't his fault I needed to get out. Or maybe it was.

"I might even have some ideas," I began, anxious with the possibility of revealing myself. But then he started on his toenail again, under the sheets this time. It was a tiny bit his fault.

It was April by the time Tia's visit plans solidified. Iris and I picked violets and drew them, coloring in the charcoal images with pastels and crayons. My own plans were still quite liquid—I'd received a packet from Outward Bound but hadn't opened it. I imagined the list of gear in there, the arrangements. I imagined telling Caius and yet I didn't. It was enough emotional turmoil to feel there must be fury over the fence at Amanda's house. I thought about Malena— missed her with a physical longing—and wondered about her as I watched the new nanny come and go. I told Iris, who asked daily, that our baby was at home with her mommy, and then distracted her with something horrible, cookies, television, ruining her with my guilt. I still couldn't decide what my family would feel when I told them I wanted to go away, so I kept myself in limbo. I could still get my deposit back from Outward Bound if I changed my mind.

Some days I considered walking over to her house just to say I was sorry, I didn't mean to leave like that. Some days I couldn't believe she'd stretched my hospitality so thin. I surreptitiously watched the house as it was resurrected from the inside out, the crash site patched, the gutters reattached, the windows rehung. The paint was unmatched, several different shades. I looked at the lights from my bedroom at night with my gaze aslant. Nothing was permanent.

The week before Tia arrived, all the doors in our house seemed to open and shut at random. There were *chirrups* and *whirs* and the furrowing of small animals in my garden, groundhogs and chipmunks, squirrels and skunks and deer at night, searching for roots and shoots. I'd discovered two dead squirrels the week before— then twice in as many days, some cat had deposited a house finch, then an expired mouse, on our doorstep. Iris found an owl pellet in the backyard. It was a little unusual, but there was no time to sketch anything, just time for cleaning up, always cleaning up. Everyone in the house was in constant motion. Carra was busier without us than she'd ever been in her life—always at practices and at friends' houses after school. On weekends the house was empty of her particular clacking footsteps, her special shuffle up the carpeted stairs, her energy of staying and of waiting to go.

I wondered about her best friends; Carra had started to keep things to herself, though I insisted on names of companions and parents and destinations. I didn't press her for who she loved most, to whom she was telling her secrets. She was often down the street at Vivian's house, but she hardly talked about her friend anymore. I remembered myself at twelve going on thirteen; Tia and I told each other everything, when there began to be things to tell that didn't issue from the realm of parents and pure imagination.

A few weeks before, I'd found Carra sitting by the washing machine at night, waiting to rescue her bathing suit before the spin cycle. I couldn't leave it any longer, my question list, my strong desire to know my daughter, though now I wondered whether I'd ever known her, even when she had relied on me for food and contentment. Her mouth was the same as it had always been, wide and tender, my husband's mouth, revealing judgments with expression instead of words.

"So, Carra-my-faira," I started, using an old pet name, Caius's pet name, in fact.

"Mom, I'm kind of busy," she said.

I looked at her posture. She looked the opposite of busy; she looked like she was simply waiting, storing all her possibilities and necessities, ready to pounce on that bathing suit and escape to her room, her phone conversations, her books and music and whatever else sustained her at nine P.M. on a Thursday night.

"Well, while you're busy, I thought we might catch up a little." I cringed even as I said it. My mother's voice issuing from my mouth, my mother's needy questions.

The first time I'd ever lied to my mother that I remembered, besides perhaps a preschooler's transparent experimentation with truth, I was twelve years old. She asked where I'd been all day. She had said it with a tone much like mine with Carra, wobbly with want. And I don't know why—I'd been in the woods with Tia, casting a spell against a girl we hated, with a leaf gall and a cottony clump of spiderweb—but I told her Tia and I had been at the library, reading and doing homework. It mattered to me that I keep my day secret, and it felt awful and delicious knowing I'd fooled her, knowing she wasn't able to keep me attached, attended to, once I'd passed our house's threshold without her.

"I mean," I said to Carra's silent pout, her mouth saying she wasn't sure whether to be annoyed or released, "I mean what do you care about these days? Is swim team good? Or—" I stopped myself. Let the last word drown in the sound of the washer's chug. It was unbearable to ask and unbearable not to know.

"Everything's fine," she said, the pout changing into a vulnerable, minuscule smile. "I'm doing the relay now, because Jill broke her ankle so she can't do backstroke. And"—here she paused and opened the washer to stop the new spinning and fish for her suit—"I totally hate Hailey, because she told everybody I like Mitch."

I remembered Hailey from a play group when Carra was less than one year old, still sitting on a mat. Hailey had no hair then, just an egg-shaped head and blond lashes and no eyebrows. Her mother always brought Entenmann's brownies and sang "Everyone loves Entenmann's!" and regaled us with stories of Hailey's newest words, how she was counting when she gazed at her fingers, how she was definitely gifted.

"Gotta go," Carra said, storming up the steps, her suit trailing soap-scented water. I stayed downstairs for a while, my hands on the washer, feeling the spin and trying to let it be enough.

One morning Iris wouldn't play with anything for more than ten minutes without me.

"No more sandbox!" she cried, flinging a handful of sand and desiccated bugs and dirt from the ground into my legs.

"Iris, that's very rude," I said, but I could see she was about to turn down the street that led to a tantrum.

"Do you want to do something inside?" I sighed. I'd been weeding. That is, I'd taken out my gloves and the lawn refuse bin, and I'd picked a single clump of crabgrass, not getting to the roots.

"Maaamaaa," said Iris.

"How about a video?" I sighed again. I was wanton, and I didn't even have the excuse of bad weather. The breeze was sweet with the first lilacs from the edge of the lawn; the sun striped the walkway. We should have been happy.

"No," said Iris, sprinting toward the front yard. "I wanna visit baby," she said.

"Iris!" I yelled. "I think baby's sleeping."

We were coming home from the preschool open-house when the next carrion appeared. Iris bounded up the steps to get the mail.

"What's that?" she reached to pick something up. It wasn't another mouse; it was much bigger.

"We don't have a cat, damnit," I said out loud. I never swore. Why was I swearing? I'd had enough of Iris's recalcitrance, enough of trying to keep the porch clean. I felt like I had when I was first pregnant, unreasonable, unable to bear the most trivial of details. But a dead groundhog on my front porch. It was too much, too much death, too suspicious, too horrible.

Iris didn't appear to hear my expletive. She was reaching for the bloody flank.

"Don't touch!" I yelled, which made her turn to me and cry.

"Don't yell at me, Mama!" yelled Iris. She flopped to the floor of the porch, weeping as I scooped her up, hoping to avoid whatever foul germs the rotting thing could spread on her soft, vulnerable fingers.

"Mom!" yelled Oliver, coming up the walkway. "I'm going to ride my bike to Kevin's house!"

"Fine," I said, collecting my angry girl, who had scraped her knee on the step. "Don't you have homework?" At that minute, I didn't care about the homework. I could see the groundhog from where I sat. Crushed, a tire print on the flank. The center was wet, and I imagined the motion of maggots. It was so foul, I wanted to do something, scream at someone, hit something. I gagged and brought Iris inside.

"I'm going, okay?" said Oliver. "And we're going to the movies later." I let him go, instead of inspecting his backpack, offering him a snack, asking him about his day. I let him leave me, wanted him to go.

Once I had wiped her hands with antibacterial wipes, taken off her shoes in case they were contaminated, cleaned up her scraped knee, and given my daughter a cookie she shouldn't have before dinner, I settled her in front of the television. Then I went outside with a blue bag from the *New York Times*, which Caius hadn't been reading and neither had I, and bagged the groundhog. I still felt angrier than I should have, almost feverish, unreasonable. It occurred to me, a grain of thought working against my mind the way a grain of sand irritates an oyster to pearl, that someone had put the dead thing there, along with the others. Not a cat but a person, someone with a grudge against me.

There was only one person like that: Amanda. I remembered how casually she'd told me she put hot sauce on her sister's toothbrush— not that this was in the same league, but still. I tried to remember what I had said to her when I quit. Had I told her off, or had I made it about me? Suddenly I couldn't remember it exactly; suddenly history was rewriting itself the way it always did after a breakup. And it had been a breakup. But it wasn't her, it was me. Or maybe it was her. She'd always been nagging me, always complaining about how I took care of Malena. About hand washing and honey and how many diapers were filled. About all the things a mother is obsessed by. I tried to imagine just how angry she was with me, just how vengeful

she might feel. What would Amanda's face look like, hoarding carrion, smuggling it to my doorstep when she knew I was gone?

I peered out the window, disgusted and afraid—and disgusted
with myself for being afraid. What right did someone have to ter-
rorize me in my own home? Should I call the police? Should I
march over there and tell her to stop it? Was I imagining things?
Was it possible that someone could be this disgusting, this *mean?*

I steamed all evening, burning my finger on the frying pan at dinner, spilling Iris's juice, which made her cry. But I couldn't say anything until the children were safely in bed; I couldn't explode with
my fearful theory, not even with Caius. He had to find it credible,
had to be willing to join with me rather than soothe and smooth
me. I didn't want to be soothed; I wanted company in my outrage,
so my approach to Caius would have to be gentle. I told him about
the groundhog.

"Do you think Amanda might be giving us those, um, dead animal gifts?" Caius was flossing his teeth in the bedroom doorway; I
was in the bathroom, washing my face. I could feel the repulsion
sneaking into my limbs like adrenaline.

"Are you serious, Thea?" he asked, sounded parental.

"No. I don't know. I guess I was just thinking if I were really mad,
I don't know, if she were really mad—do you think? I don't know,"
I said.

"Do you think she could do something like that?"

"Maybe it was just a cat," I lied.

"If it happens again, we should tell the police," he said.

"I don't know," I said, and I didn't. I was afraid I could be wrong.
The police seemed so drastic, so confrontational. If we called them,
it would be real.

"It's not such a big deal," I said.

"You're the one who thinks she's doing it. Which would be
harassment. Maybe it's her husband."

"Never mind," I said. Half of me wanted him to say, *No, you do mind, and I'll phone the police this instant!* The other half of me regretted sharing my suspicion. I had no proof.

"Your call." He pushed in front of me to spit in the sink. I didn't want it to be my call. I wanted it all to go away. I had small secrets, and I wanted to relinquish them.

It was a good time for Tia to be coming. I didn't want to be this way; I needed to put my suspicion to bed for a while. I wanted everything to be usual again, normal. I tried to stop thinking about the little corpses and concentrate on Tia's visit. The trip was officially to see her mother, now that Mrs. Larkspur had moved to the home, but I imagined our days and nights together nonetheless, eager as a girl planning a sleepover party. It was partly the company I was hungry for. Although I had always told Caius pretty much everything, lately he didn't listen well. Or he listened the same way he always had and suddenly that wasn't enough for me. And maybe, just maybe, Amanda had been a little bit of a friend. And then we'd broken up over my employment, which would have been a stretch for any friendship, or even just for neighbors. Maybe at the same time I suspected her, I missed her a little bit.

Since she was finally coming, my friend, I wanted to tell Tia everything, to tell her things I didn't know yet. The day before Tia arrived, Caius trundled through the back door in the middle of dinner. Iris was flinging bits of carrot and turkey burger from her high chair, Carra had already excused herself to go out with a friend, and I hadn't caught the friend's name and worried, and Oliver was trying to tell me about his project for school, on Hawaii. Just the week before I'd thought we were ready to put the high chair in the attic, but Iris clearly wasn't there yet.

"Can we go to Hawaii, did you ever hear of slack-key guitar playing, could I get a guitar?" Oliver asked.

Caius walked in and his look said he was surprised by all the mess. Iris's flung food and coats puddled about the kitchen and pots sat on the counters. He also seemed surprised we hadn't waited, even though he'd called in the afternoon and said he might be late. Some days "he might be late" meant go ahead without him, though once upon a time it had meant could we wait a little extra in case he managed to make it home in time to eat with us. But now wasn't once upon a time. When she was hungry, Iris wrapped herself around my legs, and Oliver got a little zany with questions and ideas and snacked on anything he could reach. So I'd given in to dinner, and now I had ketchup on my white sweater, the one I knew I shouldn't wear within a mile's radius of my children, but it was thick and the house was chilly. I was tired of waiting for it to be safe to wear white.

"Hey," said Caius. "I see we've started without me."

"And I see you're late as usual," I snapped.

"Daddy, can I get a guitar?" Oliver asked, waving his burger for punctuation.

"Where's Carra?" Caius hung his coat on his hook and reached across the table to pick up a sautéed onion with his fingers. I wanted to say, *Did you wash your hands? Did I say you could sit down yet? Where are your manners?* I wanted him to go away and let me deal with my chaos in my own way.

"She's out."

"We could go to Hawaii," said Oliver. "It's got rainbows and they grow sugar and pineapples. There's a movie set in Hawaii, but it's rated R, so I can't see it."

"I *know*," I said.

Iris threw the last of her food on the floor, having eaten nothing, and started to climb onto the high chair's tray.

"You forgot to snap her in," said Caius, picking Iris up as if rescuing her from an evil stepmother.

"You forgot to tell me you were actually coming." I stood up, wiped my mouth, and took my plate to the sink, though I'd only eaten a single bite of burger and all I'd gotten was bun.

Caius stood with Iris, defending the door to the hallway, the stairs, my escape.

"Can we go to Hawaii?" Oliver was still sitting, his face wrinkled with worry. "So you guys won't fight?"

"We're not fighting," said Caius.

"Yes we are," I said. I stuffed my burger into the garbage disposal with a fork. I put my coat on over the ketchup-stained sweater and went out the back door. I wanted to tell Oliver it would be okay. I wanted to sit with him for the rest of his dinner, to give Iris her bath, to give myself the deep satisfaction of finishing the day with them, but I couldn't be there with him anymore, in that horrible hot minute. I couldn't bear all his freedoms, to come and go at will, to be beloved without being constantly required.

I jogged a little, down the cul-de-sac and onto the woods path. I didn't want to look at the house. Let him manage for a little while. My coat smelled of turkey burger and onions, homey and good. What if I stayed out all night? What if I went away for a few days? What would he do? Would they even get out of bed in the mornings, or would they all stay camped at home, eating what they had, complaining and wallowing and getting hungry with Oreo crumbs on their cheeks? I wanted to take Oliver to Hawaii, just Oliver and me, without anyone else to make demands or requests, or to throw carrots on the floor and squish them with bare feet, tracking orange onto the rugs.

I wanted not to clean up after anyone. I wanted someone to take care of me; I wanted to quit. My mother had never seen any of my children, and it wasn't fair. She would've adored them, and she would've helped me through the milk-blurred early days. Not once had Caius's parents offered to help out, to take them so we could go off on our own. They had come to our wedding, had let my parents pay for it, offering at the end to settle the liquor bill in a grand gesture. I didn't need any of them, anyone, my useless brothers all wrapped like burritos in their lives, all full of their own needs.

Down the slope toward the river, my feet shushed through the thin brown blanket of last year's oak leaves. The air smelled sharp and filled my lungs with its coolness. It was past dusk, but a little light lingered in the forest, not yet drained from the spaces between the new-budded branches. I was wearing clogs, and frost and the slushy green business of spring—shoots and roots and mosses—squished into the back beneath my heels.

Spring was supposed to be fresh, but I smelled rot and the bitter sap of the pines attending to their wounds. The days were getting longer, determined. Any minute now the little maple fists would unfurl into green applause. The grass would grow slick and green; the woods would fill with the quiet music of growth. Soon it would be summer, with the sloppy schedule of schoolless days. We could go on a vacation after all. We could rent a house in the Catskills, the way we'd planned on doing every year, though we'd only gone two years in a row, between Oliver and Iris. Or I'd go on this trip in September by myself.

I slipped on a wet patch and yelped as I slid down to the path by the river. The mud wet my thigh through my jeans. Hikers are never this unprepared, even in the woods behind their houses—they wear real shoes and eschew white sweaters made of silk and cotton for wool, warm when wet. A chattering complaint issued from the crown of an oak as a squirrel blamed me for all its missing acorns. Its voice was so loud and particular, it almost sounded like Iris, and I almost told it, Shush Jitterbug.

I stood up and brushed myself off and saw the pumpkins. They were half-covered with leaves, some of the naked ones slumped with rot, some pale with age, some just stems, and a few still bright orange under the oak blanket. The maples and chestnuts around them shivered, shaking their bunched leaf buds. And over the river, on a tree bench, a fallen giant sleeping over the water, my daughter Carra sat swinging her legs, waiting for the boy who was scooting his way out to meet her. He didn't walk along the trunk—he was cautious. I didn't know him at all, didn't recognize his black spiky hair, his full mouth, his skinny legs as he shimmied toward her.

They didn't see me. I sat on my slope behind an elephant-skinned sassafras, watching as this boy reached Carra, touched her twelve-year-old cheek in the almost-dark woods. The water wrapped night between the fallen sticks and stones, going on and

on. I watched my daughter engaging in the surest form of separation from us, keeping the secret of love.

It was a visceral pain, Carra's betrayal, her growing into this
young woman. I had always told myself I'd know her best now, that
I'd be the one to help her through her secret times of adolescence,
but this came too soon, and I'd neglected to notice its surest sign.
Part of me wanted to run to her, to interrupt, and part of me knew I
had nothing to give her that she wasn't taking herself—freedom,
separation. I'd need to say something, needed to tell her to be careful, needed to be sure she was safe—but if I pushed my way in,
she'd push me right back out again. It wasn't me she wanted; even if
she needed me, she didn't know it now. I no longer wanted to know
who stole last Halloween's pumpkins and put them in the woods,
where they were huddled still, orange and rotted and hollow, passing neighborhood gossip between their stumped stems.

I would tell Caius about Carra, but I couldn't do it with Tia coming. I would tell Carra I knew, but I needed to think about how to
do it. Suddenly Tia's timing couldn't have been more wrong. The
busyness I'd told her about was all internal now, was all the hidden
clock-workings of a family. And the animals, the dead animals—I
was afraid she'd belittle my fears, or make them larger. She wasn't
my sounding board the way she once was. As much as I wished she
was, she wasn't safe.

On the afternoon drive to the airport, with Oliver at a friend's,
Carra officially at swim practice but probably back in the woods for
all I knew, and Iris asleep in her car seat with cookie crumbs on her
shirt and a smudge of chocolate across her forehead, I tried to
remember why I was still angry with Caius. We'd made up officially; we'd even had tender sex that morning at dawn before he got
up for work. I hadn't minded. I had sort of enjoyed it, though I kept
wondering whether Oliver might wander in, whether Iris would
call from her crib, or climb out, her new trick, drawn to the sound
of something other than sleep in the house. She was going to be

finished with the crib soon, and the high chair, and then done with needing me, just like her sister.

Driving down the Garden State toward Newark, I got off on the Lyons Avenue shortcut through the cruddy neighborhood, turning right at the nudie bar, my minivan a red advertisement for affluence as we passed buildings with wounded windows, cracked glass and boards, gravel instead of grass for lawns. I power-locked the doors and stared ahead until I got back onto Route 78. Probably there were much worse areas in Paterson and Elizabeth, and I knew I probably had nothing to be afraid of but poverty, one building burned and another with windowless holes in the walls. I tried to clarify why I was angry with my husband, to make it solid when it kept shifting in my head. I didn't want to resent him; I wanted to love him without reservation, as I had before children. We were different people then, but I ought to be able to love that way nonetheless.

Sometimes it seemed I was the only one who was different now. Caius put them to bed sometimes; when they were infants, he'd done an occasional night feeding. But he never gave over his body, all his sleep, letting their rhythms determine his. Once in a while, he took half a Saturday. But if he needed to work, he worked. If he wanted to read a book, he did, and somehow he made it through the paper almost every day. On weekends, he even read the classifieds ads. Maybe I felt he hadn't given enough up for us. And maybe it wasn't about him but me instead, my self swimming right below the surface of the family sea.

As I turned back onto Route 78 East, Iris sighed in her sleep. A deep, lost sighing, her face obscured by her curls. Letting go of something that worried her. I adored her for her intensity. I forgave her all her tantrums. Watching her face in the rearview mirror, I wanted to sleep like that, to surrender.

The traffic was making me late, and nervous. I wanted to tell Tia *everything*, out loud, all the things I was wondering; I wanted to hear myself making jokes about what motherhood really meant: having no time to go to the bathroom. Maybe Tia would understand after all. Even if we weren't as used to each other, even if there was background to review. Iris woke, sounding her frustration at having succumbed to sleep in the first place. The car in front of me honked its horn, though there was no apparent source of the slowdown.

Tia was waiting outside baggage claim, a lost look on her face that was not entirely erased as she got in the van. She had a single, chic black bag; she was thin and older and her nose looked different. My tall friend, with her widely spaced brown eyes, which she'd always wished were blue. She was finally in my car; I was finally bringing her home. And though we kissed cheeks, her smell like the ocean apparent beneath the awful scent of airplane travel, I was still nervous, as if I were on a date. It almost felt good.

Back on the Garden State, Tia was mostly the one talking, and I was listening. Iris had found her way back to sleep when we started moving.

"So I wasn't sure they'd even give me my seat," said Tia. She turned on the radio and started tuning, and I tried not to be annoyed, to mention the sleeping child, the price of waking her.

"God! I can't believe the stations are still the same! I can't believe this place, all the *green*. It's all brown in California. They call it gold, but it's really brown."

I turned the radio down, a gravely singer complaining about love. I wondered whether I'd pay for Iris's second nap, whether she'd wake inconsolable when we got home, or worse, before we arrived.

"My God, look at this town," she said, as we approached downtown Sylvan Glen. "It's like Lincoln Logs! Lego Land! You know all about that, little mommy." She was grinning. I would let her call me that. It felt warm. I'd stopped sweating and started feeling ordinary again. Calm. The town did indeed look like a child's miniature village.

We parked in the lot by her mother's retirement home. Iris sighed again, waking.

"Why haven't you made it out to see me?" asked Tia. Her voice sent familiar waves through my chest. My best friend. An adult body, the young woman's face set inside like a cameo. Tia's cheeks were tan and lightly lined. Her light brown hair was streaked with gold. It was long and slightly ragged, fashionably ragged. Her eyes looked tired but that same brown; this was the face I'd told my secrets to.

"I guess because of the kids . . ." It felt good to be able to look at her, though still I thought of Carra, of letting her be in love, of all the dangers she had let loose from the box.

"Silly," said Tia. She spoke a different language. She didn't have any kids of her own. "You should get Caius to take care of them. Or get a baby-sitter or something. You should come see the left coast."

Of course she was right, and of course she had no clue what she was asking for. She got out, waving, and went to see her mother. I brought her slick black bag home, feeling forlorn despite the fact that she was here at long last.

And looking up at my front porch, I saw there was another one, more regular than the newspaper. I felt a wave of disgust, then fury. I looked over at Amanda's house and thought I saw someone slide the curtain away from the window to see me. To see my reaction. Something dead and furry waited on my bricks, and I felt as though I were in a horror movie, afraid to leave my daughter in the back-seat while I disposed of it. Then a cat darted out from behind the Martins' and I sighed, shivered slightly with my own raging para-noia. I would wrap it in a bag, chuck it in the trash, and tell Caius all about it when he got home.

April

18

Amanda

Carole was a mom, but her daughters were grown, one living at home and attending the community college, the other working at a bank, not finding a husband, not producing grandchildren. Carole had taken a job at the bank herself for a while, but she hated the cleaning-fluid smell and the impatient gum clacking and knowing too much about her daughter as a grown-up. Her mother lived in Boca in a retirement community, where she belonged to more clubs than Carole had ever heard of in her life: Art Appreciation, Dazzling Widows, Window Decorations, Canasta, Tapestry. She told me all these details in ten-minute morning installments while she swayed with Malena in her arms and I got ready for work, forgetting my hat, searching for my keys.

"My little love!" she said to Malena. "I missed this, being *needed*. Are your keys by the door?" She looked so calm. I was going to miss the train.

"All my customers wanted was to make a deposit, cash a check, get the heck out of line so they wouldn't be late getting back to their own desk. Sweetie pie," she cooed to Malena.

Had she said heck or hell? I wondered. Should I worry about bad words? I said them all the time, but now Malena was getting older. I found my keys in the pocket of my coat and kissed Malena and darted for the door, sweating in my silk blouse.

"She's the right one," Aaron said in the evening, sighing happily over the long notes she left us, telling us Malena had pooped twice and had eaten six spoonfuls of strained peas. I pictured her opening her mouth like a perfect little chick. I tried not to mind that Carole wrote number two for a bowel movement.

Still, back at work, I looked at Malena's photo and traced her perfect tiny mouth and worried that, although Carole was confident and calm when I was around, it was an act. That once I left she was simply letting Malena sob in her crib. I cut and trimmed and arranged a bouquet of horrible thoughts: She was putting her on her front to sleep because that was what she learned with her own kids, twenty years ago; she was secretly diabetic and might succumb to coma, or worse. She was slapping the baby, she was pinching her, she was stealing and suffocating and screaming, unable to take it, psychotic, angry. Now that Malena was old enough to eat, she'd steal the food from her spoon. She was pushing her carriage down the middle of the street, letting it fly into traffic. She was using a knife to . . . All the horror movies I'd ever seen melded with my terrible imagination. That, and maybe my own secret sense of the pressure of being the caregiver.

I knew better, I'd always known better. Once I weaned Malena, my hormones began to readjust—but I wasn't normal yet. If I was ever going to be normal again.

I had a blister from my pumps when I walked into work with a thousand things on my to-do list—call an illustrator whose work had been lost when an intern sent it to a ranch in New Mexico instead of a farm in upstate New York, convince Neethi that I really wasn't the right editor for a series of hideous imports she'd fallen in love with at Frankfurt that featured Nordic mythology, find out why I could hear a maddening muted alarm going off on some other floor or maybe in some other building every afternoon at two that no one else in the office could hear, go over the galleys for the Rose manuscript, which was finally on the fall list.

"You're late!" Neethi was marching down the hallway, her vast gold hoop earrings swaying like life preservers on a sinking ship. She carried the binder. I felt a horrible swoop of déjà vu.

"No, it's only eight thirty-two!"

"It's at eight-thirty," she said. And, in case I hadn't noticed the binder, "The six-month follow-up. Get your FDP and get up to the conference room on sixteen." She smiled. It was an unusual sunburst of sympathy. "I don't want to waste the day, either, but—ah, well, it's the price of corporate-level organization."

I didn't remind her that the Franklin Day Planners had been her idea in the first place.

In the conference room, Aliza the in-house council was chewing on a cuticle.

"Now that we're all here," announced the russet-haired man with the bow lips, "we can get started. I know you don't want to waste a single day." He smiled. He looked older. "But that's exactly what we're after. Long-term planning." He wrote on the white board: What Have You Accomplished? I wanted to tell him he really didn't need to capitalize each word.

"Every six months," he pronounced. "When I return to these places of work, some dreams have become realities, souls soar—"

Sore souls, I thought. His face was ruddy, and I wondered whether he was an alcoholic or just had a skin condition.

"—and other dreams still need more work. More Planned Advancement. Let's start by looking at those first lists—you have kept them?"

I had mine, stowed in the back of the binder, folded into halves, quarters, eighths, so it was a private lump. "Healthy baby," it read. "Easy delivery. No more barfing. Good sex again. Keep my job.

Become editorial director. Have own imprint. Plumber finished by the time I get home." I laughed aloud. What had happened to us, Aaron and me—the boy from Africa and the woman who fell in love with books? We lived in the suburbs and I obsessed about plumbing and he was chewed up by his job. Though maybe there were things he loved about his job. And I supposed there were things I loved about the suburbs. Certainly not my neighbors, though.

"How's yours look?" asked the editorial assistant next to me. No, now she was an assistant editor, I'd forgotten. Rumor was she had courted the senior VP on the fourteenth floor by doing extra projects for him, and she'd ditched her editor, just a senior editor, as soon as the VP needed a new assistant. I kind of admired her. No one wanted to stay an editorial assistant, not even for the requisite one to two years. The other two assistants from the first FDP training had quit.

I covered my paper. "Where's our esteemed production director?" I asked her.

"He's gone on disability." She smiled at my covered paper. Her eyes were extravagantly green, and I wanted to ask whether her contacts were colored, even though I knew the answer. "Bleeding ulcers." How could she smile through those words? "He's gone to San Diego to live on a boat."

P art of me knew the only way I'd ever be calm, sure of things, was if I were the one caring for my baby. But a bigger part of me knew I didn't want to quit work, give it up; I'd never gotten much past a quick handwritten list calculating our requirements against Aaron's salary alone. It was actually possible, and it wasn't about money anyway. I'd only wanted that as an excuse: We couldn't really afford to live on one salary. We could. But I couldn't. I had to go out, to be a person alone with work to do—with deadlines and a paycheck and meetings, even loathsome meetings—and not just a mother.

This was my *new* normal: juggling guilt and longing. Perhaps the women who stayed home just had more guilt in the mix and succumbed to it, women like Thea, who clearly had talents other than wiping noses and making suppers. But there was more to it than food and tissues. Of course there was: teaching them how to share, to wash their hands, how to tie their shoes. It was being an example, all the time. Even if I didn't do it, there was nothing wrong with being at home, or for that matter, with being Thea.

Of course I thought about how we'd kissed. It was almost as if it was something that had happened to someone else, in a movie. It was not a kiss of love. It was about comfort. And now that she'd quit on me, we had chilled to each other like jilted lovers. I saw her children in their yard on Saturdays and Caius driving off when I did in the morning, his wide shoulders and sure stance as he unlocked his car. Usually I was coming or going, all week I was only home before light and after dark. I was glad of the distance between our houses.

Alternate Fridays were different. I worked at home every other Friday, and Carole only worked a half day, so by three o'clock I was lured outside to walk Malena in the stroller or sit on the lawn and let her see the sky as April swelled into spring. I felt that working on children's books hadn't prepared me, in any way, for talking to a child. She knew nothing, so I tried to tell her everything.

"Precipitation," I started, "is rain and snow and hail. Moisture in the clouds—" I looked at her. She was chewing on a fist and smelled like sweet bread dough.

"Okay, never mind. That's the sky. Sky! Those are clouds . . ."

Obviously she didn't understand any of it, but I pointed out cumulus and nimbus. I showed her the maple leaf and a blade of grass.

Sometimes it was a little bit boring. Not Malena herself, but being always in *charge* of Malena, the fact of having to sit still or move, to rock or hum but not give my pure attention to anything else. I felt guilty for that, for wishing I could go back to the manuscript I'd brought home. I read in pieces, but it wasn't the same. I tried to remember how all week I'd missed Malena, a dull and constant ache.

Then Carole had to stay home sick, so I had to stay home sick. I wished Aaron could do it because he didn't have an author meeting. He didn't have anything urgent, but the assumption was that I would be the one to stay home. So I did, and I resented it and loved being with Malena.

It was a Monday. I tried not to think about the rest of the week, to worry about prolonging my own fake illness.

Malena couldn't do much at the playground. I pushed her on the baby swings and she waved her arms. I put her in my lap and went down the slide, my hips scarcely fitting within the plastic parameters. The park smelled of cedar chips and sun-warmed metal.

"She's too young," called a woman sitting on the bench. She had long brown hair and a sugary voice. "Don't let her go down herself."

"Um," I said. "I know."

"And honey, it's much too cold to swing, the metal on those swings, you should be careful."

"I'm her mother," I said, carrying Malena over to the giant tic-tac-toe game. I wondered why she was telling me what to do, and a small wad of guilt and worry formed in my belly, a whole planet of guilt, starting with a speck of dust and magnetically attracting matter. Magnetically attracting comments. It was as if I were wearing a sign: Working Mommy.

I should've been flattered that she thought I was the young baby-sitter, but I wasn't the baby-sitter. I was the person who had endured all-day morning sickness, I'd felt the contractions like tsunamis of pain, I'd pushed and I had been cut, I'd been stitched, I'd made milk. I still belonged to Malena at night. I still belonged to her all the time; when I was away, I might forget temporarily, but my cells knew, the strange passion of motherhood was just behind my calm office mask.

I put her back in the swing to spite the bossy woman on the bench, and because it made Malena giggle. I pushed her in an arc, her feet purple exclamations in the sneakers Carole had picked out at the baby store in town. We left an envelope of money to pay her back; somehow it felt like an illicit transaction. I was still unused to having someone else living in my house during the day, someone else who rummaged in the fridge for lunch, someone else spooning sweet potatoes into Malena's bird mouth. When I wasn't there, I could let myself stop thinking out the minutes of her day. I liked coming home and letting Carole leave, taking my baby and shifting the evidence—moving the mail to the table where I sorted it, pushing the toy chest to the other corner, holding and bathing Malena to erase Carole's smell, a sort of salty perfume, and cover it with my own, invisible to me.

I was the mommy pushing the swing, and I tried to savor it, an orange taste on my tongue. I tried to imagine doing it every day. I would be bored. Still, I let myself go there. She could hold up her own head, she could sit, and she could eat, but she still required a whole person, absolute attention. Helplessness scared me—it was my job to take care of Malena, and I had hired someone else to do this job for me.

I parked the stroller in the backyard and put Malena out on a farm-scene mat to watch the sun and wind particularize the locust leaves. April still grew cool when clouds covered the afternoon sun. I sat on the steps by the shed and a chill seeped from the concrete through my jeans. It would be quiet to be a mother alone, quiet except for the occasional cry, for the mowers and blowers evacuating the neighborhood of excess green. I'd be lonely. I *was* a little lonely; squeezed by home and work, I'd forgotten how to just be with Malena, with anyone. Wind rattled the glass in the shed door, a little rhythm, *fix-a-me, fix-a-me.* I didn't have the energy to fix anything. I looked at Malena; she was wide eyed as she rolled onto her front and did a wobbly half push-up.

The phone rang inside the house, but I didn't feel like running in to get it. Squirrels harassed each other around an elm—maybe they were mating, but it looked almost vicious, the way they nipped at each other, screamed and bristled. Through the open back window I heard Carole's voice on the machine, her cough. It was wrong to begrudge her this, but I wasn't always sure I wanted this other person in my life.

I tried to enjoy the afternoon. Changing Malena, I thought about how a parent maintains a baby's body—inspecting, cleaning, observing the absurdly fast growth, touching and tasting the incredible new skin. I could see how someone wouldn't mind it as a job, even if the baby they cared for wasn't their own. Being with Malena for the day reminded me of the things Carole did for her, the details, the greatest intimacies, and how Carole was taking care of me, how I appreciated her, despite not wanting to think about her too often.

"You are amazing!" I said to Malena, who had just burbled and peed into her new diaper so I had to start again.

The second day, I didn't enjoy "our" sick day nearly as much. I felt as if I were in a tunnel, scrabbling through roots and stones in an unknown, clearly wrong direction. It was only a little time at home, but all my calm and ordinariness, all my day-to-day balance of being an editor and being a mother, being a woman who works and one who watches her daughter's fingers open and close, ferned around themselves, wound into a snarl of what I could do and what I *should* be doing.

Then there was the third day. I was missing the production meeting. You didn't miss a production meeting unless you had a funeral or an author's hand to hold or a heart attack. One woman in production had felt sick one Wednesday morning when she had to present some specs for her book. She stayed at work, only to be found writhing under her desk right before the meeting started. Acute appendicitis. The EMTs took her down the elevator on a stretcher. Then the meeting convened without her.

I thought about my own mother, tried to remember what she'd done when we were sick. I remembered her brushing my hair once when I had a fever. It hurt and felt delicious. Probably, Dad had been the one to stay home. Had Mom felt this guilty? Maybe it was her fault; maybe she'd transferred the guilt onto me. All along I'd faulted her for taking the easy way out, for working all the time. It was easier, and it was harder; it was awful. I was a ball of tangled twine, and I felt pulled and knotted from within and without.

"Try to enjoy it," said Aaron. "It's like a day off."

"You wouldn't say that if you had to stay home."

"If I didn't have to go to Atlanta, I would, you know I would."

I didn't know that. At least he hadn't been able to prove it yet. I did know his flight left at 8:25 A.M., and at 5:10 A.M. we were all up, Malena and me in the bed, Aaron stuffing extra socks into his garment bag.

At work, things were gnarled and gossipy; the trade division was up for sale, and everyone was worried. I was worried. When there was turnover, there was the inevitable overthrow of miscellaneous thrones; there were the pet projects placed in other people's chairs, and the higher your position, the more vulnerable you were. I knew I hadn't brought in as many well-reviewed or award-winning or unexpectedly best-selling books in the last year—*Wild Aunt Safari* was old news—in no small part because I hadn't been at work for a hefty slice of the last year.

Morning sickness felt as if it was years ago. Finding Carole felt like years ago. All the trouble with the house felt like years past, the horrific crash, the tree settling in like an unwanted guest. The nighttime anxiety I'd had just afterward—sometimes ghostly reminders briefly inhabited my body when I woke to Malena's cries, and my heart pounded horribly. But mostly, I remembered the rain on the living room rug, snow drifting into the kitchen through a big black plastic flap. Unadulterated winter sunshine on the blond wood floor. Workmen cutting and sanding and pounding.

"I think that's your limo," I said. We lived in a town so quiet I could hear the idle of an unfamiliar engine over the miniature orchestra of cardinals and black-capped chickadees.

"You'll be okay?"

"She's my daughter, I know what to do." I rested Malena's sleeping head in the crook of my neck.

I called Neethi early and left a message, sniffling as convincingly as I could, hoping she wouldn't call back, but of course she did, just as I was spooning rice cereal into Malena.

"Are you really sick, or is it your child?" she asked, forgoing the ordinary salutations. Malena smeared her cereal on my arm.

Surprised by her outright attack, I forgot my sniffling and said, "Oh, um, we both have it?"

"I thought you had contingency arrangements," said Neethi, cruel and quick.

"Oh," I said, remembering that I'd lied that my sister could take over in a pinch. Neethi had offered me the name of an emergency nanny agency in the city, which charged only one hundred dollars *an hour* to cover when your own live-in had to go back to Guatemala or wherever to help an ailing mother-in-law. I coughed, anyway.

"Yes, my sister's away. But really, I wouldn't want to be hacking on everyone there—I do have it, too." Too little, too late. I knew she was wearing her scarlet production meeting lipstick and matching suit. The new director was supposedly both a tyrant and a fox, but I hadn't met him yet.

While Malena took an afternoon nap, I called my mother, unsure of what I wanted to say. That she had done me wrong, that she had been good. When I got voice mail, I hesitated.

"I just," I said, hearing the dead air. "I just know more now." I wondered whether the recording had stopped. "Thank you."

I stared at the phone for a second, surprised.

I was making hot chocolate when she called back. I'd wanted it the way I wanted things when I was pregnant—with a longing that was almost disgust.

"It feels like the hardest thing in the world, doesn't it?" she said, and for a minute, I wondered whether someone was impersonating my mother. Did no one introduce themselves anymore? Did caller ID mean no one needed to start with hello?

"Mom?"

"Like you can hardly stand it, like it is sickeningly important and like you're making all the wrong choices."

"Not that bad."

She chuckled. I could imagine the corners of her mouth, the new wrinkles I'd noticed back at Chanukah, folds that made a smile almost unhappy. "Well, it doesn't get any easier."

"Excuse me? I thought you were supposed to finish up with a platitude."

"That's my Amanda, always looking for a summary. It doesn't, really. Gets less *big*, but it never goes away."

"Are we talking about my postbaby belly or motherhood?"

"Both," she said. "Must go, I've got a meeting, but you're welcome."

I spooned one mouthful of hot chocolate from the pan, burned my tongue as I swallowed, and poured the rest in the sink. Malena started to cry.

When I was four and a half, I wanted to learn to tie my shoelaces because Jane could already do it. My father was grading tests. He showed me twice, distracted, how to make a loop and wind the second lace around, but I couldn't copy what he'd done after he went back to the papers at his desk. All night, I thought about my shoelaces, passionate to know how to tie them. In the middle of the night, the rooms were washed by the gray-yellow glow from the street lamp outside my bedroom window, and I crept downstairs to find my sneakers and try again. My mother was at the kitchen table, drinking a glass of wine, wearing a robe. She looked soft and exhausted and she'd missed dinner and bedtime because of a conference at Brigham and Women's Hospital. I expected her to tell me to go upstairs, but she took me into her lap and showed me how to make two loops and cross them.

"Daddy said one loop," I said, trying to copy what her hands had done. Her breath smelled sweet and grapey.

"Sometimes different methods work for different people," she said, taking my small hands in hers and leading me through.

So, she taught me to tie my shoes, but she hadn't been around. Was I going to be around? There had to be a compromise.

19

Thea

Oren was the one I'd fought with the most. In the years since I came home from the trail, after he had died, I hardly remembered that, preferring instead to remember how he was golden, how he was good. He would have been the uncle who came to visit, playing horsy and bearing quirky things that could be played with instead of sending big plain presents that didn't really matter, like the ones from my surviving brothers.

I predicted in the impossible past tense: Oren would have brought a cheap Chinese kite to the birthday party. He'd get ice cream on his elegant nose. The next day he'd have gone to the broad green hill by the lake at Ramapo Reservation with the birthday child. He'd have untangled the silky string, attached the lion's head to the dragon body, launched the kite to the sky with his own sprint, brought the tether to Oliver's hand, or Carra's, or Iris's.

But having Tia here reminded me that being closest in age had meant we were closest in competition, too, that Oren had been the one hanging on my mother's other leg, that he'd gotten Dad to come to his baseball game instead of my viola recital by means of charismatic and insistent begging. Sometimes I'd wanted the attention he got, even though he was younger. Sometimes I'd wanted everything he had.

On the second night of Tia's visit, after I'd convinced myself I hadn't knocked on Carra's door to talk with her about what I'd seen because my friend was visiting, Carra brought her secret to us when I didn't expect it.

Caius came home early. Tia was out with her mother buying clothes. "She's so batty now, she wears the weirdest things," she'd told me. "This weird dirndl dress and pants and a sweatshirt all at once." I didn't like hearing Tia call her mother batty, though she'd probably done it twenty years ago as well. Caius and I were sitting on the front porch swing listening to the birds arguing over the first crop of insect hatchlings, the house creaking with the memory of living wood.

"I'm thinking about what you said," I told him, my heart hammering. "About going out and doing something for myself?"

"Good," said Caius. "Have you found us a place to go for that vacation in September yet? The kids have those Jewish holidays off, right? I can take three days in August, too. Did I tell you about the settlement on the Steinberg account?" His questions were laconic, as if he'd been drugged by the early evening light.

"Yes," I said, though he hadn't. "I wanted to tell you about something. Well, two somethings," I said, as Carra, the buds of her body invisible under a sweatshirt, came out of the house with a cookie in her mouth and another in her hand.

"Mommy," she said. She sat on my lap, leaning her head against Caius's shoulder. The swing creaked with our collective weight.

Carra let me stroke her hair, glinting with red. Her skin was so young; she still had the scent she'd had as a baby, apricot, beneath the chemical smells of her makeup, chlorine, beneath the cotton and high school hallway smells. It hurt to love someone like this, someone who was letting me go every time she walked away.

She finished her cookies and leaned into us. I looked at the enormous length of her arms, thought about the bones beneath, grown from baby bones, grown from the first tiny person I'd birthed. Sometimes she was separate from that person, but at this minute she was the same, needing us, Caius and me, needing our bodies for comfort despite her own capabilities, despite being taller and stronger than I'd ever be.

"I have a secret," she said into Caius's shoulder.

I felt fear in my limbs again, as I had when I saw her in the woods. Panic rang in my cells like a thousand invisible alarm clocks.

"Okay, Carra-my-faira," said Caius. "Tell us."

"You can't be mad," said Carra, her face against the stripes of his button-down.

"Okay," he said again. I wanted to pull her face to mine, I wanted to inspect her for damage. Instead I held her hand. She let me.

"I like a boy," she said. She sighed with the great energy of youth. Her language wasn't the language of someone having sex. I breathed. Deep in, deep out.

"Have you kissed him?" I asked.

"Yuck," she said. "Of course not. Not yet."

Then she got up and flounced inside, twelve again. "Homework," she said. "When's dinner?"

"Pizza, I think," said Caius. "Later."

"She has," I whispered to Caius.

"Really?" He sat up straight.

"Maybe she was working up to telling us that," I said.

"How do you know if she didn't tell you?"

"I saw her," I said. "But don't be mad." I wasn't sure why I was telling him that when I was mad myself. Then Tia walked up the driveway and saluted.

All along I'd wondered how other mothers, no matter how distracted, let their daughters make mistakes—get pregnant, get diseases. All along I'd secretly believed I was better than them; bad things only happened to children whose mothers let the songs of their own lives drown out plaintive calls for help. But I'd been listening, hadn't I? Now I knew how it happened: like that. She was going to be thirteen in a few weeks. *Thirteen.* Too soon to start lying to us.

Still, by consensus, we decided to let Carra's secret rest. Caius wanted me to tell and retell what I'd seen, and we stayed up that night deciding to confront her, deciding to wait until she came to us. It would be better if she laid her cards down one by one, if we didn't pull them from her hand. It would be better if she trusted us as much as she could.

"You have talked about, you know—sex?" asked Caius, as if sex wasn't something we held between us that we relied on for connection more than the walls of the house. As if sex wasn't how we'd had a Carra in the first place.

"Last year, of course," I said. "She isn't going to be stupid. I don't think this is going to go that far." I believed it, too, though I would have believed she hadn't kissed him if I hadn't seen it.

"If she doesn't tell us soon, we tell her to tell us."

"She knows about birth control, too."

"But you said she isn't having sex."

"No," I said, "but she knows."

He groaned and rolled over and then rolled back to kiss the air in my general direction. Neither of us would sleep much, but we'd both pretend.

"Why doesn't Clark come down more often?" Tia asked, referring to my brother who lived in upstate New York.

I was trying to talk with Tia; I felt we hadn't really talked yet, five days into the visit. I stood on the lawn below the back porch, trying to keep Iris from pulling all the buds off the tulips; I'd let her take one, and she'd cracked it open, fascinated for a second by the pistil, stamen, by the unhatched red inside. But then she'd move on to another bud, and another. I told her not to pick them, grabbed her wrist twice and squeezed her fist into an open hand. Still, as soon as I started talking with Tia, she quit digging her hole in the corner of the yard, cast away her plastic spade, and started for the tulip buds again.

"No, Iris, I said *no*," I said, feeling oddly that I was making everything up. Then, "Clark? Because he's busy. Because his wife doesn't like us. Because he still wishes I hadn't moved into the house. Though frankly, he was completely convinced and convincing at the time."

"I remember when we kissed in a tree," she said. "He was so shy, his lips passed over mine like a butterfly. That tree in the Burtons' yard, the beech?"

"Not there anymore. The new owners cut it down and added on."

"It is kind of weird that you're living here," said Tia.

"No, Iris, I said *no*." Iris flung herself at my feet, the split bud of a looted yellow tulip in her hand. She cried a loud, fake cry, and I wanted for a quick hot second to slap her. I wanted the tulips, they were what my mother left me, fewer coming up each year, and I looked forward to them all through leaves and buds. I was furious with her for taking them right before the gift opened itself.

"I mean, is it weird to have sex in your parents' bedroom? Not just once, but all the time?"

Tia was more annoying than my daughter. "No," I said, looking down at Iris, who was dissecting the yellow flower and smoothing her fingers along the petal. I bent down to kiss her delicious forehead.

"Who is sex?" asked Iris.

"Christ," said Tia. "I didn't know she was listening."

"She's always listening," I said. Iris got up and skipped across the lawn before I had to answer her. I knew we'd come back to the subject.

"You and Oren had that thing you did with bottle caps, that collage or something?"

"You're right, the collage, I'd forgotten." In the back corner of the yard, behind the forsythia and beneath a mottled sassafras grown wild from the woods, we'd used bottle caps to make a sort of mosaic floor beneath the trunk. Oren had come home, thrilled with his newest finds, an orange from orange soda, the sharp reds and silvers from beer bottles. Our mother had found it and was worried we were drinking the beer.

I couldn't remember when we'd stopped. I'd lost so many pieces of history, reinventing how my life had evolved, how my brothers had lived, how my mother had raised us, how my father's math had taught us measures and proof, by telling it as stories to friends, by giving it to Caius when we were in the mountains together: my dowry.

"Hey, Iris, baby, can you find the collage?" Tia's voice lilted with the fake soprano of an adult unaccustomed to speaking to a child. "Your mommy made it with your uncle when they were little kids. Look back there." She pointed to the back corner of the yard, then the other corner, at the forsythias that framed the south end of the property.

"Mommy?" Iris reached her arms up for me.

I lifted her. She smelled of grass and crushed flowers, delicious. May you never lose a brother, I thought. Or anyone. I shivered. One of the hardest things, having children, was the fact that there were more people you could lose, more dangers. When Carra was first born, I'd realized how awful the world really was, and I'd thought I was the only one who could keep her safe. But for all I knew now she wasn't at school; she could be off in the woods with the stolen pumpkins, she could be opening her mouth for that boy as we spoke.

"Lemme go," said Iris, pointing at the ground. I put her down and let her scamper off in search of the mosaic.

"Here," said Tia, patting the step beside her.

I sat down, watching Iris as she went, wanting to follow after her but wanting more to prove to Tia that I could pay attention, if only for a sliver of time.

"So," said Tia. "I've been waiting for the right minute to tell you, but there aren't very many right minutes. You're so *booked*." She touched my arm and I felt a flood of familiar warmth. We once knew each other, knew everything. Maybe it was possible to catch up, or at least to weave fifteen minutes together, to overlap, if temporarily.

"I know," I said. "Mommyhood."

"So I don't even plan to tell my Mom—not that I ever tell her most important things."

For that second, her face luminous with secrets coming to the surface, I thought I might guess. She was getting married. She was pregnant. Something big. I had expected this moment all along, the time that would feel like old times, the times that were almost romantic. And I knew it was absurd, that we'd never be Carra's age again, collecting leaves for spells and building forts out of sheets, making Tia's mother furious because we used the good blue-striped sheets—we took a whole pile of them out of the clickety-doored linen closet, pulled them out into a muddy day.

It wasn't innocence I wanted, it was the deep selfishness of childhood, it was being able to tell your best friend anything. The pillow of the future.

"I had an affair with a woman who came on a climb," Tia said.

"Oh." I started to make a sentence but swallowed the words before they strung together in any meaningful way.

"I'm kidding," said Tia. "I just wanted to see what you'd think. The truth is, it was a married man. I'm one of those awful other women. It's such a cliché. And I don't even think I love him, but there's no one else, and I'm bored, and I *probably* should leave him. He came on a trip to Utah, and then another to Joshua Tree. And then another one right into my sleeping bag. There aren't any kids or anything—I probably should leave him." She tilted her head toward the house.

"Probably," I parroted. The joke about the woman wasn't funny. I thought about kissing Amanda. *I would get so bored,* she'd said of my life. She was irritating, even if she was a little bit right. Like remembering a bad dream, my mind jumped to the animals. I would have to do something about that after Tia left; I had to stop them coming, somehow.

"Is that what you think, Thee? You always had such good advice."

I didn't know why I wasn't more focused on Tia's problem. I supposed I thought it was time for me to get the good advice instead of giving it, or perhaps because Iris had disappeared into the forsythia and I was almost panicked with the desire to follow her and to stay. No matter how hard I was trying, I was weary of listening instead of telling. Never telling. I started by shifting the subject to me. "Sometimes it's incredibly hard, being a mom. Sometimes I wish I could take a vacation, be *Thea* for a while." Right away I felt fake and selfish.

Tia nodded. "Why don't you?" she asked. It was too plain a question. Too bald. Too clear that the gulf between us was only growing wider, a continental drift.

"You deserve better than a married man," I said, afraid of what was sitting in my mouth.

"You didn't answer my question."

"So, it wasn't really serious, and I don't think it meant anything, but you know that neighbor I told you about, the woman in your mom's house? You know how I said she went back to work and I took care of her baby for a while after that horrible accident with the storm?"

"You're not having another one," said Tia. "The thing is, with David, that's my married man's name, he wants to have kids and his wife doesn't. But honestly, I'm not sure I could do it, either."

Probably not, I thought. You'd have to give up so much vanity, so much time.

"No, I'm not having another baby. The thing is, we kissed." Why was I telling her this instead of about Outward Bound? Why did kissing Amanda even matter? I was done with their family, after all. Even if I did think of Malena often, even if I did wonder whether she was sitting up, whether she'd started to babble.

"Excuse me?" Tia put her hand on my thigh, the gesture almost an exclamation.

"And now I'm not taking care of her baby—I quit, I couldn't stand her bossiness anymore—and there have been these dead animals, and I keep thinking—"

"What, like *Fatal Attraction* or something? Ooo, you better lock up the pet rabbit. I thought I told you to be careful where you put your lips."

"Never mind, it's probably just a cat leaving them. Just squirrels, mice."

"Doesn't sound like just a cat." She gave me her best Cheshire grin, enjoying herself.

I already regretted saying it. It had sounded like it meant more than it did. Perhaps I'd been sucked into her melodrama. Perhaps I was trying to compete. But I knew in my heart it wasn't a cat. That was why I couldn't let it go.

"Babe, it's no big deal. I've been with women, too. I mean, even back in high school when we were talking about Jerry and when I was going out with Clark, remember how he bit his lip so much it was all chapped? Anyway, even then I'd, you know, experimented with girls."

"With who?" Why not with me, I thought, jealous not of sex but of friends I didn't share. Of experiments without me. My cheeks hurt with tension and I exhaled, hard, trying to let go.

"Oh, at Lizzie's birthday sleepover—that was when you went away to camp that time—we all practiced kissing, all girls, French kissing and then kissing necks and down . . . well, anyway, it got a little hotter than that."

"No way," I said, jealous of history, jealous of something that happened twenty years ago. I could see a flash of Iris's yellow overalls through the green and failing yellow of the forsythia.

Tia licked her lips, as if remembering the taste of the girls' bodies. Girls we'd made fun of, girls we'd pretended to disdain. "You're probably bisexual, babe. Most people are. I can't believe you never tried it out before. It's great, it's natural, it's really only another means of expression."

No, I thought. You have no idea. You've never been married, you've never had children, you're dating a married man. Not dating, sleeping with. It isn't about sex, I thought, and realized what a relief that was. The kiss hadn't been about sex. It was all right to need something, from Amanda, from someone—but it wasn't all right for it to be about sex. Sex was what Caius and I shared, and that was enough. Sometimes, more than enough, sometimes not at its best. But most of the time, he was exactly who I needed, the way he folded me into him, the way his sweat smelled of burned sugar and limes. With Amanda, it hadn't been about sex. It had been about our differences or a temporary peace—now vanished— about what we need and what we never get. I sighed.

I let Tia go on about what she'd done with girls, with women, with her married man; I let it roll over me and I didn't care any- more, though I still loved her. She owned her own stories. We'd shared a branch, like trees grafted together in an English Fence, but we each owned our own roots, our own leaves and buds.

"Mommy! Mom-ma!" Iris ran, a yellow line of light across the yard. "Look at this this *this!*" She held up a rusted orange bottle cap.

"You're right, I'm sure," I said to Tia's last statement. I kissed her cheek and let her sit alone as I stepped down from the porch to examine Iris's find.

The night before I drove Tia to the airport, we went in to talk with Carra, Caius and me, together.

She answered her door with a pen in her mouth, chewing the end, a little blue ink on her lips, like a child. She was a child. We'd promised each other to be careful how we spoke to her; we'd prom- ised to respect her but tell her what we knew.

"Your mother was in the woods—," Caius began. "I mean, we wanted to tell you that we know you're, well, actually dating."

"My mother was in the *woods?* What does that mean? What were you doing in the woods anyway, Mom?" Carra examined her homework without looking at us.

"I just wanted you to know you can tell us anything, sweetheart, that we know you're getting older—"

"*Duh.* Like this is some brilliant deduction. *You're getting older,*" she mimicked me, her face sour. "There's so much you don't know."

"So much we don't know?" said Caius, drawing himself up so he was taller. It was a strange thing; I'd never seen him do it around our children, only around people he was trying to intimidate or impress.

"I'm not having sex, so don't get on me about that. I'm not doing drugs, so what do you care? I'm okay, okay? Just butt out." Carra looked at me then, defying me to get angry. She wanted that. And Caius might give it to her, but I couldn't. My mouth ached to kiss her head, my arms to make her small, protected. It was ridiculous; I'd never imagined wishing my daughter would not grow up, but this was sooner than I'd planned. If I ever planned anything. Tia had made me feel lost in history, lost in my own present, as if my life had happened *to* me with no driving of my own.

"Don't," said Caius. "You're too young. And you're bringing him to meet us," he said. "Or else you're not going to see him anymore. We meet all your friends." His voice was louder than necessary. I was afraid he might wake Iris. At the same time, I was moved by his fear and assertion. By his simplification of something so tangled and impossibly tenuous.

"Fine," said Carra. "You can meet him. Mitch."

Of course it would be Mitchell, Belinda the actress's little boy, the one whose nanny took him to kindergarten. Our town suddenly seemed very small, and our children, who'd been in strollers about a minute ago, were dating among themselves without regard for their parents' readiness.

Later, when Caius and I had put the issue to bed—he was beautiful to me, fathering, saying what I couldn't—we sat up with unread books, talking more about other things, about the world outside our home.

Having Tia visit, having someone else in the house gave it an energy, the drama of possibility, and we stayed in our room at night—except when Iris woke up—restless and physically close. Something about having people in the house warmed Caius with sexual energy, and he turned to me, not always interested in the actual act, but instead interested in my body, in touching, in spreading his energy across my skin like frosting.

"So, it's her last night," he said, his fingers light on my forearm, stroking the inside of my elbow. "Are you sad she's going?"

I put my book down. "Actually, not really." I touched his fingers with mine.

"I thought it was good. I mean, I thought having a friend here made you happier."

"Excuse me?" It sounded suspicious, accusatory. I sat up and rubbed my arm where he'd been stroking, pushed his hand away. "What do you mean *happier?*"

"Nothing, I didn't mean anything." Caius made a verbal retreat. I found it infuriating, even more than when he was direct in his complaints about my nature.

"You *never* mean nothing," I said, shifting further from him in the bed. I wanted to go back to feeling warm, to wanting his touch, but at the same time there was something satisfying about the general sense of strife, at mining the thin silver river of complaint below the surface of our time together.

"I just mean you haven't been so happy lately, and all I want is for you to be happy. That squirrel thing, it's got you so riled up."

"It's just not that big a deal," I lied.

"Well, if you want to, you could file a police report."

"I don't want to do anything."

"Does that mean you want me to do something?"

"No," I said. "I mean yes." It was a guilty feeling, but I wanted him to rescue me, to find out who was doing this, to protect me. I was pathetic, but I couldn't very well go over to my neighbor's house and ask whether she was depositing dead animals on my porch.

"I just want it to go away."

"The squirrels?"

"And birds and a groundhog. Everything," I said, almost weeping.

"I'll take care of it then. All I want is for you to be happy," he said, with a horrible gentleness. Condescension.

"Argh," I said.

"Please, Thee, please just listen. I was thinking you should try getting a baby-sitter, so you could have a little time to yourself."

Of course it made sense. It was infuriating. Another accusation, the assumption that I wasn't whole as things were, that I was silently brewing discontent, that he could smell my secret.

"Thee?" He reached for me again, and I let him touch my arm. I despised him for being slightly right. "Think about it from the outside for a second, from my point of view, if you can stand that."

"Of course I can stand that. I'm not unhappy with you. Do you think I'm unhappy with you?"

"I think you deserve to be happier. It isn't about me, it's about you. You don't like things to be about you."

Of course I did, I thought. I didn't often get the chance, but of course I did. I fumed and noticed how soft his fingertips were, how long his fingers, how his eyes had flecks of brown marring the infuriating blue.

"You're a wonderful mother and a wonderful wife, and sometimes I think you could use a little time to think about who else you are, spend some time with your friends or go out, I don't know—"

"Stop making suggestions," I said. I tugged on his arm, bringing him closer. "I'm not mad at you, but I don't want you to be mad at me, either."

"Why would I be mad?" he pulled away slightly.

"Because I want to use that vacation time for myself. I want you to take care of the kids. I want to go on a trip, Outward Bound. I know it's a lot of work to take care of the kids and it's your vacation, but I want to go. Just five days. I plan to go. Is that okay?"

Caius sat further away from me and looked at me as if I were some mysterious object in his bed—a mermaid, a unicorn.

"Of course it's okay," he said. "This trip—it's something you want to do? I mean, of course it's okay." He said, as if deciding. "You deserve a change. I can manage the kids easily. They have school anyway, right?"

"Some of the time. Most of the work will be Iris." My hand was shaking under the blanket. I'd finally told him. This meant I was going.

"No problem. I'm their dad, after all. Iris is no big deal. Do you know some good sitters who might help me out?"

I laughed. Then I pressed my mouth against his collarbone and let the frustration beneath my skin, the relief and complication and new anxieties—I was going!—turn into want.

"Okay," said Caius, letting me kiss him but not relaxing, not until I'd climbed atop him and we'd made love, speechless and fast, almost angry. Then he fell asleep, breathing the deep breath of satisfaction, of innocence, of being guiltlessly able to think about himself from time to time.

I couldn't sleep, so I got up and put on Caius's robe. I could still smell him, salty, the ghost of his aftershave on my cheek and my shoulder. My thighs were sore and it felt good, chapped by love. Usually, we talked things through and through. Usually I let Caius lead me to a resolution. But for this strife, for his wanting something else for me, as if I were too small to determine that for myself, for his genuine concern for the separate me, for the me who spent hours in motherhood that would become hours with myself when Iris went to school, a gradual loss and not obvious to someone not looking closely, sex was a satisfying temporary solution. A distraction. An attention. And I was going away. He was helping me so I could go away from them all, from him. He thought it was a good idea, even.

But because he was a man, there were things he wouldn't ever understand, things of the body. Like being a mother. And with someone like Amanda, for whom the initiation of absolute belonging was fresh, the motherhood was raw and visible. I supposed that was part of what attracted me to her, what made me feel something close to empathy but mixed with sympathy and some jealousy. She was a mother, and she had found a way to keep some of herself, too; she let work reel her in from the sea of her child's needs.

As happened whenever I thought of Amanda, I also thought of the dead things on my porch, and the loop of suspicion made my heart race—I would never get to sleep. When had these horrible gifts started arriving? I'd thought it was recently, but when I thought of my sketch pad I remembered the first bird—and realized it had been going on since winter. I was shocked it had gone on so long: since one winter day after one winter night—the day after Amanda came home so late, the day after we'd accidentally kissed.

I went into the living room, hoping I wouldn't wake anyone, but found Tia on the couch. She was drinking scotch; I could smell it across the room, a sharp, unpleasant smell. Caius always said it was warm, buttery, but I could never get past the terrible stench of alcohol.

"I'm sorry, I didn't want to bother you to ask." She shook the glass at me. No ice, muted sloshing in the grainy light.

"It's Caius's. You can drink it all." I laughed.

"Do I sense strife in the castle of marital bliss?" Tia sipped her drink.

"No, actually. It isn't about us. Or him. I'm just . . . thinking . . .," I said, letting the sentence peter out.

"Ah, thinking. I used to do that sometimes. I'm kind of more into doing these days."

"I hate having dead things on my doorstep," I said.

"What does Caius think of your dead animal problem?"

"He actually thinks we should file a police report."

"Really? Why don't you put up a spy camera?"

I laughed, but actually it had occurred to me. I wanted to catch someone in the act. I wanted to stop feeling attacked. Even if I minded being treated like a child, I didn't mind that Caius said he'd take care of it. Whatever that meant.

I sat on the couch by Tia, almost touching her, happy to have her, happy she'd be going. I realized what I really wanted was to have all my choices back, to know when I decided each thing—marrying and having babies and moving back to this house where who I was before followed me around like an out-of-synch shadow.

I could feel Tia's heat beside me on the couch.

"It's hard to imagine what it's like for you," she said. "I'm here and I'm watching, but I don't really know." She sighed. Then she started talking about her married boyfriend and the second of clarity was gone. It was all right not to tell her my own news, it was all right to plan something that might change me alone in my family, somewhere I'd lived for a long time.

As I drove Tia to the airport, she recounted our times in the woods behind the house. I was feeling guilty and relieved because she was almost gone—I could go back to being a mother and a wife and an abstract friend, not the kind who listened with absolute attention, but one with license to be distracted.

"And acorns! We had something with acorns! I think it was a spell about our parents, something about them doing everything we said—"

"Did it work?" Oliver asked. He and Iris were in the backseat, hearing everything as usual.

"Oh." Tia slipped out of her shoulder belt and turned around. "Your mom's parents were tough. So tough. You don't realize how easy you have it. You should have seen all the chores she had to do."

"Really?" Oliver was restless, shifting in his seat, kicking the back of mine. His voice was loud with unexpressed physical energy.

"She had to milk the cows and ride the horses."

"Horse! Horse! Neigh says horse!" said Iris.

"That's right," said Tia, laughing. "You never told me about this part of motherhood." She touched my arm.

"No way," said Oliver. "You had cows?"

"No," I said.

"And we used to play hide-and-seek on Spirit Night, and your mom was never afraid of the boys with shaving cream and eggs, like me."

"I think you've got it backward," I said to Tia.

"Nope," she said, turning away from my children to look out the window at New Jersey. "Your mom was never really afraid of anything."

But then she took it away, the stretch of warmth that had grown across my collarbone, the forgiveness, the connection.

"Now your grandmother," she said, turning to her diminutive audience, "didn't like much mess or bother."

"Oh, she wasn't that fussy," I said, feeling my defenses in my fingertips, my heated cheeks.

"You know"—Tia turned to me—"My mother never liked your mother. You know that, right?"

"I do not," I said, affronted not only by the content but the context.

"Thought all those flowers and children were a bit too perfect."

Right in front of my kids. I repressed the urge to shush her. Instead, I drove on toward her departure.

May

20

Amanda

"I am going to be fat forever," I said to Rosanna, leaning into the receiver and picking through my in-box as if there was anything I didn't already know about in there. Didn't already know about and hadn't already avoided all day. I felt tender, exhausted, irritable.

"You're just PMSing," said Rosanna. "Come to the gym with me after work."

Of course she knew better. After work I would run to make the earliest PATH. I would almost fall asleep on New Jersey Transit and would be woken by some young turk screaming into his cell phone.

"I should join the gym again," I said, but the very idea exhausted me. Rosanna and I had had exactly one lunch together since I'd been back, because if I ate lunch at my desk I could leave earlier, and I always needed to leave earlier—earlier than Neethi, earlier than Jessica Gravitas, earlier certainly than Rosanna, who came in at eleven and left around ten P.M., with long breaks in between for workouts or cocktails in the bar below street level on Broadway that I'd heard about for six months. But hadn't seen. Who needed bars, anyway? What I needed was a diet and a personal trainer. Or else a masseuse and a long, long nap.

"Babe," said Rosanna. "I've got something I want to show you for the Rose book. It's gorgeous."

"Did you settle on a photo composite?"

"No, just come see it."

Her office was still a shock, each time I entered. Piles and piles of paper, canvases leaned up against her floor lamp, one or two square feet of floor space clear in the entire room.

"I couldn't say on the phone," she said, as I stepped over to her light table in anticipation of a slide, "but I think I may be in trouble here."

"Rosanna?"

She closed the door. "I have to clean up my office. I don't think I can. But this time they actually mean it."

"Annual review?"

"Yep. Here's the jacket art."

She held up a purply sheet, a photo of a woman climbing right out of the frame, the jagged rocks in the background, the title set like cairns in the background. It was gorgeous, perfect, and suddenly I thought the Rose book was going to be big.

"Wow. Who's your freelancer?"

"Me. Will you help me clean this place up?"

"Yes," I said, knowing I would lose the rest of my afternoon now, that she'd do the same for me, and that it would be just as awful in a day or two.

I took Thursday at home instead of Friday, because Carole had a doctor's appointment in the morning. I took Malena out for a walk in the stroller after Aaron left, hoping to "tire her out with the fresh air," as my mother suggested. I was also calculating how many calories I would burn by walking, but I stopped in town for a café mocha, thereby making the point moot. I called Rosanna from my cell phone on the way back, but she wasn't in the office—or else she had already lost her phone under the paper. As I carried the carriage up the steps, I noticed a strange odor coming from behind the planter that still held last fall's dead mums. It was not the odor of a dead plant but a dead animal. We kept the spare key in that plant, in a fake rock. For a minute, I was afraid when I saw it, a tuft of incongruous fur, twitching, but only from the breeze, not from any extant life. A big, fat squirrel. It stank. I took a few tissues from my pocket to grip the thing and walked to the back of the yard with it, flung it over the fence and into the woods.

All out of kilter, I was willing Malena to nap in the Pack 'n Play in the living room when I saw the letter come in the slot. It wasn't time for the mail yet; Betty, the postal carrier, usually came around four, and UPS was midmorning, but it wasn't even ten yet. Just one envelope, just one pale hand reaching into my house to deposit it. I knew those fingers, those particular spade-shaped nails. It was Thea, dropping something into the slot in my door, probably assuming I wasn't home. And since I didn't particularly want to talk to Thea, I waited, standing like a startled animal, until I heard her steps leave my porch.

"Dear Mr. and Mrs. Katz," the letter read.

It has come to our attention that some repeated vandalism has occurred at our residence. Perhaps you are aware that carrion, or dead animals, have been repeatedly deposited at our doorstep. This is to inform you that we are going to turn this matter over to the police, as the acts appear to have malicious intent. If you have any information to report, please contact us within the next twenty-four hours, as we plan to alert the authorities after that time.

Sincerely,

Mr. and Mrs. Caius Caldwell

"What?" I said aloud, but then I felt ferociously sick. I ran to the kitchen, thinking I might actually vomit. They thought we were putting dead things on their doorstep. They thought we were that pathetic.

○

I called Aaron twice at work but couldn't bring myself to tell him. I was too confused. I wanted too much to talk about it, and there was always someone in his office, someone holding on the other line. By the time he got home, I was sure I should be really, really angry, but I just handed the letter to him, before a kiss, before handing him Malena, before saying hello.

Aaron looked at me, then the letter. He put his briefcase down and read it standing. He smelled like the train, a strange mix of bergamot and exhaust. His face looked strange, then lit. He finished, smiled at me, and laughed. He laughed.

"What's so funny?" I asked. "They think we're committing malicious deeds."

"They don't say that," said Aaron. "Technically." He laughed again, and this was why I loved him. Because he laughed.

"I found a dead squirrel today," I said.

"Two mice," said Aaron.

"You didn't tell me," I said.

"Didn't think it mattered," he said. "And a bird."

"Yuck."

"Carrion, or dead animals," he intoned, grandiose, and chuckled again.

Then, of course, he worked himself into an impenetrable fury. He kissed Malena and she cried, sensing his mood. He didn't change his clothes; instead, he went into the office and drafted his own letter in legalese. It said we were now aware of the problem; that they should indeed go to the police, because we'd had the same problem ourselves, though we hadn't leaped past the obvious conclusion that someone's cat was overzealous.

I slept badly that night and went downstairs rather than wake Aaron with my restlessness. I read the letter twice, then peeled back the curtain in the living room before I settled in to try to sleep on the couch. I glared at their house, amazed that they could carry such a thing so far. Thea, whom I'd kissed, who'd held my girl in her own arms, whose cookies I'd eaten. I thought she must be a very sad person indeed, and wondered if this was the cost of spending too much time in your house—you might begin to think people were setting siege upon your castle when really they were just trying to live their lives with as many of the ordinary pleasures as possible and keep a respectful distance from their neighbors.

For three weeks, I did as Aaron suggested and let it go. He never mailed his letter—said we shouldn't escalate matters. But each time I drove up to our house and saw theirs, that fortress of ill-directed blame and buttery guilt, I seethed. It hurt my gut; Rosanna told me I had to stop taking Mylanta or I'd ruin my chi.

"I'll ruin *her* chi," I told her. Rosanna crossed her arms in that neat way she had, folding herself up like a bird, holding warmth to her breast while suggesting the possibility of flight.

"You should save that anger for something more worthy, like Neethi's postponing Rose from the list *again*."

It was a kind attempt at distraction, but it didn't work. The only thing that made me feel any better was imagining my revenge. First, I thought of confrontation, of going to her house wearing a threatening black suit and carrying her letter and something bulky in my pocket that could ostensibly be a gun. I'd never actually handled a gun, but I'd watched enough spy dramas on TV to have learned the gun-revelation gesture, hand in pocket, sly grimace. Of course I wouldn't have a gun, but I'd scare her, I'd threaten her, I'd let her sweat out her worst fear, that someone might actually be *angry* with her and actually face up to her. With a weapon, to boot. I knew from living with her that she was afraid of confrontation, of facing what she had done. Which was why so much of what she did was beyond reproach. She was aggressively nice. Until now.

Aaron explained to me that making a fuss would only make me look guilty. I flirted with him instead of letting him know just how pathetic Thea's accusations made me feel.

"Me? Maybe they think it's you," I said.

"Nah, you're the guilty girl."

"I'll show you guilty," I said, biting his neck.

And I knew he was seething, too, that he held his own fury inside. It wore away at him like a stone in a sock, blistering soft skin. I wanted to forget, to excuse her, but it wasn't in my nature. Our houses were just too big, I thought, too cavelike, dark with nights and our body heat, and we became fierce mama bears, feral, protecting what was ours with blind intensity.

I thought about collecting our own dead animals, or roadkill, of packaging them neatly in a gift bag. I'd rest tissue paper over the corpses. I'd deposit them on her mat and ring the bell.

Or maybe it would be more effective to pack them in bakery boxes, retie that thin white-and-red string that came from a metal roll dispenser at the back of Wyckoff bakery and always smelled as though it, too, were made of butter and powdered sugar.

Finally, I had to stop imagining and do something. I wasn't someone who could contain actions for too long without letting them spring out of me somehow, without giving in. But it couldn't be traceable; it couldn't make me seem guilty when she was the only one who ought to feel ashamed.

That was it. I strolled Malena to the post office in town on a damp Saturday when Aaron was working and the streets smelled of impending rain. I bought one of those prepaid postcards, anonymous and innocuous by itself, but when I took it home, I scrolled it into my typewriter from high school, the one I'd moved from apartment to apartment as if it might someday have reason to express its letters again despite the computer age. I typed *Mrs. Thea Caldwell* and her address, thinking I couldn't blame Caius, after all, with his rummy mouth and dazzling eyes.

On the message side I typed a single word: SHAME.

It took twenty minutes to get a sleeping Malena back into her stroller, but I knew I had to do it before I changed my mind. My heart hurt with effort as I put the card in my coat pocket and buckled Malena in—she was awake now and bucking with protest. I carried the stroller down the front steps and started down the street, my heart still hard at work. I thought of all the arteries and veins at work keeping me moving, alert, all the motion required internally just to stay alive. Malena was crying as I reached the mailbox on the corner, the only mailbox for blocks and blocks. What had become of them all? Did they disappear with the addition of a second car in each driveway? As I pulled open the mouth of the big blue box Malena stopped fussing and began to croon, a sweet, quiet singing that reminded me of Thea's singing to my daughter. I'd seen the way she'd watched Malena, greedy. Her love was possessive. She was someone who attached herself to those she loved like a parasitic orchid. She bloomed only on the crowns of others. I wasn't ever going to be like that—to attach from crown to root. Nor would I be like my mother, always keeping a distance to prevent excessive attachment. I couldn't let a night go by without checking my daughter after she was asleep. I needed the last sweep of softness—my finger on her cheek, or if I dared lean over into the crib, the breathing of her breath, sweet, apricots and almonds.

I imagined bringing the card back home, tearing it into a dozen pieces, stuffing it into the empty milk carton already in the trash. I imagined Thea's face as she read it, puzzled at first, then red with recognition. I remembered how pale she was, almost fishlike. How had I ever thought her beautiful? She had an asymmetrical nose and too-thin lips. She had a hard heart, a suspicious mind.

I wasn't sure I could ever let it go. I looked at it again, my note, my retribution. She was religious at heart. I was giving her back her sin—sinner that I was myself. It was a damp day, and the drizzle was about to start as I let the card fall into the wide mouth of the mailbox. Going. Gone.

July
2001

21

Amanda

"Oh a very happy birthday to our country," said Aaron, stroking the edge of my Mother's Day silk robe as if it were part of my skin.

"I'm sleeping," I said, though I'd been listening for Malena, of course, even when Aaron and I were tangled like branches in a stream. I was on vacation with relatively little controversy, since almost no one was at work for the long weekend anyway. Carole was on vacation, visiting her mother in Boca. And wonder of wonders, after two straight months of working Saturdays and half of Sunday, Aaron was home for four whole days in a row. We hadn't had sex for so long I had wondered whether I liked it anymore. Whether he liked me anymore. Whether he was getting some somewhere else, though I knew better, because even his kisses good-bye at five-thirty in the morning or kisses hello at nine at night when I was already beached on the couch were so abrupt and hard I knew he was trying not to want me.

"Liked that," he said, grinning ridiculously.

"Me, too." Frankly, it had taken about half an hour for me to warm up. I used to be able to switch off, or switch on, as it were, to move easily from the ordinary body to the body at play. But since pregnancy, it was more complicated, like a whole house full of signals and fuses. It was worth it, though; when I finally came, I'd cried with the relief of letting go. Then I'd fallen asleep and drooled on Aaron's arm. Now he was assembling himself, that familiar body, hardly changed since we'd married, the lean curve of his shoulder as he pulled on his T-shirt, stepped into his jeans. He hadn't shaved yet, so he looked like a college kid, and I touched my face where his cheeks had scraped mine with pleasant abrasion.

"I'm going out to survey the grounds," he said.

"I'm going to continue sleeping," I said. "Don't wake her."

"Right," he said. Since he'd been home, Aaron had been buzzing around the house with purpose, painting the peeling portion of fence by the garage, planting impatiens in undivided clumps by the front walkway, fiddling with the leaky faucet in the powder room until we had to switch it off and leave a message for the plumber. I adored his handyman mode, though I resisted the urge to make him a list of things that actually needed repair.

"I'm going to tear out that poison ivy in back by the Martins'," he said.

This was actually on my mental list. "Wear gloves," I said, imagining my husband dotted with welts.

I meant to fall asleep again, but I kept hearing Malena stir, though each time I checked she was still asleep, obliging us with a three-hour nap for the first time in months. Of course, I picked at the notion that Carole was training her to sleep all day so she wouldn't have to play all the games she listed on her little My Day sheets we read like Torah when we came home. At least I did. Shape-sorter play. Water play with dishpan and spoons. What floats?!?! Having come home from work, I couldn't help thinking, *Shit floats. Shit and witches.* But then I shed my jacket and held my girl and let myself believe in wonder for a while.

I crept downstairs in my robe and poured myself a glass of apricot iced tea, then tried to stir the sugar in, but instead of melting it swirled like a sandstorm in the sun-orange liquid. I could hear Aaron thumping around outside and I sighed, wondering whether we should get Malena a water table for the backyard or whether it would attract wasps. Some kids were screaming outside, the sounds of summer play. I'd gotten used to it, to Thea hollering for her kids across the lawns, to all the chatter and argument and the striking sounds of basketballs. Sometimes Oliver had a friend over and they used the fence as a backboard for a soccer ball. Aaron had asked them to stop just yesterday. I could never bring myself to say anything; I just seethed, calculating the cost of the broken slats.

I couldn't imagine going back to work when my respite ended the next day. Of course, once Aaron was gone, it would be easy enough to imagine. He hadn't let go of the office so completely for years. But now the house stuff was filling his empty hands. I realized Aaron didn't know how to sit still anymore. When he sat on the floor to play with Malena, he always had a cup of coffee, a newspaper, a *New Yorker*, a crossword puzzle, and a jiggling leg. His best attention was divided, and I wondered what else he had been thinking about while he ran his tongue down the back of my knee. Had he been mentally measuring the surface area of the shed, which he wanted to paint? He only had one more day; he would never finish. He'd have to come home after work and go out to paint in the dark.

"Aaron?" I called out the open back window. "She's still asleep, come inside for some iced tea, Aaron. Aaron?"

As I stepped over to the back door, I saw his form, backing up, oddly bearlike, his bare arms stained with something, the green of his law school T-shirt splattered. Had he started painting the shed? Was he retarring the driveway?

He thudded against the door, so I stepped down to open it, and he was saying so quietly I almost couldn't hear him, "Nine-one-one, please. You need to call nine-one-one."

My husband wasn't splattered with paint or tar. He was bloody, even his hair had a streak like highlights. There was a bloody handprint on his arm, and he held a girl in his arms, a girl who was clutching her hand even as he gripped it, too, his hand over hers, and the source of the blood seemed to be that embrace of fingers. Someone was coming up behind him, a boy. He was tall, hollow looking, and oddly clean, gripping a red bandanna as if it were proof of something. Had the boy cut the girl? Had my husband bloodied someone? Why was it so quiet? Why wasn't there ominous music to warn me that Something Very Bad had happened?

"Give me that," barked my husband to the boy. "And Amanda, please call," he said, as he tied the bandanna around the girl's wrist.

It wasn't until I was explaining to the operator that the emergency was medical, that I didn't know what had happened, that someone was bleeding, a lot, that I realized the girl was Carra. She was a horrible gray color, but her lips looked stung, fat and worried. I wondered whether one's lips grew fat just before death. My heart was slower, my own limbs tingled.

"They're sending an ambulance," I explained, as I hung up the phone and jogged back to them. She wasn't crying so much as moaning, and the boy touched her bare leg as she lay across my husband's lap on my living room floor. The rug drank up blood like spilled wine.

"She put her hand through the glass on your shed door," said the boy, his words staccato and very, very quiet.

"Why were you by our shed door?" It wasn't meant to sound harsh, but the boy just stood there with his baby mouth and hard eyes. I still didn't understand. It wasn't an accusation. Was there some reason they needed to be in our backyard? Were they rescuing a hurt bird? Stealing sunflowers? What the hell?

"We weren't trying to steal anything," he said. "We were just, um, making out."

Carra looked at me. "Just leaned . . .," she started, but couldn't h. I was half-afraid blood would come out of her mouth, that been so sliced by our window she would start to leak and spout from every part of her body. She was still awake, and it would help no one if I panicked. I winced as Aaron retied the bandanna, wrapping and tugging fiercely, his face almost angry, his hands slick with her blood.

What the hell was this girl doing with her boyfriend in our yard—did thirteen-year-olds have sex on their neighbors' lawns?

"Go get her parents," Aaron said to the boy, but he just stood, stunned. I looked at her long face, the lovely cheekbones, her mother's lantern jaw. Was this the kind of people we were, blaming a bleeding girl for her own mistake? I had the quick ugly thought that it wasn't her mistake, it was Thea's—this happened on Thea's watch. We were horrible. No, I was horrible. Aaron was good. I could learn from my bloodied husband.

"Should we take a look at it?" I asked. "Maybe wash it off? Do you think it needs stitches?" Carra was horribly pale, almost blue. Her bruised lips opened and shut without producing words.

"Did you guys do any drugs?" I asked the boy.

"Fuck no," he said, looking away.

"It matters," my husband said.

"We just cut through the woods and made out. I smoke, but she doesn't," he said. He touched her sneaker with his own, afraid of any contact of skin. I guessed they'd licked and sucked each other, that they'd pressed against each other's bodies as if feeding their starving selves, and now he couldn't even touch her. What would I do when Malena became one of these, a dangerous, beautiful creature, protowoman? Why were boys always so afraid? Carra looked limp, one arm atop the other, her legs akimbo in my husband's lap on the living room floor.

"I think it's an artery," said Aaron. "It's gushing." And to illustrate his point, blood poured through the bandanna and onto his lap, a river of blood. Aaron, who usually passed out at the sight of blood, gripped Carra's arm as though he were holding her together. His other hand supported her back, and I couldn't help thinking that just minutes before he'd been pushing into me, holding my back as he moved. God, this was real. This was no ordinary two-stitches-and-go-home cut. This girl was really damaged.

"It just cracked into two pieces," said the boy, not looking at Carra, not comforting his girlfriend.

"Go get her parents," Aaron repeated, and the boy finally went.

"The pane was loose," I said starting to feel panicky. "I kept meaning to get it fixed."

"Never mind," said Aaron. "Never mind." And then the sirens came close and Malena, upstairs, began wailing along with them.

・ 22 ・

Thea

"It's not that I'm litigious," I whispered to Caius. "It's just—*nerve damage*, Caius. She probably won't swim next year. What if she can't write?" It was either fury or terror; I wanted to choose fury.

"No one's suggesting that," said my husband. He wore the hospital bracelet that had allowed him to spend the night. I wanted to do it but he'd insisted, and at home, curt and exhausted by my own fear, I had made Oliver and Iris macaroni and cheese from a box and frozen peas, which Iris pinched with her fingers and didn't eat. I felt as though Carra were dead, all night, as though I were with my new family, the family in the gray lens. As though Caius were dead, too. I practiced the dull motions of mourning.

But no one died. Carra was sedated; a hand surgeon had reattached a ligament while Caius stood by in scrubs. She was stitched and sent to recovery, then to her own private room in the same hospital where she was born. Caius slept on a chair. I wanted to be there, but someone had to be with the other children, and as usual, I was that someone.

"The surgeon said scarring and temporary loss of sensation. Temporary," Caius repeated. He finally looked tired, but calm and pressed nonetheless. There was a small stain on the cuff of his blue-striped button-down that could've been coffee and could've been blood.

"She said she'd been meaning to fix it, the boy told me. Mitch." I still had trouble calling him that, the toddler I'd seen babbling in Wolof in a stroller back in the days of his nanny's reign. "It was an accident waiting to happen."

I wasn't going to tolerate accidents. I wasn't going to let someone else's negligence ruin my daughter. The bandage swallowed her entire arm. She was plugged into a bag of blood, for God's sake, Caius's blood. He'd donated just before her surgery, in case she needed it, and she did, she needed us, blood and bones. Her eyes were bruised and her skin looked pallid. My girl felt cold under my hands, and I asked for blankets twice, but the nurses just gave me a look. I would tell Caius, he would make them bring blankets. Embarrassingly enough, now that I knew she was going to survive, my selfish thought was that now I couldn't go away to Outward Bound in September. I was that egocentric, and I wanted to repent, wished I could ask God to forgive me, wished I knew what I believed.

"I think, actually, Aaron saved her from much worse," said Caius, cupping my hand, then squeezing a little too hard. I pulled away. I couldn't tolerate being soothed. Coddled. I thought of coddled eggs: my mother made them, in six aluminum cups that the spoon scraped in a shivering sound that hurt me even more than the bleedy yolks.

"I need a shower," he said. "I'm going home. Did you call a sitter for this afternoon?"

"No," I said. "I did not call a sitter. I left Oliver at camp and Iris with Mrs. Chen, but we have to pick her up by noon. We don't have a sitter, they all have summer jobs. We don't just up and go to the hospital. We don't have backup," I said, almost weeping.

"Fine," said Caius. "We'll just come in shifts."

He ran a tired hand through his uncombed hair. He looked ready to be free of me, and for a minute, before I remembered why we were here, that he'd been up all night, that we were both raw nerves disguised by a thin layer of parenthood, I couldn't wait for him to go. I was scared.

She was home the next day, bandaged, doped. Mitch had come to visit. He was wearing a dress shirt even though it was July. He was so thin in his jeans I wanted to reach out and test to see if there were legs in there or just sticks. Mostly, she slept. I felt vigilant, as though I were supposed to be doing something now, after the fact. I hadn't given up on the idea that it was somehow Amanda's fault. She'd been the one to say it; she'd said the window needed fixing. And if I couldn't keep my daughter from exploring the woods of her own adolescence, at least I could reprimand those who left bear traps on their lawns.

Caius went to work for a few hours, but he was home by mid-afternoon, spraying Iris with the hose on the lawn. She wore her first-ever two-piece, her baby belly already thinned. She shrieked with pleasure as he soaked her and she ran: approach, avoidance, approach. I couldn't bear it. I brought out a towel.

"Too much sun," I said, standing beside my husband. "She'll get burned."

"I put on a gallon of sunscreen," said Caius. His nose was red; I was sure he only meant on Iris. The day was too bright and the lawn was too green. We were both ready to fight about something; maybe we needed it.

"No," I said, "between ten and three a half hour is more than enough." Iris pouted but relented. I gave her cheese and crackers and she shivered at the kitchen table in a terry cover-up. Then Caius switched on the TV for her, something I'd never have done unless there was dinner to make.

"You're done with this suing them thing, I hope," he said, once Iris was consumed by *Dora the Explorer.*

"I'm still thinking about it," I said.

"I just don't understand what you have against the woman—besides the fact that she left her things on the couch when she stayed here," said Caius. He picked up a bag of veggie chips and tugged at the top. He was going to open it, eat a few, and let the rest go stale.

"And that evil postcard," I said.

"Well, they were angry. We were kind of over the top with our letter, I think. I shouldn't have gotten so territorial." If I were honest with myself, I knew he hadn't wanted to write that letter. He'd written it for me. My protector. And in retrospect I wish he hadn't done it, an awkward, formal thing. I wasn't sure what I wanted from him these days.

"She should have fixed the window," I said, each word a stone. Caius assumed his most irritating mask of emotionlessness.

"I'm going to call them," said Caius. "I'm going to thank him. And her. He went in the ambulance, and she waited at the hospital with the baby until we got there. I know you didn't see her in the waiting room, but she was waiting there, and Malena was crying, and all she wanted to know is whether we still needed her there, whether she could *do* anything."

"He helped her, I know," I said.

"So stop it," said Caius.

I had gone straight into the room; I'd missed Malena climbing around on the waiting-room furniture, I'd missed Amanda's heavy form hovering around my moment of fear and grief. I could imagine her sitting on the chair with her leg up on another, her lushness itself a provocation.

"I kissed her," I told my husband. "Or she kissed me."

He looked up but didn't relinquish his poker face. He walked over to the phone.

"What's their number?" he asked me.

"On the mouth," I said.

Then he smiled, enigmatic. I would hate him if this turned him on.

"Okay," he said. "Are you telling me something I don't know? About you, about her? Or just that you kissed her?"

"Just that we kissed. It was a stressful moment. I mean . . . what I mean is, I don't hate her. Not that I love her. I worked for her. She was impossible." I felt like I was going to throw up. What had I thought this would resolve?

"So you kissed her," he said again, and he smiled again, and I could see he was having an autonomic response to this information, that he was unable not to like the idea. Boys were disgusting.

"Or *she* kissed *you*," he said. "And she was your boss, so that's sexual harassment." Now he was baiting me. It hurt, but he was right, I was being absurd. I wanted it to be someone else's fault Carra had almost bled out in the green of July.

"We should file a lawsuit."

"Ha-ha," I said, angry for my damaged daughter, for myself because I couldn't protect her.

Everyone was at work over there, so we waited until evening to call. Caius dialed the kitchen phone, and I stood beside him holding the phone from the living room. When Amanda answered I imagined, for a moment, that nothing had happened between us, that there had been no letters, no blood, no shame.

Caius thanked her for both of us, his voice calm, serious, charming.

"Let me get Aaron," she said.

"But first," my husband said, "I want you to know she shouldn't have been in your yard, and I apologize. And if any repairs are necessary—"

"Oh, we needed to fix that window anyway," she said, opening the loophole once again. "The pane was loose."

"I wish you had," I blurted out.

"Thea?" she said. "You were listening in?"

As if she needed to have private moments with my husband. "No, I was on all along. Not *listening in*. Calling. You. I wish you had fixed it."

"But we can pay for the repairs now," Caius said, holding up his arm, his hand, a basketball defensive posture. He was blocking me. I seethed but said no more.

"Right, then," said Amanda. "That won't be necessary."

"But thanking your husband will," said Caius. "I think he may've saved our daughter from much greater harm."

"He did," she said, and then she put down the phone. I couldn't stay on to talk to Aaron. He needed to be thanked, but Caius clearly had enough for both of us. Enough thanks and enough forgiveness for us both.

September
2001

23

Thea

"I guess I can call Jasmine to help out in the afternoons?" It was early; the kids were just getting dressed, and Caius was hovering while I packed. I filled a duffel and the internal frame pack, which belonged to my friend Vicky's older son; he'd bought it when he was planning to become an Eagle Scout, before he decided he'd rather spend all his resources on his grunge band and a motorcycle she wouldn't let him ride.

"I made a list for you already," I said. He sighed and went to take a shower.

I had also cooked and frozen dinners. And talked with Iris about it every night, that Mommy was going away but only for a few days, that I'd be back soon, that Daddy could take care of her. She'd been having trouble adjusting to preschool, the same preschool her brother and sister hadn't wanted to leave at pickup, the same bubbly Miss Leigh who made the same adorable tissue-paper butterflies and sand-art projects every fall. When I left Iris, I had to peel her from my leg. When I picked her up, she ran crying to me, as if I'd been gone for months. I resented it, as if she was trying to keep me from going on my trip after all, and I needed my trip. I needed to separate from her for more than two hours. I needed to separate from my house and the sound of the garbage truck every Tuesday at eight-fifteen and Carra's physical therapy appointments reminding me I hadn't been vigilant enough, and the impatiens still expressing their summer exuberance under the dogwood, and my neighbors' houses staring at me, fat on their frames, the same place, the same place, year after year. I needed different air, and my family didn't want to let me go. I was selfish for it, greedy, but if I didn't go soon, I might not be able to see anything clearly anymore. I was so heated up, I started to believe in all those urban myths—self-immolations, alien abduction, and my mother's least favorite idea, mental breakdown.

"People can always control their actions," she'd say, "unless they are impaired. Breakdown means losing control, and you can always maintain control if you just try hard enough."

The long underwear would help me stay in control. The bug spray, the waterproof matches, the compass, the wool socks, the hiking boots I'd been breaking in by walking them around the neighborhood. Caius called them my clodhoppers. I think he may've been worried I was leaving him. And a small, mean part of me liked his worry. I was going away, and when I came back I could forgive everyone for taking me for granted, for letting me cram myself into the small spaces between them, a paste, a grout, a mother and wife in semiliquid form. Of course it wasn't their fault, it was mine. The rain pants would help me stay in control. The wicking T-shirt. The maps. Maybe I wouldn't come back.

Carra still wore a brace for her healing wrist and the welts were noticeable, plum blooms. She said they tingled, and her writing was cramped, but she could write. She wasn't swimming this fall, but she said she didn't want to, anyway.

"I'm doing theater instead," she'd told me. I knew this was because Mitch loved theater; my girl could barely memorize the poems she needed to learn for English class, let alone a collection of lines. It would've been hard to imagine her playing a character— until this summer, when she had been someone new almost every day. I was afraid to leave her for this long, and I was also relieved. I made her promise not to change too much, and she'd winced when she said, "Okay, I promise, Mommy, promise." She'd also invited Mitch to dinner, twice. He made excellent eye contact with the silverware and answered questions in single syllables, while my daughter beamed at him and thought we didn't know she was holding his hand under the table. I wasn't sure what he did in theater— did he play the furniture onstage? I'd just have to wait for a performance.

"Going!" called Caius from downstairs. "I'll drop the kids!" It was as though he was practicing, and I thanked him aloud.

"Momma," said Iris, coming in from her bedroom. Her face was still lined from the pillowcase; she wore the special silvery fairy ballet slippers we'd bought her as a first-day-of-preschool present. When she was home, they were on her feet. They were already stained with chocolate pudding and bathwater and grass from their one unsanctioned trip onto the lawn.

"It's not a school day," she said.

"I'm afraid it is, my love. But I know you're going to have fun. You're going to do the water tables with Miss Leigh today. And after school, I'll take you to the grocery store, okay?" I'd meant to do the shopping while I had my childless hours, but already I was conceding, bargaining. If she didn't cry when I dropped her off, it would be worth it to buy six extra items she picked out, to have to take her in and out of the cart six or seven times, to forget half my coupons because she wanted to play with the credit-card machine at the checkout. I was going away.

"Can I wear that?" She picked up the wool shirt I'd borrowed from Caius. He never wore it, but he'd had it since the day I met him at Lakes of the Clouds. It came down to the floor on Iris, a checkered dress.

"I think it's a little hot for today," I said, trying to pry it from her.
"No!" cried Iris. "It's beautiful!"

I'd almost allowed myself to forget the letter, the postcard, the police interview until the doorbell rang, and it was James McBean, who graduated from the high school two years before I did, played soccer, hung out in the halls with a crowd who never smoked but stuck chewed cinnamon gum on the lockers, who took turns shouting rude bleats at passing freshmen for kicks. Now he had four kids of his own and he sat in his car by the speed-measuring sign— SPEED LIMIT: 25; YOUR SPEED: 00—with a Starbucks cup and his cell phone. He was in the local free paper, commended for special service to seniors. He sounded tired but kind. Four kids could do that to you.

"I wanted to report back to you, Mrs. Caldwell," he said, smiling reflexively at Iris in her nightgown, slippers, and the wool shirt.

"Right, the animals!" I said, and I realized I was holding a bottle of water-purification tablets in my hand, gripping them in the hope of concealing them from Iris's interest. I opened the door to Officer McBean, to Jimmy, but he held up his hand.

"Don't need to come in. It's been a bit of a misunderstanding, Ma'am," he said, scratching the back of his neck. It was going to be hot, that choice September made daily—fall or summer still. Summer. The lawn hissed with the last of the cicadas.

"The apprehended individual—okay, just between you and me, it was your old neighbor, that Tia Larkspur's mother. D'you know what ever happened to Tia? She was a nice girl. Anyway, the mother seems to be mentally altered. Senile. So I don't think it's intentional. She seems to think she's saving the animals. The other victim—same thing happened at someone else's house, anyway— isn't pressing charges. It's up to you. We don't know for sure if it was her every time, of course—"

"Of course I don't want to press charges," I said.

As I closed the door, I felt a mixture of recognition and shock. And I thought of Tia calling her mother batty. And as I cajoled Iris out of the wool and into her dress, I decided it wasn't senility only that made Mrs. Larkspur leave the animals, or rescue, but beneath it a gold vein of contempt for my mother—perhaps for me—*all those flowers and children, a bit too perfect.* Wasn't this the same contempt and competition we all carried, small eggs, when we watched other people and their children?

I'd let myself forget it until now, the letter, like purposely forgetting a worrisome mole. I never saw Amanda anymore, or if I did, I pretended not to. I realized the letter was my own dead squirrel, that maybe I should apologize; that I had been far too mean and too afraid, that I still believed deep down she'd started it. She'd degraded my way of life. She'd said she'd be so bored. She'd moved into Tia's house. And my house. And I missed Malena again, wishing I could be done with it, or that maybe I could do it over. I bundled Iris and her special toy frog into the car so I could drop her off, come home, finish packing. *Shame,* I thought. It sat on my heart like a tick, drinking and clutching. I would have to wait until it had its fill and let me go.

24

Amanda

When I filled out the 450 forms for the new obstetrician, who was going to help me determine why my period, after being regular for seven months, had disappeared entirely, I had to be honest in filling out the line that read "Who may we thank for your referral?" and write Thea's name. I almost left it blank. Then I imagined how it might feel when she came in next time, loitering in the waiting room among the boxes of well-drooled-upon stuffed bunnies and single pieces of puzzles and game parts, the few *Highlights* magazines and three racks of fresh *Parenting* and *Fit Pregnancy*. She would be trying not to think about the weigh-in, the finger stick to check sugar, the paper gown and the feel of metal stirrups on her heels, and the woman behind the glass, perhaps the same one with brittle blond hair and red-lined bright blue eyes, who might say, "Oh, thank you for sending us Amanda, by the way." Then she would have to remember that she'd had her husband send us that ridiculous letter. That my husband had saved her daughter's life. Then she would have to think of Malena and how she'd quit, and how she'd accused me of having the sort of wrath that inspired dead-animal deposits. And she'd see just how ridiculous she was being. I imagined how she had felt finding these gifts with regularity—disgusted, vaguely afraid. But I wasn't afraid, just annoyed. Then the police called to tell us they'd apprehended an elderly woman. Mentally altered. In fact, the former inhabitant of our house. I'd long since let the annoyance about the animals go. I remembered the shoes lined up on the porch when we first visited the house; I could easily forgive those strange trespasses from her world into the ordinary one. But I couldn't forgive Thea for thinking it was me.

In the doctor's office, I was too nervous to be angry. I knit a tissue, braided wound-up strands of worried cotton. I bit my cuticles, but that hurt. I was afraid in a sort of pleasant way, afraid because I'd used a pregnancy test kit after I was late, expecting it to be negative, and it had not been. And I had told Aaron and we'd both explained it away with readjusting hormones, because we'd been careful all along, at least most of the time. But who had time to remember a diaphragm every time there was a minute and enough energy for sex—the opportunity brief and occasional as an eclipse?

And the nurse took my urine away and came back to the weigh-in with a knowing look. And on my way home I stopped at the Rite Aid for prenatal vitamins, thinking perhaps I felt a little nauseated, thinking perhaps it was better to go through this now, before I had time to think too much about it. I had no idea how I would ever have enough capacity in my heart to let something, someone, as exquisitely necessary as my Malena in along with her.

Of course she'd be the first person I saw when I got out of my car. Thea stood behind her husband's silver sedan in her driveway, loading things into a huge backpack in the trunk. It was September fifth, too late for her kids to be going off to summer camp. And

Thea was alone at the trunk. I realized I'd almost never seen her alone.

"Hey," I said, and louder, "Hey, Thea." Like a girl in the school yard calling for friend or fight. It may've been aggressive, but I was a pregnant woman now.

She looked up from her trunk but didn't stop stuffing items into the backpack. A fluffy pink sweater. A box of granola bars. How dare she have ordinary comforts? She'd accused *me*.

"Hey," I said again, coming up to the fence. Of course you couldn't tell yet, but I was still worried she might magically detect my pregnancy. Aaron didn't know. He wouldn't know until he came home.

"I did *not* put dead animals on your doorstep!" I called out to her.

Could this ever be patched over, or would the roots of conflict keep raising the sidewalk squares, making a gap for kids to trick on bikes and crash into concrete or soft lawns when they missed their landings? Her kids. My kid. My kids.

"Oh," said Thea. She looked up. "I'm going on a trip," she said. "I'm going on Outward Bound, can you believe it?" As if we'd been conversing all along.

"It had nothing to do with us, you know. I still can't believe you wrote that letter."

"Oh, I didn't. It was Caius's idea. He thought—oh, never mind. Amanda, thank you for not pressing charges against Mrs. Larkspur."

Never mind? It wasn't that easy. "Thank *you* for your rude letter."

"I said it wasn't my idea." Her hands were on her hips. This was it—we'd be enemies. I could live with that. I'd will the next tree to drop on her prissy Laura Ashley living room. I'd have parties and invite the other neighbors and not her. Yeah, the lime-sucking Martins could pass out their Christian-right newsletters to all my friends. We could start a heathen intervention program.

"Right," I said, "your hunky husband thought it up all on his own."

It flashed for a second in her face, doubt. She pressed her hands against the things in her trunk. She was waiting for me to leave.

"Did you get the postcard?" I asked, finally, because I wanted to see the wound I'd aimed to inflict.

"No?" she said. For a second I wondered whether it had been lost, wedged into a catalogue, glued to the bottom of the mailbox with moisture; perhaps it went the way of a million other missing pieces of paper, or flew from her box to the street, the sewer, on the damp breeze of accident. But then I knew she was lying. Maybe she hadn't figured out it was from me. Maybe she had other things to regret.

"Really," I said. "Well, you should be ashamed anyway." I wanted to smile. I wanted to be satisfied, but my hands were shaking slightly, even as I told myself I had only done what was necessary.

"Fine," said Thea, fiddling with a strap, then heaving the trunk shut. "I'm sorry. It was silly of me, the whole thing. Quitting like that, too. Do you know, I went to visit Mrs. Larkspur yesterday— she believed she was rescuing them, like babies left for adoption at the castle door of the barren queen."

"Ha!" I couldn't help laughing. I wanted to release her, a little anyway. She *had* said she was sorry. She had read my note, she had taken shame into her house, and I knew it. And it didn't make the wound go away, but something about her would always look innocent and redeeming to me. Something about her was the good neighbor, despite her absurd accusation. "You sound like my sister," I said, relenting just a little.

"You have a sister?"

"You knew that," I said, wondering how she could've forgotten. Maybe she had never listened to me; she'd just tolerated me. I thought of how vulnerable I'd been then—and how kind she was. How lovely she seemed. I'd wanted to be like her, how could that be?

"Yuck, look," she said, pointing to a shifty silver cat that was gliding through my rhododendrons with a bird in its mouth. "I think that's the Martins' new cat."

I nodded, not ready to change the subject.

"They're really so wasteful—predators who don't need to hunt—and here it's after the little brown songbird. Eating up our music."

"Wow. Poetry of the suburbs," I said, meaning it but not forgiving her. "You should write children's books." *Don't blame me for everything*, I thought, trying to hold on to my anger in the face of her stoicism.

"Really?" she said, but she wasn't asking, she was already looking away, discarding my compliment. I could see her correspondence file with Neethi: *Oh, you wouldn't believe my glorious garden!* on scented, lilac-colored stationery. Neethi would expense her ridiculous bouquets in round-bellied vases and packets of testicular poppy seeds when her book went back for a second printing. I gagged at the thought, but then, I was pregnant. I was pregnant.

"How's Carra?" I meant it. It wasn't a dig. Carra had sent Aaron a letter. She'd come by once since she'd been out of the hospital; she'd brought the signature Thea brownies on a paper party plate, but it had felt awkward, as though her father had told her to go, and told her mother to send the silent chocolate gesture. She smiled a lot and said little. We were old, I realized. She was so complex and stunning. I wasn't going to let myself be intimidated by her youth, but I didn't really know what to say to her. She'd shown us her scars, great welts, the stitch marks like notations on a musical score. After she left I had a brownie, which tasted strange—and then I noticed the tiny note in Thea's writing: *Fat-free. Enjoy!*

"She's better, thank you," she said, looking down. We'd fixed the window. Aaron had thrown out his bloodied T-shirt, his favorite from law school, because the stains would never come out. We had a new living room rug.

"Well," said Thea, turning toward her house.

"Nice trip," I said, wanting to make it to my own door first, so much that I tripped on a flagstone and righted myself without allowing a little yelp for the pain in my toe. *Fuck you, fuck you, fuck you*, I thought, but my polite banter exposed me. I still wanted her to like me, how pathetic was that?

A new normal, I thought; it was starting all over for me. I wanted to feel that I was wrong and she was right, but I didn't. My new normal meant having things to give up, like this fight with my neighbor. It meant having inexplicable impulses and longings and the terrifying, exquisite current of another person's pulse inside my skin. Maybe our choices were only enormous because we made them. Thea's mouth on mine, perhaps, was a kiss of her choices meeting mine. Of course I felt guilty; of course she got bored. Perhaps it didn't matter who was doing motherhood the right way—though of course it was I. I leaned my briefcase by the back door and went to look for Carole and Malena. The house smelled of vanilla and the laundry was folded in a basket on the couch: a ladybug dress, Aaron's work socks. Maybe it would all be over so fast and maybe it was just beginning. All the little mountains of decisions—of leaving Malena and coming home, of all the things that would diverge now that there was someone else entering our lives—maybe they were all the quiet music of beginning.

I was on my way home from another doctor's appointment when I saw it from Route 17 South. In the morning I'd had a little bleeding, and I was afraid, less than a week after I knew for sure she or he was real, of losing this child I'd already begun to plan for, to throw up for, to include in my imagination of the future. It was okay, I was okay, she or he was okay. The doctor checked with ultrasound and told me to take the day off and to try to put my feet up on the train—right—but that everything was fine. My hands smelled from the antibacterial soap at the office, strange chemical pear. Then I got back in my car and called the office from my cell phone. I'd miss a meeting with Neethi about the annual reviews; she was asking me to do three of them this year. "A little extra responsibility we can make official after your own review," she'd hinted.

I called Aaron and left a message that everything was fine. He had a breakfast meeting downtown and wasn't answering his cell phone. I was thinking about the rest of the day, about being home with both Malena and Carole, how I'd try to stay upstairs in my own bed with the manuscript I'd brought home and not listen for them out the windows, through the walls. I didn't like being around while someone else took care of Malena now; I could hear her small sounds, her complaints, even Carole's delight as she came closer to walking, balancing against the coffee table, pulling up on a chair. She probably wouldn't walk for a little while, she was only ten months, but she could be early, and I didn't want to miss that particular birth of independence if I didn't have to. Half of me hoped Carole wouldn't tell me if she did walk when I wasn't there. I was thinking about the air conditioner, which rattled, that perhaps today was cool enough not to use it. I was hot at night again; everything about pregnancy was familiar and still new. I hadn't rinsed off all the soap, and my hands stuck to the steering wheel.

Perhaps I'd stop at the supermarket, I was thinking, I could actually cook for dinner, though I wasn't sure I could stomach the meat aisle. Parsley would be nice. Perhaps a parsley pesto. I could manage angel-hair pasta. I thought of stirring it to keep it from sticking. I drove down the hill and saw the skyline of Manhattan and saw the strange smear of smoke rising. Saw that the skyline had been battered, that something was wrong with the city. Something was wrong because one of the towers was missing. I wasn't the only one who pulled over. I stood on the side of the highway with other puzzled strangers, a woman in a red denim jacket with a wretched cough, a tall man with white hair who was sobbing already, a student who had just started classes at Ramapo College today, she told us, psychology was going to be *hard,* as if we knew her, as if this mattered, until someone told us what had happened. I listened to the radio, but it didn't seem real. This was a dream, this was someone else's life, this was not something that happened to New York, to America, to us. I could still smell the antibacterial pear soap. I tried Aaron's phone again and again, and his office, where no one answered, and then I drove home, slow and unsure as a student driver, feeling like a student, less than a student. Feeling as if I'd forgotten how to manage the small responsibilities of life, feeling as if I wouldn't be able to breathe until I knew he was safe.

25

Thea

On the airplane to Maine, I was nervous about being alone. Here I'd wanted this, even imagined the plane ride itself, the buffer between me and the rest of the world, the space, pure and elegant, of not being responsible for anyone else. But it left me with too much time to think about the kids—whether they were angry I'd left, whether Iris was crying and crying, and though I knew it wouldn't hurt her to be without me for a few days, I felt anticipatory empathy. I hurt a little for her powerlessness. And, I supposed, for my own.

Carra pretended not to need me as she recovered, but I still needed to see it, her scar, the wound of separation. I was just going hiking for five days. Backpacking. I ate a roll of Tums on the plane. Pretended to read a book. Stared out the window and hoped I could let New Jersey go, let my family go, let myself have what I needed instead of feeling tethered during my short release from house arrest.

After our flights, we met in the park and ride, six women over thirty, dragging gear off buses and shuttles and out of cars, piling our goods, careful as eggs in a crate, into the back of a big rattly van that smelled of peanut butter and wet wool. We stuck nametags on our chests.

"Memorize," said our leader, a leathery, grinning woman with watery blue eyes and a powerful stance. Only her face was open. "I'm Dora, which should be easy to remember, since you're mostly moms and you've all seen *Dora the Explorer*."

The woman next to me, Roberta, smiled. "Nope," she whispered. "My youngest is thirty."

I gulped, making the polite you're-too-young-to-have-such-an-old-kid face.

"Memorize the names. It's a small group. It won't take long. Tonight you'll set up camp together. Tomorrow you'll trust each other with your lives on the ropes. Then you'll navigate, hike, cook, eat, breathe, and dig toilet holes together. I am being polite today. Tomorrow I will call them shit spots."

The women were here for real reasons: a year since breast cancer surgery, parenting autistic twins, one's divorce was final, one had graduated from the University of Maine with her BA at age forty-six. Beside them I felt small in some ways, a midlife-crisis excuse, but also smart, smart for finally finding this for myself.

We set up tents at dusk at a wide flat campground near a lake. The air smelled piney and I had trouble with the poles, embarrassing myself. I knew how to set up a tent, only these were newer models, not the classic A-frame two-person I'd used on the trail with Tia.

This was the time I'd been aching for, this time alone in the world again, and I couldn't stop thinking of what happened the first time I'd left my family, not just for the safe containment of college, but for the great expanses of the world.

I had boyfriends in college, but I never fell in love. Tia did, in serial, regular, and absolute passions that she wrote of so earnestly I was surprised when they ended and a new name graced her pages.

It was because of her southern Californian boyfriend, Burton, who'd been rock climbing and surfing and hiking since before he could speak, that we started planning our trip along the Appalachian Trail for after graduation.

By the time we graduated, Burton was moving to Las Vegas with his new girlfriend, but Tia and I had all our maps, our training logs to compare, miles of jogging and old-style calisthenics.

It was June when we got a ride up to Maine from a man Tia met in a bar in the city. We started with fat packs and soft feet. By the end of the week, my blisters had blisters, but I felt hardened, capable, and vaguely satisfied with the map's-inch of distance behind, with yards and yards to go. The post offices in towns along the way held letters for us, and my mother, true to form, sent care packages of dried roses and chocolate bars and short letters with her artist's angular writing.

By the time we made it to New York, I didn't mind them visiting us, my baby brother Oren and my mother in her old silver Peugeot at the Bear Mountain Bridge. Oren looked tired. It was July, and he said he had the flu. Blithely, I believed him. I didn't know what lies he held beneath his skin.

On the first day of Outward Bound, I had little time to worry about what I was missing at home. We left camp and took a day hike to Table Rock, carrying only lunch and climbing equipment. We reached the big slab of granite, smooth as a new cheek. I set down my pack and thought, I wasn't sure I wanted to do this. I was already sore from sleeping on the ground. And I felt this strange resistance—almost as though all the hoping for change wasn't going to help me change, as though my desire to be here was artificial, unearned.

"Daunting, isn't it," said Adrienne. She was short and plump, and had chocolate brown eyes. She'd taken on the heaviest things for her pack—two ropes, a water sack—and had walked quietly behind me without complaining for our three miles in.

"Yeah, I haven't done this before," I said.

"Many of you have never climbed," announced Dora. "And some of you will like this more than others. Just remember, this is about learning to trust your partners, and to trust yourself. When you hear someone say they can't do it, remind her that it's just another handhold, just another step. And also, I've been taking groups here for fifteen years, and there was only one person who actually couldn't do it. She had multiple sclerosis. She did the hike in. She did twenty feet ascending, but then her legs let out. None of you have that excuse. Your only obstacle is yourselves—the rock has nothing on your personal self-doubt."

"Wow," said Adrienne, turning to me. "Will you be my partner? I think it'd be easy to trust you. Trusting myself is another story." She giggled. She had a happy giggle, reminding me of a duckling bobbing her head.

"It's going to be fun," I lied. In fact, it felt awkward. I kept imagining I wouldn't mind being a beginner, if only our climb was really for beginners. It was a long, smooth rock that went straight up in the air. I wasn't twenty-one, and my knees were stiff. Adrienne clambered up the rock like a spider, asking me for help once or twice, but only to tighten the rope. Dora coached me, telling me only to say something when she asked or faltered. Then it was my turn to rope in—clips and straps and harnesses—and after watching Adrienne, I thought it would be easy. It wasn't. I scraped both knees and my legs started to shake only halfway up.

"Crap!" I yelled, as I slipped the first time.

"You can step right there," said Adrienne. "Just above your left foot."

"Let her find her own holds," Dora said. I hated Dora. I hated rock climbing. This was humiliating and I was ready to come down. But first I had to finish going up. I gripped with sore fingers, I pulled up farther than I should have and lost my balance again.

"Crap!" I yelled again. I'd wrenched my arm.

"Um, just another handhold?" said Adrienne. She was too darn perky.

Still, when I made it to the top, I did feel satisfied. Battered, but satisfied.

"I . . . am . . . not . . . tired," chanted Roberta, one word per step. I had forgotten what real discomfort was. Sure, I remembered artificial discomforts, the house just slightly too cold, wet toes for an hour before you change your socks, hunger that didn't really count, hunger in the ordinary world. It was raining, and we were moving into backcountry, covering ground, and now it did feel like an accomplishment, like just doing this was more important than anything else. I loved that we relied on one another for navigation and cooking and encouragement. I loved the differentness of the days, even though I was so exhausted I wanted to sit on a rock and let my muscles stop, let go of the tearing sensation I felt with every step. My pack was ridiculously large; I was a turtle plodding along with a too-big shell. Rainwater made everything heavier. My toes were pruned and my heels were blistering. My arm still throbbed from our first day's climb. No one else complained, so I kept it in.

There were distractions; we talked and talked, the way women do, but for some of the time we let the conversation wane, watching heat rise in bands from the greenery. At least it was a sun shower. I trudged behind Roberta, with Susan behind me, feeling the weight of my pack, irritated by a rivulet of warm water that was working its way through my raincoat. I was sore but happy of it, and of the strange way we'd gathered. There was the excitement of the group, the giddy sense of escape we all shared. There were the brilliant green ferns on the forest floor between the silver birches; there was the crackling sound of rain on my pack; and most of all, there was the pleasure of missing them, missing Iris's face, missing the sensation of largeness as she hid behind my legs when I answered the doorbell. I missed Caius and remembered the way his forehead made lines like an empty musical score when he smiled. I missed my older children for the noises of their presence and absence. Here there were just birds announcing the arrival of drowned worms, the clatter of cooking utensils tied to the outsides of packs, the swishing of gaitered calves, boots against the mossy drum of ground.

"I miss them," I said aloud.

"But I don't miss the dishwasher!" called Adrienne.

"I don't miss the laundry!" said Beth.

"I don't miss the crack in my car windshield I need to get fixed!" Adrienne was giggling.

"I don't miss being in charge of every meal!" Susan called. "What about you, Roberta?"

"Hm," she said. "I don't miss chewing grape gum in the chemo waiting room trying not to barf."

"I don't miss feeling both essential and unimportant," I said quietly. Then Roberta stopped and I bumped into her, and we fell and muddied our knees.

"Who says you're not in charge of dinner tonight?" Beth asked Susan, and we kept trudging on.

That night it stopped raining just for dinnertime. We sat around a fire in the lushest of campsites and talked about anything but our blisters, our blackfly bites, sunburn, unaccustomed muscles. I had forgotten what it was like to meet so many new people all at once, in an intimacy rivaling college, freshman year.

Then it started raining hard again, so we dove into our tents. A river divided the tent into sides, and Susan and I stayed up chattering, voices and teeth both. She lived in Colorado and we conspired to meet up, families together, for a summer vacation next year. We planned adventures out as if anything was possible: a trip down the Amazon, our kids sleeping in hammocks on boat decks at night.

"So," she said, "solos tomorrow. Are you nervous? I'm nervous."

"No," I said, and I realized I was looking forward to being alone, as much as I loved all this company. Still, there was trepidation. "I guess I'm more solitary than I thought."

o

Tia and I had been in Hot Springs, North Carolina, when I got my mother's letter telling me to come home. She sent two oranges "for drink and food in one round," as if we couldn't buy them in North Carolina, and a short letter on thick gray paper that said Oren was dying of late-detected Hodgkin's disease. I sat on the post office steps with Tia, shaking. We blocked the doorway with our tall packs and muddy legs.

Oren died a month after I got home. I always wished my mother had told me sooner, instead of letting me almost finish the trail. I would have quit; I never cared about making the whole thing, I only cared about the days with Tia, about the birches standing all around us like a rooted chorus. It was the time I'd wanted, but when I got home, I felt like it was lost time instead of something I owned.

In the morning, I set out alone. This was it, the climax, the period of reflection. I looked at the familiar lichens on the granite. I paraded my way through puddles and couldn't stop imagining how Iris would attack them, her passion for splashing. There were wild blueberries, mostly expended but a few tiny potent berries, enough to make it worth my while to stop on the outcrop that sheltered them. I took out my sketch pad, left until now, and two charcoal pencils. It seemed sacrilegious to try to capture this world in black and white, but then I began to see it, the way everything could be broken into line, into light and shadow. I sketched the rocks against the sky, a single birch leaf up close, a blueberry's perfect shape against its twig. I flipped through the pages of my book and found the squirrel, the ruined bird that had graced my step just a few months ago. It felt distant, impossibly unimportant.

I thought about the complaints I'd registered against my family with these women I hardly knew, of how easy it was to bemoan the state of my daily life. Belonging to this group felt a little like betraying my family—my other group, my only group for the past years. It felt something like what I'd sought in childhood: some other team, not just my mother, my father, all those boys. I'd complained about Carra, worried over her accident, her not telling me about the boy; I'd complained about Iris needing me too much. I'd bitched—there was no other word—about Amanda, calling her spoiled, calling her mean, letting them agree. Hearing myself recite the story of our relationship made me realize all the mistakes I'd made. I'd judged her at her most vulnerable, I'd couched my criticism in charity, and worst, I'd suspected her of something only someone who was unbalanced might do. I wasn't the only one letting off the collected steam of years, though I felt guiltiest for ratting out Caius, his not seeing me anymore, asking me if I might be happier doing things, all the while making a silent comment that I was doing some harm through my dissatisfaction. Maybe that's all it was, a temporary dissatisfaction, a storm.

Something rustled behind me on the rock, and a furry form bustled out toward the grassy plain beyond the outcrop. I held my breath for a minute, trying to remember what we were supposed to do if we saw a bear. Was it run? Or stay still? Was it different in daytime or night? But of course, breathing now, it wasn't a bear, it was much too small— a groundhog, just like the burrowers at home who cut their tunnels under our yard and Amanda's, ignoring the fence. Perhaps all I needed was to spend more time beyond my property lines, looking in instead of out, opening my frame instead of holding everything inside.

I still didn't know what I wanted to be when I grew up. But I also knew I didn't want to be my mother, holding so tightly to everything, to everyone, that letting go meant excising a piece of herself. It wasn't her fault she'd lost a son; it was her fault she never let the living go, either, never let us love her from a distance. And this was a gift I had, for that moment, anyway: distance. I promised myself I'd leave when I needed to, drive to Ramapo State Park, up to Turkey Hill in Harriman, that I'd scoot out on the log that straddled the brook in the woods behind our house, anything to give myself more proper perspective from now on. I had to learn how to let go and how to fill myself up.

We'd taken my mother for granted—we ate her perfect meals and basked in her perfect attention and never expected her to resent it, even when we pushed her away. Somehow, despite my best intentions, I'd taught my family to do the same. I had learned from my mother's grief; perhaps I studied her grief too closely. I prepared myself for a loss that might never come, and if it did, I wasn't actually prepared. I was just practiced, which wasn't the same thing. You couldn't prepare. My children growing up wasn't something to begrudge, and neither was their needing me. What I needed to do was to stop making myself look for sorrow.

I'd always thought my father's obsession with finding something important in math—making his mark—was a vanity. His published papers were kept laminated in notebooks. That my mother's quiet work of raising children, making dinners, the garden, were mark enough. But perhaps it was as elemental a drive as that to procreate. The need to be something, make something—the preschooler's pride in a beauteous lump of feathers and clay—all on your own. Children were always separate, even as they needed you, they were their own people from the very beginning. It was only the work of leaving that required assistance. My mother's modesty had its own beauty, perhaps, but it was a mistake to think modesty could sustain me. It wasn't enough; it probably hadn't been for her, either. I wanted to make something, too. I wasn't sure what that meant, except that when I went home, I was going to find out. Community college courses, maybe architecture, graphic design, writing. Something else just for me. What Caius was trying to tell me all along, only I'd had to find it myself, my own way.

I put away my book and just looked, just let myself face the quiet world. No sound except wind, except a tree leaning against another, groaning, nothing except my own breath. It was new and it was familiar, the view a gash of blue sky and green, the silver stripes of the birches, the sky opening up to me like an offering. And I was small in all of it, and I had fourteen more hours to myself, then twelve, and then I was setting up my bivvy sack for the opera of the sunset. I picked a spot under a few birches, just in case it rained, but I scrambled up to a viewpoint a hundred feet higher to watch the sky open into orange fruit, then pink and blues.

I hadn't expected to cry. I hadn't expected anything but the relief of my aloneness after all that intense company. But I missed my new friends now, missed the celebration of our collective escape. And I was tiny in the world, slightly afraid of a night alone. It wasn't bears I expected, it wasn't ax-wielding madmen in this pristine space of woods and sky, it was the danger of my own return. I cried for the unimportance of dead groundhogs, for the time I'd willed past instead of appreciating, for Carra's growing older, for all the frustration Iris would inspire, would conduct from her own perspective, for the closeness I'd wanted with my own children, for what was there and what was missing.

Inside my sack, my clothes still damp, I watched the sky, the slow movement of the stars. I ate two cold pancakes and drank water, still warm from the day. I thought of the glow-in-the-dark planets Oliver had helped me putty up on his ceiling in their order: My Very Educated Mother Just Served Us Nine Pizza Pies. "If it's pizza pies," Oliver had said, "how come there isn't another P planet after Pluto?"

I saw how much space there was between now and the light of the stars. I saw how much I'd forgotten to look at everything—and that my shortsightedness had the celestial bodies of my children as an excuse.

Just before dawn I started to pack up my things for the walk back toward our base camp. I had four hours before we were going to meet, so I was surprised to see someone walking toward me through the dappled morning light of the skinny birches, thin silver men. It was Susan.

"They want us to come right back now," she said, with a strange urgency. "Something's happened—we have to leave early."

"Something's happened?" What could happen if you left the ordinary world for a few days? "Is everyone okay?" I meant the other women; I meant my family, too.

"I hate to say it," said Susan, "but my first thought when Beth found me was nuclear meltdown. Isn't it weird, all this distance between us and the world, and yet there's a nuclear power plant close enough to kill us, I'm sure."

We swished our way through the woods, and I wondered whether there was anything to worry about but my own small world, whether I really wanted to cut my private revelations short by a single day for something I could do nothing about. But then, of course, I worried about that very private world, which had endured enough over the summer. My stomach hurt, but it was kind of exciting at the same time. I hated to think I was as thrilled about an unknown event as I might be watching a thriller.

"Do you think it's something regional? Or should we worry about our kids?" I asked.

"We should always worry about our kids." Susan forced a chuckle.

We were back in half an hour, no meandering contemplation. It was a sharply sunny day, and I could smell the sweat of five days' effort rising from my own underarms. Everyone sat in a circle around the long-finished campfire at base camp in the sunshine, and Dora, our group leader, told us about the airplanes and that the World Trade Center in New York had been destroyed.

It wasn't how I'd intended to come home. My flight out was canceled, so I took a bus and two trains. There was an ongoing public conversation—everyone had something to say, except for the occasional Arab-looking person, who was left sitting in his or her own section of seats like a plague-bearer. And I was afraid all the way home, though I'd talked with Caius on the phone after more than a dozen attempts to get through. Most everyone we knew was okay, except for two men he'd gone to law school with who had worked in the tower that fell first—the web of phone calls still hadn't revealed their fates. The man who coached Oliver's soccer team was gone, and a girl from Carra's swim team had lost her mother. It was a gap, like torn fabric, a hole between when I'd left and now, the long return. It wasn't until I switched buses in Trenton to head back north that I thought about Amanda and Aaron, thought about how neither worked downtown but both went into the city every day.

Emergency, I said to myself. *Emergency.* I still didn't believe it, despite the descriptions that fell around me like snow. Buses and trains changed routes or were canceled or delayed. It wasn't until the bus got on Route 17 and headed north that we could see the smoke still rising from the city. It was like something in a video game, an action movie. It wasn't something that was supposed to happen here.

Home. It had taken more than thirty-five hours to get here. The white clapboards looked so clean, the shutters so shiny in their jackets of paint.

For the first minute Iris was incensed, as if my leaving was a personal affront, as if my being gone was all that had happened in the world. Then she held tight to my leg and conceded a sticky kiss directly on my lips. I was sure she'd grown an inch in my days away, my long complicated journey home. I didn't tell Caius about the National Guard inspection we'd endured in Trenton, that because of my backpack I'd been searched. I'd had to take off my bra. I'd had to give up the food in my pack and my Swiss Army knife.

Without changing, I took Iris in the backyard, where the last of the summer heat was leeching from the grass. The sky was overcast, the flowers long finished, the heavy paper heads of the day lilies listless in the last of the day. I could almost see winter in the green, new ice splitting the sap-sucked twigs, fat final buds of the trees pinched tight by the icy fingertips of autumn evenings. Chasing Iris through the yellow forest of the first-turning maple, I imagined the cold that could happen, the quick change in the sky, the cold collapsing the leaves into yellow fists.

Safety in this strange storm: I looked at my home with a little less weariness. I had all this. Still, I wanted to go again. I was not cured of wanting to escape, but the world had grown smaller, more fragile, in the last few days.

"Chase me!" Iris loved this game, and I let her go a little before I followed her. She had no idea what had happened; Caius had turned off the radio, the television, when she came in the room, he told me. I wasn't sure how long we could protect her from the awful truths of the world. She led me back by the historic site of the bottle-cap mosaic. A single purple fall-blooming iris tilted its head in search of sunlight. I crouched in the home of my histories, beside a spontaneous outburst of forget-me-nots among the dead leaves, just opening their tiny buds. I felt as if I'd been forced to look outside the frame I'd hammered around my days, around my past.

"Chase me!" Iris's voice grew smaller. I wondered what we'd ever be able to tell her about this time, what wars would consume us now, what changes in our liberties.

"Have you heard from all the neighbors?" I called out to Caius, but the screen door closed; he hadn't heard me. Every house in the neighborhood had people home, televisions on. I felt fond of everyone, afraid for everyone. I followed Iris.

"Chase me, Mommy!" Her voice was vanishing. I pushed through the maples at the back of the yard.

Then the afternoon was finished, and I'd showered and held my children to me and let them squeeze away. Iris was in bed; Caius and I sat on the porch swing holding hands and wondering about each of our friends. He'd been calling people everywhere; he'd been reminding himself of everyone for whom he cared. He'd left three messages with Aaron and Amanda, but neither of them had called back. The house stood empty, no baby, no nanny, as if it were unoccupied and up for sale. I shivered.

"Can I play basketball at Nicky's?" asked Oliver as he dropped his bike on the driveway.

"I think you should start getting ready for bed," said Caius, the father in charge of the children.

We sat, listening to the screen door wheeze as it closed after Oliver. Carra talked on the phone, her voice rising with romantic intent. I knew that sound. Our daughter was an adolescent. I creaked the swing, pulling us back, letting us go.

A car drove into the driveway across the fence. Amanda's car. The front door opened and Malena's cry fell out into the early evening. Aaron got out of the passenger's side, his face strange, wearing a suit smeared with soot. I hadn't realized I'd been holding my breath.

Caius called out to them, "I left a message—is everyone okay?" And we already knew the answer. And I breathed and breathed.

"I was on the ground floor," said Aaron, walking up and leaning against the pickets, as if we spoke every day. "I was supposed to be upstairs, at Windows on the World, but I missed my train," he said.

"You would've been up there?" Caius looked at him, then stood and walked over to our neighbor. He reached across the fence and pulled him in, a real embrace, kissed his cheek. A smudge of soot transferred to my husband's sleeve.

"It took me until now to get out of the city. The hospital—"

"Are you okay?"

"I'm fine," he said, his mouth moving but his face oddly still.

"Thank God," I said, looking at Amanda, who was now standing behind Aaron.

"We're going inside," said Amanda, reaching for her husband's hand. Malena had grown, too; she almost looked like a toddler, with enough hair to relinquish babyhood and a certain, curious face emerging from the plushness of baby fat.

"She's so beautiful—," I said, and Amanda looked at me, and a gentle smile graced her bow lips. I meant it for both of them, all of them. Their beauty was something I'd forgotten.

"Thank you," said Amanda. It was like the smallest absolution. They turned and trooped into their house.

"See you later," said Caius, as if he hadn't just kissed her husband.

As we settled back on the porch, Caius turned and brushed a hair from my mouth. The touch thrilled me, a little, just enough. I tried to brush the soot from his sleeve but it was already working its way into the fibers. We sat, not talking, listening to the final calls of the cicadas, temporarily safe, temporarily satisfied with the contents of our own changeable hearts.

ACKNOWLEDGMENTS

Giant thanks to my extremely talented agent, Jennifer Carlson; to Sally Kim, an extraordinary editor and person; to the lovely folks at Shaye Areheart Books; to friends and super-strength supporters Cynthia Starr, Linda Buckbinder, Harlan Coben, Sandy Desmond, Kim Perrone, Kris Linton, Madeleine Beresford, and Susan McBrayer; and to early readers Moira Bucciarelli and Marcia Worth-Baker. Thanks also to Alison O'Connor, Sandra Marshall, Emily Remensperger, and Melanie Segal, without whom my time to write would've fit inside an acorn. Thanks Claudia, Rebecca, Alex, and Samantha, Dad and Peg, Herb and Ethel Herman, Mom and Tom, Rosenbergs, and Filners. To Josh (reader, Web-page designer, best friend), Jacob, and Carina—you are my home.

ABOUT THE AUTHOR

Gwendolen Gross is the author of the novels *Field Guide* and *Getting Out*. She graduated from Oberlin College, was selected for the PEN West Emerging Writers Fellowship, and received an MFA in fiction and poetry from Sarah Lawrence College. Ms. Gross has worked as a snake and kinkajou demonstrator, naturalist, opera singer, editor, and mom. She lives in northern New Jersey with her family. *The Other Mother* is her third novel. Visit her Website at www.GwendolenGross.com.

A NOTE ON THE TYPE

The text of this book was set in Weiss, a typeface originally created in 1926 by Emil Rudolf Weiss (b. 1875) for the Bauer foundry in Frankfurt. The typeface was inspired by Italian Renaissance cuts and its italics based on the chancery style of writing. In metal type, it was known as "Weiss Antiqua." Emil Weiss, as well as being a type designer, was a poet and painter.